FINDING LOVE IN SPECIAL PLACES

SEVEN SHORT STORIES INCLUDED

STACY EATON

NITEWOLF NOVELS, LLC

❀ Created with Vellum

STACY EATON'S SHORT STORY SERIES

The *Finding Love in Special Places* Short Story series consists of short stories that are under 20,000 words each.

These books are mostly sweet, with a few passionate kisses and adult language from time to time.

Finding Love on Christmas Vacation

Finding Love on Christmas Vacation is a short story, and part of Stacy Eaton's Finding Love in Special Places Short Story Series.

Lucy dreads spending Christmas at her father's cabin, especially since this is the first year he won't be there. When she shows up and finds a window broken, and forest critters inhabiting the cabin, she's forced to stay with Maverick in a nearby cabin.

Maverick arrives earlier than usual this year with the hopes of finally meeting his long, time friend's daughter, Lucy. What he didn't expect was to find his friend had passed earlier in the year.

Maverick and Lucy hit it off instantly, but will her father's final wish push them apart instead of bringing them closer?

Finding Love on the Summer Surf

Finding Love on the Summer Surf is a short story, and part of Stacy Eaton's Finding Love in Special Places Short Story Series.

Cynthia was in desperate need of a few days of peace, and when her good friend, Janet, told her to take off to Ocean City Maryland for the weekend and use their condo, she takes her up on the offer. Now she's ready for sun, sand, salty water, a few bottles of wine, and a smutty story on her audio player.

The last thing Michael wanted to do was clean out the condo. It had been his wife's sanctuary, and now that she was gone, it was painful to be there—even five years later. That's why Michael ends up on the beach, trying to get into a novel, but more interested in people-watching.

When Cynthia gets caught in a rip-tide, Michael comes to the rescue. Suddenly, the weekend they both planned is pulled out to sea as these two get lost in the tumble of the surf.

When the weekend ends, will fate bring these two back together, or will their weekend of memories drift away with the ocean waves?

Finding Love with Dear Santa

When Faith McMillian returns to Merryland with her son, Luke, right before Christmas, the last thing she is looking for is love. All Faith wants to do is figure out how to get her life back on track. When her son forces her to write a Dear Santa letter with him, that is the only thing she asks for.

Peter Sterling enjoys playing Santa and making wishes come true for people in Merryland. When his high school best friend's son sits on his lap to share his Christmas wish, Peter finds himself very curious over their wishes.

Peter and Faith enjoy catching up, and it isn't long before hidden feelings come to the surface. Will Faith end up going back to New York to rebuild her life, or will Peter somehow manage to fulfill her Dear Santa's wish?

Finding Love with a Champagne Toast

After a divorce that took two years to acquire, Karen Reed is ready for a few days of solace and sunshine on the island of Lanai in Hawaii. With a long flight over and a friendly seat companion, Karen is now looking forward to a light dinner and a good night's sleep at her resort.

Hudson Forbes made a promise to his wife before she died, and he is on a mission to fulfill that wish. What he didn't expect was to find the attractive brunette from the plane walk into the restaurant at his resort.

When they sit down to share a meal, they decide to take advantage of the company, the sunshine, and the romance that quickly builds. But when the week is over, will they be able to go their separate ways after sharing a final champagne toast?

Finding Love on the High Seas

Rainey Caldwell thrived on her work as a geneticist, even though she doesn't like people. She prefers studying DNA to talking to a human. When it comes to social activity, Rainey is awkward and filled with anxiety. That feeling will only intensify when two old high school friends show up on the cruise ship that she's stuck on for six days.

Zack Wheeler had been the most popular boy in school, but even thought things had looked great for him then, a lot had happened since. On the request of his family, Zach joins his buddies on a week-long cruise and finds himself face to face with the nerdiest girl at school. Only she's not a nerd now.

When Rainey and Zack decide to forget about the past, they look to enjoy the vacation, but when the ship docks, they are unsure what to do now with their newfound appreciation for each other.

Finding Love on a Dude Ranch

When Heather Tate lands at an airport in Jackson Hole, Wyoming, she's not doing it because she wants to. She's only here to help a friend. Little does she know that when the ranch hand appears at the airport, she's about to go for the ride of her life.

Rob Heller helps run the Triple G Dude Ranch with his mother. It's more than a vacation spot, it's a real-life working ranch, and for the next week, he's going to have to deal with a city-slicker who wants to learn about life as a rancher.

Heather quickly proves that she can handle the workload and earns the respect of all the ranch hands. Heather and Rob are both dreading the end of the week that will put a halt to their blossoming relationship. When it's time for her to leave, these two have trouble saying goodbye, but Heather's life is in Baltimore behind a desk. Will Heather find a way to have all that she loves? Or lose the cowboy who rode off with her heart?

Finding Love at the Farmer's Market

Sandi Warrenton hadn't been back to her old town in many years, but when her friend Maggie called and asked for help, she hustled back to be at her side. With Maggie dealing with a horrible diagnosis, Sandi will do everything she can to help her with her small-town bakery.

Aaron Norcini wasn't in the mood to sell his jellies and jams at the Farmer's Market, but he went anyway. Luckily, he did because after helping a customer, he turns to find a childhood friend standing at his booth.

As Sandi and Aaron rekindle their friendship, they share the hard lessons they have had to learn in the twenty years since they last saw one another. When another heartbreak slams into them, they lean on each other in a way they never dreamed could happen.

Now Sandi must decide where her future will lie and how much to take on as she starts on a new path that might end with her finding love at the Farmer's Market.

1: FINDING LOVE ON CHRISTMAS VACATION

❀ Created with Vellum

This book is dedicated to Tina Rucci.
May you always have love on Christmas.

CHAPTER ONE

LUCY

I finally put my car in park and stared out the windshield. My four-hour drive had taken eight thanks to miles of bumper-to-bumper traffic, multiple car accidents, a visit to the garage to get my tire and rim replaced, and the storm that loomed overhead—half a day early.

I blinked my bleary eyes and pushed open the door. After collecting my purse and backpack, I trudged through the seven or eight inches of fresh snow toward the front door of my father's cabin —correction, my cabin. I frowned. Oh, who was I kidding, this would always be my father's cabin.

When I reached the porch, I stared at the front door. It was the same color it always had been: cobalt blue. For some mysterious reason, I had thought it would look different, somehow reflecting my loss. To me it had always been an odd choice for the front door, window trim, and flower boxes that ran along the small front porch. My father said that the color reminded him of my mother, and I had to accept his words at face value as I barely remembered her. She died when I was six, and with twenty-six additional years of life filling my brain, I only had vague memories of her left.

A pain seared through my chest. I didn't want to forget my father.

He had only been gone two months, and already, the sound of his voice seemed to have faded. I didn't want to lose anything of his.

I set my two items on the porch and returned to the car to get my suitcases. It was more of an excuse to avoid entering the cabin—and the memories.

Once all my items were on the porch, including the wooden box that held my father's ashes, I withdrew the key from my pocket. With shaking fingers, I reached for the lock and paused. As much as I wanted the warmth of indoors, and to surround myself with my father's favorite things, I wasn't sure I was ready.

Stop being a pansy, Lucy, and open the damn door! I chided myself. I shoved the key into the lock, and with two quick turns, I twisted the lock and then the knob and pushed open the door. The scent that hit me was not what I'd been expecting, and I wrinkled my nose. Yuck, talk about stale and musty and gross—yuck!

Normally, when I arrived a few days before Christmas, the house smelled of evergreen, hot chocolate, and my father's musky cologne— maybe a little cinnamon or wood smoke mixed in. Today, it smelled rank, and maybe a little bit lonely. I stared into the darkness on the other side of the threshold, afraid to take the next step.

The wind howled behind me and pushed me forward as if my father were urging me on. It's just a cabin; there are no ghosts in here. There were only happy memories of our Christmas vacations since I was an infant. I threw a hand out and swiped along the wall to find the light switch. I clicked it on and off—nothing.

"Well, crap!" All thoughts of my father and ghosts forgotten, I stepped inside and shuffled carefully toward the small kitchen area where I knew my father had kept flashlights in the first drawer. I heard rustling in the back of the house, but I figured it was the wind.

There was just enough light coming from the open door to make out the larger pieces of furniture, but I had no idea if there was anything lying haphazardly on the ground. I doubted it; my father had been a neat man.

I shivered as I approached the kitchen. It was really cold in here, colder than I had imagined it would be. I reached the drawer as I heard something scurry across the floor, and stuck my hand inside to find a flashlight quickly. The first one didn't work; I dropped it back inside the drawer and went for another one as I heard a heavy thump.

My heart began to race as I realized I was not alone in the cabin. The fact that I was exhausted from the day of travel and emotional at being here added to the adrenaline burst that flooded my system. My hands shook as I grasped the second flashlight and lifted it to the sound of another thump. I pushed the button, and a thin beam of light landed on the door as the jean-clad leg of a man came into view. A squeak left my lips as the light beam flickered and then went out.

"Lucy?" a man's deep voice called from the door.

"Yes," I replied as my heartbeat practically exploded out of my ears.

"I'm sorry, I didn't mean to scare you. I'm Maverick. I rent the cottage next door."

Maverick—his name was as sexy as his voice and the pictures I had seen of him from my dad. Although there was never much to see of him in pictures. He and my father were always outside in the cold, the two of them bundled up like Eskimos, but Maverick's eyes were a piercing blue and had always captured my attention.

"Maverick," I sighed, relieved it was my father's friend and not a stranger. "It seems the power is out, and the flashlights are all dead."

He clicked a flashlight on in his hand but directed the beam toward the floor. "Yeah, the power is off in a few of the cabins. It went off a few hours ago. I wasn't sure if Charlie was coming, or I would have put the generator on. Where is he? I expected him to be here when I arrived yesterday."

Charlie, my father, usually came to his cabin in October and stayed here until March. For some reason, he loved the wild winters and being trapped indoors for weeks at a time. Me, I preferred places where snowplows came around and I didn't have to wait for a thaw to get out of my house—but that wasn't what made me sad now, it was the fact that Maverick obviously didn't know.

He took another step into the house, and the beam of light came up higher, brightening the room to where I could almost see the features of his face. I could imagine the color of his eyes as he waited for me to speak.

I chewed on my bottom lip as I came around the counter toward him. I'd given this bad news to many people at work, but when it was about someone you loved, it was different. "Maverick, I'm sorry. I didn't know that you weren't aware, but my father passed away in October."

He literally jerked back a few inches as if I'd smacked him. "What?"

I stepped forward and wrung my hands. I hated talking about this and thought that everyone that cared about him would have heard by now.

"He passed away in early October. He was in a small plane crash."

"Oh, my god!" The beam of light dropped toward the ground, and he swiped a hand along his jaw. "I'm so sorry, Lucy. I didn't know. Wow, your father was such an incredible man. I'm at a loss."

"Thank you, and you're right, he was, and some days, I'm at a loss, too."

"Wow," he exhaled loudly. "I don't even know what to say."

I was used to that, and right now, I didn't want to talk about my father. I wanted warmth, light, pajamas, and a pillow. "Is it colder in here than it should be?"

He shined his light around the room. It looked so forlorn, as if it knew my father was gone.

"It does seem colder than it should be. You stay here, let me look around." Before I could say anything, he walked off toward the back of the cabin, and I was alone in the darkness again. There was more scurrying, and then Maverick released a string of oaths.

"Is everything okay?" I asked as I walked down the hall that led to the two bedrooms and bathroom.

"You have a problem, Lucy, but it's not something we can fix tonight." He stepped out of my bedroom and filled the hallway with his very existence. I hadn't realized he was as tall as he was until he stood right in front of me.

The hint of burning wood wafted from him, and I instantly

pictured myself rolling around in front of a fire in his arms. I cleared my throat. "What's the problem?"

"The back window is broken, and there is snow coming in, but there are also animals in the house seeking shelter from the storm."

"Animals? What kind of animals?" I glanced at my feet, suddenly afraid that a snake would slither up my pant leg. Would he think me odd if I jumped into his arms?

"There is at least one raccoon in here, but I have a feeling there might be more in the cabin."

"A raccoon?"

"Yes."

"Well, can't we get it out?"

"Lucy, there might be a family of raccoons in here, and no, that's not something that we should do in the dark."

"Oh, come on! It can't be that bad. I'll grab the broom, and I can shoo him out, then I can block up the window and get some sleep."

I had already turned to get the broom when a big hand grabbed my upper arm. "Um, Lucy, that's not going to work."

"Why not?" I sure hoped that he wasn't saying that because I was a woman I couldn't handle ridding the cabin of some vermin.

He pulled me toward the door and in front of him before shining the light inside. An awful smell filled my nose as the light beam lit up the room and two bright, black eyes stared back at me. The raccoon rose onto its back legs, spreading its arms wide and squealing to tell us to get lost, the look in his gaze feral and his jaw opening and closing as if he were going to attack and eat us.

I stumbled back against Maverick as his arm came around my waist, and he pulled us out of the doorway.

"I think you should stay at my place tonight," he said as we walked backward toward the living room. I was just about to say, "No, I can close the door and sleep on the couch," when something rushed past us on the floor and bumped into our legs.

I almost launched myself into his arms, but instead, pushed myself closer to his chest and grabbed hold of his arm for security as I responded, "Yes, please."

CHAPTER TWO

MAVERICK

I'd been waiting almost a year for this day to come. Three days before Christmas was the day that Lucy arrived to spend a week with her father. They did it every year, and this was the first year that I'd been able to rent this cabin for the same week.

Normally, I arrived at the cabin a day or two after Lucy left, and I'd spend the next week visiting with Charlie and hearing about how incredible his daughter was and what was new in her life. Charlie had more than once said that he wished we'd been able to meet. He told me that he'd love to see his daughter with someone like me. I'd started to think that maybe I was the man for her, especially after last year's tales of her disastrous love life.

Part of me may have already been in love with her, or at least I really loved the things that he said about her. His stories affected me so greatly that over the eleven months between visits, I found myself daydreaming of her or imagining myself in the tales that Charlie recounted.

None of my friends knew that I carried a torch for a woman I'd never met. Maybe Charlie did, but he'd never asked. Instead, he'd spend hours sharing photos of her that she'd sent to him over the year and telling me everything that had changed in her life since our previous visits.

I loved hearing even the smallest detail, and when I had arrived the day before and found the snow around his cabin undisturbed and no truck parked at the side of his cabin, I'd gotten a little worried.

I thought that maybe he was late, but as the day dragged on, I began to seriously worry. Charlie was usually here in late October. The woodpile beside his cabin that was normally six feet high stood only knee high and was buried under several inches of snow. When it started to get dark, the knowledge that something might have happened to him or his daughter began to set in.

It was about the time the lights went out and I got my generator started that I really began to wonder what could have happened to Charlie and if I would ever meet Lucy in person.

The sound of a car engine captured my attention, and I peered out the front window as a woman got out of an SUV and carried things to the cabin. I could barely make her out, but I knew it was Lucy.

After putting on boots and a jacket, I grabbed a flashlight and headed over to her place to check on her and find out where Charlie was.

To learn that he had died made my heart hurt and my head spin. For ten years, I'd been spending the week here after Christmas with him. A few times at the beginning, I'd brought girlfriends, but then I'd learned that I wanted this week to myself, that I preferred to spend time with Charlie snowmobiling, skiing, or sitting by the fire talking about life, and Lucy, with a beer in one hand and venison jerky in the other.

The news almost took my legs out from under me, but then sounds in the cabin helped me focus and not lose my man card in front of the woman I'd been hoping to meet for years.

If there was one raccoon, there were probably others, and by the look of the bedroom, there were others. The amount of feces in the room told me a family had probably taken up residence in the cabin.

Lucy stumbled against my chest, and I held her close as I backed us down the hallway. When another critter rushed past us, I almost yelped, and I was really thankful when she said she'd stay at my place.

"Let's grab your things and head over to my cabin. We can come back here tomorrow and check things out in the daylight."

"Okay," she replied as we rushed toward the front door. We gathered her bags and began the short trek to my place.

"Do you have more in your car?"

"Um, no, this is everything."

"You didn't bring groceries?"

She stopped and stared at me, it was a little brighter out here than in the cabin and I could see her eyes opened wide.

"Wow, I've been coming here for so many years that I didn't even think about that. Usually it's already here when I arrive." She shook her head.

"You're lucky I'm stocked up, then." I smiled as she frowned.

"I really can't believe I did that. The whole trip up here, and it was a hell of a trip, I was only worried about stepping into the cabin, not about what to do once I was here."

A gust of wind blasted us, and we turned toward the path that led to my place five hundred feet away. There was a cluster of six cabins here, all privately owned and rented out when the owners weren't using them—except Charlie's. He never rented his place out. He said it was his home away from home, and he didn't want strangers living in his house. Charlie—I couldn't believe he was gone. The thought punched me in the gut.

A few moments later, I pushed open the front door and ushered her in. Lucy set her things down and shivered as she stood brushing snow off her long wool coat.

"I didn't realize how cold I was until I felt how warm it was in here," she said as she pulled her gloves off and glanced around the room.

"The fire really warms the place up."

Lucy glanced over her shoulder, and the two of us locked eyes. It was the first time that I got to look directly into her face, and I was mesmerized. Time seemed to stop for both of us as we studied one another. She slowly turned to face me and lifted her lips into a smile as she held a hand out toward me.

"Lucy Dodds; it's nice to finally meet you, Maverick Moore."

I cocked my head to the side in surprise. "You know my last name?" I took her cool hand in mine and loved the feel of it—so much so that I was tempted to pull her closer and feel more of her.

She tossed her chin up, laughing slightly as she withdrew her hand. "You're kidding, right? My father talked about you nonstop when I was here. He constantly told me that I needed to come the week after Christmas, so I could meet you."

"He did?"

"Yes, but wait," she frowned, "you're usually here the week after Christmas. Why are you here this week?"

I laughed nervously. "Um, because for years your father has been telling me I needed to meet you, and this was the first year I could rent the cabin at the same time. I booked it a year ago."

"Wait, so you came this week to meet me?" She looked puzzled, but almost excited about the news, too.

"Is that weird?" I asked as I removed my jacket.

She laughed as she unbuttoned her coat. "No, it's not weird. That's my dad for you."

"So—he was really telling you that he wanted you to meet me?"

"Yes, he was, and you really came a week early to meet me?"

I took her jacket and hung it on the hook beside mine. "I did."

"Well, then, I'm glad I came. I almost didn't." She glanced toward the door. "I wasn't sure if I'd be able to face the cabin and all the memories yet."

"I can understand that. At least now you have another night before you have to face it, and someone here to help you do it."

She put her hand on my arm, and I felt the heat of it all the way in my heart. "Thank you, Maverick. I think that will make it easier."

"Whatever you need, Lucy, I'll help you with it." A part of me meant that for the time she was here, while another part of me was already falling head over heels for this woman and wanted to help her with everything for the rest of her life.

Was it just the stories that Charlie had told me, or was it more? As Lucy and I continued to gaze at one another, I wondered if she felt the same connection I did. Was this real or because her father had wanted us to meet? Were we connected by a shared loss, or were we already building a bridge toward one another that might lead to a future?

The next few days would tell. In the meantime, I needed to do more than just stare at the beautiful woman in front of me.

"Can I get you something to eat?" I stepped around her. "I was just thinking about making something for myself."

"Okay, that would be nice."

"I made chili before I came up to the cabin and froze a bunch of it. Just needs to be warmed."

"Chili sounds perfect," she replied as I headed toward the kitchen. I was thankful to have something to do. If I had stood there much longer, I might have pulled her into my arms and sought out those full, pink lips of hers.

I reached the small kitchen and turned briskly to ask her if she wanted onions or cheese on her chili and found her directly behind me pulling up fast.

Her hands landed on my chest as she caught herself before she plowed into me. "Sorry," she squeaked before she bit down on her bottom lip.

My hands had gone to her hips automatically, and the two of us froze. The air around us seemed to sizzle, and my focus went right to her mouth as she let go of her bottom lip and licked it slightly. I pulled my gaze to her eyes and found her watching me.

Her whispered words drifted to my ears and my heart raced. "Please tell me I'm not crazy, and that you feel it, too."

CHAPTER THREE

LUCY

Holy smokes, had I just said that out loud? By the sparkle in his eye and the twitch of his brow, I'd have to say that I had.

His fingers curled around my hips, holding on to me a little more snugly. "You mean the electrical storm that seems to be zapping around us when we get close?"

"Yeah, that."

"You're not crazy." His voice deepened slightly, and I nearly shivered with anticipation. One of his hands left my hip and cupped the side of my face, his thumb tracing over the contours of my cheek. "You're even more beautiful than your pictures." I pursed my lips, and he lifted a brow in question. "What's wrong?"

"How many pictures of me did you see?"

His lips spread into a wide grin. "How many did you send your father?"

I stumbled back a step, and his hand drifted to his side. "He showed you all those pictures?"

A twinkle winked in his eye. "Every single one of them. Many I've seen a few times. We used to sit in front of the fire, and he'd give me his computer. He had all of your pictures saved, by month, and he'd go through each one and tell me what the picture was about."

My jaw dropped, "He did that?"

His other hand left my hip and took with it my sense of gravity. I felt as if I might float away at the staggering news. I could imagine my father sharing a picture or two with someone to say, "Hey, this is my daughter," but to show someone every single picture I had sent him. Now that was kind of mind-blowing—and weird. I was instantly trying to recall every picture I had ever sent to my father to see which ones I'd be embarrassed about.

"Don't worry, Lucy, I loved every single one of them."

"But why?"

He chuckled, the deep, smooth sound taking the edge off my building hysteria. "Why not? Your father loved you very much. One of my favorite things about coming here was hearing all about you and watching him light up when he shared stories."

"But isn't that weird? I mean, you've probably seen hundreds of pictures of me, and might know more about me than my own friends, and I have only seen a couple pictures of you and know so very little."

"What do you want to know?" he asked as he leaned against the counter, hands on either side as they rested on the wood block behind him. He was totally open right now, welcoming almost, and I had this tempting need to know just how it would feel to kiss him. I doubted that was what he was asking though.

I put my palms up, "I don't know. I have no clue where to start."

"Okay, well then, why don't you think about it for a moment while I heat up dinner?"

He winked and turned away, and I crossed my arms over my chest and wandered to the couch. The fire was crackling wildly and throwing off so much heat that I was tempted to take off my sweater, but the thin camisole underneath was not made for mixed company.

Well, maybe it was, but I had a feeling that if I took off my sweater, that electrical current that zapped between us would take on a whole new level of intensity.

What the heck was that anyway? I'd been attracted to men before, quite a lot of men, but I'd never felt this level of magnetism. From the moment he had walked into my father's cabin, I'd been drawn to him.

I turned to study him as he set the timer on the microwave and removed two bowls from the cabinet. He peered my way and winked again. What was it about Maverick that was different from other men?

I was correct when I'd told him that I didn't know much about him. I knew he was a firefighter, and he'd been coming to the cabin the same week for about ten or so years. I knew he was a couple of years older than I was and that he was attractive. I also knew that he enjoyed skiing, fishing, and snowmobiling with my father—and that was where my knowledge stopped.

I felt my forehead bunch as I tried to recall anything else my father might have said but came up blank.

"Would you like cheese or onions on your chili?" his deep voice broke my concentration.

"Cheese, please." I stood abruptly and walked toward the kitchen. "Why did he tell you all those things? Why didn't you tell him to stop?"

"Stop? Why would I do that? I loved hearing about you."

"But why?"

A muscle in his jaw ticked for a second as he pulled out a block of cheese and began to grate it. I was impressed that he knew how to use a grater. I would have pictured him with a bag of pre-shredded instead.

Finally, he answered, "I don't know. I just enjoyed hearing about your life, and you. In fact, that's the reason that I changed my normal vacation schedule. I wanted to meet you this year. I'd heard so much about you that I felt like I already knew you."

"But don't you have family that you spend Christmas with? I always assumed that you came after the holiday so you could be with family."

He shook his head, putting his attention on his task. "Just the guys at the firehouse, and I see them year-round. I was always low man on the totem pole for seniority, so I never got Christmas off. Besides a lot of the guys have kids, so I wanted to make sure they were home with their families."

"You don't have *any* family?"

"I have a brother, but he lives out West. We see each other during the summer; he's not a fan of winter." He grinned my way. "We are complete opposites. I take after our mother, he takes after our father. He likes the sun, I like the moon. He works in an office, I'd die being chained to a desk. He thrives on making money, I prefer to make a difference."

"I'm like that, too, I like to make a difference. That's why I'm a nurse."

The microwave beeped, and he removed the big container. "I figured you were. Firefighters, cops, nurses, doctors, we all kind of think the same way."

"True." I watched as he served up the chili and then I carried the bowls to the table while he gathered utensils and napkins.

"Do you want a glass of wine?"

I smirked over my shoulder, "I did not take you for a wine drinker."

"Hey, I drink wine, usually only with dinner, but there is something to be said about a glass of vino, a roaring fire, and a beautiful woman to share it with."

My cheeks began to warm at his side compliment, but I didn't say anything.

A few moments later, he set the items on the table along with two wineglasses. As he walked back toward the kitchen, I took a second to check out his backside. My cheeks grew warmer as he glanced back at me as if he knew what I was doing.

Once he was settled, I scooped up a spoonful of chili and blew on it. It tasted fantastic, and I quickly scooped more into my mouth.

"Glad I had food to feed you. You look like you haven't eaten for days."

"It feels like it." I sat back a little and took a few moments to tell him how terrible the drive had been. "I almost turned around a couple times."

"Why didn't you?" he asked before he took a sip of wine.

I stared at his throat as his Adam's apple bobbed. How did I tell him that some strange voice in my head told me that I needed to be here today, or that no matter how much I wanted to turn around, something kept me from doing so?

I shrugged, "It's tradition. Besides I needed to come for my father."

He settled his hand over mine on the table. "I'm really sorry about your father, Lucy. I honestly cared a great deal for him. It hasn't really hit me yet that he's gone. I should be more sensitive about your feelings. Here I am flirting with you, and you're grieving."

"It's okay. I've been grieving for two months. It's time for me to move on. Dad wouldn't have wanted me to be sad. Actually, the only reason I came up here this year was because this is where he wanted his ashes scattered. He left explicit instructions on when and where to do it."

"When did he say to do it?"

"Christmas Day," I paused. "Did he know you would be here early this year?"

"Yeah, I told him last year that I was going to try and book the cabin a week early. Why?"

She shook her head and laughed. "That explains why he told me last year to make sure I scheduled to take Christmas off. He asked me like three times if I had done it. He wanted to make sure that we met."

The fire seemed to crackle more loudly, and we both glanced toward it.

"Well, I'm glad we have met, and I'm glad I'm here so that I can be with you when you scatter his ashes," he said hoarsely.

"You'd do that?"

He squeezed my hand, "There is no place else I'd rather be, Lucy."

CHAPTER FOUR

MAVERICK

It wasn't until the words left my mouth that I realized just how true they were. Charlie and I had shared a special bond with each other and with this place, and I wanted to be here and part of this monumental moment.

"Thank you, Maverick," Lucy's voice was filled with emotion, and her eyes grew glassy as she fought to hold back tears.

I squeezed her hand one more time and then released it to give her some space to compose herself as I went back to my dinner and thought over what we'd just talked about.

What if she hadn't come this year? I wouldn't have known what had happened to either of them. That thought really bothered me, enough that food got lodged in my throat, and I had to force it clear with a rough cough.

"Are you alright?" she immediately asked, her eyes alert and searching my face.

I cleared my throat. "Yeah, swallowed wrong."

She nodded and stared at her food before changing the subject altogether. "So how many critters do you think are living in my dad's cabin?"

"By the look of the excrement, I'd say a few."

She winced, "How do we get them out?"

I really liked that she'd included me in her plans. "Well, once it's daylight, we can check out the house better. Raccoons are nocturnal, so it shouldn't be a problem."

"But won't that mean they will be sleeping when we go in? I mean, if they are sleeping, won't they get angry if we try to wake them up? I don't really feel like getting rabies shots because one takes a chunk out of me."

"I could always shoot them."

"No!" the word burst out of her mouth as I had anticipated, and I chuckled.

"Relax, I was kidding. I wouldn't do that unless it was necessary."

"Good," she commented as she went back to eating. Once we were done, she helped me clear off the table. "I'll wash these since you fed me."

"You don't need to do that."

"It will only take a few minutes," she replied and went about rinsing the bowls. I stood back and watched her. Her long, blonde hair was mussed from traveling all day. She looked tired but breathtaking all the same.

I grabbed a towel and moved to her side to collect the dish she'd just washed, bumping into her shoulder as I did so. Both of us stopped, and I had this incredible urge to wrap my arms around her and pull her flush against my body.

The wet bowl was all but forgotten as my instincts took over, and I reached for Lucy's chin.

She turned her face toward mine, her lips open, her blue eyes bright. I leaned in and placed the softest of kisses on her lips, as if I were kissing a flower petal I didn't want to bruise. I pulled back and waited for her to yell at me, or frown and go back to washing the dishes, but she didn't say a word, just returned the stare.

Did I chance kissing her again? Something told me yes, not that I wanted to rush anything, but I had been dreaming of this moment for years. As I began to lean in, a shattering sound and then a thud had me spinning around, effectively blocking anything from getting at Lucy as her hands went to the back of my shirt, gripping it tightly.

"What was that?"

"It sounded like glass breaking." I took a step.

She pulled on my shirt. "Where are you going?"

"I need to go check it out."

"What if the raccoons came over here?"

I laughed and tapped her chin. "I don't think the raccoons came over here. Let me go look. Stay here."

She nodded but didn't say anything further as I stepped away. I walked briskly toward the bedroom door and paused outside of it as I felt a slight breeze. I peered around the corner, wondering if I'd find someone lurking inside, but the only thing I saw was the curtain fluttering in the breeze. I checked the window and found it broken in the upper right corner, a tree branch leaning against the glass on the outside. "Well, crap."

I turned around and found Lucy at the door. "What's wrong?"

"Looks like a branch fell and broke the window. It's too late to do anything about it tonight. I'll have to wait until morning when I can get over to your dad's shed or get a hold of Joshua."

"Is this your only bedroom?" She glanced around the small room.

"Yes, I was going to let you have it tonight and sleep on the couch, but I think we are both crashing in the living room to stay warm."

Our eyes collided, and I wondered if she was picturing the same thing that I was: Our bodies keeping each other warm as we snuggled on the blankets in front of the dying fire. She pulled her bottom lip under her teeth as her gaze slipped down my chest, and I had a sneaking suspicion that she was riding on the same train of thought as I. My fingers tingled to reach for her, but I held back.

"Okay," she stated casually as she turned and headed toward the living room.

I grabbed the pillows off the bed and the blankets, too, and brought them out to the couch. After getting a towel from the bathroom, I closed the bedroom door and wedged the towel under the door to keep the draft down. "That will have to do until morning."

"Wow, we're going to have a lot to work on tomorrow," Lucy said as she slipped to the floor to sit in front of the fire. "Now, there are two windows to fix."

"I think this place will be easier," I told her as I sank down beside her, "but let's not worry about all of that tonight. We will have plenty of time to deal with it tomorrow."

"Yeah, you're right."

"You probably don't want to talk about this, but can you tell me more about what happened with your father?"

She stared into the fire, her eyes losing focus. "He was heading to Maine with friends. One of the guys had his pilot's license, and they took his little four-seater up. It was way too windy that day, and they should never have gone up, but they did, and the wind brought them down."

"How did you hear about it?"

"Ironically, I saw it on the news. I was on break at work, and the news was on. It said that four locals had crashed a plane heading to Maine. I knew instantly that it was them. I was the one to drive to Vermont and identify all the men."

I reached for Lucy's hand and laced my fingers with hers. "I bet that was hard."

"Of course, but I would rather have done it then leave it for the other families to do. I see death often enough that it doesn't faze me like it does others."

"But it would faze you if it was your father."

"True, and it did," she squeezed back a little, "but it didn't really hit me until the funeral. Then all his friends started coming up to me and telling me they were sorry, and how great my dad was, and I just wanted to curl up and cry someplace."

"Did you?"

Her brow wrinkled, "No, actually, I didn't, not really."

"Have you cried at all?"

She shrugged. "Yeah, I cried a little at the funeral, and after, but I didn't fall apart or anything. That's not me."

"Lucy, that's anyone who loses a parent. I remember when my

parents died, I was eighteen by a week. I was so upset, I destroyed my bedroom. My brother came in and helped to calm me down. Maybe it hasn't really hit you yet."

"Maybe," she said softly, "or maybe it never will."

I let go of her hand and scooted closer to her, putting my arm around her shoulders and drawing her close. "Well, if you want to fall apart here, you're safe to do it. I got you."

She smiled before she laid her head onto my shoulder. "Thanks, Maverick."

I kissed the top of her head. "You're welcome, Lucy."

For a long time, the two of us sat like that, staring into the fire. I reminisced about her father and wondered what she was thinking. I stroked her hair and her arm, and from time to time, brushed my lips over her head and inhaled the sweet scent of her shampoo. If this was all I would ever have of her, I'd take it.

"I feel like he's here right now."

"Like here in the cabin?" I glanced around, knowing I wouldn't find anything, but still checking.

"Yeah, like he's watching over us, and he's happy that we are here together."

"Well, I don't know about him, but I know I am."

She lifted her head and turned to face me, our noses only a few inches apart. "I am, too. I wish we had gotten a chance to meet when he was alive."

"That would have been nice."

"It would have."

I set my wineglass aside, taking her empty one and doing the same with it. I spread my hand along the side of her face and into her long, blonde hair, letting the soft strands flow over my fingers. "I've wanted to do that for years."

"What else have you wanted?" her voice was soft.

"This," I told her right before I took her lips in a kiss that I had no intention of ending quickly.

CHAPTER FIVE

LUCY

I felt drunk. Was it my long day of travel, the emotions of being at the cabin, the warm bowl of chili filling my belly, the tangy glass of wine I'd drunk too fast, or the man that kissed me as if the world were about to end?

To be honest, I think it was a little bit of the first things and a whole lot of the last. Somehow, I found myself curled up on his lap, and then I was facing him, straddling his thighs, and he was holding me tightly, touching me tenderly as if I would break. His touch grazed sensitive parts of my body that begged for more, but not tonight.

I kissed his neck down to his collar, and the crook of his shoulder felt so good that I didn't want to move. I inhaled his woodsy scent, and then I was out like a light.

The next thing I remembered was waking up to staggeringly bright sunlight coming in through the kitchen window. I threw my arm up to block it, so I could look at my surroundings. I was on an air mattress in the center of the living room floor. The fire was still going but only barely. On the couch were my clothes from yesterday, and I quickly lifted the sheets to see that I was dressed in my pajamas.

Did he undress me? Had we had sex? My cheeks blazed at the

thought of him taking advantage of me while I was out of it. Had he spiked my wine? I didn't remember anything after kissing him. Holy crap! How could I not remember having sex with Maverick? Even if I was exhausted, I should have some recollection of it. He must have drugged me, that was the only thing I could think of. Fury began to rise inside of me at the same time that the front door opened gingerly, and his head popped in.

"You're awake." He grinned and came all the way into the living room, closing the door behind him on a gust of wind.

I shivered and pulled the covers back up over me. He came over to the couch, fully dressed in jeans and a sweater with a jacket over it that he unzipped as he took a seat. "Did you sleep well?"

I frowned. He wasn't acting like a man who had taken advantage of me. "Did we, um, last night?" My cheeks burned as I tried to ask a question that normally would be no big deal. Why did this man make me blush so much? I could talk about any body function with any person and never get tripped up, but asking this particular man if we'd had sex tied my tongue in knots.

He raised a brow. "Did we make love?" He chuckled, "No, Lucy, I prefer to have my woman conscious, and I'm pretty sure that the first time we make love, neither of us will ever forget it."

I swallowed and had this urge to throw back the covers and invite him under. "Then how did I get in my pajamas?"

"You really don't remember?" He laughed, "I knew you were out of it, but, man, I didn't think you were that far out. You fell asleep on my shoulder, and I laid you on the couch while I got the air mattress set up. Then I roused you enough to get you up, so you could change into your pajamas," he looked at me pointedly, "in the bathroom—alone. You came out, lay down, and that was it. You were out."

"Seriously?"

"Yes, seriously. Cross my heart." He made the little movement over his chest.

I felt better knowing he hadn't taken advantage of me but still felt weird that I had passed out that hard around him. "What time is it?"

He glanced toward the kitchen. "Eleven fifteen."

"What?" I sat straight up. "No way, I never sleep that late."

"Yeah, well, I guess you needed it."

I threw the covers back and scrambled out. "You should have woken me up, I have so much to get done. I can't afford to sleep all day."

"Relax, Lucy, I've already taken care of your father's place."

I froze halfway to my duffle bag. "You what?"

"I called Joshua this morning. Do you remember him? He manages the other cabins for the owners. He came over, and the two of us got all the critters out of the cabin. We've already boarded up the window, cleaned up the mess in the bedroom, and he ordered a new window for you. He needed to order one for here, so he just went ahead and ordered two."

"You did all that?"

"Yes. Is there a problem?"

Was there a problem? No, I guess not. This handsome man was more than just a decent cook, he was rather kind, too. "No, I'm just surprised."

He chuckled as he stood and approached me. "Don't be so surprised. I like to do those kinds of things. Besides," his voice lowered, "it is the least I could do for the memory of Charlie. I feel like I owe him my life in a way."

My brows pinched together. "Your life? What are you talking about?"

"Ah, that's a story for another time." Maverick stepped around me, and I reached out and pulled him back around.

"No, tell me now. Did he save your life or something?"

"How about I make you something to eat, and I'll tell you while we eat."

"Okay."

"Why don't you get dressed, and I'll fix lunch, unless you'd prefer breakfast since you missed that."

"No, lunch is fine."

31

While I showered, I pondered what he could have to say. What had my father done to help him? I rushed through getting dressed and found him in the kitchen setting plates on the table with big, crusty bread and bowls of soup.

"More chili?"

"No, homemade chicken soup."

I stopped short. "You make homemade chicken soup, too?"

He laughed and put his hand on my lower back as he led me to the table. "No, actually this was made by one of my brothers at the firehouse. We take turns cooking, and he made extra, so I could bring some here with me."

"Do you all take turns cooking?" I asked as we sat.

"Yes, most of the time. There are a few guys who can't cook to save their lives, so they prefer to do cleanup."

"That's a good tradeoff."

"It is. Everyone has their job at the firehouse."

"How often do you work?"

"We do three on and three off." He tore a piece of bread and dipped it into his soup. "Sometimes it can be a long three days."

I tapped my spoon on the bowl for a moment. "You know, I don't even know where you live."

"Saratoga Springs," he replied as he took a bite of his soup.

"Are you kidding me? I'm right down the highway from you in Hudson Falls."

He smirked, "I know."

"How did you know that?"

"Your dad told me."

I laughed, "Of course he did. What else did he tell you?"

Maverick grinned. "What didn't he tell me?"

"Ugh!" I laughed, and for a few minutes, he told me about some of the funnier moments of my life, like me pulling out my first tooth, and jumping off a trampoline and breaking my arm, along with trying to cook breakfast in bed for my dad on Father's Day when I was eight.

"Okay, fine, he told you all about me, so why didn't he tell me as much about you if he wanted us to meet?"

32

"I guess it was because you were always seeing someone." His brow furrowed. "I meant to ask you, are you seeing someone now?"

I shook my head as I wiped my mouth. "No, I broke up with Glenn right before my father died."

"So, you're not seeing anyone."

"Nope, you?"

"No." The two of us locked eyes, and a magnetic current pulled us toward one another.

I cleared my throat. "So tell me how my father saved your life. Did you fall in the lake or get trapped by a snake?"

He laughed loudly. "No, nothing like that. I met him when I was twenty-two. A buddy of mine rented one of the other cabins, and a bunch of us came up here and spent a week getting trashed, at least they did. Back then, I was kind of out of control. I hung with the wrong crowd, dated all the wrong kinds of girls, and had no idea what my future was going to be. When my parents died, I kind of went to hell in a handbasket, so to speak.

"My brother had already moved out West, and I had no clue what the hell to do with my life. I was walking down the road really early in the morning one day because I couldn't sleep and smelled smoke. That wasn't something new, of course, people always have fires going, but the odor was wrong. It was more than just wood burning, I could detect other chemical scents in the air, and I started to search for it.

"I remember I was running down the road, and your father was outside on the porch, he had his nose up in the air like he was smelling it, and I had an idea where it was coming from. He asked me what was going on, and I said that I thought something big was on fire. He jumped in his truck and told me to get in, and we raced down the road. When we came around a bend, we could see the smoke and flames. Three of the people I was with died in that fire because they were high and passed out when it started, but I helped your dad and did everything he told me to do. Afterwards, he commented on how well I did, said I had firefighting in my blood, and that I was better than the other people there. When I got home, I went straight to the fire department and signed up for the academy. The next year, I came back and set a baseball cap from my fire department on your father's porch. He saw me and called me in for coffee. While he was pouring it, I saw your picture on the mantel. He stood next to me and said, 'You know, if you keep going the way you are, one day you might be worthy of a girl like that.'"

CHAPTER SIX

MAVERICK

I couldn't believe that I was telling her this story, or that I told her what her father had said, but when tears came to her eyes, I was glad that I had. They weren't sad tears, they were tears of joy.

I knew how much it meant to know what a person thought about you, especially when that person was now gone. People always take others for granted, but once they are gone, you realize how much you never said to them. I had learned that the hard way with my own parents. I wanted Lucy to know just how important she was to her father.

"So that's how you guys became friends. I never knew. I only remember coming up for Christmas one year, and he mentioned you, and then he kept mentioning you. I didn't even know you were as young as you were until I saw a picture of you two ice fishing. I had always assumed that you were his age."

"You did?"

"Yeah, I guess that's why I never paid much attention to details of you. I wish that I had."

I shrugged. "You were busy with your career and all those guys you were dating."

"Hey," she laughed, "I didn't date all that many guys."

My jaw dropped a little, and I popped my eyes wide as if I was shocked she would say such a thing.

"Wait! Did he tell you about the guys I was dating?"

"Yes, if you were with them for any amount of time, and especially if he met them, he told me about them."

She laughed, "He did not."

"He did."

"Fine, who were they?" Her eyes sparkled mischievously over the table.

I really didn't want to think about other men with her, especially after I'd lain awake half the night watching her sleep in the firelight and wishing I was sleeping beside her and not on the couch.

"Well, there was Whack-a-doodle, at least that's what your dad called him."

Lucy barked out a laugh. "Whack-a-doodle?"

"Yeah, I think he was the dentist." Lucy laughed so hard she snorted. "And then there was Dumb Cuffs, he was the police officer, and Numb Nuts, he was the nurse you were seeing for a while. You guys almost got serious, he was really nervous about that."

"Wait, he liked Jared."

"No, he thought he was a twit; he pretended to like him for you."

"But he came up here for Christmas with us, and Dad told him he hoped he saw him again."

"Yeah, not really. He said that to be nice, but let me tell you, he told me everything about that guy the moment I got here. In fact, he talked for hours about it."

"I never knew! I thought he liked him."

"Nope," I shook my head slowly, grinning the whole time.

For the rest of lunch, we joked about the guys she'd dated, and while I didn't want to really think about them, I loved listening to her laugh.

After lunch, we cleaned up and then went over to her father's cabin. She paused at the door as if she were afraid of what she'd see when she stepped inside.

I put my arm around her shoulders. "I promise, no more raccoons."

She tried to smile, but it didn't reach her eyes. "It's not that. Last night I was so tired that I didn't really think about being here. Today, in the light of the day, I'm afraid to step inside and see the ghosts."

"Ghosts?"

"Yeah, the memories of all our times together. This was the one week every year that we both put aside everything else and it was just us. It was like the outside world didn't matter."

"He said the same thing. Said it was his favorite week of the year, wished you would stay longer."

"I wish I could have, too." She stepped forward and opened the door, going right in and then pausing a few feet inside to look around. I waited on the other side of the door until she glanced back and smiled sadly. "I can feel him here."

I joined her and put my arm around her back. "I bet you can. I can, too."

She sniffled and began to move around the cabin. "I'm actually glad that I didn't sleep here last night. It would have been weird waking up this morning to all of this and being alone." She turned to me, "I'm glad you're here with me, Maverick."

"I am, too."

She let her fingers run over different items: a couple of pictures, the back of her father's favorite chair, the blanket her grandmother had knitted when she was young thrown over the back of the couch. She stopped in front of the fireplace and stared at the empty grate.

"There was always a fire going, always. No matter how warm it was outside or how late it was, the fire was always going the entire time I was here." She sniffled again and then her shoulders began to shake.

I was at her side by the time the tears began to drip off her chin. I wrapped her in my arms. "Go ahead, Lucy, let it out. You're safe here, baby. I got you, let it go."

As if she'd been waiting for someone to give her permission, she opened the dam and let it out. She sobbed into my chest, crying as if her world had ended, and in a way, it had. I shed a few tears myself as I held her and looked at the picture of the two of us on his mantel.

Lucy cried for a long time, and I moved her over to the couch and handed her some tissues from the box on the side table. She grew so quiet that, after a time, I wondered if she'd fallen asleep, but I could see her eyes were open, blinking slowly.

"I needed that," she said, her voice husky from crying.

"I'm sure you did."

She tilted her head so she could look at my face; her cheeks were flushed, her eyes swollen and bloodshot. "I'm sorry you had to witness that."

"I'm not." I brushed a few locks of hair back from her face.

"I must look a mess."

I locked eyes with her. "You have never been more beautiful to me."

Lucy lifted herself and brought our lips together in a slow, searching kiss. A few moments later, the pace changed, and things became more urgent. She shifted so she could climb over my lap like she had last night, and I wondered if she would pass out again.

"I'm awake," she whispered as if she'd read my mind.

I laughed and pulled her closer. "I'm glad to hear that. If you fall asleep now, I'm going to think there is a problem with me."

She pulled back and looked at me with the sexiest look I'd ever seen. "There is a problem."

"What?"

"We're still dressed."

I twisted so she was now lying on the couch and I was over her. Her squeal made me laugh as I stopped an inch from her lips. "I can fix that."

"Please do."

~

After we'd made love, I held her and wondered how I could ever move forward in life if she wasn't part of it now. Fear kept the words back, but I knew without a doubt that I loved Lucy. I knew everything about her, but she barely knew me. I needed to give her a little time and share with her as much as I could, so she would see that I was worth it.

We dressed, and for the rest of the afternoon, we went through her father's place. There were more tears, and Lucy made a few piles of things that needed to be taken home and things that could be thrown away.

I asked her if she wanted to do this alone, but she promised me that it was easier with me here. I could see the toll this was taking on her, and I tried to keep the conversation as upbeat as I could. By the time the sun began to set, she was ready to call it a day.

"Do you want me to bring your things over here?"

She glanced around, "Maverick, would you mind if I stayed at your place another night? I'm not sure I'm ready to be here by myself, not after spending all day sorting through things."

"Absolutely. Joshua actually replaced my window while we were over here, so you can sleep in my bedroom."

She lifted her lips in a playful smile, then began to worry her bottom lip. "Only if you're going to be in it with me." She stepped closer and put her arms around my waist.

"I think that can be arranged, pretty lady."

"Then you have yourself a deal—so what else do you have over there in that fridge? I'm starving!"

The two of us walked out arm in arm as I itemized the contents of my fridge. After a warmup of chili and more crusty bread, we cuddled on the couch and decided to watch a movie. The two of us laughed and recited lines from *National Lampoon's Christmas Vacation* before we snuggled and kissed on the couch.

That night, I carried Lucy to my bed and laid her down. She had no idea how much this meant to me to have her here. I felt as if I had finally received the Christmas present that I had always dreamed of. I wished that I could lock us in the cabin and forget about the world beyond, but I had a feeling that our time was limited, and I needed to take advantage of every second I had.

That night, as Lucy slept on my shoulder, I kissed her forehead and whispered the words that I could no longer hold in. "I love you." I could only hope that one day she might feel the same way.

CHAPTER SEVEN

LUCY

Clearing out my father's cabin was tough but not horrible—at least not with Maverick at my side. He kept me entertained with stories that my father had told him, mostly stories of my own life, but from time to time he'd add in something I didn't know. Those were the best stories.

I wasn't sure why I didn't want to stay in the cabin that night. Everything had been cleaned, and the marauding trespassers had been evicted. Maybe it was because I'd never been at the cabin without my father, and being there alone was too hard—or maybe it was just an excuse to be with Maverick for another night.

I found it funny that we didn't live that far away from one another. It was maybe a thirty-minute drive on Interstate 87. That was close enough that we could see one another after the holiday—if we wanted to.

Granted, I enjoyed my time with Maverick, but were these feelings real, or did they stem from being here without my father and that Maverick knew him so well? I had a feeling that Maverick liked me, maybe a lot, but had my father built me up to be something I wasn't? Were his feelings toward me fantasies of a woman he'd heard about for years?

The next day, Maverick and I did some more cleaning at my father's cabin and then we spent the afternoon snowmobiling. It was exciting, and we laughed constantly. A few times, we threw snowballs at one another and ended up rolling around in the snow kissing. That's how we ended up back at his cabin and on the air mattress in front of the fire for the remainder of the evening.

The third day was much the same, and it wasn't until the next day on Christmas Eve night that I stood at the window of his cabin and stared at the darkened glass of my father's place. I'd never seen it dark unless the power had gone out, but then the generator would be turned on or candles would be flickering behind the glass.

I wasn't sure that I would ever be able to stay there again and was so thankful to Maverick for allowing me to remain at his place. Neither of us had broached the subject of me leaving again after my second night here. It just felt right.

As Maverick came up behind me, he wrapped his arms around me. "What are you thinking about?"

I snuggled against his chest. "The cabin looks so dark and lonely."

"Do you want me to go turn lights on over there?"

"No," I answered wistfully, "it's just strange to see it that way. There were always lights on, and on Christmas Eve we'd decorate the tree. It's odd not seeing a tree in the window—almost as unnerving as not seeing him walking around behind the glass." My eyes filled with tears as I whispered, "I can't believe my father is gone."

"I'm so sorry, Lucy. I know how hard the first holiday is, the first year, and trust me, it takes a long time before it doesn't feel like you've been kicked in the gut every time a memory comes to you."

"I'm glad you're here, Maverick. I don't know if I've told you this, but you have made it so much easier for me to deal with all of this. I'm not sure I could have done this without you."

"You could have, Lucy, but I'm glad I was here for you, too." He paused and squeezed me a little tighter. "So what happens tomorrow?"

"Well, tomorrow, I take his ashes out to the lake and scatter them."

"You said 'I.' Does that mean you don't want me to come?"

"I don't want you to think that you have to be there. Of course, you're welcome to come, but you don't have to."

He turned me around in his arms. "Of course I want to be there, Lucy. Why would I not want to say goodbye to my friend? In fact, Joshua asked if he could come, too."

"He did?"

"Yeah, I told him I'd let him know what time you were doing this."

"Oh, well, I don't want to upset anyone's Christmas morning."

"Come on, Lucy, we are talking about Charlie here. Your father meant a lot to the people around here. I think they would be disappointed if they didn't know it was happening."

"Okay, well, I planned on going down to the lake around nine."

"That sounds perfect. Let me send Joshua a text and let him know."

I supposed it would be all right if Joshua was there. He had been friends with my father after all, and it only made sense that Maverick be there, too. I felt better knowing I wasn't going to be doing it alone.

The memorial service that we'd had for him in Utica where he'd lived had been intimate, but I hadn't known many of the people.

That night, I was restless, and Maverick seemed to sense it. He kept his arm around me and held me more closely than previous nights. We made love two times during the night, and in the morning, I was up at daybreak, staring out the window at the cabin again.

When my father was alive, I'd wake to the smell of coffee, bacon, and pancakes. We'd eat breakfast and then open our gifts from one another. Then we'd get dressed in our snow gear and take the snowmobiles out to go from house to house around the area wishing people a Merry Christmas. By the time we arrived home, it was always late afternoon, and I would be so full from all the cider, hot chocolate, coffee, eggnog, and cookies that I wouldn't even need to eat dinner that night.

My father did have a lot of friends here. I probably should have let more of them know, or maybe I should have scheduled a memorial here so that people could have paid their respects. It was too late to do that, though. My father specifically said he wanted to have his ashes spread on Christmas morning, so that was how it would happen: His last Christmas wish granted.

Maverick and I were both quiet as we dressed and ate breakfast. I wasn't really in the mood for food, but I ate the pancakes and bacon that he cooked. Had Maverick known that was my traditional Christmas breakfast, or did it just make sense to eat that type of a meal this morning?

We had just finished eating when Maverick slipped a small package on the table and pushed it toward me.

"You have a gift for me?"

"Yes, don't sound so surprised."

"But I don't have anything for you."

He laughed and took hold of my hand. "You forget, I knew you were going to be here, so I had time to prepare. Besides, just spending time with you has been gift enough for me."

"Aw, Maverick, that's so sweet of you to say, but I still feel bad."

He leaned over the table and kissed me. "Don't. I'm serious, the fact that I was able to help you and be there for you was enough."

"Thank you, for everything," I told him and moved to unwrap the gift.

"Why don't you save that for later? I didn't realize how late it was. We need to get going."

"We can be a couple minutes late." I laughed as he pulled me out of my seat.

"No, that's okay. Leave this here, and you can open it when you get back. Let's get going. We don't want your dad to be late."

I laughed at the thought of my dad being late to his own memorial but got ready to go anyway. I slipped the urn box that held his ashes into a backpack and wrapped the straps over my shoulders before we climbed on our snowmobiles.

On the way out to the lake, I started feeling anxious, but as we got closer, I started to notice lots of tracks in the snow, fresh tracks. Had Joshua brought people with him, or had there been a group out joyriding this morning?

We crested a small hill, and Maverick had stopped at the top to wait for me. I pulled to a stop next to him and followed the direction of his pointed finger. Down below, there were at least two dozen people, maybe more, all standing around the spot where my father loved to fish.

"Maverick? Are they all here for this?"

He put his hand on my shoulder. "Your father had a lot of people around here that cared about him, Lucy. I bet more would have come if it weren't so last-minute."

"Wow, I'm just floored."

"Come on, let's not keep them waiting, it is cold out here."

The two of us headed down the hill toward the group, and as we climbed off, Joshua and several others approached me and offered hugs, handshakes, and condolences.

I felt like I was on the verge of losing it again, but luckily Maverick was right there, his arm around my waist, shaking people's hands and talking to them as if he were part of the family—and in a way, he was, at least to my father, he was. Maverick seemed to have been the son that my father had never had, and as I looked at him, I realized that I could easily fall in love with him. Was that what my father wanted? Was that what this had all been about? I wondered as we took up a circle, and I pulled the wooden urn box out of my backpack.

I looked around the circle at the mixture of smiling and sad faces. Some of these people I knew, some I didn't, but for all of them to be here on Christmas morning, I knew that my father had truly been loved.

CHAPTER EIGHT

MAVERICK

I was hoping that she wouldn't be upset that this many people had come to pay their respects, but as it turned out, she seemed grateful—possibly a bit overwhelmed—by the caring that poured from each of Charlie's friends. These people knew him well and loved him. They would mourn for him and forever talk about him over campfires or fishing.

It suddenly hit me that Charlie was gone. Since Lucy had arrived, I'd been fascinated with her. I'd kept my focus on learning more about her and making sure she was all right, but I had yet to deal with the loss of my friend, and as I stood beside her, it hit me like a ton of bricks. I literally had to gasp for air and put my hand on my chest as it ached.

"Um, I'm really in awe and quite humbled by how many of you showed up here today, thank you," Lucy said to everyone. "My father was very lucky to have so many wonderful friends here."

Murmurs went around the group as Lucy stared at the wooden box in her hands. "I'm not quite sure what to say." She looked at me, her eyes wide, "Should I just scatter his ashes?"

"Maybe someone might want to say something, share a story, or a comment," I replied, and a chorus of consent followed. Lucy nodded just as Joshua spoke up.

"I'll go first," he said and began to tell a short story about the day that he first met Charlie. The next person talked about the first time they'd gone fishing together, and another talked about how Charlie loved her berry pie. Around and around it went until everyone had shared something. There was laughter, many sniffles, and quite a few tears shed.

During that time, no one seemed to feel the cold or worry about the time. Some people only took a minute or two, while others spoke for five or six minutes, and then it came to my turn, and I looked down at the box in Lucy's hands.

"Do you mind?" I reached for it, and she handed it to me readily.

"My dear friend, you kept me from going down a path that I might not have recovered from. You were my favorite confidant, and a father to me in ways you will never know," I turned to Lucy, "and I will forever promise to make sure your daughter is taken care of."

There were a few aws that went around the group, and her cheeks seemed to grow a little pinker as she nibbled her lip and averted her face.

"You will be missed, Charlie, by all of us." I handed the box back to Lucy who sniffled and met my gaze, and I winked. "You should probably scatter them now."

She nodded and slowly opened the lid of the wooden box, removed the large clear plastic bag that held Charlie's ashes, and set the box down in the snow. We all gathered around her as she walked to the edge of the lake; it was icy, but not completely frozen through, and Lucy took a long, deep breath before she slowly upended the bag, and the dust began to filter out. Some of it fell right to the water while some of it got caught in the wind and drifted up and around us. I could just imagine Charlie there with us: watching, smiling, laughing.

Once Lucy was done, she mumbled something under her breath and then she wiped at her cheeks before she turned to me. I didn't think twice before I pulled her into my arms and held her. People took their time saying goodbye, hugging her and me, and when just about everyone had left, I went to retrieve the box.

"What are you going to do with this?" I asked as I picked it up and studied it. It had an intricate design carved in the top. I lifted the lid and noticed something on the bottom of the box. There was an envelope taped to it, and I reached in to pull it out because it had both Lucy's and my names on it.

"Lucy, did you know this was in here?"

She shook her head as she studied the envelope. "No, what is it?"

"I don't know, but it's addressed to both of us."

"What?"

"See, it's addressed to us both. Where did you get this?"

"Um," she tilted her head to the side as she approached me, "my father's attorney said that my dad had asked for this specific box. They were friends. I guess he had the box and turned it over to the mortuary after my father passed." She took the envelope from my hands. "Let's take a look at it."

She ripped it open and pulled out a single piece of paper. "It's a handwritten letter from my father."

"What does it say?" I asked as I shifted closer to look over her shoulder.

"My dearest Lucy and Maverick, I always hoped that this letter would be a long time coming and that you would have met by now, but in case you haven't, I hope that you take the time to do so. I can just imagine the type of relationship you two could have. With that in mind, I have decided to leave the cabin to you both. Contact my attorney after you find this. You can decide who uses it when, or if you wish to share the time and make memories together. It would be my hope that you would both choose to make many memories there. I love you both, Charlie."

I was stunned. I never expected Charlie to do such a thing for me. I started to look around. Was this a joke? Was Charlie really alive and trying to hook us up? Was he trying to see what we would do with this?

"I can't believe he did that," Lucy said. "Did you know he was leaving half of his cabin to you?"

"No, I had no idea. He never said anything like that to me."

She frowned, reading the letter again. "But I was planning on selling the cabin."

"Selling it?" My jaw dropped. "Why would you do that?"

"Why wouldn't I?" She turned to me, her voice rising, "This was my father's place. I already sold his other house, and I only ever came up here to spend time with him."

"But it's been in your family almost your entire life. You have spent every single Christmas here since you were a baby."

"Yeah, and now my father is gone, so my holidays are already different. It doesn't matter if I keep the cabin." She pursed her lips, "Are you saying that you want to keep the cabin?"

"Of course, I want to keep the cabin, Lucy. I love coming here, and I love that cabin. I have a lot of great memories of your dad and me hanging out there."

She sighed and snagged the box out of my hands. "Figures."

"What figures? I can't believe you wouldn't want to keep it. What about all the memories?"

"What about them?" she practically yelled at me over her shoulder. "I have all the memories in my head," she poked a finger against her skull. "I don't need a cabin to hold them." She reached her snowmobile, shoved the box in the backpack, and spun on me. "What do you think I've been doing the last couple of days?"

"I don't know, going through your father's things."

"Yes, so I could remove his personal items and sell the cabin."

I took hold of her shoulders. "But, Lucy, your father wanted us to share that cabin. He wanted us to get to know one another. Now that we do, don't you want to keep getting to know one another? Don't you want to start our own tradition?"

"Tradition? You mean us coming up here and spending a few days together having sex in front of the fireplace?"

I jerked back as my brows slammed down in confusion. "No, it's more than just sex to me, Lucy. *You're* more than just sex to me."

"Maverick, you have no idea who I am or how you feel about me. Our time here has been great, and I really appreciate everything you have done for me this week, but you don't know me. You think you might have feelings for me, but they aren't real. You have feelings for a woman you've heard stories about, not someone that you actually know. Whatever you think you feel—is not real."

Heat spread through my veins in an instant. How dare she tell me what I felt or knew. "How can you say that? I thought we were on the same page, Lucy. I thought you were starting to have feelings for me, too."

"Maverick, I barely know you. You barely know me."

"I know you a lot better than you think I do."

"No! You know stories about me. You know what my father told you, but you don't know me!" She pointed to her chest, "You don't know the real me."

I laughed briskly, "Is that what you think?" I shook my head and climbed on my snowmobile. I needed to move, or I'd lose my mind. "You have no clue how I feel about you, Lucy, but maybe you're right. Maybe I don't know a thing about you, maybe I don't really love you," I yanked my helmet off the handlebar and pulled the straps out of the center as she stared at me, her eyes wide, "but if you think I'm selling your father's cabin, you have another thing coming."

I slammed the helmet over my head and latched it quickly before I gunned the engine and tore out of there, leaving her in a wake of snow. I didn't even bother to look back. I just kept driving like a bat out of hell trying to outrun the hurt she'd just inflicted.

CHAPTER NINE

LUCY

What the hell just happened? I turned and looked back at the trampled snow beside the lake. Just a few minutes ago, I had felt serene and at peace, giving my father what I thought was his last wish. Damn you, Dad, what were you thinking?

I slung the backpack in place and climbed back on the snowmobile. I took my time riding back to the cabins for two reasons. One, I didn't particularly want to fight with Maverick anymore, and second, because this would be the last time I was here. This cabin—this way of life—had been my father's, not mine. He'd loved it here, I'd enjoyed my visits, but I didn't want to live here for half the year. I had a life in Hudson Falls, a job, and I couldn't afford to run away from it all.

Once I arrived at the cabin, I stowed the snowmobile in the shed out back and locked it up. When I came around to the front of the cabin, I glanced toward Maverick's place and stopped in my tracks. All my bags were sitting on the front porch.

"Are you kidding me?" I tossed my hands in the air and marched over to his place. "Real grown up, Maverick," I called out loudly and had no doubt he was on the other side of the door. It wasn't until I had all my items that I turned and realized that his truck was missing from its spot.

Wow! Not only had he dumped my stuff outside, but he'd fled, too. What a chicken! Good thing that nothing else was going to happen between us. He wasn't worth it. I put my things into my SUV and then went into my father's place. For a few minutes, I walked from room to room, touching a few things and smiling at the memories—until I came to the fireplace and saw not the cold fire grate, but Maverick's warm flickering fire, and the warmth and security his arms had provided.

I clenched my eyes closed. Nope, not going to think about Maverick. I'd let the attorneys deal with it. As far as I was concerned, I'd had a holiday fling to offset the sadness of the season, and nothing more. I retrieved the items I'd boxed up and filled my vehicle. I forced myself not to stop and look at the place one more time and climbed into the driver's seat.

As I pulled away, I glanced in the side mirror and got my last view of the cabin. I had all the memories that I needed, I didn't need to make any more.

When I got home later that night, I dumped all the stuff inside my tiny house before taking a hot shower and climbing into bed. As I lay staring at the shadows, sadness began to engulf me.

I'd said my final farewell to my father today, and for the first time in as long as I could remember, my Christmas had ended in something other than joy and contentment. My stomach growled, reminding me that I hadn't eaten since the fast food stop on the highway, but I was too weary to eat.

I rolled over and tried to snuggle into my pillow, but it was cold, and the room was lonely. There was no Maverick here to warm me, no strong arms to hold me, and no one to tell me it would be all right as the tears slipped from my eyes, and I drifted off to sleep.

The next day, I woke and stumbled into my living room to find it full of boxes, bags, and my luggage from the trip. "Ugh, coffee first."

What I really wanted was to get dressed and go to work, but I was still on vacation. I wasn't supposed to be back at the hospital until January 2, and now I was stuck in my house for the next week. I should have stuck it out at the cabin and enjoyed a few more days of snowmobiling and watching the snow fall while I snuggled with a good book in front of the fire.

Of course, snuggling in front of a fire brought memories of Maverick to my mind, and I sank to the sofa. What I'd said to him had been unfair. I didn't know how he felt about me or what he knew. Granted, I had a feeling that he really did like me a lot—and when I examined my feelings more closely, I felt a great deal for him, too. There was chemistry between us that couldn't be explained away by stories told over coffee and beers.

I was right that we didn't know each other very well, but hadn't I already been considering seeing him once the holiday was over and we were home? I hadn't broached the subject with him, but I had considered it since we only lived a short distance from one another.

I curled up at the end of the sofa and sipped my coffee as I stared at the boxes around me. Would it be so wrong to keep the cabin and share it with Maverick? Even if we didn't end up together, we could share the cabin. He normally always came up after I did, so we wouldn't have to change our regular vacation schedules.

The fact that my father thought so highly of Maverick to have left half of the cabin to him meant a lot, and I couldn't ignore that. My father cared enough about Maverick to include him as if he were part of the family. Had my father known that if Maverick and I had met, we would have gotten along as well as we did? I pursed my lips and then laughed. Of course, my father would have known we'd get along.

As I ruminated, I stretched out one of my legs, and one of the bags tipped over on its side. I caught sight of something red. I set my mug down and discovered that Maverick had slipped my present into my bag before he'd dumped them outside.

I took the present back to the sofa and curled up again as I began to unwrap the shiny paper. Inside was a box, and I tore it open it to reveal a metal frame. There were three parts to it that folded in on themselves. I slowly folded back the right side and found a picture of my father and me laughing in front of a Christmas tree at Joshua's house the previous year.

My vision began to blur through tears as I flipped back the left side and found a picture of Maverick and my father fishing, the two of them holding up trout and grinning like idiots. The tears spilled over as my gaze landed on the center picture. It was a picture of my father. He was sitting in his favorite chair on the front porch of the cabin, his feet kicked up on the rail, his legs crossed at the ankle with his favorite mug in one hand, a smile on his face, and his cellphone to his ear in his other hand. I had no doubt that he was talking to me on that phone. Had Maverick taken that photo? Whoever had taken that photo had captured my father in his truest sense. He was relaxed, happy, and content.

A tear dripped on the glass of the picture, and I pulled it to my chest. Maverick did know me well enough to know that this was what I would want: something to remind me of my father at his best, and not only with me, but with him, too.

My heart melted into a puddle at my feet, and I frantically looked around at all the stuff in my living room. I quickly got up and began to dig through the boxes. I found what I wanted and dug out a gift bag from my closet. I shoved the item into the bag and ran to the bedroom to shower.

An hour later, I was back in my car and heading north on the highway, anticipation racing through me as I couldn't make this trip fast enough.

It was afternoon when I finally returned to the cabin and found Maverick's truck gone again. I wondered for a second if maybe he'd gone home, but I saw his snowmobile on the side of the cabin and knew he wouldn't leave that behind.

I headed into my father's cabin and carried in a few extra bags that I'd stopped to get on my way here. Over the next few hours, I put dinner in the oven and decorated the cabin. Since it was after Christmas, I'd managed to wrangle a tree from a local lot for almost nothing. As the fire crackled and dinner cooked in the oven, I began to feel nervous. Maybe Maverick had gone someplace else for a few days.

I sat on the couch and wondered if I had done all of this for nothing when I saw the lights of a car pull into the circle. I peeked out the window and saw Maverick climbing out of his truck. I could tell by his shadow that he was looking toward the cabin, but it was too dark to see his features. I watched him walk up to his front door and then stop.

Slowly, he bent down and picked up the small bag I'd left there. There was a dim light on his porch that was just bright enough for me to watch him shove his hand into the bag and pull out the small object. He put the angel back in the bag and turned toward my cabin.

I ran back to the couch and jumped into the corner, suddenly nervous about what he would say.

CHAPTER TEN

MAVERICK

The moment I returned to my cabin, I packed her things, left them out front, and then got the hell out of there. My heart was wrecked, and I couldn't think straight, but I knew that if I stuck around, I probably would make things worse.

If Lucy didn't want to be here, then fine, she could leave. If she didn't want to share the cabin and she wanted to sell it, then I would buy her half. I had some money saved up, and I was pretty sure I could get a loan for the rest. It was a great cabin, and if I needed money to help me pay for it, I could always rent it out. Since it was a two-bedroom, it was great for small families and could bring in a nice income.

I drove around for a while and then stopped at a diner for breakfast. It was busier than I expected it to be on Christmas morning, but many families were gathered together, talking and laughing, and I longed to be part of one of them.

I'd selfishly thought that Lucy and I were the start of something, that maybe, in a couple of years, we might have a family of our own, but that fantasy was shattered all to hell.

When I finally talked myself into going back to my cabin, I was torn as to whether I wanted her there or not. When I saw her car gone, I went over and peered into the front window. All the boxes she'd packed were gone. I rubbed my chest mindlessly as I returned to my cabin.

It was a long night, but I managed to get some sleep. The next morning, I got a call from Joshua who asked for my help. There had been a water leak at one of the cabins, and he had some fixing to do. I was more than willing to pitch in, if for no other reason than to keep busy.

It was almost dinnertime when I got back, and when my headlights reflected at me from a silver SUV in Charlie's driveway, my heart skipped a beat. Did Lucy come back? Why? For me—or for the cabin?

I toyed with going straight over to see her but decided I should take a shower and see if she came to me.

On the front porch lay a small gift bag, and my heart began to race at what I saw in it. Was she calling a truce?

I didn't think twice before I took off for the other cabin. I knocked on the door and heard her call out.

When I opened the door, Lucy was sitting casually in the corner of the sofa, a glass of wine cradled between her hands and her feet curled up next to her. She looked excited but nervous as she nibbled her bottom lip.

"I didn't expect you to come back," I blurted.

"I hadn't planned on it."

"Why did you?" I closed the door and waited.

She inhaled deeply as if to give herself strength. "Have a seat." She patted the cushion beside her as I came around the couch.

She looked at me expectantly, almost wistfully, and I dared to hope.

"Lucy, what's going on? Why did you come back?" I glanced around, and for the first time, noticed that the house was filled with holiday décor. The air smelled of turkey and stuffing. I glanced at the kitchen and saw two places set at the table. "Are you expecting someone?"

"I was, and he's here. Have a seat, Maverick." She set the wineglass beside her and kicked her feet out to put them on the floor. I sank to the couch a foot away from her as she turned to face me. "I owe you an apology. What I said to you was wrong and way off base. I can't possibly know how you feel or what you think, and I'm sorry. I was overemotional and out of line."

I reached for her hand and hesitated at the last moment, wondering if she'd pull away, but she closed the last inch and took hold of mine.

"I'm sorry for leaving you out there and for dumping your things on the porch, but I was afraid if I stayed, I'd say something that I couldn't take back."

"I understand. It was actually smart because I think if the two of us had kept going, we might have said things we both would have regretted. God knows that I had already said things that I regret."

"What do you regret, Lucy?"

She smiled tenderly, "You are more than just a holiday fling, Maverick. I do care about you. Oddly enough, the moment I met you, I felt something with you that I couldn't explain. Is it some kind of early love? I don't know, but I do know that I like it, and I really like you."

I wanted to yank her into my arms and make her repeat that. "You do?"

"Yes, I do."

"Do you still want to get rid of the cabin?"

"No, not really. It was a rash decision that I made. I was trying to tie up loose ends, and I realized that if I had sold this place, I would have regretted it for the rest of my life. I don't want to live here half the year, like my father did, but I don't want to get rid of it either."

Relief washed through me. "Thank god, but if you said you did want to sell it, I was prepared to say I'd buy your half."

She touched the side of my face, "I don't think that will be necessary."

"You know what I think will be necessary?"

She tilted her head to the side. "What?"

"I think it is extremely necessary that I kiss you, right now." I cupped the back of her head and pulled her forward as she giggled. Our kiss was warm and full of promise.

"You know we could always come to visit and then rent this place out to others."

"My father paid this off, so the only expenses are upkeep and taxes, so I don't think we'd need to do that, unless you wanted to make money on it. I always liked that no one else ever stayed here. It was just our place."

"Well, then, let's keep it just our place." I kissed her again.

The buzzer went off in the kitchen. "I need to check the turkey."

I let her stand as the buzzer stopped ringing. "Do I have time to take a quick shower? I've been working all day."

"I thought I smelled smoke on you," she commented over her shoulder as she headed to the kitchen.

"Yeah, there was a small leak at one of the unoccupied cabins. I helped Joshua fix it today."

"I thought that maybe you'd left when I first got here," she said as she opened the oven and peeked inside.

"No, I wasn't going to leave." I leaned against the counter. "I was going to come over here and dig through everything here to see if you'd left something that might tell me where to find you."

She straightened and looked at me. "You were?"

"Yes."

"Why?"

I approached her slowly, taking her hands in mine as I stood in front of her. "Lucy, you might not know how I feel about you, but I know how I feel about you. I love you. I fell in love with you years ago, and it didn't matter if I had met you or not. I knew how I felt. The minute I met you, all those feelings that I'd had were cemented into my heart. I love you, Lucy Dodds, and I wasn't going to let you go just because we had a small argument."

"You love me?"

"Yes." I kissed the tip of her nose and pulled her closer.

"You really love me, not just what my father told you about me?"

I chuckled. "You know he told me bad things about you, too. It wasn't all good." I stared down at her for a moment. "Did you open my gift?"

"Yeah, that was sneaky slipping it into my bag, but I'm glad you did. It's what helped me to come back."

"It did?"

"Yes, you gave me the perfect gift: a combination of love that my father had for us both."

I leaned back. "And you gave me a Christmas ornament."

"Hey," she slapped my chest playfully, "I'll have you know that is my father's favorite ornament, and it always goes at the top of the tree."

"I know that."

"You did?"

"Yep, he told me about it. Told me it was always the last one to be put on and the most important one. Do you know why?"

She sighed happily. "Yes, it was the first ornament that my parents bought together after I was born. They bought an angel to watch out for me."

"Now you have two."

She wrapped her arms around my neck. "I'll take two."

"I love you, Lucy. I'm glad you came back."

"I'm glad I came back, too, and I'm glad that you love me, Maverick. I have no doubt that, soon, I'll be able to say those same words without any hesitation."

"You know, when I made reservations for the cabin last year, I thought I was finally going to meet you. I never anticipated finding love on Christmas vacation."

"Neither did I."

Lucy and I kissed gently before, hand in hand, we put the final ornament on the tree.

Her father might be gone, but his memory would live on forever, through us, our children, and this cabin.

The End

2: FINDING LOVE ON THE SUMMER SURF

CHAPTER ONE

CYNTHIA

It wasn't until I arrived that I realized this was exactly what I'd needed. Janet, my best friend and owner of the condo, had been bugging me for a year to get away for a long weekend. I'd never had time. Or maybe I'd had the time, but it always seemed like other things needed my attention. Well, it was time for some *me* time, before my life got crazy again.

After lugging my suitcase up the three flights of stairs, and then gathering my two bags of groceries, along with my cooler containing more food, I got it all up the flights, and I was ready for a nap. Instead of napping, I put my food away, and then popped open a bottle of wine before kicking off my sandals and throwing open the sliding door.

The fresh ocean breeze swirled around me and pulled the thin gauzy curtains out the door as I stepped out. I put my face up to the sky, closing my eyes as the hot summer sun beat down on me. God, that felt good—so damn good.

I returned to the condo and found the cushions to the chaise lounges where Janet said they would be in the hall closet, and then brought them outside. With my wine in one hand, my sunglasses in the other, and my phone containing a trashy romance novel on the audio player in my pocket, I made myself comfortable.

I sighed as I leaned back, sipping my wine. Instead of turning on my audiobook, I closed my eyes and let the sounds of the area wash over me. The call of a seagull brought a smile to my lips, and two young children laughed not far away. The crashing of the waves reached me, and I focused on that sound, ignoring all the rest.

As I listened to them roll onto the beach, it felt like they were beckoning to me, begging me to come to them. I lifted my head, looking out toward the ocean. Janet's condo was less than a block for the sea. I could see it clearly from where I was, and even the smaller condos that faced the beach didn't distract from my view. It was beautiful, and my soul instantly started to reenergize.

I watched the waves, sipped my wine, and began to fidget. For the last three years, I had been going nonstop. I couldn't remember the last time I did nothing, had no plans, no schedule, no work. It almost made me nervous, or maybe it was more anxious.

Perhaps playing in the waves would release that tension. I pushed myself to my feet and went to find one of the bathing suits I'd packed. After debating between the bright, and slightly sexy, yellow and blue or the more reserved pink and purple, I finally decided to throw caution to the win and wear the two-piece that Janet had talked me into buying.

I pulled on my cover-up, slipped my feet into my flip-flops, downed my glass of wine before grabbing a bottle of water, and then collected two towels. I'd wade in the water for a little while, perhaps swim a bit. See if the ocean waves could release the knot between my shoulders.

If that didn't work, I had a date with my wine bottle. I let myself back out, smiled at a couple who were going into the condo beside mine, and then headed to the beckoning beach.

Several families were leaving, tugging along children and beach carts, while lugging armfuls of toys, coolers, and towels tiredly past me. When I crested the dune, I was surprised to see that there weren't a lot of people in the water. Was it cold? Maybe people just weren't in the mood to swim right now. I scanned the beach, seeing a lot of people sunbathing or sitting under umbrellas to protect them from the blazing sun.

Not a bad idea, I thought as I considered it. The sun was strong, and the rays would easily cause sunburn to someone who was fair-skinned. I was of Italian descent, so my skin didn't burn quite as easily, although I should have brought sunscreen with me anyway. Well, I wouldn't stay long. I'd take a dip, swim for a little while, maybe float a bit, and then I'd head back to the condo, shower, and maybe grab that nap, or another glass of wine—maybe both.

I found a spot to drop my towels, kicked off my shoes, and decided to keep my sunglasses on. Tucking my condo key into my cover-up, I adjusted my bathing suit slightly, feeling more naked than I had expected, and then set off for the water to hide my insecurity.

The sand felt hot under my feet, and I hurried my steps to the edge of the water where the sand temperature was much cooler. The foam of a diminished wave raced toward me, tickling my toes and pulling the sand out from under my feet as it covered them to my ankles. Ah, that was refreshing. I stepped farther in, sighing as the cool water slashed against my thighs. I ran my hands over the water as it rushed past me forcefully, almost as if telling me not to go out.

Well, that wasn't happening. I pushed on and soon the water covered my chest. The waves picked me off my feet, pushing me around a bit, and I laughed slightly. The current was strong, but it didn't dissuade me from continuing. A larger wave came toward me, sucking the water in, and my feet hit the hard sand under me. I pushed myself up, rising above the wave as the crest rushed past me angrily. "Geez," I muttered to myself as I prepared for another one right after that.

I managed to get almost over it, but I got splashed in the face, the salty water partially filling my mouth, and I sputtered. "Yuck."

I barely had my feet under me when another one came at me, and I jumped again. This one twisted me slightly, and I felt the pull on my legs as it wanted to tug me farther out. Oh, shit!

I felt panic began to creep in, and I was pulled under. I kicked, trying to right myself, and I was covered with another crashing wave that pulled me farther under.

I twisted and opened my eyes. The salt burned, but I tried to figure out which way was up. Suddenly, the word bubbles exploded into my mind, and I tried to figure out which way the bubbles were going. They would go up; that would be the surface, the air! My lungs began to burn, and no matter how hard I tried to figure out which way to go, the continual waves hitting me confused my mind.

Suddenly, a strong hand grabbed my arm, and I clung to it with my other hand as I was pulled above the water. An arm wrapped around my waist, and I coughed after getting another mouthful of water.

"Kick," a deep voice said, and I tried to do what the man asked. I kicked, and he tugged me sideways, his arm still tightly wrapped around me, right under my bust. I sputtered as more water went into my mouth, and my heart drummed so hard that I thought it might explode inside my chest.

"Take a breath," the man said, and I barely had time to suck air in before we were pummeled with another wave. The sudden fear that we would both be pulled out to sea had me almost frantic.

We were above the water again, and he told me to resume kicking. I did, and he pulled me closer toward the shore. He adjusted his hold on me, bringing my back closer to his chest while his hand practically cupped my entire breast. I should have been upset by that, but if the man brought me to safety, he could squeeze my boobs as much as he wanted.

Another wave hit us, but we stayed above the water this time as we were almost thrown forward toward the shore.

We were almost close enough that I wondered if my feet would touch yet, but the grip he had on me wouldn't let me test that theory. Another couple of seconds, and his body shifted, pulling me upright. "Can you stand yet?"

I tried to put my feet down, and I almost went under the water. I shook my head, and he pulled me a little closer to the beach, his arm still securing me to his chest. As the next wave hit us, his arm slipped, and I started to twirl away from him. At the last second, he grabbed ahold of my bathing suit and yanked me to him.

Startled eyes landed on his as our bodies came in contact, face-to-face, and I clung to him like my life depended on it. The only thing I could think to say spilling from my lips. "I lost my sunglasses."

CHAPTER TWO

MICHAEL

Being here was harder than I had expected it to be. It had been five years since I'd been back to the condo. Since Annette had died, I just couldn't force myself to do it. If it weren't for the kids, I probably wouldn't have come now, but they had talked me into it.

At least while I was here, I could start clearing it out and get it ready to sell. There was no reason to keep it. This haven had been Annette's, not mine. Yeah, I might have enjoyed our time here, especially when the kids were younger, but now it held only sad memories.

That's why I was sitting on the beach and not going through the condo. I'd walked in there, looked around, and then all but ran down here. Now I sat in a chair, reading a book that I'd purchased a year ago, and letting my mind wander like my eyes were.

From under my beach umbrella, I watched a woman with shoulder-length brown hair set down a couple of towels and yank a cover-up over her head. My gaze continued to wander, right down the back of her. Well, hello sweet cheeks. Her bathing suit barely covered her backside, but that was okay with me. She had a nice rear, and as she turned, I got a good view of her body's profile.

She had gentle curves and breasts the perfect size to fill a hand. My own palm tingled at the thought. I frowned. When was the last time I even had such thoughts of a woman? Shit, it was over five years, more like six, before Annette found out she had uterine cancer and was dying.

I huffed out a sigh and tried to return to my book, but my gaze was pulled back to the waterline as the woman entered the water. Surely, she was just going in deep enough that she could get herself wet. I glanced down the beach, seeing few people out in the water.

There was a reason people weren't swimming, and as the woman went deeper, I wondered if she had a death wish. Or maybe she was a seasoned swimmer and would be able to handle the dangerous rip current that was present today. She continued on, and I set my book beside me as I watched her jump a wave.

I glanced farther down the beach. We were in a private section, and there weren't any lifeguards on duty here. Far off in the distance, I could see the red flags waving over the lifeguards' towers on the public beach, warning people of the danger. I glanced back to the woman; she got hit with a wave, and I immediately got to my feet, removing my sunglasses and dropping them to my chair as I started toward the water.

By the time I was at the waterline, I could tell she was struggling, and she was being pulled out farther. I rushed into the water, diving through a wave once it got deep enough, and I swam toward her. I spotted her head right before another wave hit her, and then she was under.

I got near the area I had last seen her and dove under the water, straining to see her through the turbulent water. I caught a flash of yellow and surfaced for another breath before I dove back under and toward her. As soon as I was close enough, I snagged her. Probably hard enough to leave a bruise on her arm, but I didn't want the violent water to rip her from my grasp.

When she was close enough, I wrapped my arm around her and started to swim parallel to the beach, trying to get us out of the dangerous current. We got walloped with another couple of waves, and I had to readjust my hold on her a couple of times. I realized after one such adjustment that I held her breast in my hand, but I was too concerned about losing her to shift my grasp. It really did fit perfectly in my palm though.

We were out of the riptide, and I began to bring us closer to land. The waves brutalized us, and she started to get pulled away from me, but I snagged on to the only thing I could, her bikini strings, and I dragged her back.

We were face-to-face, and a wave crashed over us a moment after she said, "I lost my sunglasses." I almost laughed but didn't. I could finally touch the ground, and I fought to keep us from getting swept back out. Her arms were around my neck, her breath coming in hurried puffs at my ear, and I held her with one arm, trying to navigate the harsh water with the other.

"Put your legs around me," I told her, and she immediately did. Now that her body wasn't flailing around, it was easier to get us closer to the beach. The water was only to my chest as I rose out of the water. It was then that I realized the soft tissue touching my chest wasn't just her arm or stomach. I must have dislodged her bathing suit top as I'd pulled her to me, and now her bare breast was pressed against my skin.

I lowered us back into the water. "You okay?" I said softly as her ear was right next to my mouth.

She nodded, still clinging to me as if her life depended on it. I splayed my hand on her back, rubbing it slightly up and down to help calm her. "Why did you stop?" she asked.

"Stop?" I pulled my face back so I could try to see hers. She released her death grip on me only enough that I could shift right in front of her. Her eyes were wide, her face rather pale for her darker complexion.

She nodded. "I'll let you carry me right out of the water. You can keep going."

I chuckled, and a wave hit us, bringing our faces closer together. "I would have carried you out, but you seem to have a little wardrobe malfunction. I thought you might want to fix that before I did."

She glanced down. "Oh, crap."

75

I smirked. "Sorry, I guess that happened when I grabbed you the last time."

"Can you fix it?" she asked and then gnawed on her bottom lip.

My brows went up. "You want me to cover your breast?"

She nodded. "I'm afraid if I let go of you for even one second, I'll get washed out to sea."

I chuckled. "I think you're safe. Your legs are holding me pretty tightly."

As if she had to check, she squeezed her thighs, bringing her way to close to the danger zone, and parts of my anatomy that had been previously dormant took notice. I put my hands on her hips, pushing her back slightly.

"It's okay, your hands are free, and you already got to cop a feel once; another time isn't going to make much difference," she said.

I laughed. "Okay, if you say so, but before I do that, should I at least know your first name?"

"Cynthia," she replied quickly.

"Hello, Cynthia, I'm Michael."

"Can you fix my top now, Michael? I'd really like to put my feet on dry land."

"Okay," I told her before I brought my hands to her chest. She shifted back a little to give me access. Unfortunately, that pushed her hips lower, and her eyes widened when she felt what was going on beneath the water. I tried to keep my attention on what I was doing, but my eyes flipped to hers. She had dark-blue irises, and they were staring right into mine.

I found the edge of her bathing suit and began to pull it over her breast, my thumb brushing her nipple by accident, and she gasped, her legs tightening, bringing us into a more intimate position. Her breathing shifted, coming in a couple short puffs. I covered her breast with her suit and was about to remove my hand, but at the last second, I palmed it, squeezing gently.

Her lips parted; her legs tightened, and I zeroed in on her mouth. A wave hit us, and it was like it was meant to be. Our mouths brushed, and I held her tightly to me as I tried to keep my footing. I pulled back, staring at her; she looked as shocked as I did.

"Well, Cynthia, I think maybe you can get out of the water now." I turned us toward the shore, looking away from her.

"Yeah."

I got us a little closer, and I knew she would be able to stand. "You can put your feet down now."

Very slowly she released her lock around my waist and let her legs slip down me. Unfortunately, her slow and deliberate movements made my condition rather apparent and instead of stepping away, I felt her body press closer to mine.

CHAPTER THREE

CYNTHIA

I stared into his cinnamon eyes; they were warm and intense, and I felt my heart flutter in a way it hadn't in over twenty years. I swallowed as I wondered what had come over me, asking him to fix my top. Maybe a near-death experience had banished my shyness. Whatever the reason, I would much rather deal with the embarrassment of him fixing it than try to do it myself. With my luck, some random wave would suck me back under.

I leaned back, and as his hands worked on my top, I felt something hard between my legs. Oh, snap! Had I been the cause of that? Well, of course I had. What hot-blooded man would be able to keep from having an erection when a near-naked woman was clinging to his body so desperately?

Michael replaced the cup of my suit over my breast and didn't remove his hand right away. My body clenched around his as he gently kneaded it in his palm. Wantonly, I wanted to throw my head back and let the man have his way with me. He had rescued me after all. Would it be wrong to offer my body as a thank you?

A wave hit me from behind and pushed our faces together, our mouths somehow finding one another briefly before we pulled apart.

He looked as surprised as I did and he began to pull us closer to the shore.

"You can put your feet down now." His voice was huskier than it had been, and I slid down his body, torn between wanting to run to my towel to cover my mortification, and wanting to lure him back into the water to give him that thank you.

After a moment of staring at one another, I finally came to my senses and stepped away. My gaze slipped over his chest, and while it wasn't carved and defined, I had firsthand knowledge of how strong and solid it was.

"Thank you, Michael."

"You're welcome, Cynthia."

I stepped back farther, and we were no longer touching. I turned, heading toward the beach but paused when I realized he wasn't beside me.

"You're not coming?" I tried not to wince at my words, and he sputtered out a laugh as he looked away.

"I think I'll stay in the water for a moment and calm myself down before I do just that."

"Oh," I said stupidly. "Do you—"

"No, go on out. I think it might be easier without you here."

"Yeah, maybe," I said and turned as I felt my cheeks burn.

I kept my chin down as I got out of the water, checking my suit to make sure my other boob wasn't flashing the crowd and then rushed to where I'd left my towel. I glanced to the water as I wrapped myself and saw him still out there.

The man had just saved my life, and other than the fact that I knew his name was Michael, I didn't know anything else about him. Well, I knew he was handsome and had beautiful eyes, and his body had been attracted to mine, but that meant nothing.

I gathered my stuff, wanting to put space between me and the ocean, but I didn't want to leave without saying thank you again. Sadly, he began to swim with the current, and I watched him move away from me.

The man was probably married, probably here with his kids.

Maybe he'd been running along the beach when he had seen me flopping around. I sighed and collected the rest of my things, heading back to Janet's condo. I guess my original thank you was going to have to be enough.

When I got back, my legs were still slightly shaky, and I collapsed onto the lounge chair on the deck to rest. That was the scariest thing to ever happen to me. I honestly believe that I would have died if he hadn't come along.

I replayed the incident in my mind a few times, my body quivering with the aftereffects of my adrenaline rush. Then I thought of Michael and his heroic efforts to save me, and my body shivered for a different reason. He had been handsome and strong, and his eyes had been so beautiful as he had stared at me. His touch on my skin had been incredible, and suddenly I wished that I had waited to see where he would go once he'd gotten out of the water.

Sighing, I went back into the condo and decided to shower and pour myself another glass of wine. After finishing those things, I found myself curled up on the couch and drifted off to sleep.

I woke to find the sun lower in the sky, and I poured another glass of wine before I went out on the deck to watch the sun set. I was standing at the railing when I glanced around. There were quite a few people enjoying the evening on their decks, and laughter and chatter filled the air. I paused at each deck to study the people, envying their company.

My gaze drifted over the balconies across the small street from me and jerked to a stop. Michael stood directly across from me wearing a light-blue polo shirt and dark shorts. In his hand was a glass of wine, and he was staring at me.

He raised his glass to me and smiled. I waved, surprised to see him again. My gaze went behind him, and I searched the area to see if he was with someone, but the condo behind him was dark. After a moment, he pointed at himself, and then at me.

Did he want to come over? Oh, hell yes! I nodded dramatically to make sure he could see it and saw a smile cross his lips before he turned and disappeared into his condo.

My mouth felt suddenly dry as I wondered if I had just imagined that, but a few moments later, I saw him taking the stairs down to the ground floor. In his hand was a bottle of wine, in his other, his glass. He glanced at me as he crossed the street, and my heart squeezed in my chest.

Holy smokes! He was coming over! I spun around and ran into the condo, sliding to a stop in front of the mirror in the living room to make sure I looked okay. I was wearing a gauzy tank top that was slightly see through and hip- hugging shorts. I brushed a hand over my hair and realized I didn't have time to do anything to fix the wind-blown mess that it was.

I was barely to the door when a knock sounded, and I pulled it open. For a long moment the two of us stared at one another. He was taller than I remembered, and I had to tip my face up further to see him.

He smiled. "I wasn't sure I would see you again."

"Me either," I replied and then stepped back. "Come in."

He did, and after stepping into the small living area, he glanced around and turned to me. "I know the people who own this condo."

"You do?"

"Yeah, or at least I think I do. Janet and Nelson, right?"

"Yes," I chuckled. "Janet is a good friend of mine. How do you know them?"

"I have owned the one across the way for about twelve years. We used to have dinner together once in a while."

"Wow, small world," I said. We stared at each other again.

"Um, maybe I should have asked this before I came over, not that I could have done it from over there, but are you here with someone? A husband, boyfriend?"

I shook my head. "No, it's just me. You?"

He shifted so he was facing me a little more. "No, it's just me."

The seconds seemed to go by in slow motion as we studied each other, and I felt drawn to him as I shuffled forward slightly. "I'm glad I got a chance to see you again, Michael. I can't thank you enough for helping me today."

"The pleasure was all mine." His voice was deep as he spoke. Was he talking about the fact that he had gotten a chance to feel me up? I might have been brazen enough to ask him to help me earlier, but I wasn't enough now to ask.

"Let's take our wine outside and enjoy the evening," I told him, and he held his hand out to me to proceed him.

Outside, we stepped to the railing, and for a few moments we were quiet as we each glanced around. I felt his eyes on me and turned, feeling my knees go weak as our gazes locked.

"Maybe I'm wrong about this, but maybe not." He spoke softly as he stepped closer. "Is there something going on below the surface here?"

CHAPTER FOUR

MICHAEL

I wasn't sure if it was only me, or if she felt it too. Maybe it was because I'd saved her life, but I had saved many people, so I didn't think that was it. Could it possibly be because of the circumstances in which we met? It could be. It was known that people who experienced stressful situations together sometimes felt connected.

Yet, I doubted that. Ever since she'd stepped away from me this afternoon, I hadn't been able to put her out of mind. I'd swum parallel to the beach for a little while, the currents taking me farther south than I'd expected, and when I got out and walked back, she was gone. As I went back to the condo, I checked all the balconies, looking for her. Since she had been at that part of the beach, I could only assume that she was staying someplace around here.

I wasn't sure why, but I wanted to find her again, but what if she was here with someone? Why would someone as beautiful as her be here alone? I'd let myself back into the condo, showered, and took my laptop out to the balcony to get some work done.

A few hours later, I'd put my laptop away, then pulled a bottle of wine off the shelf and uncorked it. When I stepped back on the balcony, I glanced across the way and came up short. Was that her?

On the other side of the way, a woman stood in a flowy tank top, her brown hair waving in the wind as she sipped from a stemmed glass. Damn, it was. I watched her, willing her to look my way, and when she did, she jerked back in surprise before smiling.

I wasn't going to waste this opportunity and headed over to her place. Had Janet and Nelson sold their condo? I wasn't aware that they had ever rented it out to strangers before; maybe she was family, or a friend. Or I could be way off base. It had been years since I had seen them.

As we stood on the balcony, I couldn't take my eyes off of her. From the smile on her face, to the way her lips rounded around the glass as she drank her wine, I was kind of enthralled. I couldn't remember the last time a woman had commanded this much of my attention. It didn't hurt that her shirt was practically see through and the bra she wore was low-cut and sexy as all get-out.

Never one to not say what I was thinking, I blurted out, "Maybe I'm wrong about this, but maybe not. Is there something going on below the surface here?"

Her eyes widened, and I found I loved the color of them. A deep, dark blue almost like the ocean far out away from the coast. "Yes."

I smiled down at her. "Okay, I wasn't sure." I released the breath I'd been holding and held my glass out to her. "To surviving the rip current."

She laughed, the sound striking me smack-dab in the chest. "Yes, to surviving the rip current." She tapped her glass to mine. "And to meeting new people."

"New people." We sipped from our glasses and turned back to the railing, but now we were standing a little closer, and our arms touched ever so slightly. I enjoyed the warmth that it brought, suddenly missing the physical connection with someone. Five years was a long time not to have contact with anyone, and I frowned as I contemplated that.

"You said you owned that condo, right?" she asked, and I nodded before she continued. "You must come here often."

"I do, but not really," I said softly then turned to her. "In fact, I haven't been here in five years. I really only came here this time to get it ready to sell."

"You don't enjoy the beach?" she asked.

"I love the beach, but that condo was my wife's; at least, she's the one that wanted it."

"Oh." She shifted away slightly. "She doesn't want it anymore?"

"Annette passed away about five years ago."

Her hand shot out, her gaze softening. "I'm so sorry."

"Thanks," I told her. "Annette loved bringing the kids down here for the summer, but now she's gone, and the kids have other things to keep them busy. This is the first time I've been back since she passed."

She squeezed my arm and then released it. "I bet that's hard."

I chuckled for some reason. "Yeah, it is. In fact, that's why I was down on the beach earlier. I didn't want to be there."

"That's understandable. Personally, I'm glad you were on the beach."

I eyed her, my gaze slipping back to her chest as I remembered what I had done earlier for her. "I am too."

She laughed nervously, biting her bottom lip. Damn, I wanted to kiss that mouth. I mean a real kiss, not a brush like earlier. I cleared my throat, forcing thoughts away from that incident.

"What about you? Why are you here?"

"Well, I needed a break. I haven't had one in three years, and it seemed like a good time to take one. I'm about to start a new job, and the last few years have been one thing after another. My son is away with his father, so it seemed like a good time to have a little me time."

"You're married?" I didn't need that kind of mess.

She shook her head. "Divorced, three years now."

That was good news. "How old is your son?"

"Ten. You said you had kids; how old are they?"

"Tiffany is twenty-two, and her brother Matt is about to turn twenty-one."

Her jaw dropped as her eyes ran down my face and chest. "You do *not* look old enough to have adult children."

I laughed. "Annette and I started young. We were high school sweethearts, and I was twenty when Tiffany was born."

"Wow! I was twenty-seven when I had Jack. I wasn't sure I was old enough when I had him; I can't imagine having a kid at twenty."

"It was rough, no doubt about it. Going to college and taking care of the kids was exhausting. We were fortunate that Annette's parents had money and helped us survive so we could focus on our goals and still have a roof over our heads."

"You were lucky."

"Yes, we were."

We took a seat on the chaise lounges and talked about our kids for a while. I heard her stomach growl, and we ended up working together to cook dinner. She fixed a salad and potatoes, while I fired up the grill on the balcony and cooked chicken.

The longer I was with her, the more I enjoyed myself. The laughter was abundant, and it was really dark when our conversation took on a lull. It wasn't uncomfortable; in fact, it was quite the opposite. I enjoyed being with her and found myself waiting for her next smile, her next shy glance, her beautiful laugh.

That thing that was swirling under the surface had only grown stronger as the night progressed, and I realized that now would probably be a good time to leave. I glanced at my watch, wow, ten-thirty. "I should get going."

I got to my feet as she replied, "I guess it would be about that time."

She wobbled on her feet slightly, and I took hold of her arm. "You alright?"

"Yeah, I guess the last glass of wine hit me harder than I realized."

"We did finish off two bottles. That's a lot for anyone." I slid my hand down her arm and laced my fingers with hers.

"Although we did drink it over several hours."

"True." I stepped closer. "I'm glad I don't have to drive though."

"Oh, yes, very true." She shifted toward me. "Only a few steps and you'll be home."

"Or we could take a few steps back and be in your place." Not quite sure what got into me to say that, but the words were out there now.

Her lips curled in a seductive smile. "Well, that is correct. Only a few steps for that one."

I couldn't help myself; I leaned forward, staring at her mouth. "It's not like it would be our first kiss or anything."

"No, I guess we did kind of get past first base earlier today."

"I'm pretty sure, we paused on second base," I said right before our lips touched and I brought her body to mine. After a couple of long moments, I pulled back. "I think I would prefer to call that our first kiss."

"Um, yeah," she said breathlessly. "I agree."

I rubbed my hands up and down her arms. "I should go."

She stared at me, her hair falling back from her face, her eyes darker now that there was little light. "Or you could stay."

CHAPTER FIVE

CYNTHIA

"Is that the wine talking?" he asked softly as he cupped my cheek.

I laughed. "Well, I'm pretty sure the wine is doing some of the talking here. I'm not usually so bold, but had you kissed me like that when you first arrived—and sober—I would still be asking you to stay."

"Not bold? You were pretty bold in the ocean today when you told me to fix your top."

"I was scared shitless then," I admitted with a chuckle.

"Not scared now?"

"No, not at all."

"Then I'll stay."

My reply to him was to step forward and pull his face down toward me for another kiss. This one had us shifting, and he walked us back toward the sliding glass door. Inside the condo, my hands were under his shirt, lifting it, and he pulled back long enough to toss it off.

"Your shirt has been driving me nuts all night," he said huskily as he ran his hands over the material. "I haven't been able to stop thinking about you in the ocean."

"Take it off of me." He didn't hesitate as he pulled it over my head and tossed it somewhere to the floor.

Our kisses grew more intense, and his palms came to my breasts, squeezing them as I arched into his hold. I whimpered softly, and he peeled back the cups of my bra to pinch my nipples as we landed against the wall near the hallway.

His hands left my breasts and cupped my backside, lifting me, and I once again locked my legs around him, feeling that hardness between his hips. His mouth ran down my neck as he pushed me against the wall. I clung to him, my hands in his hair, holding his mouth to my body before he pushed off the wall and carried me back to the bedroom.

Our bodies landed on the bed, our hands rushing to touch anything that we could as we rolled one way and then the other, getting the rest of our clothes off. Finally naked, Michael pulled me into the center of the bed and lowered himself over me. His hand caressed the side of my face; his lips brushed over mine tenderly, and then he pushed his hips forward.

Now that we were here, the rush was over, and we made love slowly with soft touches and gentle motions. We carried each other over the pinnacle and held on tightly afterwards. I drifted off to sleep lying sated on his chest, his fingers trailing over my side and hip repeatedly.

The last thing I remember was him kissing my forehead and saying thank you. For what, I didn't know, but in my sleepy mind I said you're welcome.

I woke up to the feel of a hard body against mine, and a slight throb in my head. For a moment, I was at a loss as to why there was someone in my bed, but then it all came back like a wave washed over me and cleared away the sand hiding the memory.

Oh, man, Michael had stayed the night. Part of me was thrilled, while the other part was wondering what he was going to say as he left this morning. Thanks for a good time; hope you enjoy the rest of your stay.

I winced and felt his hand squeeze my hip as it landed there. His lips touched my neck tenderly, and I pushed thoughts of him leaving out of my mind for a few moments. He nuzzled my ear. "Morning."

I rolled to my side, glancing at him, wondering how different he would look in the light of day. His eyes twinkled slightly as he stared at me. "Morning," I said and then cleared my throat.

"I hope you don't mind that I stayed."

I shook my head. It wasn't like it could be changed. "No, it's alright."

He winked and then threw back the sheets. "I'm going to use the bathroom."

I watched the very handsome and naked man walk out of the room and down the short hallway to the bathroom. Holy crap, I'd slept with that? Suddenly, all those girlie parts that had been sated last night were calling for a repeat performance.

Only, I had no doubt that he was going to return and gather his clothing, making an excuse to have to get going. Imagine my surprise when he returned and climbed back under the sheets, lying on his side and smiling at me.

"My turn," I said softly as his minty breath wafted over me. Obviously, he'd used my toothpaste to freshen his morning breath. I guess I should do the same. I darted out the door, feeling very exposed in my nakedness. Why was it so easy for a man to strut around in his birthday suit, but when a woman did it, she felt self-conscious?

Probably because women had no self-esteem. Okay, so most of the time, I did. I used the bathroom, brushed my teeth and hair, and then glanced at my body. Yeah, my boobs sagged a bit, and I did have a few stretch marks on my belly from my pregnancy, but my body wasn't bad. In fact, my body was pretty damn good, and last night he had wanted it. Did he still? Only one way to find out.

I returned to the bedroom, my chin up, my eyes zeroing in on his. He let them boldly drift down my body and then slowly back up. He lifted the sheet for me to join him, and as I slipped under, I noticed that his erection was back. Yay, me!

We lay on our sides, staring at one another for a long time. "You're a beautiful woman, Cynthia."

"Thank you," I replied.

"I have to admit something to you."

Had he lied that his wife was dead? That was going to be a total dealbreaker if he did. "Yes?"

"You're the first woman I have been with since Annette died."

I blinked, not expecting that and quite in awe of his confession. His words last night echoed through my mind. "Is that why you thanked me last night?"

He chuckled. "Maybe. I guess I was thanking you for being you. For being a beautiful woman who was there with me."

"Well, I'm glad that I was."

"What about you? Have you been with anyone since your divorce?"

I shook my head. "No, after John left, I was too busy to think about sex or dating."

"I get that. I threw myself into my work after Annette died. I guess this is the first time I've stopped and just thought about myself."

"Feels good to think about yourself a little, doesn't it?"

He laughed. "Yeah, actually, my kids have been telling me that I needed to do that. They have told me for years that I should start dating again."

"But you weren't ready."

"No, I wasn't."

"Are you now?" I asked playfully.

He leaned forward and kissed me. "I'm not sure I'm ready to start dating, but I'm pretty sure I'm ready to do what we did last night again."

I wrapped my arms around his neck. "I think I agree with you."

Michael and I made love again, and I felt free for the first time in a very long time. There was no pressure, no expectations, and when we were done, we silently lay in each other's arms for a long time.

"I just realized that we don't even know each other's last names," he said after a while.

I laughed as I looked up at him. "Is that a bad thing?"

He chuckled. "You think that we shouldn't share that information?"

I shrugged. "I don't know. I kind of like the air of mystery around this. It's different than anything I have ever done, and I like it. In a few days, I will go back to my life, and you will return to yours. We'll probably never see each other again. Why add something to the mix that doesn't need to be present?"

He contemplated that for a moment. "Okay, I get what you are saying. So, we just hang out for a few days together, have fun, enjoy this incredible sex, and then we say goodbye with nothing else?"

"Yeah, why not?"

He cupped my cheek and pulled me to his mouth. "I think it sounds good. We enjoy a few days, no promises, no stress. I can do that. When do you leave?"

"I have to head back on Sunday, early afternoon."

He nodded. "Well, then we have two and a half days to have fun."

"I think we should start that fun by making breakfast. I'm starving."

"Got any pancakes?"

"Aw, a man after my own heart." I laughed as I slipped out from under the covers and found underwear to slip on.

He grinned at me, and I felt something tighten in my chest. It was only for a few days, and that was going to have to be enough.

CHAPTER SIX

MICHAEL

I'd wondered what she would say when she woke up, and after a few moments of her being obviously uncomfortable, she'd returned to the bed a confident and very sexy woman.

I wasn't sure why I had told her about not being with any other woman; maybe it was because we hadn't used any protection, and I should probably broach that subject. At the age of forty-two, I wasn't sure I wanted to find out I was going to be a father again, but what was done, was done.

Her suggestion that we enjoy our time together and then go our separate ways seemed only perfect with everything else going on. I was well aware that this was a summer fling, and while I had never had one before, I thought it was perfect for both of us.

Cynthia pulled on underwear and disappeared out the door. I followed after putting on my boxers and shorts. In the kitchen, she now wore her gauzy tank top with nothing under it, and my gaze got stuck on her bare breasts underneath. Jesus, we were totally going back to the bedroom after breakfast.

It took a few moments, but our conversation finally got going again, and before I knew it, we were laughing and telling more stories about our kids. We avoided any serious conversation about work or our marriages, and just had fun.

After breakfast I headed back to my condo to change. We were going to head down to the beach and relax for a while. I'd made her promise me not to go into the ocean unless I was with her, and she was quick to agree.

After I'd let myself into the condo, I paused and glanced around. For some reason, things looked different now. I went to a picture of Annette and I that was perched on a side table and lifted it.

I miss you, Annette, I thought to myself. I knew she would not fault me for what I had done. She had told me herself to move on with my life after she died. She didn't want me to live the rest of my life without love, not that what I was doing right now involved love. I set the picture down with a sigh.

What exactly was I doing? I glanced out the back slider at Cynthia's balcony. I was enjoying myself. Finding my feet again. Maybe when I got back home, I'd be ready to take the next step and actually go out on a date. Maybe—

I dressed and collected a few things for the beach before meeting Cynthia downstairs on the street. This time she had a chair and a beach bag with her. I'd brought my umbrella with me, and we got our little space together in comfortable silence. I couldn't remember the last time I had been comfortable around someone that I didn't feel the need to fill the quiet. It didn't seem necessary with Cynthia, and I was grateful for that.

With the crash of the waves as background noise, I settled in with my book, while she slipped earbuds into her ears and fiddled with her phone. I raised a brow at her, and she grinned. "Audiobook."

I nodded as she leaned back under the umbrella and got lost in her story. Unlike yesterday, I was able to get into my story, and the two of us enjoyed the moment.

A while later, she was wiggling in her seat and pulled her earbuds out of her ears. "I need to get in the water; you want to come?"

I grinned at her. "You want me in the water with you, or do you really want me to come?"

She giggled and said something under her breath that I didn't hear. I set aside my book, and we headed down to the waterline. The two of us waded out until she was almost chest height in the water.

"I think that's far enough," I commented as I squatted down under the water and glanced down the beach. The red flags were down, but that didn't mean the current wasn't still dangerous.

We jumped the waves a little, and one brought her toward me. I wrapped my arms around her, and she locked her legs around my waist, her arms around my neck.

"This reminds me of something," I said softly to her.

"Yes, it does," she replied just as quietly. She squeezed her legs around my waist, pulling my hips to that soft spot between hers.

I groaned and kissed her tenderly. She nipped at my bottom lip. "You keep that up, and I'm going to take you right here."

She lifted a brow. "Promise?"

"Shit, Cynthia," I muttered as I got rock-hard, and she pulled me tighter to her. I glanced back to the shore; there were quite a few people on the beach, but no one was paying any attention to us.

I slipped my hands down her backside, pulling her bathing suit bottoms to the side so I could touch her. She gasped, and her eyes closed as her lips parted.

"You like that?"

She nodded.

I shifted her hips away slightly as we bobbed with a wave, and I yanked on the tie to my suit, pulling back the Velcro and releasing myself. She grinned at me as I brought her hips back to mine and shifted into her.

A sound released from her mouth, and I kissed her softly as I moved my hips under the water. I hadn't had sex in the ocean in a very long time, probably since I was in my twenties, and it was more exciting than I had remembered.

I held her tightly to me, feeling her body move with me and with the help of the rocking ocean. I paused. "I probably should have asked this earlier, like way earlier, but are you on birth control?"

She pulled her face back, laughing slightly. "Yes."

I pushed my hips forward, filling her as her eyes closed. "Good." The two of us remained locked together, moving slowly, our eyes locked with one another's until the release began to build. Then I pulled her to me, kissing her hard and hoping that we looked like lovers just enjoying a romantic moment, and not two horny teenagers going at it in the surf.

After we'd finished, I put a little space between us, and she laughed. "I feel like a naughty kid. I've never done that."

"What, had sex in the ocean or in public?"

"Either, both!" She laughed.

"Kind of exciting, isn't it?"

"Yes, it was, very."

We held on to one another for a few more moments and then slipped apart, both of us readjusting our suits before climbing out of the water. I held her hand as we returned to our chairs, and then we went back to our respective books.

She had packed some snacks, and for the next two hours, we relaxed, ate, read, and then took another dip. Although that time we did behave ourselves.

It was almost two in the afternoon when she yawned. "I think I need a nap. All this fresh air is making me tired."

"Sure it's not all the sex?" I said quietly toward her.

She laughed. "Well, that could be helping."

"Why don't we head back? You can shower and take a nap, and then I'll take you out to dinner later."

"That would be nice."

"We can go to a restaurant, or we can hit the boardwalk."

Her eyes widened excitedly. "I've never been to the boardwalk."

"Well, then that is where we will go. You can't visit the beach and not go down to the boardwalk."

"Perfect."

We packed our stuff and headed back to the condos. On the street between the two, we paused, and I kissed her briefly before I told her I'd collect her around five.

I let myself back into the condo and came up short when I saw my daughter standing there with a smirk on her face. "And who were you just kissing?"

"Tiffany? What are you doing here?"

"I was worried about you. Thought maybe you needed some help down here, but obviously, you don't need my help. Who was that?"

I chuckled. "Cynthia."

"And who is Cynthia?" she asked with a wide grin.

"Just a friend."

She nodded dramatically. "Yeah, a friend. That's what it looked like from up here."

I set my stuff down, ignoring her comment. "Did you really come down to help me?"

"Yes, I thought you might be having a hard time being here since Mom is not here."

"Well, it has been hard."

She laughed. "Not that hard, obviously."

Oh, she had no idea just how hard it had been. I cleared my throat. "I need to shower. Why don't you get some snacks out while I do?"

She nodded, and I went into the bathroom, wondering how I was going to be able to hang out with Cynthia now that Tiffany was here.

CHAPTER SEVEN

CYNTHIA

The man brought out something in me. That naughty, playful side that had been hidden since I was in college, and it felt great!

Wait until I told Janet about my weekend. Wait, I couldn't tell her about this. What would she think about me hooking up with a stranger for the weekend? Although he wasn't a stranger; she knew him. Hmm, I'd have to think about that. Maybe I could just tell her that I had met someone, and we'd had a nice time. I snorted; a nice time was barely touching the surface.

After a wonderful, leisurely nap, I took a shower and dressed in a sundress that looked great with my slightly sun-kissed shoulders. I was ready when there was a knock on the door, and I opened it with a wide smile, ready to throw myself into the arms of the man on the other side. Only problem was, he wasn't alone.

He looked slightly tense. "Cynthia, my daughter surprised me today by showing up."

"Oh," I said and held my hand out to her. "You're Tiffany. Your father has told me so much about you."

Her eyes had checked me out from head to toe before she stepped forward and put her hand into mine. "Nice to hear that he didn't forget about me. It's nice to meet you."

"Tiff wants to ride down with us to the boardwalk. She's going to meet friends down there."

"Oh, okay," I said, trying to keep a smile on my face, and I noticed the begging look in his eyes. "That sounds like fun. Let me get my purse."

I frowned as I collected it, wondering how I was going to be able to enjoy the rest of my weekend with Michael if his daughter was hanging around. Pasting the smile back on my lips, I joined them on the landing outside my door.

Michael winked at me, and I realized that he was probably thinking the same thing that I had been. I wonder if his daughter was upset about me joining her father. I hoped not.

Michael had his hand on my lower back as we reached the ground level, but he removed it, and his daughter laughed. "You two don't need to pretend. I did *see* you two kissing earlier."

Busted! I glanced quickly at him and saw he was trying to hide a smile behind his hand as he wiped at his mouth.

"You saw that, huh?" I replied to her, not knowing what else to say.

She grinned. "Yeah, and I think it's great. Dad needs to start living his life again."

"Hey, I'm right here," he said. "Don't talk about me like I'm not."

"I'm not. I meant that I'm glad you aren't sitting around being all sad. It's nice to see you smile."

Michael looked at me, his eyes warming, and then he reached over and took my hand in his. His daughter glanced around him and smiled at our hands.

We took the bus to the boardwalk, and Tiffany and I talked about the things she liked to do down there and how she was meeting friends. At least Michael and I would have a little more time alone together.

When we arrived, it was busier than I had anticipated, and I was mesmerized by the sights, sounds, and smells. Small shops lined the boardwalk with trinkets and food, and families pushed strollers or chased after toddlers. There were a ton of teens and young adults in groups along the way, and I took them all in.

Vacation for us had always been visiting family in other states. We had never done anything like this before, and I felt slightly sad that Jack had never experienced this. Maybe Janet would let me borrow the condo another time, and I could bring him down here.

It was probably going to be a while since I started my new job on Monday and wasn't sure when I would get any vacation time. Perhaps next summer. I turned to say as much to Michael and noticed him staring off in the distance.

I stepped closer, squeezing his hand. "You okay?"

He snapped his attention to mine. "Yeah, I'm fine." He glanced around, and I wondered if he was searching for his daughter before he leaned down and kissed me.

Tiffany had departed from us shortly after we arrived, telling her dad she'd see him sometime and then laughing.

"Are you upset that your daughter saw us together?"

He touched the side of my face. "Not at all. I have to admit I was surprised to see her, but she wants me to be happy."

"Are you?"

"Happy?" He cocked his head, and I nodded. "Yes, right now I am."

"Then where were you just a minute ago? You didn't look so happy."

"Ah, just lost in some thoughts. Annette loved being at the beach, but she wasn't a fan of crowds. She hated coming down here during the busy season."

"What about you? Do you like this?"

"Actually, I do." He smirked. "While I don't love crowds, I do like to people watch, and you see all kinds of people here."

I glanced around, my eyes caught on a couple rollerblading past. "Oh, yes, you do."

"Do you like it?"

"Like it?" I shook my head. "No, I love this. I'm like you; I love to watch people, and holy cow, it smells so good down here. I was wondering if I might be able to borrow Janet's condo again and bring Jack. He's never been anywhere like this."

He opened his mouth as if he was going to say something, and I saw a thought pass before my eyes, but it was immediately gone. "Well, then we need to let you try some of those great smells. There is nothing better than boardwalk fries. Come on." He pulled me toward a stand and then glanced down at me. "What do you think of Ferris wheels?"

My gaze slipped past him to the large one on the pier. "I love them!"

He squeezed my hand. "This weekend just keeps getting better and better."

The fries were wonderful, and so was the cotton candy that he bought me. I was laughing when he sucked my sticky fingers into his mouth, and I didn't tell him that over his shoulder, I could see his daughter watching us with her friends. They were giggling and happy, and I let it go at that. I was glad she wasn't upset with her father being with me, not that it would last, but for now, this was what I wanted.

Michael took me on the Ferris wheel, and then we did a few more of the rides and played a couple of the games along the pier. We ate dinner in one of the seafood restaurants along the boardwalk, and just when I thought we should head back, he surprised me by pulling me into a small photo booth, and I sat on his lap while we stared at the camera and made funny faces for the first two pictures. He turned my face at the last second and kissed me for the final two shots.

We laughed as we looked at the photos after they were spit out of the machine, and I wondered who was going to keep them. He tore off the last one, slipping it into his pocket and handed me the others. I held it to my breast for a moment, a keepsake from my wonderful weekend.

We strolled the boardwalk, wandered through some shops, and I paused in front a large glass display. "This is beautiful."

He put his arm around me. "Sea glass. It's pretty popular around here."

"It's beautiful." I fingered the pendant of one of the necklaces.

"Do you like that one?"

"Yes, I love them all, but this lighter brown color reminds me of your eyes."

He pulled it off the display. "Then you should have it."

"Wait! You aren't going to buy me a gift."

"Yes, I am," he said and winked. "I don't want you to forget my eyes."

I laughed and let him purchase the necklace. He told them not to even bag it up and instead pulled the tag off and slipped it around my neck.

The cool glass landed on my chest, and I touched it. "Thank you," I whispered to him, and he wrapped his arm around me, kissing my brow.

"My pleasure."

We were leaving the store when he paused. I glanced to where his gaze was and saw it on a large glass sculptor of a wave. "Wow, that's beautiful."

He nodded and then led me out of the store just as fireworks began to burst in the sky outside. Could my night be any more incredible?

CHAPTER EIGHT

MICHAEL

It was the perfect afternoon, and I had the perfect company beside me. After the fireworks, we piled onto the public transportation bus and made our way back to our condo. I wasn't sure if she would want me to stay with her again, but I knew I wanted that.

As we walked hand in hand down the short street to our places, she spoke softly. "So, would your daughter mind if you didn't come home tonight?"

"I'm not sure I care what she thinks, but to be honest, I think she would be alright with it. If that's what you want."

"Oh, that's what I want."

"I was hoping you'd say that."

I made love to her again, twice, and held her tightly in my arms as we drifted off. In the morning, I found myself alone in bed, and I found her pouring two cups of coffee, my polo from yesterday covering her body.

My chest hummed with appreciation of her in my clothing, something that Annette had never really done. We ate breakfast, made love again, and then headed out for an afternoon adventure. Tiffany and her boyfriend, Jarrett, joined us at the mini golf place, and we played a round of eighteen holes before having lunch together.

Cynthia and I returned to her place, and we couldn't keep our hands off one another and didn't even make it to the bedroom this time. Then we headed down to the beach before dressing and having a nice dinner at a small restaurant within walking distance.

In the back of my mind, I knew that she would be leaving the next day, but I tried to block that out. That night when we got back, I stood on her balcony, looking over the way at my place. Maybe I should keep it. Perhaps if she did come back with her son, I'd run into her again.

During the last two days, we had talked no further of what would happen once we left. I guess she was content with a weekend affair, but something in my chest said it was more. Maybe that was just to me. I'd fallen in love with Annette in high school and had never thought of another woman. Now, Cynthia was all I could think about. Was it possible to have something with this woman? Would she want it?

I kissed the back of her head. "I was thinking." I turned her in my arms, and she raised a brow. Suddenly, I felt slightly nervous. "What if we saw each other again after this?"

Her lips parted in surprise. "Are you serious?"

"Yeah, I think I am."

She chuckled. "You think, huh? That's kind of dangerous for a man to think sometimes."

A laughed rolled through me. "Once in a while, maybe."

The humor left, and she looked contemplative. "I'm not sure, Michael. This whole time I've been telling myself this was just the weekend. While we have been together for two days, what do we really know about each other? We don't even know where the other lives, or what they do." She put her fingers to my lips as I was about to supply the answers. "And I think it was smarter for us not to."

"Why?"

"Because what we have right now is incredible. It's intense and romantic, and it doesn't exist in the real world. I'd hate for us to make a promise to each other and then find out it won't work later. I'd rather us keep this wonderful weekend to ourselves to forever cherish."

I couldn't fault her on that. I knew so many people who struggled with life and relationships while dealing with the daily grind and careers. "I guess you're right."

She smiled sadly and cupped my cheek. "I will never forget you, Michael."

"I hope you don't, Cynthia. I know I will never forget you."

I'd kissed her, and the two of us had gone back to her bedroom. Making love to her that night, it was like we were on the countdown to the end, and in the back of my mind, I fought with the realization that I didn't want to let her go. I didn't want this to end.

In the morning, we made love one more time, and then I had gone back to my place to let her get things packed in peace. We were going to have lunch before she left, and I'd invited her back to my condo to do that.

Nervously, I glanced around. Was that a good idea? Was having her here, in Annette's space, the right thing to do?

"What are you thinking about? I can see smoke coming out of your ears." My daughter breezed past me into the kitchen.

I laughed. "Actually, I was wondering if I should sell this place or not."

"I think you should keep it. If you don't want to use it, I will."

"I'm sure your brother would like me to keep it too."

"Yeah, Matt said he was going to come down next week." She paused. "I told him that you met someone."

"It's not what you think, Tiffany."

Her brows jumped. "Not what I think? You have been with her every moment since I arrived."

"Yeah, but she leaves today."

"So." She shrugged. "You'll see her later."

I shook my head. "Actually, I won't. We decided to keep it right here, and when we leave, it stays here."

Her jaw dropped. "Are you serious? You guys look so happy together."

111

I didn't tell her that I agreed with her; instead, I said, "We have had a good time."

"A good time." She snickered and rolled her eyes. "Dad, I think it's much more than a good time. I really like her. I thought you did, too."

"I do, Tiff, but we both have busy lives. We have no idea if it would really work out in the real world."

She paused in front of me. "And you have no idea that it won't." She slapped my chest and called out over her shoulder as she left that she was going to hang with her friends.

What would Cynthia say if I told her I wanted to get to know her more? Did I want more? Did I really want to get to know her or have more of her in my life? Hell, for all I knew she lived three hours south of here, and not north like I did.

Pushing the thoughts to the side, I went into the kitchen to make a pasta salad for lunch. The whole time I did, I dwelled over what I wanted to do, and when she arrived, I still didn't have an answer.

I let her in, and she scanned the living room. "This is beautiful."

"Thanks, like I said, it was Annette's haven."

She turned to me. "Are you sure you want me here?"

"Yes, it was her haven. Looks like it's mine now."

"You're not going to sell it?"

I shook my head. "No, I think I'm going to keep it a little longer. Tiffany said that her and her brother wanted to use it. Might as well keep it in the family for a while."

"I think that's a good idea." She wandered over to the picture of Annette and me. "She was a beautiful woman."

Much like Cynthia was, only in a much different way. Cynthia was much more down-to-earth than Annette had been, but I didn't say that.

"Lunch is ready," I told her, and we filled our plates and went to sit under the umbrella outside.

She glanced around, laughing. "It looks so different from this angle."

"Does it?"

She nodded, and we sat to eat quietly. I felt tension beginning to form in my shoulders as the minutes passed by. "Cynthia," I started to say, and she lifted her gaze.

She put her hand over mine. "Don't."

"Don't what? You have no idea what I was going to say."

She grinned. "I am pretty sure you were going to bring up the subject of seeing one another again. I told you that we need to let that go."

"What if it's not meant to be let go?"

"Michael, you are such an incredible man. You will never know how much this weekend meant to me, but it needs to remain that way."

I sighed. "Are you really divorced?"

She looked surprised. "Do you think I lied to you?"

"No, but I'm just trying to figure out why you are so hell-bent on us not seeing one another again."

She set her napkin on her plate and stood, pulling my hand so I did the same. "When I went into the water, and you showed up, that was fate. I want to believe that fate brought us together for a reason. Whether it was for an incredible weekend of love, or something else. I don't want to test fate, though. Do you?"

CHAPTER NINE

CYNTHIA

Since he had left me this morning, it was all I could think about. I didn't want to leave him, but I also wasn't sure that what we had shared would be able to continue into the real world. I had to start a new job, and Jack would be home in a few days. My first priority was to him, and then my job. My personal life was about to be put back on the shelf until I was able to find a few more spare moments for me time.

I had no doubt that in those moments, Michael would come to mind and remind me of the wonderful time that we had. I didn't want to ruin those memories.

Michael stared down at me, and I wanted to fall into him. I wanted to fall all the way into him, from head to toe and with every beat of my heart. I could fall in love with this man; maybe part of me was already on the edge, looking down, ready to take that leap, but I couldn't.

"Fate, huh?"

I nodded.

"Yeah, I guess I believe in it." He grew quiet, and I could see his mind turning behind his beautiful brown eyes. "Okay, how about this.

We let fate take its course. If we see each other again, you have to promise me that you'll accept it, and we'll see what happens."

"You think that we really will see each other again?"

"I'd like to think so." He cupped my face, brushing hair behind my ears, and then staring at me. "I really like you, Cynthia, and I don't want this to be all there ever is between us."

"Then if it's meant to be, fate will bring us back together."

"You agree that if it does, we'll see where things go?"

"Yes. If something brings us back together, then I will take that as a sign, and I promise I will see where it goes."

"Deal," he said before he kissed me. I curled myself around him, praying silently that fate would bring us back to one another one day.

"I should get on the road. I have a lot to get done today, and I have no idea how traffic is going to be."

"Alright, I'll help you load your car."

"I already did that," I commented.

"Why? I would have helped you."

I shrugged. "I had time to kill before I came over."

It was so much harder to drive away from him than I had imagined. I'd also pictured myself doing a U-turn and going back, but that wasn't going to happen. If Michael and I were meant to meet again, we would. It might take years for it to happen, and in the meantime, I would enjoy my life.

On my drive home, I replayed our moments together, cherishing them. Sometimes laughing, sometimes swallowing the deep emotion as it got caught in my throat. I'd never been loved like that before. He had consumed me, brought out my inner desires, my fantasies, and he'd been right there with me through every step.

His touch had been incredible, his voice the kind you would never tire of, and I silently prayed that one day we did meet again.

When I got home, I thanked Janet immensely, telling her that it was exactly what I needed and leaving it at that. Since we were on the phone, she couldn't see my face and had no idea that the smile that was on my lips was for anything other than my enjoyment of my weekend alone.

I started my new job the next day, and while I knew I would love it, I was slightly overwhelmed by the amount of information that I would need to retain. There was so much that I might have learned in books but doing it all firsthand was something else entirely. By the end of the first day, I was wiped out and passed out shortly after dinner.

Even thoughts of Michael couldn't keep me awake as I fell into a deep slumber. The second day was slightly better, and when I got home, I was excited for Jack to be home. Even the sight of my ex-husband, John, didn't detract from my good mood.

Jack told me about his trip to see his aunt and uncle and the fun things that they had done on their seven-day trip. "I wish you could have been there; Nancy isn't as fun as you are."

I laughed. "I'm glad you had fun, kiddo."

"Who is this guy?"

I turned to see him staring at the pictures of Michael and me. Whoops, forgot to put those away. "Oh, just a friend." I removed them from his hand and slipped them into my purse on the counter.

"I didn't know you had a boyfriend."

"I don't. I told you that he's just a friend."

"Yeah, but you were kissing him."

I shrugged. "Friends do that sometimes."

He grew quiet. "Mom, I know you and Dad aren't getting back together. It's okay if you do have a boyfriend."

I turned back to him, then rubbed my hand over his head. "I appreciate that, Jack, but he really is just a friend."

"Okay, but just so you know."

"Thanks, kiddo. Now are you ready for camp tomorrow?"

Jack changed gears and started talking about all the things he was looking forward to at summer camp. By the time he was in bed, I was looking forward to hitting the pillows myself, and I removed the pictures of Michael and me from my purse and put them in my bedside drawer.

I drifted off on a wave of passion and desire and for a moment wished that I had at least gotten his phone number.

CHAPTER TEN

MICHAEL

I chuckled. "Okay, well, at least let me walk you to your car."

"You can do that." I held her to my side, wanting to drag my feet the whole way, and way too soon we were stopping beside a small blue SUV.

I pulled her into my arms, holding her close, hating that I had to say goodbye. "Drive safely, Cynthia."

"I will. You too when you leave."

"I will." I pulled back and looked down into her beautiful face. "Thank you for helping me move forward."

"I think I can say the same for you. I guess we both needed the assistance."

"Yeah, I guess we did." For a moment I wondered if she would start dating, but I pushed those thoughts to the side. I had no claim on her, and she was free to do what she wanted, as was I.

I kissed her long and hard, ingraining the feel of her into my memory one more time. As we stepped apart, I smiled sadly at her. "Until fate brings us together again."

"Yes," she said, and she blinked quickly before she turned for her vehicle. I held the door open and watched her climb in. I didn't want to close the door, and I leaned in and kissed her again.

"Bye, Cynthia."

She ran her hand over my cheek. "Goodbye, Michael."

I stepped back and pushed the door closed. For a moment, we stared at each other through the window, and then she shook her head and started the engine. She waved at me slightly before she backed out of the space, and I suddenly wanted to run after her, but her vehicle picked up speed, and she began to drive down the short road.

My gaze landed on the bumper sticker on the left side. It was a youth sports team, and my gaze jumped to her license plate. Holy crap, she didn't live too far away if her son played for the Marsh Creek Eagles and she lived in Pennsylvania. I found myself grinning as I watched her turn onto the main road and disappear.

I had a feeling that fate was going to come back in play, and I was going to make sure that she held up her side of the bargain when it did.

~

A week later I was back into the swing of things at work. While from time to time, I would think of Cynthia, I didn't dwell on it. I reserved those memories for when I was alone and could enjoy them.

The phone on my desk rang, and I picked it up as my gaze drifted to my side credenza. In the center was the glass wave that I had seen when I was with Cynthia. I had gone back that Sunday afternoon and purchased it. I wanted something more than the small picture I had of us to remember that weekend.

"Yes?"

"Dr. Grandison, they need you down in surgery."

"Alright, I'll be right there." I hung up and stood, pausing beside the glass wave and brushing my fingers over it. I shifted to look at the picture of the two of us kissing that I had set beside it. I smiled and then headed down to surgery.

I was depending on fate to bring Cynthia back to me. I knew that it was only a matter of time before it happened. Then I would prove to her that we were meant to be more.

I pushed through the doors of surgery. "What's going on?"

One of the nurses turned to me. "A woman was just brought in from a vehicle crash. She's pretty banged up, and Dr. Brentway is already in surgery."

"Okay, I'll start washing; someone come give me the details."

All thoughts of Cynthia were brushed aside as I shucked my white coat and focused on what I was about to do.

CHAPTER ELEVEN

CYNTHIA

The week had gone by in a snap, and before I knew it, it was Friday afternoon. I was looking forward to sleeping in tomorrow and spending the day with Jack. Maybe we could go down to the pool and relax. The thought of swimming brought Michael to my mind instantly.

I sighed as I shifted things around on my desk and then put my hand to my chest where the sea glass pendant hung. I fingered it and could almost feel the heat of the sun, the touch of his body against mine, and I closed my eyes for a moment to cherish the memory and hold on to it for just one more moment. Who knew that I would miss him this much? I sure hadn't.

"Hey, Cynthia, I need your help. Can you get these packets to the heads of department? I need signatures from these three as soon as possible," my boss Veronica said.

"Sure."

"If you can, stand over them and make sure they do it right then. We don't have time to wait. They were supposed to sign these earlier this week, and they know that."

I laughed. "No problem. I'll lord over them and get it done."

"Thanks!" She took a moment to tell me where I'd find each

person, and I headed out. On the third floor, I learned that the woman I needed to see was in a meeting. I told her assistant that I'd be back shortly. On the fourth floor, I waited while the young woman spoke to someone on the phone and nodded before hanging up.

She gave me a wide smile. "Can I help you?"

"Hi, I'm Cynthia. I just started in the administration office. I have papers for Dr.—" I paused and glanced at the paperwork in my hands. "Grandison to sign."

"Oh, that was him on the phone. He is on his way back from surgery. You can wait in his office."

"Okay, thank you."

"Welcome to the hospital," she said sweetly, and I thanked her again and stepped around her desk. So far, everyone had been friendly, and I was enjoying my job.

I glanced around the room and headed toward a chair in front of the large mahogany desk. I was just about to take a seat when my eyes landed on a glass sculpture on the other side of the room. No way! Was it the same, or just so similar that it jolted me?

I went directly to it, reaching out and touching the cool glass that brought me back to the shop where I'd seen it with Michael. My gaze traveled over it, and then I saw the picture beside it. I gasped! Was it possible?

A sound behind me had me spinning around, and my knees went weak as he stepped inside. "Michael!"

"Cynthia?" We stared at each other for a moment. "What are you doing here?"

"I work here now. My new job is in the administration office. I had no idea you were a doctor, let alone a doctor here."

He stepped back to his door and said something to his assistant that I couldn't hear before he closed the door and walked toward me. He stopped a foot away, and I couldn't tear my eyes from his. Those beautiful cinnamon eyes.

He held his hand out. "Hi, I'm Doctor Michael Grandison, and you are?"

I juggled the papers to my left arm as I chuckled, sticking my hand out. "Cynthia Palazzo, Dr. Grandison. It's a pleasure to meet you."

He pulled me toward him, then let go of my hand before removing the papers from my arm and setting them on his desk. He put his hands on my hips.

"The pleasure is all mine."

"I can't believe you are here," I whispered. "Did I fall asleep at my desk?"

He gave me a lopsided grin and leaned down, brushing his lips against mine. "Does this feel like you're dreaming?"

A bubble of laughter burst out. "Well, I have to admit I've had this dream a few times since I last saw you."

"Glad I'm not alone," he said huskily. "I'm going to kiss you again now, Cynthia."

"Please," I sighed out.

Michael brought our bodies together, and I reveled in the feel of his mouth against mine. In all honesty, I had never thought I would feel it again, and I was overwhelmed and overjoyed at the same time.

He pulled back a few moments later. "Not bad for a second first kiss."

"Yeah, not too bad."

"You know, I knew you lived somewhere around here."

"You did?"

He nodded. "Yes, when you left last Sunday, I saw the Marsh Creek Eagles sticker and your license plate. My son used to play for Marsh Creek years ago."

"He did?" I squeaked.

"Yep, and I had this serious temptation to start going to the games just to see if I could find you there."

"You did?"

He chuckled, brushing his knuckles over my cheek. "I did. So, are you going to hold up your side of the bargain?"

"You mean about us?"

He nodded.

"Yes," I breathed toward him before I pulled his face back to mine. "Oh, god, yes!"

Fate had brought us back together, and I had missed him so much this last week. To find that my brush with death would lead me to this amazing man, and that my job would bring me back. There was no doubt about it. Fate was working here.

He grinned as he glanced at his desk. "You ever have sex on a doctor's desk?"

I tossed my head back and laughed. As I opened my eyes to him, I opened the door to my heart, and I stepped out. I felt myself fall, fall for him, fall to him, and I knew that he would be there to catch me and keep me safe.

Who knew when I took that impromptu vacation that I'd find love in the summer surf?

The End

3: FINDING LOVE WITH DEAR SANTA

DEDICATION

This book has a special dedication as part of the set. Nancy Krueger was the winner of our Dedication contest, and requested the following dedication:

I'd love to dedicate the book to my mother Leila H. Colvin, who taught me about love and always filled Christmas with magic, wonder and joy.

CHAPTER ONE

FAITH

It had been twelve years since I had last walked through the gates into Merryland's Santa Depot, and I was doing so tonight with mixed feelings. I wasn't sure I wanted to feel the excitement, or magic in the air, but it was hard not to get sucked into the festive atmosphere around me. The colorful lights twinkled from every direction, while the decorations crowded the edges of the sidewalks. Music floated through the air from the open doors of the shops, and carolers wandered along the cobblestones. From where I stood, at least half a dozen songs collided in my ears, and I felt overwhelmed by sight, sound, and memories—oh, the bittersweet memories!

"Wow, Mom!" I turned to my five-year-old son, Luke. "This is awesome! Is this where Santa lives?"

"Um, no, he lives in the North Pole; this is just where he comes to work."

"And we are going to see him, right?"

"Yep, that's the plan," I told him with forced enthusiasm. I was all for him sitting on Santa's lap and telling him what he wanted for Christmas; I just hated that he was going to be disappointed. Between my finances and the hottest new Mighty Mark Conquers the Ocean

131

playset that he asked for—along with every other boy his age—there was no way I could get it for him.

When the set first released, it was seventy dollars. I had hesitated the one time that I'd had it in my hands and walked out of the store without it. I had hoped it would go on sale before Christmas, and it had, only I didn't know that you had to be camped in front of the store two hours before it opened to get one.

Now you couldn't find the set, and if you could, the price was almost double from scammers who had bought all the playsets they could get their greedy hands on to make a profit. Those people deserved a special Christmas present in their stocking, and it wasn't anything nice like coal.

We were a little over a week away from Christmas, and I had finally concluded that it just wasn't happening. Luke was going to be sad, but hopefully, the few other things that I had been able to get would ease his disappointment.

That was one of the reasons that I didn't want to come tonight. I didn't want Luke to sit on Santa's lap or to mail his Dear Santa letter, and I sure as hell did not want to send the one that Luke had forced me to write. Yes, my five-year-old had forced me to write a letter to Santa, too.

My request was short and sweet, and I knew that when one of the Depot workers opened it, it would get tossed into the yeah-that's-never-gonna-happen pile. I knew they had a pile like that firsthand. When I was eighteen, I had volunteered here during winter break, and I had been the lucky person to put letters there.

There were five stacks that letters were sorted into. The first was for wishes to fulfill. The second was requests that could *possibly* be fulfilled. The next two were desires that required a miracle and yearnings for love—that one was always big and sometimes X-rated. Then there was the yeah-that's-never-gonna-happen pile. I had no doubt mine would get dropped into that one.

If they still did the same thing that they did sixteen years ago when I volunteered here, then the teenagers would snigger over the wishing for love, and the adults would sigh and shake their heads over the never-happening pile. It wasn't because they were irritated with those wishes, but because they knew they couldn't do anything about them. I had heard one person say that he hated that pile because it depressed him.

I had to agree with him. It was a depressing pile, but so was my wish this year. I couldn't wait for the new year to ring in so I could forget this year even happened. Hell, I'd be happy to fast-forward another one if it would help heal my tired and sad soul.

Luke coughed and immediately captured my attention. "You alright?"

"Yeah, it's just a little cough."

A little cough for him usually meant that his asthma was going to kick up. I glanced around at the festive tree trimmings—all were from live trees. Luke had horrible allergies, and one of them was to trees—like almost every kind of tree. The poor kid had been on allergy medicine and received shots to combat those allergies for three years already, with no end in sight. I had hoped that when we moved back here to Merryland, that his allergies might have gotten a little better, but they hadn't.

"Your chest isn't tight, is it?" I squatted next to him as he shook his head, although his eyes told me something different. "Luke, is your chest bothering you? If it is, we should go."

He grabbed my hand. "No, Mom! I want to see Santa. I'm okay. I'll use my inhaler, and I'll be okay."

I pursed my lips and removed the inhaler from my purse. Luke had been using one for two years too, so when I pulled him off to the side, he snagged it out of my hand, turned his back on me, and used his device. His way of showing me that he was a big kid now.

When he finished, he practically threw the inhaler back at me and started to hustle away. "Come on, Mom! Let's go find Santa!"

I shoved it into my purse and took a few strides to catch up to him. He coughed a few more times, but I knew that was because his lungs were breaking up what had been causing the problem. My nose twitched as we passed a shop that was a little heavy on the cinnamon.

I was acutely aware of scents these days because I was always on the watch for something that would set him off. Heavy spices, trees, grass, floral scents could easily cause a reaction. We'd been to the ER more times than I could count for breathing treatments. I'd even had to use an Epi-Pen on him twice to keep his airways open.

Another reason for us to get this over with quickly. If Luke's lungs were aggravated five minutes after we arrived, what were they going to be like in thirty minutes? I didn't want to imagine.

Luke and I bypassed the shops and food stands, although his eyes seemed to devour the sweet treats for sale in the displays. I had promised him hot chocolate, and I hoped the one store was still here. It had been the best hot chocolate I had ever had, and I could not wait to taste it again.

At the back of the little shopping village—that went deck-the-halls-crazy this time of the year—was Santa's court. We were lucky, it was still early, and there were only three people in front of us. With luck, Luke could tell him what he wanted, and we could grab our hot cocoa and be back in the car in twenty minutes.

"Mom, do you have our Dear Santa letters?" Luke asked as he tugged my hand closer to the line.

"Yes, I do. I just need to find the box for them." I dug around in my purse and removed the two envelopes. Mine was lavender, and Luke had added a bunch of Mighty Mark stickers to it. He said the more stickers, the more important it looked. His letter was also covered in similar stickers, although he had opted for a blue envelope.

As we eased our way to the line, I saw the mailbox on the opposite side. After Luke sat on Santa's lap, we could drop the letters and be on our way. While we waited, I searched for the shop that had the cocoa that I wanted. I could have sworn it was on the left side, just a couple doors down, but I couldn't see it.

Luke yanked on my hand. "Come on, Mom! It's my turn next!" I pasted an automatic smile to my lips as I glanced at him, and then it immediately disappeared as I began to search for the shop again.

I tapped the envelopes in my hand as I waited impatiently for the child ahead of us to finish. Santa chuckled, the sound deep and joyful, and for the first time, I looked at him.

The man seated in the big chair had blue eyes that sparkled at the little girl on his lap. He had one hand on her back between her shoulder blades, and the other hand on her knee to keep her balanced. The little girl was talking at superspeed, and I wasn't sure if Santa was even able to understand half of what she was saying.

When she paused to suck in a breath, he found his spot to jump in and gave an big ole jolly laugh. "Wow, Jill, there sure is a lot on your list. Are you sure you've been a good girl this year?"

The little girl nodded dramatically. "Yes, Santa! I've been perfect, except when I hid my brother's hockey stick in the trash can, and the trashmen took it, and when I gave the cat a bath with Mommy's favorite shampoo, and I told Todd that I'd give him my lunch if he did my homework." She cocked her head. "Oh, and I don't always eat my meat. Sometimes I give it to the cat under the table."

I tuned the little girl out as she rambled on, and I peered at the child's mother. She was elegant and stylish in knee-high boots, tight jeans, and a glamorous sweater. She was also on her phone, totally ignoring both Santa and her daughter. I was pretty sure her lack of attention might have been the reason the little girl got herself in trouble.

Finally, Santa found a way to get the little girl off his lap, and I saw him shake his head at his elf, who was snickering behind her hand as she approached Luke.

"Hi, there!" the female elf dressed in a cute little green outfit said to Luke. "What's your name?" She bent over, and Luke grinned.

"Luke McMillian." I found myself smiling as the elf took Luke's hand and brought him toward Santa. I glanced at Santa and found his mouth parted as if surprised, and his eyes shifted to me quickly. The surprise in his features seemed to grow, but then he blinked and returned his attention to Luke.

"Luke McMillian, it sure is good to see you, young man. Come on up on Santa's lap and tell me if you've been a good boy this year."

Luke practically jumped onto Santa's lap, and I hastily dug into my purse to find my phone so that I could take a picture. I ended up dropping both of the Dear Santa letters, but I did manage to get a shot. When I bent down to pick up the letters, Santa watched me, and I gave him a brief smile before I started looking around at the shops again.

I stepped over to the elf. "Um, do you know where the cocoa store is? It's been here for years, but it used to be down on the left."

The elf who looked like she wasn't more than seventeen years old looked baffled. "Quite a few of the stores have hot cocoa," she finally replied.

I tried not to frown as I turned back to Santa and found Luke climbing off his lap. "Mom! Santa said he wants to have my Dear Santa letter right now! He said he would take yours too and deliver it to the elves in person."

My brow popped. "Oh, he did, huh? Well, isn't that nice of him?" I peered at Santa and found him observing me.

"It would be my pleasure to read over them and make sure that they get fulfilled," Santa said in a deep jovial voice.

Yeah, I doubted that would happen. Santa stood and stepped forward, and I found myself surprised to see how tall he was. Most men weren't tall to me since I was five foot ten, so to find a man standing at least six inches taller than me was surprising.

"Mrs. McMillian," he said huskily, and I wasn't sure why, but I was oddly aroused by the way he was looking at me. Thoughts of doing dirty things to Santa slipped through my mind, and I chastised myself.

"Um, here." I handed him the letters quickly and then pulled Luke back by the shoulder.

Santa stared at me for a moment longer. "The cocoa shop that you want is down on the right now. They moved into a bigger storefront." I frowned. How did he know which one I wanted? He winked. "Santa always knows what you want, Faith."

CHAPTER TWO

PETER

Santa always knows what he wants too, and right then, it was to ditch the itchy suit and beard and find out why Faith McMillian was back in Merryland. Faith and my best friend, Jeremy, had left town for good when they had graduated from college and moved to New York City so Jeremy could work on Wall Street. His dream since he was old enough to understand what a market was and that you could win big or lose everything in one bad investment.

Jeremy had said he would never come back to this small town, and he hadn't for twelve years. Why was he back now? While I hadn't seen Jeremy in years, we traded Christmas cards and the occasional email. I remember when Luke was born, he had sent emails out to everyone he knew, sharing his joy. While the kid was cute, I'd been more interested in the woman holding the baby.

I'd had it bad for Faith all through high school, but she had been with Jeremy since ninth grade. They were the perfect pair—at least to everyone else—voted most likely to celebrate a fiftieth wedding anniversary together, as well as prom king and queen. No one knew that I'd been fascinated with Faith since the eighth grade. It was something that I had buried deep within me, especially after Jeremy made it known that he liked her. When they started dating, I had held off hope that one day I would get my chance. Sadly, that never happened.

It was evident that Faith didn't recognize me, but it had taken me about two seconds to pull up the last photo I had seen of her from my internal memory banks and put two and two together. I should have said something to her, should have found a way to let her know who I was. Something had stopped me, though.

I looked at the two envelopes and set them beside my chair. At least I could figure out what they wished for this year. Maybe it would give me a clue as to why they were in town. I'd have to reach out to Jeremy tomorrow and see how he was doing.

After I took a seat, the line began to grow, and I happily went from one child to the next while keeping my eye on the passing people to see if Faith and Luke would come by again. Unfortunately, they never did, and when it was time to close down the line, I was quick to grab the two envelopes and bring them with me.

One of the assistants in the Santa Depot helped me get out of my costume and then brought me a plate of food. I sat at Santa's desk and ate while I skimmed over a few letters left for me. A few times, I glanced to the side at the two envelopes I'd collected myself. Something told me to hold off on opening those until later.

"Busy night tonight, wasn't it, Peter?" Donna, the manager of the Santa Depot, said as she breezed into the room, her Santa cap askew.

"Busier than I thought it would be on a Tuesday night. Did you guys have a lot of presents to wrap tonight?"

"Holy crap, did we." She sighed and sank into the chair on the side of my desk. "Every year, I say that I'm going to find someone else to manage this, and every year, I find myself cutting, folding, taping, and making bows by the hundreds. You know, at this time of year, I can do it in my freaking sleep."

I chuckled. "So you don't want me to bring mine in for you to do?"

She gave me a stern look. "Not if you want me to continue to be your friend!"

I leaned back in my chair and kicked my feet up on the desk. "I wouldn't do that to you. Besides, I enjoy wrapping—"

"You want to trade jobs? I think I could rock the Santa suit." She grinned.

"No, I do not. I was going to say, I enjoy wrapping my ten or so gifts. I would not enjoy wrapping hundreds. And unless you can grow about ten inches, you would be swallowed up by the suit. You know the only reason they asked me to do this was that I was tall enough and they wouldn't have to have the suit adjusted after Mr. Griffith passed away."

A dramatic sigh escaped her. "It was worth a try." She lifted her face to mine. "Is that the only reason you do this?"

"No." I laughed. "I do it because you asked me, and I enjoy helping."

"Speaking of helping, we haven't gotten as many requests as we normally do. I bet we are going to have a mad rush over the next couple of days."

I glanced at the two envelopes on my desk, and Donna followed my line of focus. "What are those?"

"Two more letters."

"Where did they come from?"

I picked them up, staring at the arrangements of stickers all over them. "Do you remember Jeremy McMillian from high school?"

"Yeah, of course."

"Do you remember Faith?"

She rolled her eyes. "Who wouldn't remember Miss Perfect? She was pretty, nice, popular, athletic, and smart. I wanted to hate her, but I couldn't."

I chuckled. "Yeah, that's her."

"Why are you asking me about them?"

"Well, because these letters are from Faith McMillian and her son, Luke."

"What? No way! Did they come back to town? I swear I remember Faith saying she was never coming back here."

"Well, it looks like they did. Faith didn't know it was me, but she dropped the letters while Luke was on my lap. I told her I'd take them."

"Well, are you going to open them and see what Mrs. Perfect and her son want? I doubt we can help them, but who knows."

I tore open the envelope from Luke and pulled out the piece of paper. The handwriting was rather neat for a young kid, but it was still a little all over the place.

"Dear Santa, it's Luke McMillian. I moved. I hope you find me! I have been good this year. I had to be so that my mom wouldn't be sad. I really, REALLY want the Mighty Mark Conquers the Ocean set!! You can take it in the water and everything! I also want a new skateboard and helmet because mine got sold. A bike would be good. I've never had a bike before. And if you can make my mom happy, I'd like that too. Maybe I might like that more than a bike or skateboard, but not as much as the Mighty Mark Conquers the Ocean! Here is my new address so you can find me 675 Elm Street, Merryland. Bye, Santa, Luke McMillian."

"Wow!" Donna said when I finished reading it out loud. "Maybe Faith and Jeremy got a divorce."

I frowned as I skimmed over the letter again and stopped at the part about making his mom happy. Why was she unhappy? That thought bothered me. "Looks like she's back at her mom's house. Maybe they did get a divorce."

"You going to visit?"

"Yeah, of course. Faith and I were good friends. I wasn't just friends with Jeremy."

She gave me a sly smile. "Yeah, I know how much of a *friend* she was to you. You forget that *we* have been friends for a long time, and you had more than once drunkenly expressed your feelings for her when you were in college."

I laughed. "That was a long time ago, Donna."

Mary popped her head into the room. "Donna, someone needs you out here."

She sighed and stood as Mary disappeared. "Don't even try to deny that if that woman gave you five seconds of her time, you wouldn't be in heaven."

"Whatever, Donna, go help your customer."

"I want to know what her letter says." She pointed to it and gave me a very intent look before she walked out.

I slipped Luke's letter back into his envelope and stared at hers. What was she going to ask for? Reconciliation with her husband? Her son to behave better? A new car?

I tore the envelope open and pulled out the note. Faith's flourishing cursive was only a single line.

Dear Santa, I want my life back. Faith

I frowned. That comment said so much—yet, it didn't tell me a damn thing. Was she sick? Did she want her marriage fixed? Was there something else going on?

I folded the paper and put it back in the envelope, then collected both of the letters, grabbed my jacket, and headed toward the door. The address that Luke had put in his letter was Faith's childhood home, and I had every intention of driving past the house.

Not that I was going to knock on the door, but because I just wanted to see if she was there. Maybe I would send Jeremy an email tonight and see how he was. Perhaps I could tell him I saw Faith and wondered where he was. Perhaps he would fill me in on what was going on without me asking.

I drove down Elm Street and found my palms a bit damp. I didn't know why I was nervous; I didn't intend to stop—at least not tonight. I slowed to a stop one door down from her mother's house. It was dark now, and I couldn't see much of the outside, but the lights were on inside the house, and the curtains were still open in the living room. I cut the lights on my vehicle and watched her and Luke through the window.

He was in pajamas and standing next to her chair. She was smiling at him, and the minute he turned to walk away, the smile disappeared, and she leaned forward and put her hands over her face, rubbing them up and down for a moment before she followed Luke from the room.

A light in the back corner of the house turned on, and a few minutes later, it went off. That room had been the guest room; her bedroom was beside that. Quite a few times, Jeremy and I had visited in the middle of the night and whispered to her through the guest room window. It was further from her parents' room and wouldn't be as easy to hear us talking. We had even convinced her to sneak out a few times by climbing out the window.

The memory of one of those times hit me hard. Jeremy was holding the screen up, and Faith lost her balance as she came over the windowsill. She fell forward, and I caught her. The two of us went to the ground. Her face and mine were only an inch away, and we stared at one another for a few seconds before Jeremy grabbed her by the arm and pulled her up. I could have sworn there had been something in her gaze, and for the rest of the night, we avoided each other.

Faith appeared in the living room again, a wine glass in her hand as she curled herself into the chair and put her head back, closing her eyes. I started my car and pulled away. I didn't want to be creepy; I knew she wouldn't appreciate that.

When I got home, I went right to my computer and woke it up, bringing my email up immediately. I started a new one and typed in Jeremy's name to populate the address field. In the subject field, I put *Checking In.*

Then I typed a quick message about seeing Luke and Faith and wondering how he was. It was short and didn't mention anything about the Santa letters. I hit send, and then got up and was about to head to the bathroom when my email pinged a moment later. I turned back and saw a notification that the email was invalid.

I frowned as I sat down. "What do you mean it's not valid? That's the one I always use." I checked the email to make sure it was right and tried it one more time. It bounced back again. "What the hell, Jeremy?"

Well, I guess the only way to find out what was going on was to see her tomorrow morning in person. With that decided, I turned off my computer and went to shower as memories of Faith slipped through my mind.

CHAPTER THREE

FAITH

I was cleaning up the breakfast dishes when there was a knock at the front door. Luke took off for the entryway. "Don't you open that door!" I shouted but knew he would ignore it. He was notorious for opening the door to strangers. It was something I had gotten on him about over and over again in New York.

I was wiping my hands on a towel as I came around the corner and heard the door open. A man stood on the opposite side, and my feet practically glued themselves to the floor as I stared at the man's face. Peter Sterling, holy smokes!

"Hey, buddy. Is your mom here?" Peter was looking down at Luke through the storm door.

"Mom!" Peter shouted and then opened the storm door for him. "She's washing dishes."

Peter took hold of the door and paused, glancing up and finding me rooted to my spot. A handsome smile filled his face. "Hi, Faith."

"Peter, what a surprise," I said as I finally managed to move forward again. "Come in." I glanced at Luke. "I told you not to open the door, Luke."

"Come on, Mom." He rolled his eyes. "We aren't in New York City anymore; no one is going to kidnap me here."

"Kidnappings happen everywhere, Luke, not just in cities." I smiled at Peter, shocked to see him, but happily so. "What are you doing here? How did you even know I was here?"

He stepped in. "You forget this is a relatively small town. Someone saw you last night at Santa's Depot."

"Ah, figures. Well, come in."

"Do I get a hug?" he asked, and I shook my head.

"I'm sorry, yes! Of course, you surprised me." I stepped forward, and for a moment, I wanted to stay right there. God, I missed being held. I pulled away before it got weird. "So you met Luke already. Luke, this is an old friend of Mom's, Peter Sterling."

"Hi." He waved.

"How are you, Luke?"

"Fine," he said as he turned and began to walk down the hall toward his bedroom. Obviously, having an adult visitor wasn't of interest to him.

"Get dressed, Luke, and clean your room," I called after him, but he didn't respond. "Would you like a cup of coffee, Peter? I was just getting ready to pour myself another cup."

"Sure, I'd love that. When did you get to town?" he asked as he followed me back to the kitchen.

"Um, three days ago."

"Did you come back for the holidays?" he asked as he shrugged out of his coat, and I studied him for a moment. Peter had always been an attractive man with his sandy blond hair and bright-blue eyes. Now he was even more so, with a short, neatly trimmed beard. I'd often thought as a teenager that if things didn't work with Jeremy, I might have tested the waters with him. I frowned and turned away.

As I poured coffee, I tried to remember what he had asked me. "I guess you could say that." He waited until I brought our cups to the table before taking a seat. "What do you want in your coffee?"

"Cream if you have it."

I collected the cream container and returned to the table. "So, how are you? Married?" My eyes cut to his left hand, which did not hold a ring. "A half dozen kids? Or are you still a stud muffin and have several ladies to call on?"

He laughed as he set the creamer down and stirred it with the spoon that I gave him before I took my seat. "I'm fine. Divorced, no kids, and far from a stud muffin these days. Is Jeremy here with you?" He grinned at me as he asked, and something pinched in my chest. Peter didn't know.

"No, Jeremy isn't here, Peter. Jeremy died almost a year ago, a week after Christmas."

Peter looked shocked as he stared back at me, his coffee mug halfway to his lips. He lowered it. "Holy shit, Faith. I had no idea. What happened?"

"He had a brain tumor. He went very quickly; it was aggressive."

He laid his hand over my wrist and squeezed. "I'm so sorry, Faith. I had spoken to him a few times over the years, but not often. I think the last time we spoke, Luke was two or three."

"Well, I'm sorry to be the bearer of bad news. When it happened, I was dealing with a lot and didn't reach out to some of the people that I should have."

"That's okay; I get that. Are you back here visiting your mother?"

I sighed, and my shoulders dropped. "My mother passed the day after Thanksgiving. I came back to figure out what to do and finish settling her estate."

His eyes closed, and he lowered his head momentarily. "Damn, Faith. I am so sorry. I don't know why I hadn't heard about your mom."

"It's okay. She had a stroke, was in the hospital for a few days, then a nursing home where she suffered another one and passed."

His hand was still on my wrist, and his thumb brushed over the skin. It had been a long time since I let someone comfort me, and it felt wonderful. In fact, so incredible that tears filled my eyes. I pulled my hand away from his and wiped at my eyes. I couldn't cry now.

I knew that if I opened my mouth to talk, I would have started spilling everything, and while Peter might have wanted to catch up, I doubted he would want all the dirt and drama of my last few years.

"Hey." He reached for my hand again. "Faith, how are you holding up?"

I cleared my throat. "I'm fine if I don't think about it," I told him before I sipped from my cup.

"I can't even imagine what you are dealing with. What can I do to help?"

I laughed a little. "Nothing. I'll be fine; we'll be fine. I just need to figure out what to do now."

"What do you need to decide on?"

"Well, I have to figure out if I want to sell this house or move back here permanently. All my stuff is in storage in New York, so its easy to move when I decide where."

"Then stay here. Do you have to sell this house?"

I shook my head. "No, I don't think I could get much for it if I did try to sell it. It is paid off, but it needs so much work."

"Then you should stay here and work on it."

I sighed. "I don't know. It depends on if I can find a job. I never planned to come back here, and I'm not sure I want to be here, but it is all I have right now."

"Why is your stuff in storage in New York?"

I bristled and looked away from him. I did not want to air my dirty laundry to him. "Do you mind if we don't talk about this right now? It's a touchy subject. Why don't you tell me what you have been up to?"

He was thoughtful for a moment, then he sat back in his seat and grinned. "Okay, I can do that. I got engaged when I took over my father's construction business when I was twenty-five, and he had a heart attack. He's still alive but enjoying retirement now. I was twenty-six when I got married and twenty-eight when I got divorced."

I laughed. "You were married for two years? What happened?"

"Oh, it was less than that. I caught my bride blowing my partner in one of our work trailers. I quickly found out that she had handed out that favor to quite a few of the guys that worked for me."

I blurted out a laugh and clapped a hand over my mouth. "I'm sorry, I shouldn't laugh."

He snickered. "It's okay. I laugh about it now. I have no clue what I saw in her, but whatever it was, it disappeared that day. It took longer to get divorced than the amount of time we were living as husband and wife."

"Where is she now?"

"No clue, she moved away. I haven't heard from her since."

"So, no one else special in your life?"

He shook his head, his eyes staring into mine. "No. You?"

I scoffed. "Yeah, like I would have time to think about getting involved with someone. I haven't been in the best headspace in the last couple of years."

"You want to talk about it? You might not remember this, but I'm a pretty good listener. Do you remember all the times you used to call me and gripe about Jeremy or your parents?"

I chuckled. "I do remember that. You were a good friend."

"I'm still a good friend, Faith, and if you need someone to talk to, I'm here. I can even give you my phone number, and you can call me tonight and pretend like we are seventeen again."

I laughed harder. "Oh, I'm not sure I would want to go back that far in my life. Maybe a couple of years, but not quite that far."

"Well, I can still give you my phone number."

"I would appreciate that. Maybe you can give me some idea of who can take care of a few things around here."

"Um, Faith, you did just hear that I own my own construction business, right?"

"Yes, but I'm sure you're busy."

"I'm never too busy to help a friend. What work do you need done?"

I barked out a laugh. "Wow, I don't even know where to start."

"Well, how about you start by making a list? I'll take a look at it and see what I can help you with."

"You don't need to do that, Peter."

"I want to."

I pursed my lips. "I appreciate that, but right now, I'm a little tight on funds, so I'm not sure what I can afford to get done." I felt my cheeks warming from embarrassment.

Lines creased his brow for a split second. "Look, make a list, let's see what's on it, what would be the most important things to fix, and I can help you approximate the costs so you can make a game plan. How does that sound?"

"Actually, that sounds good." He grinned, and I took a moment to enjoy it. "I'm glad you stopped over, Peter."

"Would you have contacted me if I hadn't?"

I averted my gaze. "I don't know. Honestly, I'm not sure how long I'm going to stay."

"Well, will you at least be here tonight?"

"Um, yeah, I'm pretty sure I'll be here tonight," I said with a light laugh.

"Good, then I'll come by tonight, and we can go over that list."

My brows jumped. "You want me to make that list today?"

"Yeah, is there something else you need to do?" He glanced around a little. "Besides putting some Christmas decorations up?"

I laughed a little uneasily. "Mom always had a real tree. Luke is allergic to trees, so that's not an option, and artificial trees are kind of expensive, and I didn't think to have our tree shipped out here."

"Ah, I get that. Makes sense." He nodded slowly. "Will you work on that list, though?"

"Peter, I do appreciate your wanting to help me, but I'm serious about not being in a place to do anything right now financially. Especially without a job."

He again took hold of my wrist. "Faith, how about you just make that list, and I help you put it in order, and then you can figure out when you can afford to do things? If you decide to sell the house, you're going to have to do some of these things anyway."

I winced. "Yeah, that's true."

"Alright, so I can come by tonight."

"At least let me cook you dinner if you are going to help me figure this out."

He cocked his head. "Do you cook better than you did at twenty? I remember you cooking at our apartment once, and you almost burned the place down."

The memory came back immediately, and I laughed. "I'll have you know, I would not have burned the food if you had left me alone. If I'm not mistaken, you were teasing me about something."

"Not me!" He looked comically affronted. "I would never."

"Yeah, right, Peter, and you should know that I'm an excellent cook. Would six-thirty work for you?"

"Six-thirty would be great," I told her and glanced at my watch. "And with that, I need to get out of here. I have to get to work."

He finished his coffee and then carried the mug to the sink before he came back for his jacket. I slipped out of my chair as he put it on.

"I really am sorry about Jeremy and your mother, Faith."

"Thank you, Peter." I touched his arm, and the two of us stared at one another for a moment. Did I hug him again?

CHAPTER FOUR

PETER

The sad, haunted eyes that stared back at me screamed for me to take her in my arms and protect her, but I wasn't sure that would be received very well. So instead, I put my hand on her shoulder, squeezed, and told her I'd see her tonight.

As I let myself out of the house, I realized that in less than a day, all my unresolved feelings for Faith had exploded back into place. I sat in the cab of my truck as I realized that my hands shook slightly, and my heart was pumping fast. She did that to me, she always had. Seeing her again, having her look into my eyes, touch me, speak to me, and laugh —holy shit, that laugh—about tore me to shreds. At least a dozen times, I had wanted to pull her to me and comfort her.

I was confused, but not about my feelings for Faith. What confused me is how she was in a bad financial situation. Jeremy had bragged many times about his expensive condo, thousand-dollar suits, and high-paying job. Did he not have life insurance? How could he pass away, and she now be in such dire straits? It didn't make sense. She had worked too, for a corporation, I was pretty sure, but I didn't know the details. Jeremy had always glossed over things about her. When we spoke, he stuck to himself.

Back in high school, it was no big deal, but in college, it had started to get on my nerves. I had still considered Jeremy to be my best friend, but when he moved away, I almost felt relieved. I would have felt better if Faith hadn't gone with him, but she had made her decision.

Now she was back—for how long I did not know—but I wasn't going to let her leave so easy the next time. Hopefully I could convince her to stay and raise Luke here. Give him a solid foundation and a safe place to grow up. Even if it wasn't with me, this was a great town to grow up in, where kids could get a good education. I'm sure she could find a job someplace around here; maybe I could help.

With that thought in my mind, I headed off to work. I was two hours later than usual, but I had called my foreman and told him I'd be late.

Throughout the day, Faith kept coming back to mind. Along with that, memories of Jeremy and I growing up. I was having a hard time comprehending his death, and as much as Faith probably didn't want to talk about it, I hoped that she would. I needed to understand it more so that I could let it go, or perhaps find a way to help her. Now her Dear Santa letter made much more sense.

Typically, I was only Santa on the weekends, but Ben had a prior engagement he needed to do last night, and I'd taken his place. Damn, am I glad I did. I could not imagine finding out that Faith had been in town for weeks or months and I hadn't known.

It made me think about what she said earlier about not being sure if she would have contacted me. Why wouldn't she have? I added that to my mental list to ask her tonight.

The day sped by, and I made it home and showered with enough time to hit the florist on the way to her place. I had no trouble remembering what her favorite flowers were and was standing at the counter, getting ready to pay when I paused. Faith said Luke was allergic to trees. What were the chances that he was also allergic to flowers? Well, damn. I apologized to the shop clerk and hustled out with empty hands.

I was about to climb in my truck when I remembered that she had been drinking a glass of wine last night. I shut my door and crossed the street to walk a block down to the liquor store. Maybe a glass of wine or two would do us both good.

I arrived only a couple of minutes late and knocked on the front door. I heard Luke's feet slapping on the hardwood of the entryway as he raced toward the door, screaming, "I'll get it!"

When he opened the door, he stared at me and frowned. "Oh, it's you again."

I tried not to take that personally as I laughed and reached for the door handle. "Yes, it's me again. How are you, Luke?"

"Fine." He turned from me as I stepped inside. "Mom, it's that guy from this morning, the one that made you cry!"

I froze. I made Faith cry? What the hell?

Her head popped out of the kitchen doorway down the short hallway. "He did not make me cry, Luke. Hi, Peter, come on back."

Luke shrugged and looked at me after she disappeared again. "She was crying. Don't make her cry again. I hate when my mom cries."

"I'm gonna try hard not to make her cry again, Luke. You have my word."

He studied me as if he was trying to gauge whether he could trust me or not. Finally, he nodded once and then took off into the living room.

I removed my jacket and put it on a hook by the door before making my way down the hallway. Faith had her back to me and was cutting something on the far counter. Steam billowed up from a pot on the stove, and the aroma of garlic filled the air.

I took in her wild long brown hair. This morning and yesterday, it had been pulled back, but tonight, it was down. My fingers ached to comb through the wavy strands that went halfway down her back.

I stepped to her side, barely placing my hand to her lower back as I held up the wine bottle. "Good thing that I got red since it smells like we are having Italian."

She glanced at the bottle and then peered at me quickly. Her hazel eyes cut away as if she were nervous. Glad I wasn't the only one. "Thank you, that will be perfect."

I took a step back and then another so that I wasn't crowding her, even though I wanted nothing more than to be up close and personal with her. "How was your day?" I asked, hoping to cut some of the tension that filled the room.

"It was alright, I guess. I managed to make that list that you wanted me to make."

"Did that take you all day?"

"No." She chuckled. "I had other things to do too. I needed to get Luke registered for kindergarten, too. They only have three more days until Christmas break, so he won't start until after the New Year, but he got a chance to meet his teacher today and see his classroom."

That was good news. It meant that at least she was considering sticking around for a little while.

"Although after Christmas, we might have other plans and be leaving again."

And damn— "To where?"

She glanced at me as she cupped the vegetables she'd been cutting and dumped them in a bowl for salad. "Back to New York. I have a video interview with a firm tomorrow."

"Oh, what exactly do you do?" I asked, preparing to check one of my questions off my list.

"Corporate finance, mostly. I also do a little nonprofit work, or I used to."

"Did you lose your job, Faith?"

Her hands froze as she retrieved the knife again. "Um, that's kind of a complicated question and answer." She shot me a grimace.

"Okay, would you prefer not to answer it right now?"

"Yes, I would prefer that. I don't want Luke to walk in and hear it."

"Okay, then we will table that question for later. How about you tell me what's on your list?"

She finished cutting the tomato and scooped it into the salad bowl before she washed her hands and turned to me. "Are you in a rush?"

"Not at all, why?"

"Okay, can we wait until after dinner to discuss that? I'm afraid that if I think about any of that before we eat, I'll lose my appetite."

"Absolutely," I told her, and she gave me a full smile before she headed to the stove. "There is a wine opener in this drawer." She pointed to the one beside her. "And glasses above me, if you want to pour us some wine."

"I can do that." I eyed what she had on the stove, chicken parmesan. "Wow, I'm impressed. You do know how to cook."

"Ha-ha!" she said as I located the wine opener. I stepped toward her to get to the cabinet over her head at the same time that she made a slight side step, and our bodies came in contact. Her eyes slammed into mine over her shoulder, and we both remained still for two seconds. Her eyes slipped down my face to my mouth and then away as she muttered, "Sorry."

Although she had looked away, she didn't move her body. To retrieve the wine glasses, I had to lean more into her and reach over her head. The whole time, I was very aware of the feel of her shoulder pressing against my chest and the way her buttocks brushed my groin. Maybe it took me a few seconds longer than it should have to gather the two long-stemmed glasses, but it didn't appear that either of us was in a hurry to move.

When I finally did step away, I saw her shiver and wondered if that had to do with me or her being near the stove. Could I be lucky enough that it was because of me?

I poured the wine in silence and then helped her put everything on the table.

"Luke, wash your hands, it's time to eat," Faith called as I approached the table, and she spun around abruptly. Her hands landed on my chest, and her gaze snapped to mine again.

The thought of wrapping my arms around her and kissing her until she couldn't stand straight ripped through me, but instead, I put my arms around her lightly. "How about a hug since I didn't get one when I arrived."

She laughed and slipped her arms around my neck, hugging me briefly. When we pulled back, we locked gazes again, and this time, it was mine that dropped to her mouth. Her lips parted, and I was ready to dive into them, but loud footsteps raced toward us, and Faith jumped back.

"Did you wash your hands?" she asked Luke as he climbed into his seat.

"Yeah."

"You sure didn't wash them very long," she admonished.

I wondered briefly if she would send him back to the bathroom, and if so, how I could get her back in my arms again. Unfortunately, she didn't.

Luke took command of the conversation over dinner, and I realized quickly that he was a lot like his father. While I understood that kids were internally focused on themselves, Luke seemed even more so as he told me all his wishes and wants.

As we finished, Faith spoke. "Luke, I didn't tell you before, but Peter was your father's best friend in high school."

Luke looked between the both of us. "I thought he was your friend."

"He is my friend, but he was also your dad's friend."

A sadness slipped through his eyes for a moment. "Cool."

"Maybe sometime I can tell you some stories about when he was little. Your dad and I knew each other since we were your age."

"That long?" he asked.

"Yep, that long." I peered at Faith and smiled. "I can even tell you a few stories about your mom."

Luke grinned. "I want to hear those!"

Was it odd that he didn't want to hear stories about his father? Maybe his death was too painful to think about.

CHAPTER FIVE

FAITH

I wasn't sure why I was nervous about Peter coming to dinner, but I was. Maybe it was due to my embarrassment over my current financial situation. Or perhaps it was because I didn't want Peter to ask about my relationship with Jeremy. It could be either of those, but I had a feeling it was another reason altogether.

Over the years, I had thought of Peter often. Especially as my marriage turned to shit. Ironically, I'd wondered several times if my life would have been better if I'd dated Peter rather than Jeremy. When Jeremy had first asked me out in ninth grade, I'd said yes. Not because I was interested in Jeremy, but rather I'd been hoping to make Peter jealous. I never expected my relationship to grow with Jeremy, and when Peter didn't seem the least bit bothered by my dating his best friend, I gave up on him.

Until a night in college, when I had been drunk, and so was Peter. Jeremy had already passed out, and Peter and I had been curled on the couch side by side, watching a stupid movie and laughing our asses off. Somehow, I had ended up in his lap, and the two of us had kissed. I had felt that kiss all the way to my toes and absently wondered why Jeremy's kisses didn't feel that way. Our kiss took on a life of its own, and the two of us were practically naked on the couch when I suddenly had to pee and pulled my t-shirt back on.

In the bathroom, I'd paused and wondered what I was doing. Jeremy would be pissed if he found out about this, and I knew that as much as I wished it could continue, it couldn't. I stepped out of the bathroom, intent on telling Peter it wasn't going to happen. Only I didn't need to. He was passed out on the couch when I stepped back into the room. I quickly grabbed my bra off the floor and my shoes and slipped out the door.

The next day when I spoke to Jeremy, he didn't mention it, and later that week, when I saw Peter, he acted like it hadn't happened. I assumed that he was too drunk to remember and chalked it up as a missed fantasy.

Over the last two years, I had thought about that quite often, and on those long lonely nights where I couldn't sleep, I'd fantasized about what might have been.

The knock at the door startled me, and since I knew it was Peter, I didn't give Luke a hard time about opening the door. I made myself busy as I tried to put the memories back into the closet in my mind, but it was hard with him standing so near and touching me. Would his lips make my body tingle again, or had that been the alcohol? I had sometimes wondered if I had felt so much in the kiss because it had been forbidden. It wouldn't be now; would it feel the same?

Not that Peter was even a little interested in me. Or maybe he was. When he hugged me and then stood back staring at me, was I reading what was in his eyes correctly?

Thankfully, I didn't have to carry on too much conversation over dinner because Luke controlled that. Peter listened, laughed, and winked at me once in a while while I watched him covertly.

When I mentioned that Jeremy and Peter had been friends, I had hoped it would make Luke happy, but not so much. His father had hurt him, and as much as I wished he would forget that, he didn't.

Peter told Luke that he would search his memory banks for some good stories to share with him, and Luke's good mood returned. After dinner, he disappeared into the living room to watch one of his favorite programs while we cleaned the kitchen.

My nerves were no longer jangled, and Peter filled me in on some of our friends who were still in the area as we cleaned up. By the time we finished, I had realized that I felt more at ease with Peter than I had with Jeremy in the last two years of our marriage.

Peter and I were on our second glass of wine, and it was going down a little too easy. It was also making me laugh more, and once, I turned to find him right behind me. Peter cupped my cheek. "God, I love the sound of your laugh. I don't think I have ever heard another woman laugh the way you do, Faith."

My heart sighed, and my body drifted closer to his without thought. His hand shifted from my cheek, and he curled his fingers around my neck as he leaned forward. I warred with myself. I wanted to see what it would feel like, and yet, I worried that it would destroy the fantasy that I had lived off for years.

"Mom!" Luke yelled, and I jumped out of Peter's grasp. "Can I have some cookies before bed?"

"Um," I turned away from Peter quickly. "Yes, hold on." I went to get the cookies, my hand shaking as I dug into the package.

"Why don't you let me take these out to him?" Peter said softly from beside me.

"Oh, okay," I said and pushed the bowl toward him without looking in his direction.

"Faith," Peter said softly. "Look at me."

I swallowed and turned toward him. The desire that I had seen in his eyes a moment ago was still there, and his voice was husky, "We will take that back up from where we left off once he is in bed."

My brows jumped, and he stared hard at me for one more moment before walking out of the room. My knees felt weak. Did I want to kiss Peter?

Oh, God, yes! I glanced at the clock; another hour before Luke would be off to bed. After I finished the kitchen, I wandered into the living room to see Peter sitting on the couch, Luke leaning beside him like they were best buddies, and both of them glued to the television.

I sank into a chair, watching them from the corner of my eye. Luke had never been close to his father, and seeing him beside Peter now made me wonder again what my life could have been like if I had said no to Jeremy all those years ago.

I remained quiet, keeping an eye on them, the show, and thoughts running rampant in my mind. I looked at the clock a dozen times and had to force myself not to burst out of my chair and race Luke to bed when his show ended.

As it ended up, he took his time getting ready and then asked Peter to read him a story. I almost groaned out loud and opened my mouth to tell Luke no, but Peter stepped forward and said he'd love to. I kissed Luke good night and then turned off the light.

I polished off the wine bottle between our glasses and brought them to the living room after I gathered the list that I had made for Peter. I stood in the middle of the room and glanced around. The room was weathered and aged. My mom hadn't changed anything in here in years, and I wondered what Peter thought of it.

I wandered over to a shelf and picked up an old photograph. It was my prom picture, and it included Peter and his date, Sarah. Peter had his arm around Sarah, but his shoulder touched mine. There was a gap between him and Sarah. There was also space between Jeremy and I. Was it odd that I had never noticed that before? Was I making more out of it than what it was?

I jumped when I felt his hand on my lower back, and he laughed. "Wow, that was a long time ago. Did your mom still have that up?"

"Mom hasn't changed anything in this house in twenty years. She just added more," I said with a laugh.

He grinned down at the picture. "You know it almost looks like you and I were going together with as much room as there is between us and our dates."

My face snapped up. "I just thought the same thing. I never noticed it before."

"Neither did I," he said as he handed the picture back to me and then went to sit on the couch. "Okay, where is that list?"

What happened to taking that kiss back up? Had he changed his mind? Probably. I shoved my disappointment away and handed him the list.

"Okay, the fireplace flue needs to be cleaned. That's easy enough and not that expensive. The roof leaks into the master bedroom. How bad?"

I winced. "Pretty bad."

"I'll look at it later." I went through the rest of the list. There were ten items in total, and some of them were extensive and were going to be expensive. He told me I could keep the costs down if I would let him do most of the repairs and just cover material costs. I just wasn't sure about that.

"So, what do you think?" I asked.

"I think you have a lot that needs to be done. Some of these are serious, like the pipe in the basement, the gutters, and the roof leaking. Those all need attention immediately. They are also the most expensive ones, except for the oil burner. That one is going to be costly too."

I sighed and rubbed my hands over my face. "I know."

Peter took one of my hands as I dropped them away from my face. "Faith, did neither Jeremy or your mother have life insurance that could help with this?"

I barked out a laugh and then groaned. "My mother's was just enough to pay for her burial and the back taxes she owed on the house. As for Jeremy's, well, that's a whole different story."

"Tell me the story, Faith," he said softly.

"Peter, you don't want to hear this, because if I'm going to tell you part of it, I have to tell you all of it."

He shifted closer, and took my other hand in his. "Then tell me all of it. I'm here for you, Faith. Tell me what happened."

Did I dare? Did I dare tell Peter all about his best friend? It would either ruin his image of Jeremy, or he wouldn't believe me. Part of me was more concerned that he wouldn't believe me. "If I tell you this, Peter, you can never unhear it. There are days when I wish I could forget it all, but you won't be able to. I'm afraid that if I told you, you'd think differently of me, or him."

He contemplated that for a moment. "What did he do to hurt you, Faith?"

"Man, that is a loaded question, Peter."

"You need to tell me, Faith. There is nothing you can tell me that would make me feel differently about you."

How did he feel? I wanted to ask him, but I couldn't bring myself to. After a moment, Peter cupped my cheek again. "I will do everything in my power to take the sadness out of your eyes, Faith. Talk to me, sweetheart."

My heart sighed at his endearment, and my body drifted toward him again. This time I knew we wouldn't be interrupted, and butterflies crowded in my belly.

"I know this is probably wrong in so many ways, Faith, but I need to kiss you."

"Please," I replied breathlessly.

Peter brushed his lips over mine once, and the butterflies exploded into firecrackers. My body vibrated as they blasted outward, and any fears I had vanished as he deepened the kiss.

CHAPTER SIX

PETER

I'd never read a children's book so fast. Luke didn't seem to notice or care, and as soon as I finished, he curled on his side and closed his eyes. I wanted to run straight to Faith and take her back into my arms, but I didn't. I remained a gentleman—until I couldn't stand the sad look in her eyes anymore.

The feel of her lips was everything I had dreamed of and more, and the whimper that sounded in her throat drove me wild as I cupped the back of her head and deepened our kiss. She wound her arms around me and pressed her chest to mine as she shifted on the couch to get closer. The kiss was explosive, and my mouth left hers to cover her jaw and neck. She gasped, and her breathing was heavy as she clung to me, her head thrown back.

My hand brushed the side of her breast, and she arched her chest toward mine and whimpered again. She began to lean back on the couch and pulled my body with hers. A moment later, my body covered hers like a blanket, and she ground her hips against mine.

"Faith," I breathed into her ear as I curled my hand around her hip and pressed myself firmer against her. Her foot curled around my calf as she kissed a line down my throat. She nipped and then sucked at the skin near my collar, and I hissed. The pleasure and pain of it almost too much. "Faith," I repeated her name as I leaned back slightly as her desire-filled eyes opened.

"Yes?"

"I want this, I mean, I really want this, Faith. You have no idea how long I have dreamed of holding you like this, making love to you all damn night." Her body tensed, and I brushed my hand over the side of her face. "But I think we need to talk before this happens."

She closed her eyes, her body practically vibrating with sudden tension. A moment later, she spoke softly. "I don't want to talk." She opened her eyes again. "I want to *feel*, Peter. I *need* to feel, please. Tonight just let me feel loved, needed, and I'll explain it all later?"

She wanted and needed to feel loved? What had Jeremy done to her? If this woman needed to feel loved, then by god, I was going to give her what she wanted.

"Is that what you want, Faith? You aren't going to regret it in the morning?"

She shook her head. "No. I want you, Peter. Part of me has wanted you for a long time. Since even before we made out on the couch in college."

I jerked back a few more inches. "What are you talking about, Faith? We never made out on the couch in college."

She laughed, the sound curling around my heart. "Oh, yes, we did. Jeremy was asleep, and the two of us were pretty drunk. We made out, even took off a few pieces of clothing, and then I had to pee. When I got back, you were snoring, and I left. I was glad you were asleep because I was going to tell you that no matter how much I wanted to be with you, I was with Jeremy."

I stared at her, the event a muddled memory. "When I woke up the next day, I thought I had dreamed the whole thing. It seriously messed with my head. This might seem weird, but I was totally into you in the eighth grade, and then you started dating Jeremy in high school. I constantly hoped that you two would break up, and I'd finally get my chance."

She gaped at me. "Are you serious?"

"Oh, yeah. I was head over heels in love with you in high school, but I wanted you to be happy. I didn't want to come between you two."

"Peter, the only reason I started dating Jeremy in the first place was that I was hoping to make you jealous enough to ask me out. When you didn't seem bothered by me dating Jeremy, I figured you didn't like me."

"You're kidding?"

"No! Man, back then, if you had told me that you were interested in me, I probably would have broken up with Jeremy in a heartbeat."

I sat up, pulling her to a sitting position. "You're serious?"

She nodded.

"Then why did you marry Jeremy?"

"Because you never showed an interest in me. You never told me not to. You didn't even remember us making out. I did love Jeremy, and he did make me happy, but—"

She paused, and I stared at her as she scanned the room. "But what?"

She shifted away from me but continued to hold my hand. "There were many times that I wondered what life would have been like if things had been different."

"Different? You mean, if I had asked you out? Or if you had told me that you were interested in me? Or something else?"

She looked me straight in the eye. "I used to fantasize about you when I was married. I would dream of what life would be like—if you were the one I'd married."

"Shit, Faith," I muttered as I squeezed her hand. "Are you seriously telling me that you weren't happy with Jeremy?"

"I loved Jeremy—when we first got married." She sighed and let go of my hand, grabbing her glass and guzzling the last of the contents. "I didn't want to tell you this, but maybe it would be better to do so."

"I think it would be, not that I don't want to take back up where we were, but I'd like to understand better where your head is."

She laughed. "My head? My head is everywhere right now." She pushed off the couch. "If I'm going to tell you all of this, I need another bottle of wine."

"A bottle? Not just a glass?"

She made a gurgling noise in her throat as she left the room. I sank back on the couch, frowning as I thought about what she had said. That make-out session had been real, not a drunken fantasy. Shit! If I had known that, I would have done something. Instead, I'd been embarrassed at the lifelike dream and had avoided her for a while.

Faith returned with a brand-new bottle of wine in her hand. She filled her glass and glanced at me, brow hiked. "Do you think I will need it?" She laughed and filled my glass without a word.

She curled herself into the corner of the couch, and I shifted so that I was sitting more sideways, a foot of space between us. "Okay, lay it on me."

She moved her lips back and forth like she was concentrating hard, then she blew a raspberry with her lips. "Fine, god, I can't believe I am going to tell you this."

"Faith, I'm your friend. There is nothing you can say that is going to bother me."

"We'll see," she murmured and shook her head. "Jeremy and I were happy. His new job in the city was hard, and he worked long hours, but after I found a job—a great job—I worked almost as long and as hard as him. We could go a few days without speaking to one other except through a text or email, but we were happy—or so I thought. Then Jeremy started talking about starting a family. It was something that we had discussed, and we wanted kids, but the timing wasn't right for me. I was working toward a promotion and working longer hours than him. He kept pushing; I kept resisting. I started to see an ugly side of him; the selfish side that I already knew existed, but had tried to ignore, came out with a vengeance. He harped on me about how I wasn't there *for him*, wasn't home to cook *for him*, to listen *to him*, to bend over the couch *for him*. Anything you could think of, he would toss in my face.

"He didn't understand that I needed time to get my career on a more solid footing. He had his career, but he didn't care about mine. He even suggested that I quit, but that wasn't happening."

"I can't imagine you not working, Faith, especially if you enjoy what you're doing."

"Right?" She grew quiet as she sipped from her glass and stared sightlessly across the room. "Then, a few months later, his attitude changed, and Jeremy did a one-eighty. He was happy and encouraged me to pursue my career. We stopped fighting, and he told me that when I was ready, we'd have a child. I was thankful and didn't think any more about it."

"What caused the change?"

She laughed. "Oh, we'll get to that soon."

"Alright."

"So we went back to working our asses off, and while he didn't work the same long hours that I did, he was out almost every night with his work buddies. I didn't care; I was too tired when I got home after twelve- to fourteen-hour days. Then I finally got the promotion that I'd been working toward for three years. Jeremy was excited for me, and we went away for the weekend to celebrate. I ended up getting pregnant that weekend—by accident—and while I wasn't sure I was ready for it, Jeremy was thrilled. Our relationship was perfect for a few months, and we were closer than we'd been since we got married. My life was good, and then Luke was born, and within a few months, Jeremy was back to being an absentee husband.

"Now I was working long hours, dealing with a baby and then a toddler, and having no help. Jeremy was around when *he* wanted to be, not when *I* needed him. We argued constantly, and we talked about divorce several times too."

"Why didn't you divorce him?"

She frowned. "I don't know. I guess I thought that things would get better, or maybe I was in denial or just didn't care. I don't know, Peter. I do know that I was miserable and lonely, and then Luke was three, and Jeremy learned he had cancer. Luke was four when Jeremy died, and he barely knew his father because he was never around. Even when Jeremy was so sick, he would disappear for hours. I didn't understand it, but Jeremy knew he was dying, and he said there were things in life he needed to do before he died. I accepted that and let it go. While we were living together, we were more like roommates. I took care of him when I was home, but I wasn't in love with him anymore. Of course, I loved him, but I wasn't *in love* with him."

"I understand the difference. What happened when Jeremy died?"

She laughed harshly. "This is where it gets good, Peter. After Jeremy died, I learned what he was doing with his time away from home."

"What was that?"

"Jeremy was spending time with his other family."

"His what?"

"His mistress and seven-year-old son."

I blinked and blinked again. Had I heard Faith correctly? "Jeremy had an affair on you?"

"Oh, yes, for eight years, he had been with this other woman. When she got pregnant with his child, that is when he backed off from pressuring me."

"Holy shit, Faith. How did you find out? Did she come to the funeral? Did she confront you?"

"She was there, but she melted into the crowd. I didn't learn about her until I went to the attorney to sign the papers for his will. She was there, and I was bewildered at her presence until the attorney explained that two-thirds of his life insurance policy was to go to Margaret and their son, Tripp. The other third was to go into a college fund for Luke."

"Wait, Jeremy left you with nothing?"

"Oh, he left me with something, almost two hundred thousand dollars of debt. Jeremy had a lot of medical bills, of course, but he had opened several lines of credit to help support his other family. I got saddled with his debt because I was his wife. But that's not the worst part."

"There is worse than that?"

"Yep, when my company found out about the situation, it triggered a clause in my contract. We weren't eligible to be in their employment if our debt ratio was above a certain level. His debt put me way over that level, and I got fired. It didn't matter the circumstances behind it.

I lost my job, had to sell our condo, and just about everything that we owned, but I cleared all the debt—just barely. I thought I was going to be able to get back on my feet, and then my mother passed, and here I am. Without a job, barely any money in the bank, and having to start over. In just over a year, I went from my dream position to hell, all because Jeremy couldn't keep his dick in his pants."

I wasn't sure what to say, but I knew if Jeremy were alive, I would have kicked his ass.

CHAPTER SEVEN

FAITH

I would blame my loose lips on the alcohol. I was waiting for Peter to say he heard enough and jump off the couch to storm off. Why would he believe me when Jeremy had been his best friend? Although from our earlier conversation, Peter had been interested in me too way back when. What did that mean now?

After hearing his thoughts, part of me sincerely wished that things had been different. Would Peter have done something like that to me? No, he had divorced his wife after he caught her being unfaithful; he wouldn't have cheated on me. Although, if I had been with Peter, I wouldn't have Luke.

Peter kept shaking his head as if he were unable to comprehend or accept what I'd said.

"I'm sorry, Peter. I know Jeremy was your friend, and it's probably hard to imagine him doing any of that, but it's the truth. It's too crazy for me to have made up."

Peter grabbed my hand. "I believe you, Faith. I do not doubt that what you are telling me is the truth. You know, I pretty much stopped talking to Jeremy a few years ago because I got tired of his life-is-about-me attitude. It got to the point that it was out of control. I can

171

see him doing this. What I can't understand is how he could have done it to you. Jeremy loved you. I know how much he loved you."

"It was the brain tumor, Peter. It changed him. Made him even more narcissistic than he was. In his mind, he wasn't doing anything wrong."

"You act as if you have forgiven him."

I shrugged. "He's dead, Peter. Why should I hold a grudge? I forgave him for his adultery and his other family. What I don't forgive him for is ruining my career. I couldn't care less if I received money from his life insurance. Luke got enough to help with college; I just wish that he hadn't destroyed everything I built."

"Does Luke know he has a half-brother?"

"No, he met Tripp once. Margaret and I met at the park, and the boys played while we talked. She told me that she had known about us. She said she never wanted to break up our marriage and never asked him to leave me. She was happy with the little time she got with him and the money he gave her to live a comfortable life."

Peter's features turned dark. "I can't believe he did that, tumor or not. He gave that other woman everything you should have had."

"Maybe."

"You guys were together since you were fifteen. That's over half your life that you were with him, Faith. How are you not upset?"

"I was upset, Peter, but I got over it. I have more important things to worry about now. I need to figure out what I'm going to do. I have to find a job and a new place to live."

"Didn't you just put Luke in school? Don't you think it might be a good idea to stick around here for a little while, Faith? You have a house to live in, and I can help you get it fixed up. You can find a job around here; it might not be your dream job, but I bet you can find one. You and Luke could get back on your feet, grow some roots. You might find that you like this small town now after years in the city, and if you don't, then get the house fixed up, sell it, and move then."

"I don't know about liking this town, but I get what you're saying." I took another sip of my wine, finishing my glass. "I guess I feel like a failure, and I can't imagine what people would say if they knew what happened with Jeremy."

"No one needs to know," he replied. "As far as anyone knows, Jeremy died from a brain tumor. No one has to know anything else unless you want to tell them. I'm sure as hell not going to say a word."

"Yeah, I guess. When was the last time that you heard from Jeremy?"

"At least a year, maybe a bit longer. Come to think of it, it was an odd letter. Jeremy was talking about all the great things that he had accomplished in life. I remember him talking about a lot of random things. I guess that makes sense now, knowing he died from a brain tumor. I never replied to it; I guess I should have."

"In the end, he was very random with his thoughts and his words. It was kind of sad to see the brilliant and vibrant man dissolve and change so much."

Peter put his hand on my knee. "Faith. I'm sorry you had to deal with that."

I shrugged. "I was his wife; it was my responsibility to care for him."

"Bullshit. That guy treated you like crap, tumor or not. You deserved so much better. Tell me what I can do to help you?"

I eyed him for a moment and then set my glass down before I shifted to my knees, taking his face between my palms. "Make me feel something, Peter."

His lips parted as I pushed him back to the cushion and climbed over his lap. I ran my fingertips over his short beard, pressing tender kisses along his jawline. "Make love to me, Peter. Give me what I have fantasized about for so many years."

"Jesus, Faith," he breathed out before he took hold of my face and brought our lips together in a rush. I clung to him, melting into him as his hands drifted over my back and hips.

After a few minutes of kissing, Peter shifted me back slightly and looked apprehensive. "What if it doesn't measure up to your fantasies?"

I laced our fingers together. "It already has."

He looked confused. "How can you know that?"

"Remember when we had our little drunk make-out session?"

"Yes."

"When you kissed me that night, I felt it to my toes." I kissed the back of one of his hands.

"When you whispered my name, you gave me chills." I kissed the other.

He smiled slightly. "When you touched me, you made me crave more." He shivered as I brought our foreheads together, breathing him in. "Right now, my toes are tingling; I have goosebumps down my spine, and I want you more than I have ever wanted someone before. You have already made me feel more in the last few minutes than I have felt in years."

"Faith—" My name was a whisper over his lips as he began to kiss me again. His arms banded around my back, and he shifted us to the edge of the couch. "Take me to your room."

I slipped off his lap, lacing our fingers, and brought him back to my mother's old room. It felt weird to step into the room with someone, but then as I turned toward Peter, it felt right.

We shifted toward one another as if we were two pieces of a puzzle ready to click into place. We fit. Peter kissed me with a tenderness that I hadn't ever felt before—even with healthy Jeremy. It was as if Peter were cherishing me, and I welcomed it.

As we undressed each other, we didn't speak words, but our eyes spoke volumes, and as we lay down on the bed, I wanted to lay open my soul to him. Part of me had loved this man since I was fifteen; now, I finally had a chance to show him how much. And I did.

I woke before him, used to getting up at four-thirty even though I hadn't been working for two months. I had gotten up that early for so long, it was normal. Back when I was working, I would be up the moment the alarm went off. I'd race to the kitchen, put on the coffee, pour a large bottle of water, change clothes, and then run on the treadmill for thirty minutes. After that, I'd pour my coffee, take a shower, dress, get breakfast ready, pack lunch, and I was out the door by six-thirty when the nanny arrived for Luke.

I would return home at six-thirty and would devour the dinner that the nanny had prepared, get Luke off to bed, and work again from about eight until ten. At ten-thirty, I'd pass out and start everything again the next morning at four-thirty.

Now, I lay there and stared at Peter's profile, listening to the sound of his slow, deep breathing. Peter had awoken something deep inside of me last night, but I wasn't sure that was good. In the light of the morning, without the haze of alcohol, I wondered if this was a mistake.

What if he expected me to stay here now? I didn't know if I wanted that. I had an interview for a job in New York today via video. If they offered the position to me, it would get me back on track to where I had been—not exactly there, but a step closer. Did I still want that? Did I still want the hustle and bustle of the big city, where nannies raised my son?

Or did I want to do as Peter suggested and find something here where life would be harder, but not as rushed. No matter what job I acquired, I'd have to work hard, but maybe if I changed what I wanted out of a job, I could be happy working fewer hours. Would I be satisfied enough?

Peter shifted slightly, curling his arm around my waist and pulling me tightly to him. What about Peter? Now that the night was over, had it ruined the fantasy?

Absolutely not.

The man had made my body sing. I had asked him to make me feel, and he had made me feel things I had only dreamed. He had made my heart, mind, and body soar. I could picture making love to Peter a thousand times, and it would always be incredible—I just knew it.

He turned his head and brushed a kiss over my forehead. "You're thinking too loudly, hush."

I chuckled, and his hand began to caress my side slowly. His fingertips teased the curve of my breast, and I shifted my leg over his.

He needed no further invitation as he rolled me to my back and brought our mouths together.

After he made love to me again, he snuggled up behind me and promptly fell back asleep, sated in a way that I had never been.

❧

I woke to an empty bed and sat straight up to see the clock on the side table. It was almost eight! Holy smokes! I threw back the covers and grabbed my robe off the end of the bed, tying it as I rushed from the room.

I could hear the television in the living room as I came down the hall and found Luke sitting on the couch, alone. "Hey, buddy. How are you?"

"I'm good." He sat up like a jack-in-the-box. "Peter made me breakfast so you could sleep."

"He did? Is he still here?"

"No, he left. He told me that if I stayed quiet and let you sleep, then he would take me ice skating this weekend."

"He did, did he?"

He nodded excitedly. "He said you could come too."

"Well, that's nice to hear. What did he make you for breakfast?"

"French toast."

I peaked a brow. "Did you like it?"

"Yeah, it was awesome. You should make it. I'm sure Peter could teach you." Obviously, my son didn't know that you soaked the bread in eggs. He was not a fan of eggs. "He let me help him make it."

"Wait? You helped him make it?"

"Yeah, he let me crack the eggs."

I stared at Luke. "And you ate it even though it had egg on it?"

He nodded dramatically. "Yeah. Peter told me that kids have to eat egg protein, or they won't grow up tall and strong."

I ruffled his hair. "Well, he's right. I'm going to get my coffee."

Luke flopped back on the couch and immediately dismissed me for his cartoon. I expected to see the kitchen a disaster, but it was the opposite. It was cleaner than I had left it last night, and our wine glasses were in the strainer. The coffee was on, and there was a note on the counter.

Faith – I hope you slept well. I hated leaving you this morning, but I had an early meeting. Hope you don't mind me using your kitchen to prepare breakfast. Luke and I were both starving. I left your plate in the fridge. One minute in the microwave should be good. I'll talk to you later. Peter P.S. Luke wants to know when we are going to have another sleepover. XOXO

I chuckled as I turned to the fridge and pulled it open. On the shelf was a covered plate. I pulled it out and uncovered it to find two pieces of French toast with pads of butter on them waiting to be melted. On the side of the plate was a small bowl with a few cut strawberries and whipped cream.

Well, damn. If Peter was going to cook breakfast like this, he could sleep over every night.

CHAPTER EIGHT

PETER

I woke up and wanted to pinch myself. I was lying beside Faith McMillian, and not only that, but I had made love to her several times last night. My heart was full, but my stomach was empty. It gurgled loudly as I slipped carefully out of bed.

After I dressed, I used her bathroom and intended to slip out of the house before Luke saw me, but he was standing in the hallway as I closed her door. Whoops.

"Did you have a sleepover with my mom?"

"Um…" Well, shit. "Yeah, I did. Let's go in the other room so that we don't wake your mom."

In the kitchen, I wondered what I should say, but Luke didn't seem at all concerned about me being with his mom. "Is my mom up?"

"No, she's sleeping."

Luke frowned. "My mother never sleeps. She's always awake."

I chuckled. "She sleeps, Luke, just enough. Are you hungry?"

"Yes!"

"I am too, so why don't we cook breakfast together and let Mom sleep."

"Okay!"

I glanced in the cupboards and fridge and quickly got breakfast underway and coffee brewing. Luke balked at the eggs, but I told him that it was important for boys to eat protein first thing in the morning. I think allowing him to prepare it helped encourage him to try it when it was done. I was glad that he liked it and ate both slices I made for him. I set a plate for Faith in the fridge, made Luke promise me that he would stay quiet while she slept, and then wrote her a quick note.

I wasn't sure if she would regret our night together, and I hoped not, but I had no clue what she was going to be thinking today. Hopefully, breakfast waiting for her would ease any concerns she had.

Before I left, I paused at the side counter and retrieved one of her old business cards, Senior Corporate Finance Analyst. Pretty impressive title, I thought as I slipped one of the cards into my pocket, checked on Luke again, and then headed back to my place to change so I could make my meeting with my client.

The client, Thomas Sanders, owned a company that was expanding, and we were constructing his new office building. He had contacted me yesterday, saying he wanted a few changes to the interior made before we got too far, so we were going to discuss them this morning. Bruce, my architect; Will, my engineer; and Dutch, my site foreman, were all present when Mr. Sanders soared into the room, looking flustered.

Without preamble, we dug into the changes he wanted. I didn't know the guy well, but I could tell that he was preoccupied with something and not too happy. We were almost done with our meeting when his cellphone rang, and he excused himself for a moment.

He came back into the room, shaking his head. "I'm sorry. My CFO quit this morning, and my board is in an uproar. It's been a hell of a morning."

"I'm sorry to hear that. Do you need to get going?" I asked him.

"No, we're almost done. I'd rather get this done; at least something positive will happen today if we do."

As we got back on topic, it felt like that business card in my pocket was going to burn a hole in my pants. When I had changed my clothes this morning, I had slipped it back in. I wasn't sure why I had, but I did.

As we finished the meeting, and I assured him that we'd be able to make all the changes he requested, I hesitated. Would Faith get mad if I said something to him? He put his hand out to shake, and I shoved my hand into my pocket and pulled out the card.

"Mr. Sanders, I'm not sure if this would help you or not, but a friend of mine just moved back to town. She was in New York City for years and recently came back after her husband and mother passed away. She worked in finance. I'm not sure if she's qualified for what you are looking for, but here is her card if you'd like to speak with her."

He took the card, glancing at it, and his brows popped. "Senior Corporate Finance Analyst for the Wellington Corporation; that's rather impressive. You said she just moved back here?"

"Yes, her husband passed last year, and her mother last month. She is in between jobs right now. I know she's trying to decide if she wants to go back to the city or stay here." He stared at me for a long moment. "Personally, I'd prefer that her and her son stay here."

He smiled. "I'll check into her and give her a call. I appreciate you letting me know about"—he glanced at the card—"Faith McMillian. Any relation to Stewart McMillian?"

"Yeah, that was her father-in-law."

He nodded. "I knew him well; sorry to hear about his son. I will definitely give her a call. If she was married to a McMillian, I bet she is a hard worker." We shook, and he was on his way, and I wondered again if Faith was going to be upset with me for doing that.

The rest of the day was a blur, and I was on my way home when I did a double take at a store, an idea popping into my head. I did a U-turn and went back to the store. Inside, I picked up a medium-sized artificial tree that already had lights on it and loaded it into my truck along with something else I found by accident. She could consider the tree a housewarming present if she wanted to give me grief about buying one.

I showered at home, changed into jeans and a long-sleeved shirt, and headed to her house. I hadn't spoken to her today, and I had no idea if I would be welcomed or not, but I was going to try. At least I could drop off the tree.

Her car was gone when I arrived, but the lights were on inside the house. Luke was jumping up and down in the living room. Was he alone? I climbed out, lugged the tree box to the door, and knocked. A few seconds later, the door jerked open, and Luke stared up at me.

"Are we going to have another sleepover?" he asked excitedly. Behind Luke, a teenaged girl approached the door.

"Hi, Luke. I guess Mom's not home?"

"Hi, I'm Laura, the babysitter. She had a meeting tonight."

"Ah, okay."

"What's that?" Luke asked, pushing the door open to check out the box. "Is that is a Christmas tree?"

"Yep, your mom said she hadn't had time to get one yet. I saw this one and thought she might like it."

"Cool! Can we put it up before she gets home?"

"Um, I'm not sure about that."

"Please! Mom will be so excited to see it up. She loves Christmas tree lights, and she was sad this afternoon. This will make her happy, please!"

Gah! I hated hearing that she was sad. "Okay, as long as Laura doesn't mind me coming in."

"No, that's okay," she said and glanced at her watch. "Actually, she's later than she said she was going to be, and I was starting to stress about it. I have to get to my other job at the movie theater. I am supposed to be there at seven."

"Well, then you go, Laura, and I can stay with Luke."

"I'm not sure Mrs. McMillian would like that."

"It's okay, Laura. Peter does sleepovers with my mom. He cooked me breakfast this morning while Mom was sleeping."

The girl giggled, knowing what he meant. I tried not to blush. "I'm sure Faith will understand. Luke and I can get dinner cooking and get the tree up."

"You wouldn't mind?"

"Not at all. What time did you get here?" I asked as I pulled my wallet out. She told me the time, and I handed her a twenty. "I have no idea how much babysitters cost these days; is this enough?"

"More than enough," she stated.

"Okay, you get to work, and I can take over here."

"Thank you!" she said and rushed to collect her things and leave as Luke helped me get the tree inside the house.

Luke and I started by checking out the kitchen and seeing what we could make for dinner. There was enough leftover from the night before that we could all eat again. With that decided, we began to work on the tree. We were almost done with that when the house phone rang, and Luke dove to answer it.

"Hello?" He was quiet for a moment and smiled.

"Hi, Mom. I'm fine. Laura had to leave, but I'm okay."

Her voice raised enough that I could hear it and put my hand out. "Luke, let me speak to your mom."

"Peter wants to talk to you," he blurted and then tossed me the phone.

"Hi, Faith, don't worry, he's fine."

"Why are you there, and where is Laura?"

"I stopped by to drop something off, and Laura was getting a little anxious because she had to work at the movie theater tonight and wasn't sure when you would be home. I told her I'd stay until you did. I was going to warm up leftovers from last night. Are you on your way home?"

"Oh, crap! I forgot about her other job. I got so tied up in what I was doing. Yes, I'm on my way home. I'll be there in about fifteen minutes. You have no idea how much I appreciate your help."

"No problem. We will get dinner warmed up and see you when you get home."

She was quiet for a moment. "Thank you, Peter. You have no idea what this means to me."

"You can thank me later," I said huskily, and she chuckled.

"I'm glad you are there. I have a bone to pick with you."

"Oh, really? Just one?"

183

"Funny, I'll see you soon."

"Okay, Luke, we need to get dinner ready and turn off all the lights."

"Why?"

"Because we're going to surprise your mom."

"Cool!" He followed me into the kitchen, and we set up the plates so that they were ready to warm. I gave him silverware and napkins, and he went to put them on the dining room table.

"Nope, let's take them to the living room."

"What?"

"We're going to have a picnic by the tree."

His eyes went wide as saucers. "Really? Can we have just the tree lights on?"

"Yep! That's the plan." I glanced at my watch. "Okay, let's turn all the lights off in the living room, and when she comes in, I'll tell you when and you turn on the tree. What do you think?"

"Yes!" He pumped a hand into the air. We turned all the lights off, and I went back to the kitchen to get drinks ready while he waited by the front window. I found another bottle of wine and poured two glasses.

"She's here!" Luke yelled.

"Okay, get near the light switch. Can you find it in the dark?"

"Yeah. I have it in my hand."

"Good, don't turn it on until I tell you to, okay?"

"Okay." He sounded so excited, and I smiled into the darkness.

I could see her through the window, walking up to the door, frowning at the dark window. Her key rattled in the door, and then it opened. Luke giggled next to me as she called out.

"Luke! Peter! I'm home!" Hearing her say she was home made my chest tighten. I wanted this to remain her home; I wanted to be her home.

The door closed, and she flipped the light switch on in the hallway. "Why is it dark in here?"

"Now, Luke," I said softly as she stepped forward and glanced toward the living room.

Luke flipped the switch and began to jump up and down. "Surprise!"

Faith was noticeably shocked and stared at the tree for a long moment before she glanced at her son, the coffee table, and then me. As her eyes hit mine, I saw the emotion fill them, and she put her hands over her face and began to cry.

Luke sounded dejected as he spoke from my side. "Oh, boy, we made her cry again."

CHAPTER NINE

FAITH

After breakfast, I made a few lists. One list was to put the items on the to-be-fixed list into an order of importance after speaking with Peter. The second list was what I needed to do before Christmas. The third list were other ideas on where to find a job.

As I sipped the last of my coffee, I took out a fresh piece of paper and drew a line down the center and wrote NYC on one side and Merryland on the other. What were the pros and cons of going back to the city?

I could find a new job; I just wasn't sure how long it would take. My friends were there, although I didn't have too many of them. I loved the city, but it was sometimes exhausting. I would need to find a new nanny for Luke. I couldn't afford the private school that he had been in before, so he would have to go to a public school—a very large public school.

There were a few more that I added to the column and added plus or minus off to the side. Then I stared at the Merryland column; the first thing that came to mind was Peter. Was that a pro or con? I put a question mark. I had a house, but it needed a lot of work. I winced; it would need a lot of work, whether I left or stayed. I needed to find a job but probably wouldn't make anywhere near what I was making. It was cheaper to live here, and I probably wouldn't need a nanny, but maybe just some after-school care. I didn't know anyone here, but I wasn't shy, and I did know Peter. I tapped my pen on the paper as I thought about him. Was I really adding him to my list?

I glanced at my watch and shuffled my papers together. I needed to get dressed and then finish doing some research on the company I was interviewing with today. The only reason they had been willing to do a video interview was that Carl Hundsberg was out of the office for the holiday. He had suggested it, and I had jumped right on.

I got myself ready, found the best place in the house to sit so that my background wouldn't be too busy, and then made Luke promise he would go to his room as soon as I got the email that he was ready. As I waited, I read more about the company. It was an up-and-coming engineering company in the city and had been steadily gaining both revenue and employees over the last two years.

I kept glancing at the clock, refreshing my email to see if I had missed the notification for the meeting link. Fifteen minutes after the scheduled time, I checked my calendar and my email that listed the time. Another fifteen minutes and I picked up the phone and called.

"Carl Hundsberg's office," a woman answered.

"Hi, my name is Faith McMillian. I had a video interview scheduled with Mr. Hundsberg today at eleven, and I never received a link to the meeting room."

"What position?"

"The comptroller position."

"Oh, that position was filled yesterday. Sorry for the inconvenience." She hung up before I could say another word.

I stared at my phone as I pulled it away from my ear. What a bitch! I couldn't believe that I didn't even get an email to cancel the interview. I dropped the cellphone to the table and rubbed my temples. Back to the drawing board.

Luke popped his head into the kitchen. "Are you done now, Mom? I'm hungry."

"Yeah, I'm done," I muttered softly. "I'll get you a sandwich."

I changed my clothes and made lunch. After lunch, I did some laundry and parked my butt on the couch to do some job searching. My cellphone rang, and I almost sent it to voicemail, but I realized it was a local number. Peter hadn't left me his number, so this might be him.

"Mrs. McMillian?"

"Yes, this is she."

"Mrs. McMillian, my name is Thomas Sanders, and I own Brighton Technologies. I'm sorry for calling you like this, but your name was passed along to me today."

"It was? For what?"

"My current chief financial officer quit rather unexpectedly, and I need to find someone as quickly as I can."

I blinked and blinked again as the words sunk into my mind. I sat up quickly. "Wow, um, okay. I'm sorry, you surprised me. Mr. Sanders, I apologize for not knowing much about your company, but I'd be delighted to supply you with my resume and speak with you about your company and the position."

"Would you be able to send your resume over now and then meet with me at four-thirty this afternoon?"

"Absolutely," I told him and grabbed my pen to jot down the information. When I got off the phone, I immediately brought up my email and sent over my resume with a quick cover letter. Then I began to search the company as I sent a text to Laura to see if she would be available for an hour or so.

With the details ironed out, I started reading about Brighton Technologies. I devoured their website, then searched them through some other sources and read everything I could until I had to change again quickly. Laura no sooner stepped in than I was stepping out.

I was ten minutes early for the interview and was asked to have a seat until his secretary could retrieve me. The office was nice, but as I was led down a hallway by a sweet, older woman, I realized it was packed. People and boxes were everywhere.

I was shown into his office, and he came around the desk with a wide smile. I liked him instantly. "Mrs. McMillian, it is a pleasure to meet you, and I am sorry to hear about your husband and your mother."

I was surprised that he knew of both of them. "Well, thank you, sir."

"Have a seat, and so that you are aware, I was a good friend of Steward McMillian's. We played golf quite often together."

"Oh, you know, I thought you looked familiar. I probably saw you at one of their events."

"Yes, I am sure that we did cross paths. So, let's get down to business."

We went over my resume; he asked questions, I asked questions. He was very impressed that I had spent the afternoon researching their company and already knew quite a bit about it, and I was equally impressed by him and the company. When we finished, he asked me a question that made me feel like the floor was about to drop out from under me.

"Why were you terminated from your last employer?"

I forced myself not to squirm. "Do you want the real answer or the sugar-coated one?"

He chuckled. "Let me hear the real one."

So I gave him an abbreviated explanation about the debt and stated only that his life insurance wasn't enough to cover it all. Then I made sure he knew that all of the debt was paid off. "I have practically nothing in my account, and we are living very cheaply right now, but all of the debt is gone."

He studied me carefully. "That was a tremendous burden to have left on your shoulders while you dealt with your grief. I have one question for you, Faith. Would you ever steal from me?"

"Never, sir."

He nodded. "I am very impressed with you, Faith. Normally, I would never do this, but I am so impressed with you, and I know you would be the perfect fit for our company. I would like to recommend you to the board for the position. They would have to vote on it, but I have no doubt that they will approve. You are everything that we could want."

I wanted to cry, and it took everything in me not to. "Thank you, Mr. Sanders. You don't know how much that means to me."

"Well, when Peter gave me your card this morning, it was like fate was shining down on us."

"Peter?"

"Yes, he's handling the construction of our new office building. It will be ready in February. I mentioned in a meeting with him that my CFO had taken a dramatic hike, and he passed me your card."

"I didn't realize that."

"Well, I think he might be happy to hear that you are considering staying in town. I will get your information to the board, and one of them should be in contact tomorrow to set everything up. As far as I'm concerned, you have the job if you want it, but we do have to go through proper channels."

"Thank you, Mr. Sanders, I am very interested." And I was. I liked him and his company, and the benefits package was more than I had expected. I knew I would enjoy working with him.

When I found out Peter was at the house, I was both thrilled and scared. What if I told him that I was going to stay, and he didn't want me to stay? But hadn't Peter given Mr. Sanders my card? How had he gotten my card in the first place? I was wondering what I was going to say to him as I pulled into the driveway and found the house dark.

Did we lose electricity? I peered into the house and saw the light on in the back; maybe they were in the kitchen and forgot to turn the front lights on. I stepped in and called out to them, flipping on the light switch and stepping toward the archway of the living room.

"Now, Luke." Peter's deep voice drifted through the dark, and then lights turned on. Only they weren't table lamps; they were colorful little bulbs on an artificial tree. Luke was jumping up and down, and Peter looked slightly nervous, but also proud of himself. On the table were drinks and silverware.

I opened my mouth to speak, and instead covered my face and started to cry.

"Oh, boy, we made her cry again," I heard Luke say as I began to cry softly, and then Peter's arms were around me.

"Hey, what's wrong? We thought you would be excited."

"I am," I said around a sob.

"Then why are you crying?"

"Because you did all of this."

He smiled and shrugged. "I bought a tree, no biggie. Luke helped me put it up and get dinner ready. We just need to warm our plates, and then we can sit in here and eat."

"Do you like it, Mom?" Luke asked from my side.

"I love it, Luke." I ruffled his hair.

"Okay, can we eat now?" he asked.

"Let me get dinner warmed, and you get changed, and then you can tell me where you were all dressed for business." Peter went to step back, and I grabbed his face and pulled it to me, surprising him with a kiss.

"Thank you," I whispered as Luke muttered yuck and then laughed. I turned before I started crying again and went to the bedroom to change. I put on leggings and a sweater and found the food waiting for me on the coffee table. Luke and Peter were just sitting down. The only lights on were that from the Christmas tree.

"So I might have gotten a job," I said as I got settled on the floor beside Peter.

Peter's face snapped my way. "Around here?"

I nodded as I chewed. "Would that bother you if I stayed around?"

He grinned at me. "I think you already know the answer to that question, and if you don't, I can show you."

My toes instantly tingled, and I glanced at Luke; he watched us with oblivion written on his face. I laughed.

"So, where is the job? What did they say?"

"Well, the man I spoke with said if it were up to him, he'd hire me immediately, but he needs to get it approved with the board."

"That's fantastic, Faith. Do you like the company?"

"Yes, very much."

"How did you find them?" he asked right before he shoved food into his mouth.

I stared at him for a moment. "Funny that you should ask that. I didn't find them; they found me. It seems that someone handed Mr. Sanders my business card this morning."

Peter tried not to grin as he chewed, but after he swallowed, he couldn't hold it back. "Well, that was nice of someone to do that."

"Where did you get my card?"

"It was on the counter when I made breakfast. Are you upset with me?"

I shook my head. "No, I'm not upset. I'm rather in your debt. You have cooked for me twice, let me sleep in, watched my son, bought me a Christmas tree, and you might have found me a job."

"Sounds like your Christmas wish might be coming true, then," he said softly and winked.

I frowned at him, and he glanced at Luke and then back at me a little nervously.

CHAPTER TEN

PETER

W hoops, I hadn't meant to say that.

"What do you mean by that, Peter?"

I nodded my head toward Luke. "Might be better to discuss that later, but I sometimes play a part."

Her jaw dropped after a few seconds, and she had put two and two together. "As soon as Luke goes to bed, you are going to explain that."

Two hours later, and one Christmas tree decorated, Luke was tucked in bed, and Faith joined me on the couch with a glass of wine. "Okay, why didn't you tell me that you were Santa when you saw me the other day?"

"How would that have looked if Santa wanted to put his hands all over a little boy's mom?"

She laughed. "That's how you knew I was in town."

"Yes. Luke had his new address in his Dear Santa letter."

She winced. "You read mine, didn't you?"

"I did, and I hated it."

"I figured it would get dropped in the dead pile. Do you all still have one of those it's-never-gonna-happen piles?"

"Yeah, we do, but no. I kept it with me."

"Why?" She stared at me, and I cupped her cheek.

195

"Because even though I haven't seen you in almost twelve years, I wanted to make your wish come true. I know that I can't give you the life that you had, Faith, but I can help you build a new life here—one filled with laughter and fun and picnics in the living room."

"Is that what you want?"

"Right now, more than I want anything else in the world. I know we aren't in love with each other, but I know we care about one another, and I have no doubt that we will fall in love with one another. I know it's crazy, Faith, but I want that with you. I want you, I want Luke, I want us to be a family."

"Do you want children?"

I paused for only a second. "I always saw myself having a child, but maybe Luke will be that child. I would never pressure you to have one."

She smiled slowly, running her fingers over my ear. "And for that reason alone, I would want one with you, because you would never pressure me to have one."

"So, what do you say you take the job, and you and Luke move in with me—when you are ready—and we fix this place up and sell it, and we can live happily ever after together?"

She seemed to be contemplating that for a moment. "Okay, on one condition."

"What?"

"You help me talk Santa into finding one of those damn Mighty Mark playsets that Luke wants. I can't find one anywhere that won't cost me an arm and a leg."

I laughed. "You got yourself a deal. If I told you I already had one, how would you thank me?"

"You have one?"

I nodded. "Yep, grabbed the last one on the shelf when I bought your tree."

Faith took my wine glass and set it on the table before she climbed onto my lap. "I don't have any money to pay for that, but would you take my heart as payment?"

I brushed back her hair. "Oh, yeah, I would most definitely take that."

"Then it sounds like you have a deal," she whispered against my lips.

"Let's seal it with a kiss, what do you think?"

Faith pressed her lips to mine, and the two of us sighed as our bodies came together. It might have taken us a lot of time to get to this point, but we were here now, and I had a feeling that our future wishes were only going to get better.

THE END

4: FINDING LOVE WITH A CHAMPAGNE TOAST

CHAPTER ONE

KAREN

The holidays were always busy with my family. My two daughters, Amy and Sarah, their husbands, and their five children dominated the month of December. Well, not just December. They dominated my life, but I didn't mind. I sat back in the plane seat, and I sighed. I loved them all dearly, but it was time for me to recharge. This vacation was a gift to myself after a hell of a year.

I smiled at the flight attendant as he drifted past, glancing at my lap to see if my belt was fastened. "Ma'am, may I get you something to drink?"

"No, thank you, maybe after we take off." First class did have its advantages, and being supplied with a beverage before we even took off was one of them.

I turned to look out the window, watching the employees walk around under the plane as they prepared things. There were no small dirty piles of snow lining the terminal here like there was back in New York where my trip started. Here in Denver, where I'd connected with another flight, it was clear and dry outside. I itched to be off the plane and relaxing on the beautiful island of Lanai for a week.

I felt someone drop something into the seat beside me and turned to watch a man push a small bag into the compartment above our heads. On the seat was a handsome leather briefcase, very similar to the last one I bought my husband—scratch that—ex-husband, and make that a big freaking ex!

One month ago, my divorce had been finalized, and the day I received the paperwork in the mail, I'd called my best friend and sobbed over the phone. The entire time that I poured my heart out about the fact that I was so happy it was over, she'd been logged into her travel agent software and booking me this trip. She had made me promise that once the divorce was final, I would let her book me a trip to Hawaii. How she managed to get me such a good deal the day after Christmas was beyond me, but she had.

The man peered at me, nodded politely, and then proceeded to settle into the seat beside me. I turned my gaze away from him to give him his space, but that didn't mean I wasn't watching him from the corner of my eye. Not that I was being a creeper. I had met him someplace, but I couldn't remember where.

He was an attractive man, not my type, but handsome all the same with his dark hair heavily salted with silver, a rugged face with deep laugh lines, and a nose that looked like it had gone a couple of rounds in the ring.

He was very masculine, and I'd always been attracted to that type of man. Not that I had a type, I was open to possibilities—well, I would be if I were looking for a relationship. After just getting out of a marriage that had taken almost two years—two years—to dissolve, I wasn't looking for an entanglement. I'd only told myself that my seatmate wasn't my type because he had a thick platinum wedding band on his left hand.

I had learned a long time ago to avoid men who wore bands or men who had band marks. I traveled a lot for business and did many tradeshows where there were a lot of lonely men. I'd been hit on more times than I cared to admit and had never been tempted to stray. Okay, maybe I had been tempted a time or two—but I had never done so.

Everyone was tempted once in a while; it was how you dealt with the temptation that mattered. I chose to go back to my hotel room early and call home or enjoy a nice dinner in my room instead of hitting the hotel lounge with my co-workers or other people in my industry.

It was lonely, but I didn't mind. I liked spending time with myself. What I did mind was that my husband of thirty years had not been as inclined to avoid the temptation. I had no clue how many affairs he'd had over the years, but I didn't doubt that there were many.

While I'd had the feeling that Richard was cheating on me, I'd never confronted him. Not until his latest woman—fifteen years younger than me—showed up on our doorstep with a baby in her arms that had bright-blue eyes. Those baby blues gave me little doubt that Richard was the father. I pursed my lips, sighed again, and looked out the window as the memories filled my mind.

More people boarded the plane, and I let my mind dwell over the many fights and drama of the last two years. Richard had denied everything, but how could he deny a child—a child I had seen with my own eyes? Had he not known about the child, maybe I might have forgiven him for this one act, but he had been there for the delivery while I was working a tradeshow in Alabama. He had helped decorate the damn nursery for Christ's sake.

I'd only learned that when Mari—with an I, not a Y—had told me and shared a picture of him doing so. She wanted what he had promised her—a family for her child—I gave him to her. Of course, by the time our divorce was finalized, she saw that the grass was not always greener on the other side. I wasn't sure that their relationship would make it, but that was the least of my worries.

The day I had filed for divorce had been rough. He had pleaded with me to forgive him. I wasn't sure why he still wanted me around, not when he'd had numerous women through the years, and to be quite honest, we hadn't been all that close since the kids had gone to college. Was that part my fault?

I didn't think so. After our youngest daughter, Sarah, had left for college, I had taken on more work, volunteering for more travel. It wasn't that I liked to travel; I preferred not being there without my kids home.

The man beside me sniffed and then cleared his throat. Great, he was sick, which meant I would probably get ill too. Whatever. It wasn't like I had anything planned once I hit the resort on the island of Lanai. My agenda included relaxing in a comfortable chair, reading, sleeping, and enjoying the sunshine. I could still do that if I was sick.

He shifted in his seat, pulling a handkerchief from his pocket and swiping at his nose. He glanced at me. "Sorry, I'm afraid my allergies are a little off the chart this time of year. All the damn evergreen and cinnamon around is making them go a little crazy."

So he wasn't sick, well, that was good to know. "Those are tough things to be allergic to at this time of year."

He laughed slightly. "You're telling me. My wife was always disappointed that we couldn't have a real tree at home."

Was? I picked up on that word. Where was she now? I gave him a polite smile and turned away. We weren't even off the ground, and he was already putting social distance between himself and his wife. Well, he'd better be ready for a long quiet flight, because I wasn't interested in idle chitchat with a cheater.

CHAPTER TWO

HUDSON

When I had first seen a woman in the seat beside mine, I'd frowned. My allergies were already a mess, and the last thing I needed was a woman with strong perfume bothering them more. Luckily, as I'd gotten situated beside her, I couldn't detect any strong fragrance coming from her.

What was even better was that she seemed to want to be left alone. I was okay with that. I'd prefer to be anywhere but here myself, but I was doing this as a favor to my wife. That thought made my chest ache for a moment. Donna's dream had always been to vacation in Hawaii, and we'd had her dream trip planned to celebrate our twenty-fifth wedding anniversary.

We never made it. Instead, I spent our twenty-fifth anniversary tossing back shots of whiskey like they were jelly beans and trying to hide from the memories.

I glanced at the woman beside me, noting her profile. She was pretty, not as pretty as Donna had been, but still very attractive with shoulder-length chestnut hair, a thin nose that sloped up at the end, and full lips. I turned back to my briefcase and removed the book that I had brought with me. I had a lot of work to get done, but I didn't feel like doing that until we were up in the air and flying smoothly.

I wasn't a fan of flying, never had been. In fact, if I never got on another plane after this trip, it would be alright with me. Donna was the one that liked to travel. I enjoyed traveling too, but by car or train or even boat. I was not a fan of being up in the air. I just didn't think it was right that a huge metal object could streak through the sky and stay airborne.

So to keep my mind occupied during takeoff, I'd read. Then I could attempt to relax and work while we took the seven-plus-hour flight to Maui from Denver.

I crossed my legs and pulled my glasses out of my pocket, peering sideways at my companion again. She had her eyes closed and was resting back against the seat. I took a moment to study her; she looked vaguely familiar, but so did many people. I often traveled for work, always in a car, unless I absolutely had to get there quickly. I preferred to drive all night to reach my destination than to take a two-hour flight on a metal bird of death.

I returned my attention to my book and tried to ignore the other passengers boarding the plane. I got knocked into half a dozen times, by luggage, elbows, and purses and finally leaned to the left. I bumped her arm slightly. "Sorry." I murmured.

She opened her eyes, took in the crowd still trying to get to their seats, and shifted her arm to give me more room without saying anything. In fact, she didn't speak until the flight attendant came around thirty minutes later and asked if she wanted anything.

She asked for white wine, a bottle of water, and a cheese and meat snack tray. I watched as the attendant handed it past me. "That looks good; I'd like the same, although I'd prefer a Jack and Coke, please."

"Yes, sir." She nodded to me and went to the small galley to get my order. I glanced at the tray.

"Have you had that before?"

She peered up as she peeled back the covering. "I have. They are very good."

"You fly a lot?" I asked, attempting casual conversation.

"I do. I travel a lot for work," she replied.

I noticed that she didn't ask me in return. "I am not a fan of flying. I travel a lot, too, but I prefer to do it by car."

She smirked. "Hard to travel to Hawaii by car."

"That is very true." I chuckled, and then the laughter faded. "But I'm only going because I made a promise."

She chewed the cracker that she'd put in her mouth as the attendant put my order in front of me, and I thanked her.

"Kind of you to keep your promises, even though you aren't a fan of flying."

I inhaled deeply. "Yeah, I guess so." I began to peel back the covering of the tray and glanced her way. "Where are you from?"

"New York."

I grinned. "Thought so. Upstate, right?"

"Correct, again."

I grinned at her. "Good time to be going to Hawaii."

She chuckled softly. "That it is."

"Is this a business trip? Or are you meeting people to enjoy the rest of the holiday season?" A frown line crossed her brow as I glanced her way, and I found myself watching her for a moment. "I'm sorry, that is none of my business. I was just making conversation, not trying to delve into your personal life."

She lifted her slate-blue eyes to mine, and for a moment, we regarded each other closely. Finally, she leaned back in her seat and sighed as if she'd made a decision. "I'm sorry. I don't mean to be rude, but because I do travel a lot, I'm used to handsome men coming on to me—not that you are doing that—but I did notice your ring, and I—"

"Wanted me to know that you were not interested." I nodded. "I get that, and as attractive as you are, I'm honestly not trying to hit on you. I'm merely making conversation with someone to pass the time."

"Okay, as long as we are on the same wavelength. I'm taking a holiday, alone, to unwind after a very long, stressful year."

"I can relate to that." I paused and then held my hand out. "Hudson Forbes, and you are?"

She slipped her hand into mine, gave it a firm shake that told me she was definitely a businessperson, and smiled. "Karen Reed."

I lifted my glass to her. "Well, Karen, to the start of a new year that I hope is better for the both of us."

She laughed softly and lifted her plastic cup. "Yes, to a better year to come."

We tapped cups, and as I sipped mine, my eyes locked with hers, and I saw pain and sadness in them. It didn't take a psychology degree to tell me that she had lost someone, too.

CHAPTER THREE

KAREN

Seven hours was a long time to keep to myself when I was sitting six inches from someone. Once we had broken the ice and made it clear that I wasn't interested in anything other than casual conversation, we quickly entered an easy conversation.

We discussed traveling, and that led to talk of our jobs. He was a psychologist who worked with businesses to help focus employees on the proper way to market to customers. As soon as he told me what he did, I remembered that I had attended one of his seminars a few years ago.

"The minute you sat down, I knew I had seen you before but couldn't place it. I attended one of your seminars. I remember after, we had a short conversation about ploys."

He chuckled, the sound deep and husky as he glanced my way. "I remember that, Karen. It's funny, I thought the same as you when I sat down, but I meet so many people, it's hard to keep them straight without a reference."

For a while, we continued talking about that. It had been a fascinating seminar, and I had even read a book that Hudson had written. I wonder where that book was now? Had Richard taken it, or was it on a shelf someplace in my new house?

"So, Karen, other than having a long year, why are you heading to Hawaii by yourself the day after Christmas?"

I smirked. "I could ask you the same thing, Hudson."

He blinked and shifted slightly in his seat, glancing down at his wedding ring and fingering it slightly. "It was my wife's final wish."

Her final wish? Oh, no! I automatically put my hand on his forearm. "I'm so sorry, Hudson. When did she pass?"

"Almost two years ago. I finally got up the courage to take this trip." He glanced at my hand and smiled, then looked away before he turned back to me as I was slipping my hand back to my lap. "We had made plans to go to Hawaii for our twenty-fifth anniversary, and well, we never made it. Donna found out four months before our anniversary that she had cancer. It was fast." He sighed. "Which was good and bad."

"I'm so sorry, Hudson."

"Thank you. Donna made me promise that I would come out here and spread a little of her ashes on the beach. It was someplace she always wanted to visit, and I kept putting it off because I didn't want to fly. Can't tell you how many times I had cursed myself for not having gotten on a damn plane earlier and brought her out here when she was alive."

"I'm sure. I can only imagine how difficult that has been, or how hard the decision to do it was for you. You are a good man to keep that promise to her."

He peered my way. "Thanks."

"In answer to your question, my divorce was finalized a month ago, and my best friend is a travel agent. The minute she found out that my divorce decree was signed, she booked me on this trip. It wasn't my idea, but once she made plans, it started sounding really good. I needed to get away and find myself again."

"How long were you married?"

"Thirty years," I muttered. "Probably twenty-three years longer than we should have been."

"Do you have children?"

"I do, two girls, both married, one had two children, the other has three. What about you?"

"Donna and I had four children, two boys, two girls. Two are married, one is hopelessly single, and the youngest passed away when he was only a child."

I gasped. "Hudson, I'm so sorry. Was he ill?"

"No, got hit by a car riding his bike at night."

My hand flew to my mouth. "That's horrible!"

"Yeah, that was a rough year for all of us, but we managed to get through it, and I think it made us all a little stronger. I know that Donna and I leaned on each other pretty hard that year."

"I can only imagine."

He finished his drink and held the glass up, getting the attendant's eyes for another one. "Do you want another glass of wine?"

"Um, not right now, but thank you."

After the attendant walked away, he turned to me. "So what was wrong with your marriage if you think it should have been over years earlier?"

"I had a philandering husband."

He chuckled. "Hence the reason you told me you weren't interested when I first sat down."

"Exactly. I've had enough of that to last a lifetime. I think I knew that Richard was cheating on me, but I just ignored it. Maybe part of me didn't care as long as he kept it away from our children and me."

"What happened for you to end it, or did he call it quits?"

I laughed. "Oh, no, when I finally decided I was done, he begged and pleaded for me to take him back. By then, I had met Mari, the mother of his newborn son, and heard a few stories of their wonderful life. I was over it—all of it."

"Were you sad when your divorce decree showed up?"

"I'll admit that I was. Only because it was an end to something that I had known for so long."

Suddenly, the plane hit a pocket of turbulence and began to pop around. Hudson's face went stark white as his hands gripped the armrests. The bumping kept on, and I swear he started praying as he closed his eyes. I instantly felt for him. I'd had a few come to Jesus moments in my years flying, but we'd always made it through the turbulence and landed safely.

I reached over and put my hand on his. "It's okay; it will be over in a minute."

He cupped my hand between his two, holding on for dear life as the seat belt sign came on and the pilot announced that it would be bumpy for a few minutes.

Hudson glanced at me, his lips pressed in a firm line before he spoke gruffly. "You said a minute, he said a few. I like your answer better."

CHAPTER FOUR

HUDSON

I only made it through the turbulence because Karen had been kind enough to lend me her strength. She allowed me to hold her hand until things finally evened out, and then I had downed my new drink.

How ironic would it have been if our plane had gone down as I was on my way to fulfill Donna's dying request? I asked for one more drink, and while I didn't gulp it down, I did drink it fast. By the time I finished, I felt better, and I turned to Karen, who had her eyes closed.

"Thank you," I said softly, not sure if she was awake or sleeping.

She opened her eyes, smiled softly at me, and replied, "You're welcome." Then she closed her eyes again, and I studied her face. She really was an attractive woman, and her eye color was very close to mine. Too bad we were both meeting one another at a difficult time.

I frowned as I looked away and settled myself back in my seat, closing my own eyes. Somehow I managed to drift off to sleep, and when I woke up, I felt something in my hand. It was another hand, and I blinked a couple of times before realizing that I was holding on to Karen again.

I released it immediately and lifted my eyes to find her watching me. "I'm so sorry."

She grinned. "It's okay. It got bumpy a few minutes ago."

"Did I just grab your hand?" I asked, mortified that I had been so forward.

"Yes, but that's okay, Hudson. It really is."

"I'm glad you are so understanding." I shook my head and glanced at my watch to find that I'd been asleep at least an hour. We would be landing in less than two hours. The flight was going faster than I expected. "Thank you for your support."

"You're welcome."

I pulled my briefcase out from under the seat in front of me and removed my laptop so that I could get some work done. What did Karen think of me after I'd grabbed her hand and held on to it like I was a child? I couldn't even imagine.

I lost myself in my work and only came up from it when the pilot announced that we would be landing in about thirty minutes. Wow, the time had flown. I finished up what I was doing and started to pack up my laptop. I noticed Karen was staring out the window.

I glanced through the window in front of her. "Wow, water as far as you can see."

She glanced at me. "There have been a few small islands, but not many."

"I'm sorry about earlier."

She smiled, and it caused me to return it. "It really is alright. It actually eased me too."

"Well, at least I was able to help you in return."

The idea that maybe the two of us might have the opportunity to have a drink on land came to me. "Are you staying on Maui?"

"No, I have a connecting flight."

"Ah, okay." I nodded, slightly disappointed that I wouldn't see her again, not that I was staying on Maui myself, but I wasn't taking another plane.

We were quiet as we finished the flight, and then I found myself glued to the side window as I leaned her way. "So many palm trees."

"There sure are," she commented as she turned toward me and jumped slightly when she saw how close I was. This sudden urge came over me to lean forward and kiss her. I hadn't kissed another woman in twenty-eight years, and I pulled myself out of the way of temptation.

I leaned toward the aisle so that we had distance between us, and I frowned. Why had I wanted to kiss Karen? Because she had been kind to me?

I was a fool. Once the plane landed, I gathered my briefcase and my small bag from the overhead storage. "Do you have something up here?"

"I do, the navy bag." I pulled out her small carry-on and put it on the ground for her, extending the handle. "Thank you, Hudson."

"You're welcome, Karen." I nodded to her as the door opened, and I waved my hand in front of me after the first-row passengers disembarked. Karen stepped into the aisle and took her bag, pulling it behind her, and I followed. She was taller than Donna, almost my height. Donna had only been five feet tall. I glanced at her shoes and found her wearing flats. Yep, she was probably around five-six; I was only five-eight.

I followed her down the walkway into the main terminal. After getting away from the gate, she paused and looked around before turning to me. "Well, I guess this is goodbye." She put her hand out. "I hope that your vacation goes well, Hudson. It was a pleasure meeting you."

I took Karen's hand. "You too, Karen." Our handshake was less professional this time as the two of us locked eyes, and I couldn't help but glance at her lips. They parted as I did, and the two of us released our hands at the same time. "Enjoy your vacation, Karen."

"Thank you, Hudson."

I nodded and quickly turned before I did something stupid, like asking if I could have her number. What had gotten into me? I'd sat next to the woman for seven hours in the air, and now I was interested in having dinner with her on land? I sighed as I looked for a sign to tell me where I needed to meet my party.

I finally found it and walked up to the counter to check in. "Hello, Hudson Forbes, I have a reservation for a boat to take me to the island of Lanai."

"Aloha, Mr. Forbes. Welcome to Hawaii. We have a shuttle ready for you right out this door. We are waiting for two more passengers, and then we will take you to the dock for your transportation. How many bags did you check?"

I handed him my ticket stub with my luggage tag on it. "Only one."

"Very good, we will acquire it for you. Have a nice visit on Lanai; it is a beautiful island."

I nodded to him and stepped out the door to outside. I paused as the heat of the island engulfed me. The smell of jet fuel filled the air, but at least it wasn't evergreen and cinnamon.

I sat in the transport van and turned my cellphone on to check messages. I was skimming through email when a young couple climbed into the van and said hello. Great, I was going to share my ride with newlyweds. For the first time since I had set out on this journey, I wished that I wasn't alone, and for some odd reason, Karen's face entered my mind.

CHAPTER FIVE

KAREN

I wasn't sure why I felt slightly disappointed as I walked away from Hudson. Maybe because I had found myself surprisingly attracted to the man. Or perhaps it was because he had reached out to me unconsciously when he needed support. It had been a long time since someone leaned on me for something other than babysitting.

Whatever it was, it didn't matter. We had gone our separate ways like two ships in the night. I chuckled to myself like we'd had some grand love affair and then gone in opposite directions. I pushed thoughts of Hudson out of my head as I found the check-in for my connecting flight. I was taking a ten-seater puddle jumper to the island.

I had an hour to wait until my boarding time, so I took a seat and checked in with my kids to let them know I was in Hawaii. Amy told me to prove it, and I took a selfie of the planes behind me and all the palm trees and mountains in the distance. Neither one of my girls thought I would go on vacation alone. They both thought it was odd that I would travel someplace as romantic as Hawaii without someone to share it with. Neither of them would have done such a thing.

They were more like their father, needing other people to supply their happiness. I preferred to get my joy by watching others and doing small things for myself.

Before I knew it, we were boarding the plane and taxing down the runway. I was excited and a bit nervous about flying in such a tiny plane over the vast ocean. I wondered if Hudson would ever get on a flight like this and quickly vetoed that thought with a chuckle.

The flight over was smooth and beautiful, and before I knew it, we were landing on the tiny island. The pilot had taken us around the island quickly, telling us where things were.

When we got off the plane on the tarmac, several drivers stood around waiting. I was the only single passenger, and a driver immediately came to me. "Mrs. Reed?"

"Yes, that's me."

"Which are your bags? I'll gather them for you. We are in the silver sedan at the back."

I pointed out my two bags and followed him to the waiting car as I inhaled the salty fresh air. I was already feeling better, and I wasn't even at the resort. The driver was kind enough to share more history of the island as we drove and answered a few questions about the resort, like how early they serve dinner.

After traveling for fourteen hours, I was exhausted, and even though it was early afternoon here, I was ready for dinner and bed. Tomorrow would be soon enough to venture through the resort and check things out.

Only when I arrived, I found myself fascinated with the quaint resort. I received a lei and a big Hawaiian welcome before I was served a pina colada in a real coconut. Fresh pineapple was being carried around for all the guests, and I moaned around the sweet treat as I put a chunk into my mouth. It was amazing. Never had I ever had such fresh pineapple.

I saw a small coffee bar off to the side, and the tantalizing scent of Hawaiian coffee wafted over to me. Oh, man. I'd be happy to just hang out in the lobby for hours. I might need a couple of cups of that to help me get through the afternoon.

My check-in was quick, and before I knew it, I was being whisked away to my room. When Marie had booked my vacation, she had wanted me to stay in a fancy suite, but I told her that a standard hotel room was just fine. I didn't need an elaborate room to sleep in. Of course, when I stepped into my room, I had to wonder if she had somehow upgraded me because it was gorgeous, and the view was exquisite.

The porter left my things, collected the tip I had for him, and quickly vanished as I moved to the glass doors and opened them to step out on the balcony. It was an incredible view, and for a moment, I was sad that I didn't have anyone to share it with. Did Hudson have a view as equally breathtaking at his resort?

I chastised myself for thinking of him and returned to the room to unpack a few things. It didn't take long; as a seasoned traveler, I had it down to a science, and ten minutes later, I changed into a sundress and sandals, grabbed my room key, and decided to take a walk around the resort—maybe grab that cup of coffee.

I returned to the lobby, went straight to the coffee counter, and made myself a large cup. For a moment, I stood there, inhaling the deep aroma. It was worth the flight just for this.

I made my way around the resort, finding the restaurants, multiple pools, the spa, gym, a night club, and several quaint shops that I looked forward to shopping in.

I was returning to the lobby to get another cup of coffee when I heard a voice, and I turned to see someone disappear around the corner. I hadn't seen the person, but it sure had sounded like Hudson. I shook my head as I scolded myself once again for thinking of the man.

After getting more coffee, I walked out toward the beach. I made my way along the pathway that wound down toward the water. It was a glorious sight, and I stood on the stone path for a while, enjoying the playful breeze and watching the waves come in. I turned as a couple passed by, and I smiled and nodded to them. I noticed that everyone was with someone, and for the first time in a long time, I missed having a companion.

I sighed and returned to the resort, knowing that the restaurant would now be open for early diners. I was starting to feel weary and wanted a light meal before closing my curtains tight and getting a good night's sleep.

As the host took me to a table along the balcony, I tried not to notice the few couples already seated. The host paused at a table, and I glanced past him to see surprised eyes staring back at me. "Hudson!"

He stood. "Karen." He laughed. "I didn't know you were staying here."

I laughed. "I guess neither of us mentioned where we were staying."

The gentleman beside me leaned forward. "Would you two care to dine together?"

Hudson and I eyed one another, and then Hudson began to smile. "I would love to have your company for dinner, Karen."

I joined Hudson at his table, and the host held my chair out for me. As I took a seat, I glanced over the table, taking in the broad smile on his handsome face as I felt something warm seep through my body.

CHAPTER SIX

HUDSON

The boat ride to the island was fantastic, and I looked forward to taking a sailing trip in the next few days. When I arrived at the resort, I checked in, unpacked my stuff, and stood on the balcony of my incredible suite. I could see the pathway that led down to the beach, and off in the distance, a woman with dark hair stood alone in a sundress. She reminded me of Karen, but I knew that was just my wishful thinking.

Ever since I'd left her at the airport, she'd been on my mind. Oddly enough, I'd thought more about Karen than Donna, and my wife was the reason I was here. I shook my head and went inside to shower and change before going to dinner.

After that, I would take a quick walk on the beach. Tomorrow I would figure out what I wanted to do in the way of activities.

I was just about to crack open the menu when I glanced up and saw Karen standing there. A bright smile graced her lips, and she looked as happy to see me as I was her. What were the odds that we were in the same resort?

"What room are you in?" I asked as we sat staring at one another.

"I'm in the east wing."

"Ah, I'm in the west. How is your room?"

"Incredible. This entire resort is wonderful. How did you get here?" she asked as she leaned forward.

"I took a boat." I grinned. "I assume you took a plane."

"I did. I thought about you while I was on it. I tried to picture you in one of the ten seats."

He winced. "Yeah, you picturing it is the only way that would ever happen."

She laughed, and the sound went straight to my heart. "That is kind of what I figured. How was your boat ride?"

"It was great. I was thinking of finding a boat to charter over the next few days and going fishing. You ever fished?"

"I haven't been fishing in years, but once the company I was working for had a company fishing trip. It was fun when the guys weren't puking over the side."

I laughed. "Would you like to come with me? I promise not to puke over the side."

She blinked, leaning back slightly as she took in the surprise. "Um—"

I reached over the table, touching the tips of my fingers against her hand as it sat next to her water glass. "Karen, I'm not sure what you think, but I know that I'm old enough not to play games. I enjoyed talking to you today, and after we parted, I found that I missed you and wished that I had a way to contact you again. I think that for some reason, we ended up here together. Maybe it's to help one another get through a rough period, or perhaps to give us hope of a future. Whatever it is, I'd like to spend time with you. Unless you'd rather not."

She stared at me, her slate-blue eyes bright with the sun shining into them from the water. "It's funny that you say that, Hudson. A few times today, I noticed all the couples around me and found myself missing a companion. I've always been the kind of person to do things independently, but this is different. I have thought of you several times today too." She shifted her hand so that her fingers lay over mine. "I'd love to spend time with you, share the island, as long as I don't interfere with what you need to do for your wife."

"I promise when it comes time to do that, I'll let you know."

"Then, what else does this island have to offer?" she said, smiling widely over the table, and I felt something funny tickling around my heart.

Karen and I enjoyed a wonderful dinner of fresh seafood and salad, and then after, we walked down the pathway to the beach. The sun was getting low in the sky, and we walked along the water, shoes in hand as our feet sank into the soft sand along the waterline.

We laughed and shared stories of our children and grandchildren. As the sun began to crest the horizon, we both stopped and watched it descend. Karen brushed a strand of hair back from her face, and I turned to her, watching the glow of the sun in her eyes.

I couldn't remember the last time that I wanted to kiss a woman as much as I did then. It had been so long since I had shared that with anyone besides Donna. What would it even be like?

Karen turned her face toward mine, the wind twirling her hair across her face, and I brushed the hair back, cupping her cheek. I leaned forward, brushing my lips over hers like it was the most natural thing in the world. It was a gentle kiss, tentative for both of us, and I pulled back and stared at her.

Karen caressed the side of my face, and then I was leaning forward again. This time, her arm slipped around my neck, and I wound an arm around her waist, pulling her closer, but not tightly to my body. I wasn't sure I was ready for that level of intimacy yet.

The kiss was beautiful, and when we pulled back, we smiled at one another and then stood close to each other with my arm around her waist, cupping her hip as we watched the sun set on another day. A day I would never forget.

We walked back to the resort, hand in hand, and Karen yawned, which in turn caused me to do so also. I walked her to her room and paused at her door. "I'll call you in the morning; maybe we can meet for breakfast and look into what the island has to offer."

"I think that would be wonderful."

I kissed her one more time. "Night, Karen."

"Good night, Hudson." She turned and entered her room, and I grinned like an idiot all the way back to my room.

CHAPTER SEVEN

KAREN

I wasn't sure the night could have been any more romantic. I washed my face and stared into the mirror, remembering the kiss on the beach. It was perfect. Nothing overwhelming but refreshing and exciting. How long had it been since I was excited about kissing someone?

I tried to remember that feeling associated with Richard, but our first kiss had been so long ago. We'd been high school sweethearts, and we'd gotten married as soon as we graduated from college. Our first kiss was a forgotten memory.

The kiss that I had shared with Hudson would be far from a forgotten memory, and the walk back to the resort had felt so natural with his fingers intertwined with mine. Since meeting him, I had yet to experience any uncomfortable moments, and I looked forward to seeing him the next morning.

As I lay down, I looked over the messages on my phone. I had left it in my room, and I had a dozen from the girls wondering if I was okay. I told them I was fine and that I had a pleasant dinner and watched the sunset on the beach. It was two in the morning where they were, and they would not see it until the morning. I turned off my sound and curled up to sleep with a smile on my lips.

The next morning a knock on my door woke me. I glanced out the peephole and found an employee standing outside with a small tray and flowers.

I pulled open the door. "Yes?"

"Aloha, Ms. Reed."

"Aloha."

"These are for you. May I bring them in?"

"Yes, please." I held the door open wider. He set the tray down near the French doors. I took in a small carafe along with a single coffee mug and a small arrangement of flowers.

"There is a note on the tray for you too, ma'am."

"Thank you." I paused and then began to look for my purse. "Let me get you a tip."

"Thank you, ma'am, but that has already been taken care of. Enjoy your morning coffee." He bowed and then let himself out of the room.

I found the note on the tray, unfolded it, and read it aloud. "If you are anything like me, you need that first cup of coffee before you can be human with anyone else. Enjoy this and meet me for breakfast in the garden café in thirty minutes."

I was grinning as I poured and took that first sip. Delicious. I took another sip and then went to my closet to find something to wear today. I decided on shorts and a blouse until we decided what we were going to do today. Thirty minutes later, with one of the flowers from the arrangement tucked into my hair, I entered the garden café and found Hudson sitting near the far railing. A soft breeze ruffled his damp hair. He stood as soon as he saw me, and I wondered if this would be an awkward greeting, but the minute we were close enough, we came together with a brief soft kiss. For a few moments, we regarded one another, then he winked and held out my chair.

"How are you this morning?" he asked as he poured me a coffee from the carafe on the table.

"I'm wonderful. Thank you so much for the flowers and coffee. That was a very nice treat this morning."

"You're welcome. I like doing little things."

"Well, as one that never had anyone do little things for them, I greatly appreciate them."

"Your husband didn't do little things for you?"

I laughed. "Oh, no. Richard's idea of doing something for me was remembering to take the trash to the curb without me reminding him."

"What about gifts? Did he give you gifts just because?"

I shook my head. "No. I was lucky he remembered my birthday, but that's okay. I didn't do those kinds of things for him, either."

Hudson frowned. "When is your birthday?"

"March, yours?"

"It's next week. I'll be fifty-four."

"I'll be fifty-two on my next birthday. Did you spoil your wife often?"

He chuckled. "I did, or at least I tried to remember to do it. I always brought home something small with me from my trips. Even if the items were for the kids, she always appreciated them, but I would surprise her with things too. Not all the time, but once in a while."

"You are a kind man, Hudson."

"Thank you, Karen."

Once again, we slipped into a comfortable conversation over breakfast, and then we went to the front desk to speak to someone about what they had to offer at the resort. An hour later, we had all kinds of activities planned for the the next few days, from fishing, to snorkeling, to archery and 4-wheel adventures.

A few minutes later, we parted ways to change clothes and gather what we needed for our trip to the island's Adventureland. It was a park that offered ziplining and other climbing adventures. I was glad to see that Hudson's fear didn't spread to a fear of heights.

Thirty minutes later, we had a private car taking us out to the adventure park, and Hudson and I sat in the back of the Jeep holding hands. I glanced at them, finding it comforting to have someone's hand to hold. Hudson turned to me, brushing hair back from my face that the wind was whipping around.

He leaned forward, pressing his lips to mine, and I felt my heart sigh with contentment. When we arrived, he helped me out of the Jeep, and then we looked around at all the excitement before us.

"You ready for an adventure, Karen?"

I squeezed his hand, staring into his gray eyes. "I think my adventure started the moment you sat beside me on the plane."

Hudson's smile softened, and he leaned forward, kissing me gently before saying, "I think you are right."

CHAPTER EIGHT

HUDSON

I was walking on air, literally. Well, I had a rope under the balls of my feet and a harness around me to keep me from falling fifty feet to my death, but for the most part, I was walking on air.

I glanced back, taking a second to watch Karen as she tackled the rope wall behind me. We were about twenty feet apart, so we could safely do the course. I was happily surprised that she wanted to do the full rope course. Donna had never been a very physically active person unless it was yoga or swimming. Those she loved, but anything else, and she'd rather sit on the sidelines patiently and watch.

Karen was turning out to be the total opposite. She wanted to try everything and put her hand into every task. I really enjoyed her excitement and go-getter attitude; in fact, I found that I loved it. I also loved the smiles, winks, and kisses we stole from one another off and on through the course.

We had only spent half the day together, and I was already excited to see what the next five days would bring us. I had a feeling that Karen was going to approach every single activity with the same excitement. I sure hope she did.

Right before we got on the final zipline, I stepped away to the side of the platform and removed a small baggie from my pocket. I stared down at the ashes inside, and my heart ached for a moment. This is what Donna had made me promise her. She had told me to have the best time of my life, and everywhere I went, she wanted me to spread a little bit of her ashes so she could be there with me. Was it weird to do this while Karen was with me?

I glanced sideways and found Karen observing me; she glanced at my hand and then nodded with a tender smile on her lips. I made sure the breeze was not blowing toward us and then slowly let the ashes go into the air. Maybe I should have said something before I did that, but at the moment, I didn't know the words.

I pushed the baggy into my pocket and turned to find Karen watching me, a tear rolling down her cheek. "Why are you crying?" I swiped the tear from her face.

"Because your wife was a very lucky woman to have a man like you in her life. I hope you don't feel like I am intruding on your goodbye to her."

"No, not at all. I think you are making it bearable, Karen. I was just wondering what Donna would have thought of it though."

"If you'd rather me not join you for the rest of your trip, I can bow out. I do not want to cause you stress."

I cupped her cheek. "Honestly, Karen, I think Donna had something to do with us meeting. She knew this would be hard, and she led me to someone who could make it easier to let her go."

Karen blinked back moisture from her eyes. "Well, if you ever want me to step away and give you privacy, you let me know."

"I will," I told her, and then I kissed the tip of her nose. "Now, you ready to zipline across this canyon?"

"I've been waiting for you," she said playfully. "You know I will beat you, right."

"You think so, huh?"

"I know so!" She grinned back.

"Alright, what can we bet?"

"Whoever loses gives the other a back rub," she said quickly and then bit her bottom lip like she hadn't meant to say that out loud.

Before she could take it back, I jumped on it. "You got yourself a bet, sweetheart!"

Her eyes sparkled as she stepped forward to get strapped into the harness that took us over the canyon in a superman pose. The employees did a countdown and then shoved us off the platform side by side.

She seemed to understand the dynamics a bit more than I did and made herself more streamlined, getting out in front of me, but I didn't mind. I actually would prefer to be the one giving the massage. The thought of putting my hands on her body was waking up all kinds of things that had been asleep for over two years.

She squealed as she looked back, approaching the finish line, and put her hands up to apply the brake when she reached the slow down zone. When we were finally back on our feet, she squealed, "Wasn't that view awesome?"

"It was!" I said as I wrapped my arm around her, but I wasn't thinking of the view below us. My gaze had been locked on her the entire time.

We took a few selfies once we were back on the ground and had someone take a couple of pictures of us. I looked over her shoulder as she pulled them up on her phone, and damn, if we didn't look like a real couple. Like we'd been together for years, and not just met two days ago..

The more the day went on, the more we found ourselves touching the other, and when we returned to the hotel, we stood outside her door for a moment. The temptation to ask her if I could come in was on the tip of my tongue, but I didn't. I didn't want to push this because I wasn't sure if I was ready for that step yet.

"Dinner?"

"If you aren't tired of me yet, I would love dinner," she replied.

"Are you kidding me? I don't think I could ever get tired of you, Karen." I pulled her closer to me. "Have dinner with me."

"I'd like that."

"Alright, then I'll be back to pick you up at seven-thirty. Is that alright?"

"That will be perfect."

"I'll see you then." I kissed her slowly, then stepped back, letting her hands slip through mine.

"I'll see you at seven-thirty," she said and then disappeared into her room.

I wanted to hop, skip, and jump in the air, but instead, I turned and found myself whistling as I headed down the hallway. As I reached the elevator, I paused and frowned. I hadn't whistled in over two years. I pushed my hand into my pocket and pulled out the small baggie that had carried some of Donna's ashes earlier today.

"Did you lead me to her, Donna?" The elevator door opened, and I stepped inside. Donna had told me that she wanted me to fall in love again and be happy. She didn't want me to be alone, but she didn't want me to forget her either.

I had no idea what this was with Karen or what would happen in a few days when we went our separate ways, but I did know that I finally felt like I was ready to take that next step and move on with my life.

CHAPTER NINE

KAREN

It was a fantasy vacation. My time with Hudson was incredible, and I'd have nothing but fond memories of this trip when it was over.

I knew that once we left this island, our lives would go back to what they were. I didn't expect anything more from him, and I was sure he didn't expect anything from me.

For the next few days, I would live in the moment, and as I dressed for dinner, I decided to go all out. I wanted to let my heart soar and do what it pleased, and if that meant falling into bed with Hudson, then so be it.

It had been almost three years since I'd had sex with a person and not a toy, and I found myself both excited and nervous as the knock sounded on my door and I opened it to find a very handsome Hudson standing before me.

He wore white linen slacks and a soft-peach linen shirt. His skin, already tan from only a day on the island, looked warm and inviting. He looked at me from head to toe. "Wow, you look beautiful, Karen."

"Thank you, you look very handsome yourself, Hudson. Come in for a moment." I held the door for him, and he paused as I closed the door; when I turned around to face him, I found myself oddly nervous. "I just need to get my earrings and my purse."

I started to walk past him, but his hand snaked out and grabbed my arm. I turned, and he stepped forward, taking my face into his hands and pulling it to his. I clung to him as he kissed me with a bit more passion than he had previously done so, and I felt my toes begin to tingle and curl. In all my life I didn't ever remember feeling my toes curl.

When Husdon pulled back, he stared at me. "I'm sorry about that. I felt like I had to break the ice."

"So, I wasn't the only one nervous?"

He laughed, the sound so husky and low that it was like a low vibration that made its way down my spine inch by delicious inch. "No, you weren't. Which I think is odd. We spent all day together, so why be nervous about tonight?"

I nibbled on my bottom lip for a moment. "Maybe because you owe me a back rub, and neither of us knows whether we are ready for the intimacy that implies."

He grinned. "You are a very intelligent woman, Karen Reed, and I appreciate that you speak so forward. No beating around the bush for you."

"Why should we? You said it last night; we are too old for games. All afternoon I have considered the possibility of sleeping with you, but I don't know if you are ready for that or if you are even interested. I know that I am, on both counts."

He took my hands as he stepped back and squeezed them. "I don't know how I got so lucky to meet someone like you on this trip. Like you, I have thought about the possibilities between us. I've only been with one woman in the last twenty-eight years. The thought of having sex with someone else is both terrifying and exciting."

"Well, then we both know where we stand, Hudson. We won't push it. If it happens, then it happens. If it does not, I'll always be happy about our time together." I stepped forward and kissed him soundly. "But no matter what happens, you do owe me a back rub, and

I am not letting you get out of that. Now, let's go eat, and then we will see what happens."

Dinner was fantastic, and as with everything else we had done together, it felt natural as we laughed and shared. We discussed his job, my job, and our marriages. There didn't seem to be a topic that we didn't touch on, and after dinner, we wandered by one of the night clubs and found ourselves out on the dance floor for a little while, enjoying the music.

I was not in the least surprised that Hudson could dance, and as a fast dance led into a slow one, I wrapped myself around him. "Did you and Donna dance a lot?"

He shook his head. "No, not really. I mean, at weddings or things like that we'd dance." He frowned. "I can't honestly remember the last time we danced together. Probably Matt's wedding. What about you and Richard?"

I laughed. "Rich had two left feet. I didn't even slow dance with him."

He grinned at me. "Well, then he missed out because having your body up against mine is quickly becoming one of my favorite parts of dancing."

I hiked a brow. "Oh, really?"

His voice lowered. "Yes, you can't tell?"

I guess I hadn't been paying attention, but I suddenly did as he pressed himself tighter to my body. "Oh, I can tell."

He leaned forward, pressing his lips to my ear. "You ready for that back rub?"

I was breathless as I responded, "I believe I am."

He brushed his lips over my cheek as he stepped back and took my hand, leading me off the floor and out of the club. Neither of us spoke as we entered the elevator, and when we got off at the fourth floor, instead of the third, I knew he was taking me back to his room.

Butterflies began to flit around in my midsection, and I found myself gnawing on my bottom lip. Hudson pulled my lip out from under my teeth. "That's for me to chew on later."

A nervous laugh filtered out of my mouth, and he winked. He

escorted me down the hallway to his room and slipped his key card out, handing it to me. "You can open the door and see what happens next, or you can say good night, and we can enjoy our fishing trip tomorrow."

I looked him deeply in the eye and then reached for the key card. Like I was going to say no to a night with him. Ha!

I turned and put the key card to the door, and Hudson stepped behind me, putting his hands on my hips and his mouth to my neck. It was as if by me taking the card, I had already opened the door.

I barely got the door open before I was turning in his arms and accepting his eager mouth over mine. He pressed me against the wall as the door clicked closed. "Karen—" His voice was deeper than I had ever heard it. "I can't remember ever wanting someone so much."

His mouth went to my neck, and I let my head drop back against the wall behind me. "Then take me, Hudson."

A moment later, his hand scooped under my knees, and he lifted me in his arms and carried me into his room. I barely took in that he was in a suite of some kind before he was setting my feet back on the floor, the bed to our side.

"Last chance, Karen."

I stepped back from him and saw a slight change in his eyes. I think he expected me to tell him no. Instead, I was putting room between us so that I could untie my dress. When I parted the front, his hands came to my breasts, and I knew that neither of us was going anywhere tonight.

CHAPTER TEN

HUDSON

I don't know when I decided to sleep with Karen. Maybe it was while I was getting dressed, or perhaps it was when she opened her door and I saw how beautiful she was. It didn't much matter when it had occurred. All I knew was that as I lay with her in the crook of my arm and my fingers drifted softly over her skin, I'd made the right decision.

There was a moment when we had first started that I wondered if I was ready, and Karen had felt the change. She'd taken my hands, shifted us apart for a moment, and asked me if I was okay. The fact that she had noticed and had asked was enough to tell me that this was right. She was an amazing woman, and while the sex was different than what I had shared with Donna for so many years, it was exciting on its own.

After so many years, learning a new body, hearing new sounds, trying new things, was intense and satisfying, and I had to hope that Karen thought so too.

She sighed against me, and I asked, "You okay?"

"Oh, I'm fine. More than fine."

I chuckled. "Yeah, me too." I paused. "Can I ask you a question?"

"Of course."

"Was that alright?"

"Was what alright? The sex?"

I nodded.

She pulled her head back and cupped my cheek, forcing me to look down at her. "That was amazing, Hudson. The best sex that I personally have had in forever."

"Really?"

"Yes. Sex with Richard was always vanilla; even when I tried to add some sprinkles, he just wanted vanilla."

I laughed. "He doesn't know what he was missing out on."

She frowned for a second. "Did I disappoint you? Is that why you are asking?"

I took hold of her face and lifted my head to kiss her. "No! Not in the slightest bit. You were fantastic. I always enjoyed sex with my wife, but this was something else. It was unique and different and special, and I loved it, Karen."

She rested her chin on my chest. "Okay, well, as long as we both agree that it was pretty fantastic, then maybe we can do it once or twice more this week."

I laughed and rolled her over. "Only once or twice?"

Four days later, I was stepping out of the shower after our eleventh lovemaking session. Yep, eleven times in four days. I hadn't had that much sex ever—including when I was a horny teenager.

Karen and I couldn't keep our hands off each other. Both of us were eager to try new things and laughed openly at ones that didn't quite work out the way they were supposed to.

We started our days in each other's arms and ended them that way too. Sometimes we'd find ourselves in the bed or shower in the middle of the day also.

This morning as I dried off, I fretted. It was New Year's Eve, and Karen was set to leave tomorrow. I still had another day before returning to the mainland, and I couldn't imagine being here for one hour without her. She had gone back to her room to shower and dress, and then we were going to spend a quiet day on the beach.

The last four days had been incredible, some of the best of my life, and through each activity, she had been there as I let another piece of Donna go. Tonight, I would release her final baggie of ashes.

Karen and I had discussed it. At midnight, I would release her final ashes into the sea, and then I would say goodbye and move on with my life.

But had I not already done that with Karen? I didn't know. Karen and I had not spoken of anything after our time together here. I'd never asked her what her thoughts were on seeing one another again, and she had never brought up the subject either.

What if we went our separate ways when this was over and never saw one another again? I wasn't sure I wanted that. I also wasn't sure what other possibilities there were.

Karen lived hours from me, and her children were close to her. Her family was important to her. My kids were scattered within an hour of me in Ohio. While I wasn't as involved in their daily life as she was with hers, I was close to my children. Was it even possible for us to continue this? Or would what we felt for one another fizzle out once we returned to the cold winter?

Maybe Karen had come into my life to ease the process of saying goodbye to Donna, and only for that reason.

No, I didn't want to think that was her only purpose. I wanted to believe that we would figure something out. I didn't want our time to be over, and I hoped that Karen didn't either.

At the beach, Karen had seemed more reserved, but so did I. I think that both of us felt the clock ticking, and we held each other's hands a bit tighter, kissed a little bit longer. Neither of us spoke about what the next day would bring, and I feared mentioning it.

I knew that I should, but I also knew that it would make it real if I did. I wasn't ready for reality. Tomorrow morning, we could discuss it over breakfast. Make plans, figure something out. I had every intention of figuring something out.

Right before midnight, I waded out into the water and said goodbye to the last of Donna's ashes. I felt at peace with what I had done, and as I returned to shore, Karen had held out a champagne flute to me.

"May the rest of your years be as beautiful as this moment is. May you have all you ever wish for, Hudson."

I smiled at her. "And may your years bring you nothing but love and happiness, Karen."

We had tapped glasses, sipped the fine champagne, and then come together in a bittersweet kiss.

Shortly after midnight, I had made love to Karen and felt the change in her. The sighs were softer, the words quieter, and our eyes had remained open and locked on one another the entire time. I fell asleep with her curled against me, feeling like I was on the verge of losing someone all over again.

When I woke the next morning, the bed was empty. I felt an uneasy sensation begin to fill my chest, even though I assumed that Karen had gone to her room to finish packing. I showered as quickly as I could and then went in search of her.

When I entered her hallway, my steps slowed. Near where her room was located, there was a housekeeping cart. That couldn't be her room. She couldn't have left already, could she? No!

I picked up my step and found myself confused as I stood in front of her open door. "Excuse me, do you know when this guest checked out?"

"Aloha, sir. I'm sorry, I do not know what time; I just know that she checked out early."

"Thank you." I spun and rushed back to the elevator, opting for the stairs and taking them to the lobby. I searched the area, hoping that maybe Karen was hanging out in the lobby waiting for me. She wouldn't have left without saying goodbye, right?

My feet took me to the front desk. "Can you please tell me when Mrs. Karen Reed checked out this morning?" Anger was starting to creep in, and I was forcing myself to remain calm.

"Sir, are you Hudson Forbes?"

"Yes, why?"

"Mrs. Reed left you a note." He reached for an envelope that was off to the side and passed it over to me.

I took it without a word and tore it open as I stepped away from the desk.

Hudson – I'm sorry for leaving without saying goodbye, but I just couldn't do it. You have given me the best days of my life, and I didn't want to say goodbye to that. I couldn't say goodbye to that. Please know that I will forever treasure our memories. I wish you all the happiness in the world. All my love- Karen

I spun around. "Mrs. Reed is on a plane to Maui, right? What time will it leave?"

He glanced at the clock. "In about twenty minutes, sir."

I almost leaned over the counter and grabbed the guy by his collar but held myself back. "You stop that plane and get me a spot on it!"

"But, sir—"

"Do not sir me! I don't care what it costs! You stop that damn plane and get a car ready for me. I need ten minutes!"

"Sir, does this mean you are checking out early?"

I shouted over my shoulder as I began to run toward the stairs, "Yes!"

CHAPTER ELEVEN

KAREN

My eyes were leaking. I didn't want them to, but they were. I didn't want to leave Hudson without saying goodbye—but how could I say it to his face?

Last night when he had said his final goodbye to Donna, I had stood back and cried. He would always love her and always think of her. How could I compete with that? I knew I couldn't.

When we had made our toast to each other, neither of us had included the other in our words. He had not mentioned wanting to see me again after we left here. If he felt as I did, would he not want to see if we could work things out?

What held me back from asking him was knowing that I hadn't been in love with my husband in years. I knew I was ready to move forward. Hudson loved his wife dearly, and while he had made advances to a new future, was he ready to fall in love with another woman and start a new life?

That was the real reason that I had left him after slipping my name and phone number into his shaving kit. Once he got home, if he missed me or wanted to find me, he could.

I knew that somewhere between grabbing my hand on the plane in his sleep, and the toast we had given to each other last night, I had fallen in love with Hudson Forbes. I doubted that he felt the same.

I had even whispered it to him after he'd fallen asleep, and I'd spent hours watching him sleep before I tiptoed out of his room and life.

Last night when I had come to change for dinner, I had packed everything except my toiletries and traveling clothes. It took me fifteen minutes to be ready and out the door. It took me longer to write the simple note to Hudson to apologize for leaving without a goodbye.

As I handed it to the man behind the counter, I fought the tears. I climbed into a car and was driven to the airfield. There were only six passengers this early in the morning, and they were loading the plane when a few of the people around the aircraft started talking, waving hands, and looking frustrated. A few of the passengers and I shared curious looks, but the men were too far away for us to hear what they were saying.

Finally, they let us head out on the tarmac as a flurry of activity began near the small terminal entrance.

"Karen Reed!" I froze and spun at the voice that called my name. Hudson was on the other side of security, waving for me to stop.

I stepped toward the railing that separated the area. "Hudson, what the hell are you doing here?"

"Karen, do you love me?" he yelled across the room.

"What?" I glanced around me at all the people watching. He held his hand up and spoke to the people at security, quickly removing his shoes and belt and everything else that might set it off.

I stood stock-still waiting for him to come through, replaying what he'd asked me. Why did he want to know if I loved him?

He rushed around the corner once he was through, stopping a few inches from me, shoes in hand and dropping them to the floor. "Do you love me, Karen?"

"What does that have to do with anything, Hudson?"

He stepped forward. "It has everything do with anything, Karen. You left me without saying goodbye, and I understand why. It doesn't mean that I'm not upset that you tried to do that. After the time that we had, I think I deserved a goodbye. So, you can make it up to me by telling me if you love me."

I glanced around me and found all the passengers and a few crew members still watching us. "Um, I'm about to board this plane, Hudson. We are already late. Can we not discuss this another time?"

He laughed. "Yeah, how? Did you leave me your phone number? Your email? No, you didn't. If you don't love me, that's fine. I just need to know if I was the only one to realize how much I loved you under the stars last night as we started this new day."

"You love me?" I queried back.

He shuffled forward slightly. "Yes. I didn't mean for it to happen, but I did. I fell in love with your love of adventure, your joy, your self-less attitude." He looked at the plane. "Although it was kind of selfish to leave without a goodbye."

I chuckled as tears began to fill my eyes, and he came forward and took my face. "Karen Reed, do you love me, or do you think that you could love me?" He glanced past me out the door. "That's a really small plane." He swallowed and returned his gaze to mine. "And before I get on it, I need to know how you feel."

"You are going to get on the plane?"

"That depends on you," he said.

"I love you, Hudson. I fell in love with you too. I didn't mean for it to happen either, but I did. I wasn't sure if you would ever be ready to love again after Donna, and I wanted to give you space. I had put my phone number on a small slip of paper in your shaving kit in case you wanted to find me later."

"You did?"

I nodded.

"Yeah, I guess I won't need that now because I'm coming home with you."

My jaw dropped. "What?"

"I'm ready for a new life, Karen, and if you love me and you want to see this work, then I want our adventure to start today. I want our future to start today. Right now."

I was speechless. Had I found love on an island in the Pacific? Was he asking me to share a future with him?

"Well?"

"Yes!" I said softly and nodded. "Yes!" I threw myself into his arms and kissed him as claps came from all around us.

They hustled us to the plane, and as we got settled, Hudson turned white as a ghost as he looked around the tiny space.

"How did you all meet?" a woman asked as the plane began to taxi out to the runaway. We told our story to everyone on the plane, and even the men seemed touched by the story. We were in the air when Hudson turned and looked out the window, clasping my hand tightly. "Okay, it is pretty cool up here." The plane banked heavily to our side, and Hudson gasped. "Okay, not that pretty!"

The pilot chuckled, and for the rest of the ride, Hudson and I chatted quietly between ourselves. "What are you going to tell your children?" I asked him after we'd gotten off the plane.

He shrugged. "I'm going to tell them that I found an incredible woman, and they are going to love her as much as I do."

"Do you think they will be upset?"

"Do you think I care? They have their lives; this is mine—and yours. What about you? Do you think your girls will care?"

"I don't know. Why don't I call them and find out?" He nodded, and we found a quiet place in the airport near the gate. Hudson went to find someone to help him get his flight changed, and I called Amy.

"Oh, my god! You're alive! I thought that you had fallen off a cliff. Do they not have cellphone signal out there?"

"Yes, of course they do, but I have been busy, and I put my phone away so I could enjoy myself."

"What have you been doing?"

"Fishing, shooting arrows, ziplining, four-wheel driving, dancing, drinking, dining, and lying on the beach." And lots of sex, I added to myself.

Amy told me to hold on a second, and then my video call button buzzed. I clicked it over to video. "I had to see if it was really you, or if someone had taken over your body."

246

I laughed. "It's me, silly."

"You look so different," she said, and then she called loudly for Sarah. "They just came over for dinner."

"Hey, Mom! Glad to see you are alive. Wow, you have a nice tan."

"Yes, I am alive."

Amy looked at Sarah. "Does she look different?"

"Yeah, she kind of does. Did you change your hair?"

I chuckled. "No, I did not change my hair." Hudson slipped into the seat beside me and winked.

"Who are you smiling at?" Amy asked. "Is someone there with you?"

Hudson and I both chuckled, and I glanced at him, raising an eyebrow, as if to say, are you ready for this.

He put his arm around my shoulders, leaning toward me to get into the camera. "Who is who?"

Both girls dropped their jaws, but Sarah recovered quicker. "Mom! Who is that?"

"Girls," I turned to Hudson briefly. "Amy is on the right, Sarah the left. This is Hudson Forbes."

"Um, hi," Sarah said with a frown. "Mom, who is this guy?"

I grinned at my girls. "This is my future. Let's just say that I fell in love with a champagne toast. I'm on my way home. We will see you at the airport tomorrow. Bye!"

"We? Did she say we?" Amy asked quickly as I was searching for the disconnect button.

I turned the phone off and slipped it into my purse. "That was fun."

He laughed and leaned forward. "You know we could detour to Las Vegas."

I laughed. "As tempting as that is, I think one surprise is enough right now. I don't think adding in a quickie marriage will make it any easier."

"There is that."

"Yes, there is that."

"Okay, I have a proposition for you."

"What is that?" I asked as I cozied my head against his shoulder.

"That when we do get married, because we will, I can promise you that. We take a honeymoon someplace where we don't have to fly."

I chuckled and leaned my head back to smile up at him. "How do you feel about cruises?"

"Cruises are almost as perfect as you are," Hudson said as he cupped my cheek and kissed me until my toes curled again.

The End

5: FINDING LOVE ON THE HIGH SEAS

CHAPTER ONE

RAINEY

"Put your phone away, Rainey!" Marsha growled at me as we stood in line to board the ship.

"I told you I would put it away once the ship set sail, Marsha. We aren't even on the boat yet."

She leaned closer to me and whispered, "Yeah, well, you are totally missing out on the merchandise here."

I doubted that. I glanced over the top of my phone and scanned the area. What merchandise? All I saw were men either with their women, or men wanting to be *away* from their women. I went back to reading the article that someone had emailed me on eyeless roundworms being able to sense color. It was much more interesting than the people around me.

"You know," she huffed, "for a geneticist, you sure hate to be around people."

I frowned at her. "What does my career have to do with anything?"

"You study genetics. You should be looking around at all the people here to see what you can figure out about them."

"Marsha, I study genetics at the cellular level, not at a population level. I don't come anywhere near people in my line of work."

She snorted. "Well, that's obvious! You need to learn how to

251

socialize and relax, Rainey. You do know that is what this vacation is about, right?"

Well, that wasn't going to happen anytime soon. I was thirty-four now and hadn't been interested in socializing for, oh, about twenty years. I lost my urge to hang out with people when I was a teenager. You could thank my high school classmates for that.

I also wasn't one for crowds, and usually, anything over two people —including me—was a crowd. Keeping my nose to the glass of my phone was an attempt to undermine my anxiety—not that it was working at the moment.

Marsha turned her attention elsewhere after giving me a dirty look that I pretended not to notice. I heard her talking a couple of moments later to the couple in front of us, and although I was glad that she wasn't speaking to me, part of me was annoyed. Not that she was conversing with someone, but because she could do it so effortlessly. To this day, I still struggled to speak to strangers about anything other than my passion—genetics.

Most times, when people asked what I did, I would tell them, and they'd say, oh really, and what do you study about them? I'd start explaining, and they'd get that boggled look in their eye that said they had no clue what I was talking about, and then they would begin to fidget. That was always the sign that they had to get away from me as quickly as possible before I blew their minds or bored them to death. I was used to it. It happened every time I spoke about my work.

The line started to move as our group was finally called to board. I slipped my phone into my purse and shuffled forward with the rest of the cattle. I couldn't believe that I had let Marsha talk me into this. My idea of a vacation was alone on a beach with medical journals, or maybe a juicy medical mystery.

The only reason I had agreed to this was that Marsha had caught me looking at vacation getaways and talked me into it in a weak moment. It'll be fun, she said. You'll meet some great people, she said. Maybe even a handsome man who could whisk you away from your drab life. Blah! Men didn't come on cruises looking for women. They were usually here *with* a woman.

"Get that grim look off your face. You look like you are being punished. This is going to be fun."

"Yeah, fun. Stuck in the middle of the ocean with three thousand other people. I don't call that fun, Marsha."

"Once you get on the boat, you won't even be able to tell there are that many people there. They are spread out all over the place. You'll get lots of peace and quiet and have plenty of room to avoid them." She paused. "Not that I am going to allow you to avoid people."

"Please don't push, Marsha. I'm here. Can't you be happy with that?"

"Ha! Nope!" she roared, and quite a few people glanced our way. I felt my cheeks start to warm as I stared at my feet. "I will not be happy until you have a pina colada in your hand and the ship is shoving off from the pier."

I sighed, and she rolled her eyes. Quite honestly, I could use a fruity drink with an umbrella in it, maybe a couple. I worked long hours to finish a project before this trip, and I worked late last night to get the final parts done. I'd only gotten a couple of hours of sleep before we had to get up and catch a plane.

I kept my eyes forward as we made our way through security and handed over our boarding passes and passports at the gangway. Before I stepped onto the boat, I paused. If I took this step, I was going to be stuck on there for six nights. Was I going to be able to handle being unplugged from my life for that long?

Marsha reached back and yanked my arm, pulling me onto the boat before I could make my decision. "You are not going anywhere," she hissed at me, then squealed as she pulled me into the main entryway.

I had to admit that it was glorious. I admired all the sparkling crystal chandeliers and shiny gold trim of the three-story area. The carpets were plush, and the wood was dark and elegant. Maybe this wouldn't be so bad after all. I mean, the place *was* huge.

"Come on. I'm starving. Let's hit the buffet. We can't be in our room for another hour."

"Why not?"

"Because they are still cleaning the rooms, and our luggage will take a little while to arrive. Relax, Rainey. We will get lunch, drop off our stuff, and then we can go to the top deck and order a drink so we can say goodbye to the world as we float away."

I wasn't sure I was prepared to say goodbye to the world, and I glanced back at the gangway entrance, wondering if I could slip off before she noticed.

Four men stood at the security check-in, all of them laughing, and I squinted. The guy closest to me looked familiar, but I didn't know why. It wasn't the first time I felt like I saw someone I knew in a crowd, but I was wrong. It was just another reason I avoided crowds. I didn't want to see people I knew.

I let Marsha lead me to the elevator, and we piled in with others heading up to the upper deck where the food court was open and waiting to help us gain our vacation weight.

With us packed into elevator like sardines my tension began to climb, but I kept myself calm by reciting genetic mutations in my mind. If people knew what I did to calm myself, they would probably think I had a genetic mutation myself. Maybe I did.

The elevator door opened, and we all spilled out to the sounds of loud Caribbean music and squeals of laughter. I'd like to think the squeals were coming from children, but it looked like quite a few of the adults had already partaken in an array of alcoholic drinks to lower their inhibitions. Or maybe that was just how they were.

"Look at that pool!" Marsha said excitedly. It was nice, but there were way too many people around it for my taste. "Holy smokes, look at that guy, blue shorts, near the stairs. Oh, please let him be single."

Just after she said that, a curvy blond snaked her arm around his waist, and he smirked at her, placing a kiss on her mouth that should have been reserved for behind closed doors. I laughed as Marsha made a gagging noise in her throat.

We followed the crowd toward another door, sanitized our hands as we went in, and then walked along the buffet, ogling the food. Wow, there was so much to choose from. Where did you even start? We started by finding a table, and then Marsha went up to the buffet to get her meal while I watched our carry-on bags. She came back with a plate stacked high with food.

"I didn't know what to get, so I got a little of a lot." She giggled.

I walked along the line and found what I wanted. Unlike Marsha, who could eat just about anything and never gain an ounce, I had to watch the calories that went into my body. I envied her genetics. Even making good choices, my plate was almost as full as hers.

We chatted about the food as we ate, and I occasionally would look around and check out the other passengers. There were all shapes and sizes, nationalities, and ages here. It was an excellent place to study people if you were into population genetics. The table next to us had a man with brown hair and a woman with red. Two of their three children had red hair too, and the third one was blond. The father must have blond in his family someplace, I thought as we finished up.

We put our plates away and were heading out of the cabana, as they called it on the ship. As we did, we passed the four men that had been boarding as we got on the elevator. I studied the one that I had seen downstairs. Something niggled at the back of my mind, but I couldn't put my finger on how I might know him.

Marsha was staring at them and turned to look more as they passed us. It wasn't until the door was almost closed behind us that I thought I heard something that made my heart sink. "Holy crap, was that Rainbow?"

CHAPTER TWO

ZACK

"Yeah, yeah, yeah, I heard you for like the twentieth time," I said to Bobby as we entered the central part of the ship.

"I know, but I can't stop thinking that this is a great idea."

"Every idea that you have, you think is great," I responded as I slapped him on the back.

"You know," Mark said, "He might be right this time. There are a lot of hot women who look like they are alone."

"Yeah, I've seen a few too," John added.

"I'm sure there are quite a few attractive women on the ship, but I'm not interested."

"Hey, come on. Loosen up. Forget about home and have some fun. You know that what happens on a cruise ship stays on the cruise ship," Bobby joked.

"Yeah, that means you can't be posting stuff on your social media," John reminded him.

I didn't care what he posted. I wasn't looking for trouble. I had enough to deal with at home.

We made our way to the elevator and took it up to the pool deck. We were all grinning as we stepped out and surveyed the fun. A ton of people were already in their bathing suits and enjoying the sun and water. What did they do, wear their suits under their clothes so that they were ready the minute they stepped onboard?

Bobby directed us to the bar, and we ordered our first drinks. This week was going to be one long hangover, I could tell. After a few toasts to friends and freedom, we finished our beers and headed toward the cabana to eat before checking out our cabins.

A couple of attractive women came out as we went in, and I gave the brunette a good once-over before I glanced at her blond companion and did a double take. No way!

"Holy crap! Was that Rainbow?" The door was closed now, but I could still see her through the glass. I was tempted to run out and check, but the guys were already heading toward the food.

"Rainbow who?" John asked.

"Um, a girl I knew in high school," I replied, and Bobby turned to me.

"Rainbow? Wasn't she that total nerd who was always in a freaking good mood? It was almost disgusting how she always smiled and wanted to be so helpful."

"Hey, she was nice."

He laughed. "Dude, nice in high school did *not* get you laid."

Mark snickered. "Yeah, but nice could help you with a good test score."

I shook my head at them and glanced back toward the door again. It probably wasn't her, but if it was, I'm sure I'd run into her again during the week. Maybe we'd be able to catch up. She had been kind, and she'd been pretty—in an awkward kind of way. If it was her, she had changed from awkward-pretty to drop-dead gorgeous.

I put thoughts of Rainbow out of my head as we ate and then found our cabins to drop off a few of our things. I checked my cellphone one last time and then sighed as I turned it off. I had promised myself I would put it away and not stress over things. I needed a few days without stress—I deserved it.

I changed into shorts and then headed next door to find John and Mark. They were sharing a room, whereas Bobby and I had our own.

The four of us returned to the upper deck and got another round of beers. We were hanging around on the pool deck, laughing at the people taking part in a game around the pool. As we did, a flash of pink grabbed my attention, and I followed the woman in the pink bikini top as she carried two drinks up the stairs to the top deck. Her slim hips shifted back and forth, making the floral wrap she wore around them swish playfully. Her brown hair was piled up on the back of her head now, with tendrils blowing in the breeze.

I followed her steps until she disappeared from view, and then I couldn't help myself. I made an excuse that I was going to use the bathroom and slipped away from the group. I took a closer set of steps and scanned the deck as I came up, walking in the direction she'd gone.

I kept searching and found the girl with the pink bikini top near the bow. Beside her was the other woman, her shiny blond hair blowing in the wind. She wore a gauzy skirt and heeled sandals. Her blouse was cream and see-through. Under it, I could see the black lines of her bathing suit.

She turned to her friend, and they clinked their plastic glasses together and laughed about something. That smile—I knew that smile or I should say I remembered that smile.

I approached them, hanging back for a minute to be sure it was her. She laughed again, and the sound brought back memories of biology class when she'd get nervous and giggle. I grinned to myself. No one knew it, but I had secretly loved her giggle and the way her eyes had lit up.

I was only a few steps behind her when the horn of the ship went off, signally that we were pulling away from the shore. Her shoulders went up and then down as if she were resigned to something.

"Rainbow?" I said as I took another step closer.

Her entire body tensed from head to toe, and her friend turned to look at me. "Hi."

"Hey," I said absently to her, throwing a quick smile her way. I was waiting for Rainbow to turn around, but her head had lowered as if she were staring down at the water, then her shoulders rolled back slightly before she twisted toward me.

"That's a name I never thought I would hear again," she replied.

I stared, amazed at how beautiful she had become. The awkward stage was far gone, and she was elegant and beautiful now.

I smiled. "I'm not sure if you remember me."

She put her hand up. "Oh, I remember you."

"How are you, Rainbow?"

Her brows popped, and she pursed her lips. "It's Rainey, *not* Rainbow."

"Rainey, I'm sorry," I said with a smile, and the two of us stared at one another for another few moments. Then her friend stuck her hand out.

"Hi, I'm Marsha, Rainey's best friend. Who are you?"

"I'm Zack Wheeler, Rainb—Rainey and I went to high school together."

Rainey made a scoffing noise. "Being in the same school with you does not qualify us as going to school together."

Marsha laughed. "Yes, it does, Rainey."

Rainey looked away, then back at me. "Well, it was nice seeing you, Zack. I hope you enjoy your vacation." She turned and put her back to me just as Bobby and the other two showed up.

"Damn, it is Rainbow! Wow, girl, you really grew into yourself." Bobby whistled, and I saw her cheeks instantly pinken.

She turned to him, gave him a once-over, and then said, "Bobby McDade, I see you are still your immature self, only now you're in an adult body."

He laughed. "Hey, I resemble that."

Marsha introduced herself to the guys, smiling a little more at Mark as she did, and Rainey put her back to us, looking tense.

I stepped to her other side as Marsha started a conversation with my friends.

"How are you doing, Rainey?"

"Fine, thank you," she replied without looking my way.

"Ironic that we are on the same ship together, huh?"

She looked at her drink and then glanced back at Marsha and my friends before she turned to me. "What do you want, Zack?"

"Nothing. I just wanted to say hello."

She raised a brow. "Well, you did that. Like I said, enjoy your vacation." She stepped around me and started to walk away, but I took hold of her arm.

"Hey, what's wrong? I'm sorry if I upset you by calling you Rainbow."

She stared at my hand, and it was then that I felt this incredible pull to be closer to her burning through my veins. Her blue eyes followed my hand, up to my arm and then to my face.

"That was a time in my life that I'd like to forget. Now, if you wouldn't mind, please let go of me, Zack."

I released her immediately, and she turned and started walking away as quickly as she could. As she began to go around a corner, she touched her arm where I had been holding her. Had I hurt her, or had she felt it too?

Bobby laughed as I stood there. "Damn, you scared her away already?"

I frowned because, for some odd reason, the last thing I wanted to do was scare her away.

CHAPTER THREE

RAINEY

I was waiting for Marsha at the railing, staring out at the land we were about to leave. This trip was going to be good; I tried to convince myself of that. I needed a break, and being stuck on a ship was going to force me to do just that. I had been working sixty-hour weeks for almost a year, and I honestly couldn't remember the last time I took off more than one day in a row. Maybe two years ago—possibly three.

I did know that the last real vacation I took was when I was with Craig. We'd just gotten engaged, and we decided to take a pre-honey-moon. At least, that is what he called it. Now I called it a pre-breakup trip.

Four days into our Cancun trip, I came out of our cabana to find a scantily clad woman hanging all over him in our private pool. Not just her hands either; her mouth and other parts of her almost-naked body were pressing in all the wrong places, and he was sitting back and enjoying it.

He hadn't seen me, but after ten seconds, I had seen enough. I quietly went back inside the cabana where I'd been napping and hastily packed my stuff. Just before I left, I glanced back outside to see her sitting on his lap, his hands cupping her butt, and that was all I needed to see. Twenty minutes after I'd first witnessed the scene, I was in a taxi and heading to the airport.

The tricky part of that breakup was that we worked together, or I thought that was going to be the tricky part. Craig never even called to apologize, and I learned two days after he was supposed to return that he had transferred to a different lab location. Fine by me!

I hadn't been on a date since, and I had no urge to go on one anytime soon.

Marsha returned and handed me my long-awaited drink. "Ah," I said on a sigh after taking a long, sweet sip.

"Just what you needed, huh?"

I laughed. "Yeah, just what I needed. After a few of these, I won't care where I am. Thank you for forcing me to do this. I really needed it."

She bumped shoulders with me. "You're welcome. We are going to have a great time. I just know it."

The ship's horn blew, and then someone spoke behind me. There was no mistaking what was said this time. I stared at the dock, watching it get farther away, and wondered if I jumped now, would I be rescued quickly? That fate might be better than being stuck on a boat with someone from high school.

I turned and wanted to melt to my knees. How was it possible for Zack Wheeler—high school heartthrob—to have gotten any more handsome? His hair was still dark, but a few lighter colors were blended in there now from age. He had a short beard and a smile that melted my knees. "That's a name I never thought I would hear again."

I almost laughed in his face as he spoke. How could I not remember him? He really was the heartthrob of our high school, and practically every month he had a new girl on his arm. Whoever that girl was, she was instantly the most popular—loved and hated—girl in school when she showed up by his side. I'd had some really off-the-wall fantasies about him picking me, and I'm pretty positive I wasn't the only girl to have them.

"How are you, Rainbow?" Was he seriously right here talking to me with that handsome smile?

"It's Rainey, *not* Rainbow," I managed to get out.

He apologized and blessed me with one of his award-winning smiles. I would have forgiven him anything at that moment—well, almost anything.

It wasn't that he was handsome, as he had been gorgeous since the seventh grade. It wasn't because he was athletic, although I wasn't sure there was a sport he couldn't excel at, and it wasn't because he had been a bad boy. He never got in trouble or fights, as far as I knew. I'd also never seen him smoke or heard anyone say anything about him doing drugs. It was just because Zack was Zack.

"Being in the same school with you does not qualify us as going to school together." Had he forgotten just how low down the totem pole I was compared to him and his buddies? I glanced over him quickly. Yeah, he was doing well for himself: expensive watch, designer swim trunks, name-brand sunglasses.

Marsha gave me an I-can't-believe-you look as she laughed. "Yes, it does, Rainey."

I was not doing this. I glanced over Zack's shoulder as three more men approached us, and panic began to swell in my stomach. Now I remembered who the other guy was. Bobby McDade. He had been Zack's best friend and his polar opposite. "Well, it was nice seeing you, Zack. I hope you enjoy your vacation." I quickly spun around and gathered my strength to run away, hoping that I could do so gracefully, and the boat wouldn't pitch and toss me overboard; the shore was much farther now.

When Bobby spoke, I rethought that. Maybe going over would be a better idea. We weren't *that* far from land, and there were some small boats around that I could swim to.

I seriously wanted to climb over the railing when Zack appeared next to me. I could feel the heat of his body radiating off his arm, and he was several inches away. I had to get away from this man before saying something stupid, like pick me for once.

When I did try to go, he stopped me, and it was like he was branding me with his touch. The body heat I had felt moments ago was magnified now by a hundred times. Before I could stumble into his arms, I found my voice. "That was a time in my life that I'd like to forget."

The moment he let me go, I rushed away, wishing the boat would rock and hide the shaking of my legs. My arm burned as if I'd been touched with hot coals, and I covered the area as I slipped around the corner. Luckily, I found the restroom right around that corner and hightailed it inside and behind a stall door.

Zack Wheeler had been a really nice guy. The ultimate boy next door from a wealthy family with beautiful and influential parents and two attractive siblings. Back in elementary school, his sister Valerie and I used to play on the playground together almost every day. However, once my nerdiness kicked in around sixth grade, she moved on to hang with the more popular kids. I didn't blame them for being popular. The entire family was loved and envied by the community.

Because he was so lovely, and his family was incredibly fantastic, that put him in a league above me by staggering amounts. My single mother cared for me around her hours at the diner. As I got older, she started working two jobs. She was determined that I get a college education and make something of myself—a chance she never had because she got pregnant with me at seventeen.

As soon as I was old enough, I got a job and saved every penny I could. Since I only had a couple of friends, I didn't do much other than study. Once in a while, I'd see a movie or get ice cream, but other than that, my money stayed in the bank.

I did pay for bus fare, but that wasn't a frivolous spend. That was a necessity. With my mom working two jobs, and no car available, the bus and my feet were my only transportation, but I didn't mind. I wasn't even interested in buying a car until I was a junior in college and was required to drive to an internship off the beaten path.

My first car had cost me two grand. It had lasted me almost eight years. By the time it died an ugly death, I was making almost six figures. I looked long and hard and finally chose one that was reliable, safe, and a little elegant.

When I hit that six-figure income two years later, I talked my mother into retiring and helped her find a nice apartment in a safe building near friends. I even bought her a new car, not as fancy as mine, but something safe and reliable. She had cried when I had delivered it and told me that all her sacrifice had been worth it to see me succeed. Now, if only I could find myself a man and give her grandbabies. No amount of money would achieve that goal.

The door opened, and the music got louder for a moment and then faded. I stayed quiet until there was a knock on my door. "I know you are in there," Marsha said.

"I had to use the restroom." I flushed the toilet and made my way out to wash my hands.

"Zack is gorgeous."

I shrugged. "I guess."

She barked out a laugh. "You guess? Have you gone blind working in that lab for so long? That man is cotton candy on a stick!"

"So, go enjoy yourself."

She leaned closer to me. "Oh, it's not me he wants to share his treat with."

I glanced up, and she was grinning at me. "What are you talking about?"

"That man was all about you, Rainbow."

My eyes snapped back up. "Don't you dare call me that."

"Whoa, testy. Why was he calling you that anyway?"

"No reason." I tried to step around her, but she jumped to block me. Water ran down my arms and dripped from my elbows as I stood there like a doctor preparing for surgery.

"Obviously, it was a nickname in high school."

"Yeah, so?"

"So, was it a good nickname or a bad one?"

I laughed and stepped around her. "Trust me, it was not good."

"I can't believe it was bad coming from a hottie like him. They said it was because you were always happy. Were you?"

I sighed and shook my head. "It wasn't a compliment." I dried my hands and turned to look at her. "Can we please not talk about Zack anymore?"

"Okay, but that might be a little hard."

"Why?"

"Because we are supposed to eat dinner with them tonight."

"What? Marsha, do not make me sit at that table with them."

"Look, you promised you would socialize and have fun. Who cares what those guys thought of you in high school? Show them who you are *now*. You're a beautiful inside-and-out, kick-ass geneticist. You probably make more than all four of them combined."

I laughed. "I doubt that."

"Besides, I already told them that if they pissed you off or called you Rainbow again that I was going to play dirty."

I raised a brow. "That sounds more like a sex game than a punishment."

She laughed and turned, saying over her shoulder, "Maybe it is."

CHAPTER FOUR

ZACK

"Don't mind her. She doesn't get out much," her friend stated from beside me.

I grinned at her. "How long have you known her?"

She thought about that for a moment. "Since sophomore year in college. We were roommates and hit it off immediately. So why were you calling her Rainbow?" she asked with a bright smile. Had I not just seen Rainey, I might have been interested in her. After looking into Rainey's serious blue eyes for only a moment, I knew that her friend was nothing compared to her.

"It was just a nickname."

Bobby slapped my back. "Dude, it was more than a nickname. The girl was all sunshine and rainbows. There wasn't one person in our school who was as happy as she was—like all the time! She always had a damn smile plastered on her lips. It was almost disgusting that someone could be that happy all the time."

Her friend cocked her head and frowned slightly, then she laughed. "You sure you got the same person?"

"Oh, yeah, that was Rainbow, alright," Bobby said with a lascivious grin. "Although she doesn't look as homely as she used to."

I frowned at the side of Bobby's head as Marsha glanced at me and then back at him.

He turned to me. "She sure did have a thing for you though, Zack. You should go for it."

"Go for it?" John laughed. "I kind of got the feeling she doesn't want to have anything to do with either of you. Now, she doesn't know me."

I wanted to growl at him to stay away from her, but I didn't because I didn't understand that feeling in the slightest.

"Well, maybe she needs to get to know you," Marsha said to John. "What about having dinner with us tonight?"

"Sure," John said with a shrug, and I noticed the grin on Mark's face as he checked out Marsha's legs. I looked away, shaking my head slightly.

"Okay, good. What floor are you guys on?"

I tuned out the conversation as I shifted back to the railing and stared down at the boats and people on the docks below as we headed out of the canal into open water. For a moment, I shifted my gaze back toward the vast land and wondered if I should have stayed home. With so much going on, it had felt wrong to leave. However, I'd been persuaded to relax and enjoy my life for a little while. I'd been assured that my problems would still be there when I returned.

Marsha walked away a moment later to find her friend, and the guys crowded around the railing with me as we enjoyed the sounds of the music and the ocean breeze. I was here, so I needed to trust that things were okay at home and enjoy myself.

We were standing outside one of the dining rooms a couple of hours later when Marsha and a very anxious Rainey began approaching. Rainey's shiny hair was pulled back and twisted up behind her head, and she wore a simple sundress in cream and peach that showed off her shoulders, neck, and chest.

John whistled next to me softly, and I had to agree, although I wasn't sure if he was doing that for Rainey or Marsha. A glance toward him showed me that he was observing Rainey, and I frowned.

"Ladies," Mark said as they reached us, "glad you are joining us."

Marsha was all smiles and relaxed, while Rainey looked like she would jump and run away at any moment. Where was the girl who used to smile at everything?

"Hello, gentlemen," Marsha said, encompassing us all in a bright smile. Rainey glanced at me, then John, and gave me a timid smile before looking away. John bumped his shoulder into mine, then stepped toward Rainey.

"Rainey, may I escort you to our table?" He held his arm out to Rainey, and she stared at it momentarily before slipping her hand into the crook of his arm. As she stepped away with him, she glanced toward me briefly. Had she wished that I had offered my arm instead?

The rest of us followed behind them and the employee who showed us to our table. John helped her take a seat and sat on her left side while I took the chair on her right. Marsha sat between Mark and Bobby on the opposite side of our round table.

The group slipped into a generic conversation about cruising while we decided what to order. After our orders were in and drinks were received, I finally turned to Rainey and spoke.

"Where are you living now?"

"Um, Ypsilanti."

"Really?"

She nodded.

"Do you work there?"

She shook her head. "No, I work in Ann Arbor. What about you?"

"I still live in Plymouth; so do these guys."

She frowned. "You never moved away? I figured you would move away after college."

"I did, but not far. I was living in Lansing but moved back a few years ago."

She nodded and reached for her wineglass. "How are your siblings?"

An ache spread through my chest as I spoke. "You remember them?"

She laughed slightly. "How could I forget them? Your sister and I were good friends in elementary school."

"That's right, you were." I nodded slowly, immediately shifting the subject. "What about your family?"

"My mother is doing well and living in an apartment at a nice retirement community. She's happy there."

"That's good."

I wanted to ask her if she was married or seeing someone, but I wasn't sure how to broach that subject as things grew quiet between us. John took that moment to jump into the conversation.

"What do you do, Rainey?"

She chewed on her bottom lip for a moment. "I'm a geneticist."

He grinned. "Wow, where?"

I forced myself not to frown. Of course, those two would have something in common. John was a doctor and would know a lot more about genetics than I would.

"A hospital in Ann Arbor."

"What part of genetics do you study?"

She smiled brightly at him, the first genuine smile that I'd seen, and I wished it had been directed toward me.

"I study the variations of genetics. It's not very interesting to someone who isn't in my field."

He smirked. "Well, I'm an oncologist, and I happen to find genetics fascinating."

She seemed rather impressed by his answer, and within moments, the two of them were neck-deep in conversation that was so far over my head that I'd never understand it. Give me numbers any day over science. If it hadn't been for Rainey, I'd have failed algebra, biology, and chemistry class in high school.

Over dinner, Rainey stayed primarily quiet but did join in on the conversation once in a while. We had barely finished dessert when Rainey asked everyone to excuse her as she stood from the table to use the restroom.

I was on my feet a moment later. "I have to head there myself. I'll walk you out."

Her eyes had gone wide, but she kept her mouth closed. Unlike John, I didn't give her my elbow, although I should have. I was afraid that if I did, I'd feel that strange current under the skin again, and I wasn't sure I wanted that. Not with how interested she seemed to be in John.

She gave me a nervous smile as she stepped toward the restroom, and I kept walking to the men's room. I didn't have to use it. It was an excuse to get her alone. I stepped in and then right back out to find her doing the same thing.

Her eyes went wide, and she chuckled as I asked, "Was that a ruse to get away from the table?"

"Maybe," she replied and then sighed. "Yes, it was. I'm not big on groups of people."

I laughed. "Yeah, well, normally I'm not either." I paused and looked around. "Can I interest you in a walk, just the two of us? I could use a few minutes of walking to digest all that rich food."

"Um, thank you, Zack, but I'm sure you can find better company than me."

"Better than you? Come on, Rainey, you used to make me laugh all the time in high school. I always enjoyed talking to you."

"No, you didn't," she replied.

"I did." I sighed. "Well, may I at least walk you to your stateroom?"

"Fine."

"Okay, and on the way, we should take the scenic route so we can view the ocean at night."

I put my hand to her lower back and led her to a door that went outside. That intense energy was back as my hand hovered just millimeters from the small of her back. A few couples were walking along the deck, and an older couple stood at the railing. I let my hand drop to my side and then tucked it into my pocket to keep from reaching for her as we strolled along the deck.

The waves were crashing into the side of the ship, and I detoured

273

to the railing to look over. Rainey followed me and stood with her hands on the varnished wood, staring out at the sky.

"Are you married? Or seeing someone?" I blurted the questions out after a moment of silence.

Her gaze cut to mine briefly, and she shook her head. "No. I'm not very good with relationships."

"Oh, come on. You can't be that bad?"

She turned to me, her hip leaned against the railing. "Oh yes, I'm awful. I'm awkward in social settings, and I get very stressed around a lot of people. I'm never comfortable about talking to anyone, and the only time I am comfortable is if I'm talking about my work."

"So talk about your work."

She laughed. "When I talk about my work, it freaks people out."

I grinned. "You didn't freak John out at dinner."

She rolled her eyes. "Because he's a doctor and understands it."

"So, you are saying that if you talked to me about it, it would freak me out."

"Quite possibly, yes. Then you'd think I was even more of a nerd than you used to."

"Rainey." I studied her, taking a small step closer to her and clenching my hands at my sides to keep from touching her face. "I never thought you were a nerd."

CHAPTER FIVE

RAINEY

I laughed. "That is such a lie, Zack."

His gray eyes were bright as he watched me, a soft grin on his lips. "No, seriously. I never thought you were a nerd. I was secretly jealous that everything was so easy for you."

"Easy for me?" I barked out the words as my laughter stopped, and I leaned on the railing and stared out over the water. "Nothing was easy for me, Zack."

"How is that possible?" He leaned next to me, pressing his shoulder into mine just enough for me to notice. "You got straight A's on everything. You were always happy and trying to make others that way."

"I got good grades because I worked hard." I thought for a moment and then sighed. "I didn't have anything else to do other than study or work. I don't know if you remember or not, but I didn't really have any friends. My mom was never home, and school was all I had. I was lonely and bored."

"You had friends."

I turned to him. "Name one."

After a moment, he said softly, "Me. I was your friend."

"Oh, Zack." I leaned back from the rail and shook my head with a dry laugh. "I was not your friend. I helped you with your studies, but we weren't friends. I wasn't anywhere in your league, and I knew that. I was alright with that."

"No, Rainey, I believed that you were my friend."

"Why? Because I helped with homework? Because I laughed at your jokes?"

"No, because you listened to me when other people didn't."

I pursed my lips as I locked eyes with him. Maybe that was true. I did remember listening with bated breath as he went on about the frustration of picking the right college and the stress from his coaches. I shrugged as I looked away from him.

"Well, like I said, I was bored and lonely. That's why I listened. Besides, I wasn't going to tell you to go away. You were the most popular boy in school."

"No, I wasn't." He chuckled.

I turned back to him, hiking a brow. "Yes, you were. There wasn't a girl in that school that didn't have a crush on you."

He lifted his chin, his eyes a little daring as he asked, "Does that include you?"

"Me? No!" I laughed as I felt my cheeks begin to heat, and I turned as far from him as I could. "Not me."

"Liar!" he joked and pushed against my shoulder, but I remained looking away from him. "Look at me, Rainey."

I refused to do as he asked, and he reached over and took hold of my chin, turning it so that I was facing him. "Tell me the truth; did you have a crush on me too?"

That was twenty years ago. What difference did it make if he knew I did. "I might have."

"Oh, so there is hope for me now."

"Hope for you now?" I laughed and shifted away from his touch, putting a couple of feet between us as I moved away. He caught up, and we resumed our walk along the deck.

"What? You don't like me?"

"I don't know you, Zack. It's been years since we've seen each other. That's a lot of life to live, and it changes a person. Maybe I had a crush on you in high school, but that doesn't mean anything now. We're adults with careers and lives. We aren't teenagers anymore."

"That's true, but it is nice to know you liked me back then."

"Whatever," I told him as I reached for the door that would take us back into the interior of the ship. Zack stepped in front of me so that I couldn't pull it open. "What?"

"I liked you, too, Rainey."

"You did not." I shook my head. Were we really having this conversation?

"I did, and you are right. We were at two different levels in high school, but that was high school. None of that means anything now."

"You're right. It doesn't, so why are we even talking about it?"

"Okay. Let's not talk about it anymore. Let's just enjoy our vacation."

"Great. You go hang with your friends, and I'll go do my thing."

He shook his head. "No."

"No? Why not?"

"Because seeing you again reminded me that I *did* like you, and I want to get to know you again, Rainey. I want to know the woman that you have become."

"Zack." I sighed. "There is no reason for us to do that."

"Do we have to have a reason to be friends? No. I want us to be friends. I'm not asking for more. Just hang out with me and have fun."

Was it possible to do that? I had a feeling that if I hung with him, I'd find that I still had a crush on him. Would that be bad? What if I let my hair down a little and let myself enjoy my vacation? What if I let myself be who I always wanted to be, and I flirted with Zack? Would having sex on vacation be such a bad thing? I didn't think so.

"Besides, you would be helping me out."

I eyed him sideways. "How would hanging out be helping you?"

"You'd be saving my liver from all the drinking my buddies plan to do. Plus, I'm not interested in running around chasing women. I came on vacation to relax."

He seemed to genuinely mean that. "Fine, I'll hang out with you a little bit."

"Great! What are you planning on doing tomorrow?"

"Sitting by the back pool and relaxing in the sun."

"What time are you going up there?"

I chuckled. "I have no idea. After I wake up and eat breakfast, I guess."

"Well, what if I met you up there at around ten-thirty."

"You want to lie in the sun with me?"

He shrugged. "I told myself I was going to take it easy and relax this vacation. Lying in the sun and watching the water sounds right up my alley. You got a problem with that?"

I shook my head. "Not at all." I couldn't help it, but I yawned. "I'm sorry, but it's been a very long day, and I'm exhausted. I'm going to head back to my room."

"I'll walk you."

"You don't have to, Zack."

"I want to, Rainey."

We cut through one of the main floors, and the lounge had a singer who was changing the song as we passed by. Zack captured my hand and pulled me toward the dance floor.

"What are you doing?"

"Dancing one dance with you before you head off to bed."

"You don't have to do that, Zack."

He pulled me as he turned on the floor and brought my body to his. His hand curled around mine, and his other slipped onto the small of my back. "I want to, Rainey."

We stared at each other for a moment, and then I cozied up to him and rested my head against his shoulder. This right here had been a fantasy when I was a young girl. Now it was finally happening. What would my childhood diary think about this now?

We moved slowly, the two of us remaining quiet as we did. Finally, the song ended, and I pulled back. "Thank you for the dance."

"No, thank you for the dance, Rainey."

I went to let go of him, but he laced his fingers with mine and led me off the floor and back to the hallway. We were quiet as we reached the elevator bank. Inside, he asked my floor, and I told him ninth deck.

We stood in the back of the elevator car silently. Our fingers still entwined until the doors opened on my floor. He led me out again and asked which way.

When we reached my door, he stopped and tugged me to keep me from walking past him. He took hold of my other hand and studied me carefully. "Thank you for the dance, Rainey. I hope you sleep well, and I look forward to seeing you tomorrow."

Before I knew what he was doing, he leaned forward and brushed his lips over mine, not once but twice. Then he breathed the word, "Night," in my direction before he released my hands and walked away.

I watched him until he turned off the hallway, and then I slipped into my stateroom. I set down my small purse and turned on the light above the mirror to find myself smiling.

Zack Wheeler had just kissed me. I had dreamed of that moment a thousand times but had never expected it to happen, and I sure as hell didn't expect to feel like a giddy schoolgirl who wanted to throw herself on the bed and squeal as she kicked her feet into the air.

CHAPTER SIX

ZACK

I found myself wanting to prove something to Rainey. I didn't have to, but I wanted to. As I reflected on high school, I realized how I might have come across.

I was from a prominent family, and I was popular. People followed me, and at times I let that go to my head. I knew that girls liked me, and I took advantage of that—maybe too much advantage. I was a total jock and cocky about my abilities.

What I wasn't good at was math, which was odd since I worked in finance now. It wasn't the basic calculations that tripped me up. It was higher algebraic equations that had confused the hell out of me. Rainey had helped me many times try to understand them for tests. I swear I only passed those classes because of her.

Needless to say, we had spent a lot of time together in my senior year, which was her junior year. I had always enjoyed her companionship, even though she was trying to cram equations down my throat.

I frowned as I climbed back on the elevator alone. After I left high school, I didn't think much about her again. Maybe a few times in college, she might have crossed my mind, but that was when I thought, oh, man, I bet Rainbow could help me with this.

At that time, I had no idea what had happened to her, and my thoughts were fleeting of her. I wish they hadn't been. What would my life have been like if I had paid more attention to her?

I shook my head as I got off the elevator and wound my way along the main floor, searching for my friends. I found them in one of the clubs on deck five.

Bobby slapped me on the back. "Where the hell did you go? We thought you fell in. You left for the bathroom and never came back." He grinned at me and waggled his brows. "Or did you go get lucky with Rainbow?"

"Hey, it's Rainey. We aren't in high school anymore, Bobby. Rainey and I took a walk on the deck, and I made sure she got back to her room okay."

John poked his head into the conversation. "You making a move on my woman?"

I shifted so that I was squared off with John. "She's not your woman."

He shrugged, smiled like he didn't care, and turned back to the brunette who was hanging on his arm. Jesus, it was like high school all over again. I shook my head and went to order a drink. Marsha joined me a moment later. "You saw Rainey?"

"I did. We took a walk, and Rainey was exhausted, so I walked her back to her room."

She lifted a brow. "You didn't go in to tuck her in?"

"No," I told her, then ordered my drink and asked Marsha what she was having since her glass was almost empty.

"Shame you didn't." Marsha brought our conversation back around after she ordered. "She could use a good roll in the hay."

"What's her story?"

"What do you mean, 'what's her story?'"

I collected my gin and tonic, and she retrieved her rum and coke, and we stepped off to the side where it was a little easier to talk.

"I mean, is she single? Does she have kids? What does she do with herself all day?"

"That last one is easy. She works. Rainey is a workaholic who hates to socialize. Anytime she is around people, her anxiety goes through the roof. If she's not working, she's home taking care of her plants, her dog and cat, and has her nose stuck in a medical journal." She sipped her drink. "It's rather boring and answers your other questions."

"So she's not in a relationship, and she doesn't have kids." She shook her head and glanced at a man who passed us. Her eyes went all the way to his feet and then back up, where she smiled appreciatively. She followed him with her eyes until he stopped to speak with another man and then turned back to me. "She's single, very single. Almost got married once, except when they were on vacation a few months before their wedding, she found him screwing another woman in their cabana pool. She hasn't dated anyone since."

I stared, my jaw hanging open slightly. "Are you serious?"

She nodded, and her eyes kept going back to the guy who had walked past us. Finally, she turned to me. "If you want to know any more, you're going to have to ask her. I have a man to meet." She winked and walked away.

For a moment, I wondered what happened with her and Mark, but then I looked back at Mark. He was chatting up a woman with auburn hair and legs that were half a mile long. Yep, high school.

I joined my friends and enjoyed my drink, and then a few more before we finally made our way into the casino to try our luck.

My luck wasn't all that bad, but it wasn't great either. I couldn't say the same for John and Bobby. Both of them had lost a few hundred bucks. Mark had cashed in his chips to score five hundred, and I had tallied up about one hundred and fifteen. Not bad. It would cover my bar bill so far on this trip.

The next morning, I rushed to brush my teeth and get changed as it was already after ten. I had told Rainey I would be hitting the pool around ten-thirty. As I started to walk out of the stateroom, I did an about-face and made sure to bring my sunglasses and threw back two acetaminophens. My head was banging a little bit from the night before.

My stomach gurgled slightly as I waited for the elevator, and I debated grabbing something to eat first. Maybe a little bit of food would help the alcohol absorb in my stomach. Then I thought of what I might eat, and anything I thought of didn't sound good.

I made my way to the top pool deck and grabbed a towel as I glanced around. I didn't see her yet, so I grabbed another one and went to find a place to sit. I was about to pick a lounge chair but then hesitated. Rainey didn't like to be front and center. She preferred to be off to the side or in the back.

I walked to the back row and tossed the towels down before turning the chairs so that they were facing toward the rear of the boat. I smiled to myself as I leaned against the railing and waited for her.

When she showed up, she took my breath away, and luckily she didn't see me. She collected a towel and passed right by the front lounge chairs, heading to the back. It wasn't until she reached that row that her gaze found mine, and she stopped in midstep. I waved and pointed at the two chairs I had reserved.

"I didn't expect you to be here this morning," she said when she approached at a slower pace. Her sunglasses hid her bright-blue eyes, and I wished she would take them off.

"I told you I wanted to spend more time with you. Is this location alright?"

She was quiet for a moment, and then her voice flowed toward me on the breeze. "It's perfect."

No, I was pretty sure that she was the perfect one.

"Why did you turn the chairs around, though?"

I shrugged and looked over my shoulder. "Because I didn't think staring at the back of other lounge chairs was an adequate picture. I'd much rather stare out over the ocean."

She looked both ways and then smiled. "I see your point." She dropped her small beach bag to the lounge chair, put her towel on another one, and turned it to face the back area.

"You need a second chair? Or is the one in the middle the buffer so that I don't get too close?"

She laughed slightly. "No, Marsha is coming up in a few minutes."

"Ah, okay." I began to unbutton my shirt to remove it while she grabbed the bottom of her shirt and whipped it over her head. My breath was sucked from my lungs as I stared at her black bikini top. I quickly looked away before I dropped to my knees and began to beg.

When I had known Rainey as a teenager, she had braces, glasses, acne, and a few extra pounds. Now the woman had smooth skin from her head to her toes, and those extra pounds had shifted into beautiful and voluptuous curves. Holy cow, she was gorgeous.

"What did you do last night?" I asked as we got settled on our chairs, and she brought out sunscreen to put on. I wondered what she would think if I offered to do that for her.

"I went to bed. I told you I was tired. I stayed up late the night before to get a project finished before we left. It caught up to me during that second glass of wine at dinner. What about you? Did you have a nice evening?"

As I stared at her, she glanced away. "Yeah, it was nice." But probably not as nice as my day was going to be with her.

CHAPTER SEVEN

RAINEY

I really didn't expect to see Zack this morning, at least not here this early. Marsha had muttered something about a few hours in the casino last night, and I swore she said Zack had been there too. If I was right, I was probably the only one without a hangover—which was fine by me.

Although Zack seemed to be doing pretty good—okay, damn good—as he removed his shirt and took a seat. I felt slightly uncomfortable as I removed my shirt. Zack turned away right after I did so I didn't need to worry about him checking me out. He hadn't been interested in high school, so I doubted he would be interested now—despite what he had said and done last night.

As I slathered on the sunscreen, we started to talk, and he told me about his night in the casino and how Mark and he had won, but the other two hadn't.

I held my sunscreen out to him. "You might want to put this on. The sun is pretty strong out here."

"Thanks. I didn't even think about that when I came up."

I tried not to watch him put it on, but it was hard not to. Finally, I flipped my sunglasses up, and that forced me to close my eyes to the bright sun. Within the next twenty minutes, the pool area began to fill up, and I had three people ask me if I was using my other lounge chair. Luckily, Marsha finally showed up and claimed it.

She was in her chair for less than ten minutes before she dozed off on her stomach and started to snore. Zack and I chuckled together, and my stomach growled.

"I think I'm going to grab some food. I'm pretty sure the burger place is open one deck down now."

"I'll come with you. I could use some water."

I pulled my lacy wrap out of my bag and pulled it on before I slipped my feet into my sandals. As we walked away, Zack put his hand to my lower back, and I had to admit that I sure liked it there. One thing that I realized last night before I drifted off was that my little crush on Zack was still there and raging.

After we ordered, we stood off to the side, and Zack stood close to me. So close that as I turned, my shoulder brushed his naked chest, the light covering of hair tickling my skin. The two of us glanced at one another for a moment, and Zack winked before he turned to look away. That might have been a great moment to steal a kiss, but did I seriously think that Zack might want to kiss me?

His hand shifted to my lower back again, curling around my hip slightly and tucking me closer to his side. Well, maybe he did want to kiss me again. If he tried, would I let him?

Oh, hell yes, I would! I had wanted Zack to kiss me since I was eleven years old and played with his sister.

"You never told me how your family was," I stated after I thought of Valerie.

A shadow passed over his face momentarily, and he looked away, dropping his hand. Oh, no! Something wasn't good with his family. I faced him. "Zack? What's wrong?"

"Rainey." He sighed and then touched my face briefly with two fingers. "Let's just say it's not a great story, and I don't want to ruin a beautiful day thinking about it."

"Okay," I said slowly. I knew his family. I had been to his house many times when I was young, and his parents were kind, generous people. His sister, Valerie, and his brother, Jake, were so fun when they were younger, although both had become snobbier as they grew up. Zack was the only one who hadn't been snobby—well, not as much.

We collected our food and drinks and returned to our seats without another word. Zack seemed distracted the entire time we ate, and I was sorry that I had asked about his family.

Two of his friends wandered past, said hello, and talked to Zack for a few minutes before moving on to find food for themselves. After they left, Zack seemed a little more relaxed and even suggested we visit the pool to cool down.

At the edge of the pool, I stopped and dipped my toe in. Zack stepped right over the edge and dropped into the five-foot-deep area. He shook the water off his head as he came up and squinted at me. "Get in here. It feels amazing." I went to sit down, and he stopped me. "No! Just jump in!"

I laughed. "I don't just jump, Zack."

He came to the side. "Try something new. It will make you feel good."

I sighed but then took his advice and jumped into the water. I let myself go all the way under and allowed the refreshing water to cool my hot skin. When I came up for air, Zack was right there.

"Feels good, doesn't it?"

A slight wave to the water pushed me forward and into his body, and he chuckled. Oh, it felt good, but I wasn't just talking about the cool water.

"Yes, it feels good," I said as I moved away from him and against the wall to hold on. There was a little more motion at the back of the boat, and the water rocked from side to side steadily. It might make a few people seasick, but I enjoyed it.

Occasionally, Zack or I would lose our footing as we talked about our favorite movies, music, and foods, and we'd end up bumping into one another. At one point, I lost my balance entirely and crashed into him. His arm came around my body and held me tightly. Once I had my feet back under me, he kept his hand on my hip, and I remained close to him, enjoying the feel of his touch.

The water would rock us closer to one another, and from time to time, our bodies would be pressed against one another briefly. I wasn't sure what he was thinking, but he had grown quiet, and I had grown—well, slightly turned on by it all. I might not like people, but I did enjoy sex, and it had been a long time since I'd had any.

"I'm going to go lie back down," I told him, and he nodded and said he'd be there in a few. I was pretty sure he was hanging back to get something back in order, as the last time we'd come torso to torso, I'd felt something hard under his shorts bump into my hip.

I grinned to myself on the way back to my seat, glad that I wasn't the only one turned on by the choppy water bouncing us off one another in the pool.

When Zack returned to his chair, he asked if we were ready for a drink yet, and Marsha perked right back up from practically a dead sleep. "Yep, I'll take one. Whatever cold, sweet drink they have on special."

"Make that two," I told him, but as he turned, a server was passing by, and he gave the man his order and took his seat.

For the next few hours, we had a few drinks, shared some chatter, and relaxed in the sun. By two, I was ready for a nap. The sun, breeze, and alcohol having calmed me so much that all I wanted to do was curl up in bed and doze off.

"I'll walk you back to your room. Marsha, you coming back?"

"No, I'm going to go down to the main pool and find myself some companionship. You two have a nice nap." She grinned at me as she walked away.

I was pretty sure she expected us to go back to my room and have sex, but I seriously needed a nap. Zack placed his hand on my back, his thumb brushing over my spine, and I began to wonder if I wanted to take that nap alone.

I already knew that Zack had a single room, and I wouldn't put it past Marsha to come back to ours for something. As we climbed into the elevator, I tilted my head toward him. "What floor are you on?"

He studied me for a moment, and I wondered if I had the invitation obvious enough in my eyes. He turned to the panel, and instead of pushing nine for my floor, he hit seven. When he stepped back to me, he curled his hand around my hip and held me closer to him.

On the seventh floor, we stepped off, and he laced his fingers with mine, leading me down the hallway. He stopped in front of a door and turned to me again. "This is my room."

I was pretty sure that I was getting the audaciousness to be so blunt from the alcohol. I leaned forward, my lips only an inch away, and whispered, "Then open the door, Zack."

CHAPTER EIGHT

ZACK

It was the best day that I had had in years. In fact, it ended up being the best week of my entire life.

Rainey and I spent every moment we could together. Several of our meals were room service, many more on one of the decks. We danced, drank, played games, watched shows, hit the three ports side by side, and held hands every step of the way.

I honestly hadn't laughed this much or felt this free in a very long time. Sadly though, all that would end in a few hours. My bags had been packed and put out in the hallway early this morning when Rainey had left to pack her suitcases. I didn't want to say goodbye to her then because I knew that our real goodbye would come soon.

I brought my carry-on bag with me with the last of my things and waited for her up on the cabana deck so we could have breakfast together. Bobby and John joined Rainey, Marsha, and me, but Mark was off someplace else with a woman he had met on the trip. We would catch up with him at the airport.

Rainey was quiet, but I had expected that. Over the last day, we had both gotten quieter, although we held hands longer, and our kisses seemed sweeter. Neither of us had talked about what happened after we left here.

I didn't want it to be over, but our lives were very different. I still hadn't explained what my life entailed back home, and she had never asked again after that first day. I figured that she wasn't interested in knowing or taking what we had built this week any further.

To be quite honest, I didn't have the time to continue to build a relationship. Not right now. Maybe in a year or two when things finally calmed down.

After breakfast, we all made our way to the main lounge. My disembarkation was before hers, and we sat off to the side holding hands and staying quiet.

"You have my email and my cellphone if you ever want to reach out," I said to her. "Make sure you send me those pictures you took."

"I'll put them into an album and share it with you."

I nodded. What else should I say? I'm crazy about you? Can you wait until my life calms down a little more? I stared at my cellphone. For the entire trip, I had wondered how many messages there would be for me when I finally checked. Now that we were back on land and had a signal, I was afraid to turn it on.

When I get off and I'm away from Rainey, I'll turn it on. I'll find out then. Even though Rainey and I were going to the same state, we took two different airlines and landed at other airports. When they called me to get off the ship, it would be goodbye.

That announcement came too soon, and I stood staring down into her face. "Thank you for the most amazing vacation, Rainey. I loved every minute of it." I almost added that I loved her, but that wouldn't have been fair to either of us.

"Me, too, Zack. Thank you for sharing it with me."

I took her face in my palms and kissed her one last time. "Bye, Rainey."

"Bye, Zack." She gave me a sad smile, and I walked away. I hated doing it, but I had to. I didn't want to think about this as just a vacation fling, but honestly, that was what it was. I wasn't capable of giving more to her.

I was quiet on the way to the airport, but by the time I got there, the melancholy was wearing off, and the anxiety was building. I turned on my phone and waited for the emails and messages to download. Twenty-six. That's the number of phone messages that I had. One hundred and fifty-two is the number of text messages that waited for me.

Most of those messages were from my sister, asking me why I wasn't answering her. She kept saying she needed my help but didn't say what it was she needed. Then they stopped two days ago. Maybe she had finally remembered that I was on vacation.

I started listening to the messages. There were several work-related, two about my car needing service, a reminder from the vet that Bruno, my dog, had an appointment tomorrow, a few wrong numbers and telemarketers. Then there were several from my sister, short and sweet, demanding I call her back. The last few were from my father's nurse.

Those were the ones I was most concerned with. I would have called then, but our bus was pulling up to the airport, so once we checked in, I stepped off to the side to call.

All the memories of my trip were tucked neatly away as I called my house to speak with the nurse staying with my father. "Beverly, it's Zack. I just got your messages."

"Hi, Zack, I hope you had a good time. I hated to leave you those last messages."

"It's okay. How is he?"

"Well, I had the doctor come out yesterday and check in, and well, he has another infection. We are treating that, but it's a rough one."

"Another UTI?"

"Yeah, those damn bladder infections are horrible. If he wasn't confined to a bed, then he might not get so many."

"Yeah, I know. How is everything else going?"

"As well as can be expected. He has his good days and his bad, but he's alright. He keeps asking for you, and I keep reminding him that he told you to go on vacation."

I chuckled. "Yeah, he did pretty much kick me out the door."

"Because you've been taking care of him for three years, Zack. He knew you needed a break."

"He was right. I did."

"Well, did you have fun?"

"I had a great time. If all goes well and flights are on time, I should be home around three."

"We will see you then. Have a safe trip."

I hung up with Beverly, so thankful for having such a great live-in nurse, and went to stand in line at security. While I stood there, I wondered what would happen with my father now. He had started the progression downhill with Parkinson's about two years ago, and recently, it had started moving faster.

Both Beverly and my father had urged me to take a break and get some me-time. For the last three years, I had worked and focused on my father and the house that I had grown up in. It was just the two of us now; well, my sister was around, but she was high-level drama, and I didn't let her in the house because it stressed my father.

I wondered as I made it through security if the reason they wanted me to take a break was that I was about to go through the hardest thing I had ever endured, the loss of my father.

Part of me wished that I had told Rainey about my family and the loss of my mother two years ago. Or how my brother had passed when he was twenty-nine in a car accident, and how my sister had ruined her life with drugs and alcohol, but I just hadn't wanted to destroy what we had. For that week, I wanted just to be me and her to be her.

On the flight home, I thought back on my week, and as I landed, I tucked the memories into safekeeping so that I could revisit them someday. Maybe after my life calmed down some, I could see if she'd be open to meet me for lunch, and I could tell her then why I hadn't asked to see her again. Or maybe by then she would have moved on and found someone else.

It was always great to leave on vacation, but that feeling that you got when you stepped into your door, that feeling of being home, being safe, being back that usually descended over me, didn't this time. Instead, as I stepped in, I smelled the antiseptic odor in the air. I heard the oxygen pump on upstairs, and also the television in his room.

I set down my things and hustled up the stairs. When I stepped inside, I came up short. My father looked like he had aged another ten years in the week I was gone. He also looked like he had lost another five pounds, and on him, that was a lot of weight.

Beverly sat on the opposite side of the bed. Her eyes held understanding. Suddenly, guilt washed over me. Here I was happy and enjoying life this last week, and my father was stepping closer and closer to his grave. By the look of him, he might not even last the month.

CHAPTER NINE

RAINEY

I watched Zack walk away and wanted to cry, but I didn't. I knew that good things didn't last forever—they never did. I was lucky to have had this fantastic week with this man, and I would be thankful for that. My mind was packed with beautiful memories that would have to last me a lifetime.

I was pretty sure that no man would ever measure up the way that Zack did for me. I had fallen in love with him in less than a week. In fact, I felt more for him than I did for Craig, and we'd been together for two years.

The problem was that Zack never once mentioned seeing me after the trip was over. We only lived around an hour away from one another, but he never brought it up. However, he had asked me to send him pictures that I had taken with my phone. Maybe he would ask to see me then. I realized as he disappeared out of sight that I might have to resign myself with my memories.

~

Two weeks later, I was in the hospital cafeteria finishing lunch when someone approached my table. "Rainey?" I lifted my head from the tablet I had been reading on and blinked in surprise as Bobby McDade smiled down at me. "I thought that was you. I forgot you worked here."

"Bobby, how are you?" I glanced past him, secretly wishing that Zack would show up behind him.

"I'm doing alright. I just saw a specialist about my shoulder. Remember when I torqued it jet-skiing?"

"I do, and you crashed rather ungracefully, I might add."

He chuckled. "Yeah, well, I tore something. This doc is one of the best. He works on a lot of college athletes. It looks like I might have to have surgery."

"Well, I hope he can fix it."

Bobby pointed at the chair. "Mind if I sit?"

I shook my head. "Not at all."

He set the tray down that he had with him. "I thought I'd grab a bite before I get this other test that he wants me to have this afternoon."

I nodded, not having anything intelligent to say in response. He didn't seem to mind that I didn't speak, as he went right on with his conversation. "I'm actually glad I ran into you. I never did get to apologize to you on the boat."

"Ship. It was a ship, and what would you have to apologize for?"

"For the way that I treated you in high school. I was a dick." I didn't want to tell him that he still was, but the thought was there. "So, I'm sorry. You're a pretty cool chick."

"You know that is why you are single, right?"

"What?"

"Because you call grown, intelligent women chicks."

He smirked at me. "Okay, you are a pretty cool, supersmart woman."

"Better, and thank you. Not that it matters all these years later but thank you."

"You know, I'm not surprised that you and Zack got together. I used to tease him that he had a thing for you in high school because he always wanted your help."

"Oh, he just wanted to use my brain."

"He did. I'm surprised you two aren't hanging out now."

I shrugged.

"I guess after his dad passes, you guys will get together, huh?"

I sat up straight. "What? His dad is ill?"

"His father is dying. It should be any day. He was doing alright before we left, and his father is the one that told him to go on vacation. I think maybe the old man wanted to die while he was gone. Zack didn't want to leave him, but he had a good nurse who watched over him. Unfortunately, he took a downward turn. I spoke with Zack last night. He doesn't think his father will last much longer."

"I hope his sister and brother are helping him," I stated, and Bobby stared at me, his jaw hanging open.

"Did you two do anything other than have sex on the ship?"

"What are you talking about?"

"I'm asking you if you guys talked at all?"

"We did."

"Then how do you not know that his brother died several years ago and his sister is a crack addict living on the streets?"

I fell back in my chair as if someone had just kicked me in the chest. "Bobby, Zack said he didn't want to talk about his family when I asked about them, and I respected that. He never brought them up again. I had no idea about any of that. What about his mother?"

"She died two years ago."

"Oh, my God!" I couldn't wrap my head around the fact that Valerie was a drug addict or that his younger brother Jake was dead. No wonder he didn't want to tell me. "What's wrong with his father?"

"Other than he's dying?"

"Yes, what medical condition does he have?"

"He has Parkinson's. It's pretty advanced."

I winced. That was a horrible disease to die from. "Bobby, where is Zack living?"

301

"At home."

I rolled my eyes. "Yes, I'm sure he's living at home, but where is his home?"

"No, he's at home. He moved back into his parents' house after his mom died to help take care of his father. They had a rough year that year. Jake had died not too much before that, and then his father was diagnosed, then his mother suffered a heart attack. Val wasn't anywhere to be found. Zack was the only one around to help his father."

I began to gather my things. "Thank you, Bobby. I appreciate you telling me."

"Where are you going?"

"I have to get back to work," I told him and then rushed away. The only thing I was going to do when I got back to work was tell them that I needed the afternoon off.

Fifteen minutes after I arrived in the lab, I was heading out to the parking lot. I had to know why Zack had held back all that information. Was it because he was embarrassed? Or because he was upset? Either way, if what Bobby said was true, Zack dealt with all of this on his own.

Well, not anymore.

I had every intention of telling him that I would help him as much as he needed. Even if it was only a shoulder to cry on, I would be there for him.

I drove straight out to Plymouth and glanced at my old apartment complex as I drove past. How far I had come since high school.

On the other side of town, I slowed, trying to remember what street they lived on. It had been a very long time since I'd been over here, and normally, I'd been walking and not in a car. I finally found the street I thought was right, but had to do a U-turn, and then the next street I picked was the right one.

In the driveway were two cars, a charcoal gray SUV and a dark-blue sedan. Did one of them belong to a woman? For the first time since I'd made the rash decision to come out here, I wavered. What if Zack was involved with someone? Bobby hadn't mentioned it, but I hadn't asked either. Maybe that was the real reason Zack didn't want to see me.

Well, I was here, and I was an old friend of the family. If there was a woman here, I'd say I came to pay my respects to Mr. Wheeler and then be on my way. Of course, it would be a lie, but whatever.

I got out, straightened my skirt, and headed to the front door. I hesitated just a moment before I knocked, and then I waited as nerves tingled through my body, making my knees quiver. A few moments later, an older woman opened the door.

"Can I help you?"

"Yes, I'm wondering if Zack is home."

She gave a tired smile. "He is, but he's not accepting visitors at the moment."

"I'm sorry. I just found out about Zack's father. I wanted to come by and check on them both."

"Sadly, he's not doing so well."

"Is he actively passing?"

She seemed surprised that I knew the terminology. "Yes, he is."

"Would you mind letting Zack know that Rainey is here? Just let him know that I'm here and I'd like to see him for a moment. I won't keep him. I promise."

"Sure, I'll let him know."

I turned from the doorway and stepped off the step as she closed the door. Chances were that Zack would send back a message and tell me thanks for stopping by, but what did I have to lose?

A few moments later, the door whipped open and Zack stepped out. His clothes were wrinkled, and his hair looked like he'd been running his hand through it for two days, but damn, did he look good to me.

"Rainey! What are you doing here?"

I approached him slowly, taking his face in my hands. "I heard that you might have use for a little rainbow in your life."

Zack immediately began to crumble, and I pulled him into my arms.

CHAPTER TEN

ZACK

My dad was in and out, but Beverly warned me that we were getting close, and it would only be a matter of time before he slipped into a coma. The infection he was fighting was too much, and since he had a DNR in place, there wasn't much I could do. He had set it up that he could get antibiotics as long as he could swallow them. Once he was unable to take his medication, he was to be kept comfortable only.

He had struggled with his meds this morning. I sighed as I leaned back in the chair and stared sightlessly at the television. One of his favorite crime shows was on, but it was just for noise.

Bev stepped into the room. "Zack, you have a friend at the door."

"Can you just let them know that I'm busy?"

"I did, but she said her name was Rainey," Bev replied after I spoke.

"Rainey?" I was on my feet and moving toward the door. I had told Beverly a little about my cruise. What was Rainey doing here? How did she know where to find me? I ran down the steps and threw open the door.

I could not believe that she was here, I mean really here. But was she? Had I maybe imagined her because I was so tired? I'd been sitting at my father's bedside for four days, night and day.

"Rainey! What are you doing here?"

She was wearing a cream skirt and a light-pink blouse, and her hair was pulled up behind her head. I wanted to grab her face and kiss her lips, but I held myself back until she spoke.

"I heard that you might have use for a little rainbow in your life."

My arms wrapped around her, and I buried my head into her shoulder as I sobbed. Rainey held me tightly, brushing her hand over my head and shoulders and kissing the side of my head and neck.

After I gained control of myself, I stepped back and sniffed as I wiped my cheeks. The smile she gave me went straight to my heart and made me want to cry all over again.

"Can I come in? I'll understand if you want me to go."

"No, don't go." I took her arm and led her inside, then into the living room.

"Why didn't you tell me, Zack?"

"About my father?"

"About any of it?"

"How do you even know?"

"I ran into Bobby today at the hospital where I work. He was surprised we hadn't been in touch but figured it was because of all that you were going through. He gave me a very brief rundown."

"Of what?"

"Everything."

I winced. "I guess I didn't tell you because I was always the guy who had his shit straight, and now everything is falling apart."

"Damn, Zack. I wish I had known what you were going through."

"What would you have done? Bailed my sister out of jail like I had to do when I got home? Come here to sit with me while I watch my father waste away?"

"I would have listened, Zack. Like I did all those years ago when we were kids and you were frustrated about something. I would have listened so you could get it off your chest. No, I wouldn't have bailed Valerie out. If she was in jail, then maybe she needs to stay there to get sober. I would have come to see you and your father, though, so you knew you weren't alone."

"I didn't want to bother you with my problems, Rainey."

"Zack, can I ask you a question?"

I nodded.

"Do you like me? Or was what we had on vacation just a holiday affair?"

"No." I shifted closer to her. "It was far from just an affair, Rainey. I do like you. Hell, I feel a lot more for you than just like, but my life is a mess, and I can't give you what you deserve right now."

"Give me what I deserve?" She leaned back. "Zack, there is nothing that I want from you besides your love or your feelings toward me. I didn't mean to say love—sorry for implying that I meant that."

I grabbed her face. "I do love you, Rainey. I think I loved you back in high school, but I was afraid of what everyone else would say. I've always had feelings for you."

"Do you care what people say now, Zack?"

I shook my head. "No."

"Then don't push me away. Let me be here for you."

"Why would you want to? What I'm dealing with is horrible."

"I want to because I love you, Zack. I've been in love with you since seventh grade, and I would do anything for you. That includes being here with you as you go through one of the toughest moments of your life."

I smiled down at her, and then I leaned forward and kissed her tenderly. "You are incredible. You know that?"

"Not really."

"No, you are. You always have been."

Beverly popped her head into the room. "Your father is awake."

I stood, taking Rainey's hand in mine. "Do you want to come up and see my father with me?"

She curled her fingers around mine. "Of course I do. I'd love to see your father again."

Upstairs we stepped in, and my father turned watery eyes our way. "Dad, I'm not sure if you remember Rainey Caldwell, but she was friends with us when we were kids. She stopped by to see you."

He studied Rainey for a moment, and the hint of a smile touched his lips. "Rainbow," he said as he held out his hand to her.

"Yes, Rainbow is what they used to call me," Rainey said as she came around the hospital bed and took my father's hand without hesitation.

He searched her face. "You're still a beautiful girl." He looked at me. "I always thought you should have dated her in high school. She would have been the perfect girl for you."

I laughed slightly. "You should have told me that. Might have saved me quite a few years of bad relationships."

He smiled a little bigger. "I did try to tell you that, but—" He paused and closed his eyes, struggling to breathe for a moment. "You wouldn't listen."

I sank beside him, putting my hand over the one that held Rainey's. "Yeah, well, you'll be happy to know that I'm listening now, Dad."

My father smiled and looked between us for a moment. "About time." A tear slipped down his cheek before he closed his eyes and drifted back off to sleep.

My father never opened his eyes again, and four days later, he passed peacefully when Rainey and I were out of the room eating. It was heartbreaking to know he was gone, but as Rainey hugged me tightly, I realized that the one thing I feared the most about his death wasn't going to happen. I wasn't going to be alone.

My father had practically forced me to go on that cruise, and I hadn't wanted to go, but now as I think about it, maybe he knew that I'd find the love that I'd been searching for on the high seas. It's too bad I hadn't listened to him when I was younger, but at least I'd been able to let him know I'd be alright after he was gone. I knew that was all he worried about anyway. Maybe the fact that Rainey had come here and he'd seen us together had given him the peace to move on.

Rainey and I stood at my father's gravesite two months later when his gravestone was finally delivered. After I'd placed flowers in his vase, I turned on my shaky knee and removed a ring from my pocket.

"Rainey, I honestly think that it was my father that helped me bring you back into my life, and it only seems fitting to do this here for him to bear witness."

Rainey's eyes misted as she covered her lips with the tips of her fingers.

"Will you marry me, Rainbow Caldwell, and make all my days sunshine and happiness?"

She laughed, the sound so bright and cheery that I knew my father could not only hear it but feel it in heaven. "Yes, Zack, I'll marry you, even if you have to use that stupid nickname."

I slipped the ring on her finger and then stood, taking her face in my hands. "That nickname defines you, the most incredible beauty on this earth."

"I love you, Zack."

"I love you, too, Rainey."

After we kissed, we started back to the car, but Rainey gasped and looked off to the east. I followed her line of vision, and tears filled my eyes as I followed the beautiful lines of the rainbow from one side to the other.

"Thanks, Dad," I whispered huskily as I tucked her against me, and we stood right there watching it until it faded away.

The End

6: FINDING LOVE ON A DUDE RANCH

❀ Created with Vellum

CHAPTER ONE

HEATHER

I stepped off the plane in Jackson Hole, Wyoming, wondering how I let myself get talked into going on this trip. I was a city girl born and bred. The closest I'd ever gotten to the Wild West was a chain steakhouse restaurant. On your birthday, they wheeled in a makeshift horse and made you sit in a saddle while everyone around you sang happy birthday.

Mortifyingly, I knew that firsthand. I might have been three sheets to the wind that night. I don't recall doing it, but sadly, pictures were taken that even I couldn't refute.

My kind of vacation was at least a week on a cruise ship. I had plenty of things to do to be social, or I could find myself a chair, park my derriere in it, and catch up on my reading as I soaked up the rays of the sun. People waited on you hand and foot—not that I needed that, but it was nice to be pampered on vacation.

This was not going to be anything like that. Kari had signed herself up for a whole week of immersive treatment at the Triple G Ranch. She was supposed to be on this vacation, but she had broken her leg three days ago. She had begged and pleaded with me to go in her place since she couldn't get a refund.

The only reason I had said yes was because I needed to get away from the city. I was an attorney working my butt off for a private firm, and work was a nightmare recently. I'd also broken up with my boyfriend three weeks ago, and the guy was practically stalking me now, trying to get me back. It honestly made no sense since I barely ever saw the guy. It was hard having any type of relationship when you worked twelve to fourteen hours a day. Hence the reason I had made the split.

Now I was here putting my detailed mind and eye on this vacation for Kari. She was a writer, and she had been planning this series for over a year. It was supposed to be about the workings of a dude ranch, and she had said that she wanted to learn everything that she could to make it authentic. With my eye for detail and ability to remember just about everything, she made me promise to record my endeavors in full detail so that she could live vicariously through me.

I walked through the small terminal, noting the wood that was everywhere. From the ceiling to the pillars, everything was constructed from timber. This was also the first airport I'd visited in the north, where you exited the plane on the tarmac and walked into the terminal. What did they do when it was snowing outside?

I followed the crowd through the building. My gaze drifted around as I walked at a subdued pace behind the people in front of me. My gaze shifted out the glass to something I hadn't noticed before.

How had I not seen the incredible mountain range? Perhaps it was because I was trying to bolt away from the guy who had sat next to me. He had talked my ear off the entire flight from Chicago. I would have slid down the stair railing if I could have managed it, but luckily, a couple got in between us.

While I wasn't a mountain girl, I had to admit that the view was incredible. There was a lot of green out the window—from the grass of the fields to the trees climbing the mountain. Near the top of the slope, the terrain changed from wooded to stone and then to snow. It was odd to see snow in June, especially since I had just come from balmy ninety-degree weather in Maryland.

If it were already ninety in early June, it would be a scorcher this summer, but I didn't mind. I would much prefer hot weather to the cold any day.

As I glanced around, I chuckled. At least half the men in the building were wearing cowboy hats. Even the men dressed in suits wore big-brimmed hats atop their heads. It was somewhat surreal to me. Most of the men I knew wore suits regularly, but I couldn't imagine any of the men I worked for at the firm having something sitting on top of their fancy-styled hair. Well, maybe Tom would.

Tom was a young paralegal that I worked with most often and probably my closest friend at the firm. We had spent many nights working till midnight to prepare documents for cases or get ready for a trial to start. I could picture him here. He was the one that had talked me into this venture in the first place.

I followed the people through the terminal and located the baggage claim. Off to the side were car rental stations, and outside of the front glass were three vans, each with the name of a ranch on them. The blue one at the front of the line had the Triple G logo. However, I didn't see a driver near the vehicle.

I glanced around, searching for someone who might be holding a sign with my name or Kari's on it but I didn't see that either. Maybe he needed to use the restroom. I wouldn't worry about it until after I'd collected my luggage.

Ten minutes later, I struggled with the two large bags and carry-on. Somehow, I made it outside and wheeled my load over to the van. I peered inside the van to see if the driver was inside somewhere, but he didn't seem to be, and I frowned as I looked around again.

Alright, time is money, and money is time. Where the hell was the guy? I went to the back of the van and tried the rear door. It was unlocked, so I opened it and then collected my suitcases, dragging them back to the open doors. The large one about killed me, but I managed to get it up. I glanced around slightly to see if anyone was watching but didn't see anyone close by. The second suitcase was a bit easier, and after I loaded them, I closed the door and went to open the side door.

I was about to climb inside when I looked past the parking lot at the terrain in the distance. It was slightly awe-inspiring, and I stepped to the front of the van and stared out at the Teton Mountain Range. It was mesmerizing, and as I inhaled deeply, I found the air was fresh and clean. You'd never attempt to do that at the Baltimore airport. Nope, you'd get a mouthful of fumes.

"That's quite a view," a deep voice said from behind me, and I turned to find a man watching me from under this chocolate-colored cowboy hat. His blue eyes were striking, and for a moment, I couldn't tear my gaze from them. He continued to watch me for a long moment as if waiting for a reply, but words seemed to have vanished from my list of capabilities.

My eyes finally dropped from his to take in his clean-shaven jaw and the plaid shirt he wore that was tucked into a pair of worn jeans. On his feet, he wore well-worn cowboy boots that had probably at one time matched his hat but were now scuffed and faded from years of wear.

"Or do you like this view better?" His chuckle was husky, and when my eyes flashed up to his face, I saw lines creased around his eyes. Was that from years of squinting in the sun or smiling?

I cleared my drool out of my throat and lifted my chin. "They are both quite nice."

He hiked a brow. "Good to know. You must be Heather Tate."

I stuck my hand out. "Yes, Heather Tate, and you are?"

He glanced at my hand, then stepped forward, taking it. "Your personal guide and ranch hand for the next week, Rob Heller."

"Personal?" I echoed the word back as he continued to hold my hand in his calloused palm.

"Yes, ma'am. You will spend the week right beside me. Whatever I do, you do."

I chuckled, slightly uneasy as I removed my hand from his. "Well, I know my friend wanted that experience, but I'm only here to observe for her."

He chuckled as he began to move around me. "You get what was paid for, Ms. Tate." He paused in front of the van, letting his gaze drift down my body and then back up. "And I sure look forward to showing you every moment of it." He winked and spun around to head to the driver's seat, leaving me something I rarely ever was —speechless.

CHAPTER TWO

ROB

I sat in a chair near the luggage carousel and watched the latest group of people converge on it from under the brim of my hat. My eyes scanned the faces, skipping over any woman who wasn't alone. I knew that our newest guest was a single woman with dark-brown hair, and that was about all I knew of her, other than her name was Heather Tate.

The original woman who had booked the trip had called to say that she wouldn't make it, and her friend was coming in her place. The owner of the Triple G, my mother Patricia, had been disappointed to hear that. Kari had told my mom that she was researching a book series and wanted to use our dude ranch as the location.

When Kari had first spoken to Patricia, she had asked that she get a one hundred percent behind-the-scenes look at how a ranch worked. I could understand her reasoning, but what was this other woman going to want to do?

My gaze landed on a woman dressed in dark jeans, sneakers, and a light-blue button-down shirt. She seemed to fit the bill, and she was focused on the window where the van was parked. I watched her scan the area, searching for something. As her face turned my way, I got my first good look at her and shifted in my seat. She was beautiful, but she was completely off-limits.

Guests always were. Most times, that wasn't an issue since they came as couples, but once in a while, we'd get an all-girls group in, and it would be hard to resist their charms. Especially when you knew that the happier they were, the more of a tip you might get at the end.

I hadn't succumbed to the pressure, but a few of the ranch hands had. Unless it caused a problem, we generally looked the other way. It didn't happen often, but we all knew that sometimes sexual chemistry did rear its head, and it wasn't like there were many single women in our area to choose from these days—especially with the hours we worked at the ranch.

The woman I believed was our guest managed to wrangle her luggage and drag it out of the airport. I was glad that she seemed to handle it and wasn't standing around in a huff waiting for someone to take care of her.

I shifted in my seat as she left the terminal, then turned to watch her outside. She peered inside the van and then looked around again. Finally, she went to the back of the vehicle and opened the doors. "Well, I'll be damned," I said under my breath.

I watched her struggle with her first piece and wondered if she'd give up, but she pushed through and then tossed the second one in beside it before shutting the door. I appreciated the woman taking the bull by the horns and getting stuff done without waiting. That said a lot about her.

Outside, I found her standing in front of the van and staring out over the horizon. I had always been a sucker for the view. Today, my gaze was locked on her, not the mountains.

"That's quite a view," I said to her, but I wasn't sure if I was talking about the mountain range or her body. She spun around, her long brown hair whipping over her shoulders and her warm chocolate eyes coming to rest on mine. An intense jolt of electricity shot through me, and I was glad that she didn't say anything. I wasn't sure I would have been capable of responding if she had.

I watched her the whole time she checked me out, more thrilled with it than I should have been until I finally got my wits about me and cracked a joke. "Or do you like this view better?"

Well, hello, darling. I wanted to reply, but I kept myself in check. She might be a beautiful woman, but she was a client, and I'd been paid to be her guide and show her everything that I could about living and working on a dude ranch.

She was quiet as she climbed into the van, and I could have invited her to sit in the front with me, but I didn't. From where she was seated, I could peer at her in the rearview mirror without turning my head to seek her out.

"I was sorry to hear about your friend. I think Patricia said she broke her leg."

"Thanks, yeah, she did. She wasn't paying attention, and she fell down a flight of stairs. She's lucky that's all she broke."

"Ouch. Hope she mends quickly."

"Thanks," she replied as she stared out the window for a moment. When I next looked up, she locked eyes with me in the mirror. "I know she wanted to learn it all, but I'm really just here to observe and take notes for her."

"You would get better notes if you could describe the work you were doing."

"Why do you say that?" she asked.

I shrugged. "Because watching is one thing, but doing is another. When you do something, you have firsthand knowledge of its mechanics. You experience not only the visual stimulation but the physical also. I think knowing how something feels is a better way to understand it."

Her brows popped over her eyes, and I wondered what she was thinking, but then she nodded.

"Okay, visual *and* physical stimulation, check."

I couldn't help but chuckle and peered back to see her sighing, but she had a smile on her face as she looked out the window.

"You must be a good friend to do this for her."

"We have been best friends since high school. We'd do anything for each other, including go to a dude ranch and remember every detail."

"Were you not interested in coming here yourself?"

"Me?" Her voice rose slightly, and she shook her head as she laughed. "Not in the least bit, but don't take that personally. I'm just not an outdoorsy person. My idea of a vacation is not working but relaxing in the sun with a drink in my hand."

"You might surprise yourself and find you enjoy it here."

"I will say that it is beautiful."

I stared in the rearview for a moment. "Yes, it is." I looked away before she saw me.

"Have you worked at Triple G long?" she asked.

"I have."

"Oh, good, then you should be a wealth of knowledge."

"There is nothing that I don't know about the ranch."

"That's good. Are there other guests?"

"Yes, they all joined us Sunday. Most guests arrive on Sunday afternoon, spend the week, and leave the following Sunday morning."

"How many people are guests?"

"We have fourteen right now."

"How many people work on the ranch?"

"Twenty-three."

"Do each of your guests get a personal guide?"

I chuckled. "No, only you, Ms. Tate. We have guys that focus on livestock, someone who works in the kitchen, ranch hands that focus on the upkeep of the property, and then those of us that oversee the guests."

"Heather, please call me Heather."

"Ma'am, Heather, it is."

Her cellphone rang, and she answered it. "Hey, Kari."

She listened for a moment. "Flight was fine, except for the guy in the seat beside me that kept asking me out for a drink once we arrived."

I kept my eyes on the road, listening to the one-sided conversation and wondering if I had been in the seat beside her if she would have said yes to me. I frowned to myself as I peered back at her. Heather Tate wasn't the kind of woman I should ever set my sights on. She had already told me that she wasn't an outdoorsy person, so the last thing I should be thinking about was spending more time with her than I had to.

That was until she spoke next, and our eyes locked in the mirror again. "Oh, yes. My personal guide is driving me to the ranch now, and Kari, he could have been your cover model."

CHAPTER THREE

HEATHER

K ari laughed loudly in my ear. "Seriously?"
"Yep."
"Describe him?"

"No." I laughed. "I'm not going to describe him."

"Come on!"

I sighed, and I noticed Rob smile. "Fine, he's about five-ten, blond hair cut very short, bright-blue eyes, and he's clean-shaven."

"I know who you are talking about! I saw his picture on the website. Is he as cute in real life?"

"Probably better."

"I'm dying right now! That could be me with him."

"Yep, it could have been if you hadn't fallen down the stairs, but guess who is the lucky one now?" I joked with her.

"Oh, I hope you get lucky. You could use a good roll in the hay." She started laughing.

"That's funny," I replied, suddenly picturing Rob and me rolling around in a horse stall. "Not going to happen."

"I know you are out there to get information for me, but you can have fun, you know."

"You're right. I can have fun. Look, I'll talk to you later. We are pulling into the ranch."

"Fine! I can't wait to see your notes. I want extensive ones about him."

"Bye, Kari," I told her quickly and hung up.

No sooner did I put the phone back in my purse than Rob spoke. "So, you're feeling lucky, huh?"

I pursed my lips, giving him a partial glare in the mirror. "Don't get yourself all excited. I was doing that for her benefit, not yours."

"Aw, too bad." He was still smiling as he turned off the main road and drove under a gate with the Triple G logo on it. "Am I better looking than her cover model?"

A bark of laughter exploded from my mouth. "Eavesdrop much?"

"Well, it's not like I couldn't hear you talking, Heather."

He drove down the long driveway, and I glanced around at the property. It was situated on the side of a mountain, with lush prairies all around. Fencing ran along the roadway, and in the distance, there were two men on horseback near cattle.

"How many cows do you have?"

"Two hundred and sixteen Angus at present count, but that will change later this week."

"Are you getting more?"

"No, we have a few that are heading off to slaughter at the end of the week and two calves coming soon."

I stared out the window. "You're going to slaughter them?"

He laughed. "Don't tell me you're a vegetarian."

"No, I'm not, but I think I prefer not to know where my dinner comes from."

"Well, on this ranch, about seventy percent of what you eat comes from the property."

"Seventy percent?"

"Yep, we have dairy cows. We have chickens, pigs, goats, lots of Angus, and of course, we have horses."

My jaw dropped. "You don't eat the horses, do you?"

He laughed, and the sound was music to my ears. "No, ma'am, we don't eat the horses. Our horses are like family to us. Speaking of which, have you ridden before?"

"Yes, I have. When I was younger, I took horseback lessons."

"Okay, that's good to know. How long did you do that?"

"About three months, and then we moved, and I didn't have a place to ride."

"That's too bad, but it's good that you have some experience. I'll pair you up with a good horse."

"I didn't say I was any good, and besides, that was like twenty years ago."

He parked the van in front of a large building. "You know that old adage, it's like riding a bike?"

"Yes."

"Well, it's like that, but it's a horse. A few minutes back in the saddle, and you will feel like you never left."

"We'll see about that," I replied.

Rob helped me get my luggage out and told me to leave it on the front porch while I checked into the lodge. I stood on the front porch for a moment, letting my eyes drift over the property. There were about twenty cabins off to the side, two large barns on the other side, and fields as far as the eye could see.

I wasn't sure I wanted to admit it, but it was beautiful. I pulled out my phone and snapped a picture before sending it off to Kari.

Rob had already gone inside, so I opened the squeaky screen door and entered. Inside the place was all lumber—not just the ceilings, but the walls and floors too. Rob had disappeared, so I popped my head into a side room that looked to be a gathering area with lots of seating and a large stone fireplace. I snapped another picture and then heard a sound behind me.

When I turned, I found a woman approaching me. She wore jeans, a plaid shirt, and worn tan cowboy boots. Her blond hair, while curly at the ends, was matted down around the crown of her head like she'd been wearing a cowboy hat.

"Heather." She stuck her hand out. "I'm Patricia Heller. Welcome to the Triple G."

I shook her hand, slightly shocked that her palms were rough too. "Thank you for having me. I'm sorry you got stuck with me and not Kari. She was so heartbroken to miss this trip."

"Hopefully, she will come to visit another time, but we are so glad to have you here. Your accommodations are ready, and Rob will take you over to your cabin. He can give you a tour of the place before dinner, and tomorrow, you will be up before the sun to start working."

"What time is before the sun?"

Rob chuckled from behind Patricia. "We are up at four. You going to be able to do that?"

What kind of a vacation made you get up at four in the morning? Ugh! I smiled. "Four works for me."

"Alright." Patricia smiled widely. "I'll let Rob show you around, and I'll see you at dinner. If you need anything"—she handed me a card—"here are the phone numbers of several of the employees on the ranch. You can call them directly."

I glanced at the card, noting seven numbers, including Rob's. "I appreciate your hospitality," I told her.

"You are most welcome," she replied as she brushed an affectionate hand down Rob's arm and then walked away. It wasn't until then that a few things clicked. Like his last name and how similar their facial features were.

"Is that your mother?"

He nodded. "Yep."

I laughed. "You said you worked here for a long time. You could have said you grew up on the ranch."

He shrugged. "I've been working on this ranch for as long as I can remember. Come on, let me show you to your cabin."

I followed Rob out to the porch, noting how his jeans hugged his hips and tore my gaze away from his backside as he turned my way. "Stay here for a moment. I'm going to get the Gator."

I eyed him suspiciously. "Gator? What do you need an alligator for?"

He chuckled, the sound slipping down my spine, making me want to shiver. "It's an ATV of sorts."

"Oh," I said stupidly and wanted to smack myself in the head as I watched him walk away toward one of the barns. I didn't tear my eyes from him until he was out of sight, then I grabbed my phone and sent Kari a message.

Holy smokes! I'm not sure if it's the air, the altitude, or what, but I'm suddenly in the mood to ride a cowboy.

CHAPTER FOUR

ROB

I left Heather on the front porch, needing a moment. I had been all too aware of the woman seated in the row behind my seat. I shouldn't have felt flattered that she said I was worthy of being on a book cover, but I was.

Every time we locked eyes in my mirror, I felt this funny zing straight down my spine. If I had met Heather at a local tavern, I might have thought that maybe she was worth getting to know better. However, she lived on the East Coast, and nothing would ever come of the attraction I felt for her.

The best I would get is a woman in my bed for a couple of nights, and that was if I were lucky. I wasn't generally lucky—not in love.

I had been engaged once, but the woman had called it off the week before the wedding. She told me she was moving to Los Angeles to work on her acting career. Until that moment, I hadn't even known she was interested in acting. I gave up trying to figure women out after that.

That was four years ago, and even though I had dated a handful of women, they were more for fun than anything serious. My mother had said that someday a woman would appear at the ranch and steal my heart. She said we'd ride off into the sunset and take over the ranch together once she was gone.

I told her my life wasn't a movie and that was never happening.

"You're back!" my mother said as I stepped into her office.

"Yeah, just got back," I told her and sat my butt on the corner of a hutch she had in her room.

"How is she?"

I frowned, staring at the floor and the dirt on my boots. "She's a guest," I said and lifted my head. My mother was observing me.

She laughed. "Just a guest? Usually, you have more to say about one when they show up."

"I don't have an opinion of her, but I guess she is nice enough."

"Pfft, nice enough. Did she give you a hard time? Is she going to be tough to work with this week?"

"No, I don't think so." I chuckled. "She put her own luggage into the van."

She frowned. "You didn't help her?"

"Nope, I watched. She didn't know I was doing that, but I wanted to see if she was going to be one of those high-and-mighty types that needed pampering or if she might actually do work and take things seriously."

"And?" my mother asked as she raised a blond brow.

"I think she's going to be fun to have around for a little while."

"Oh, good," she responded. "Let me go say hello to her. Then I have to come back here and call the attorney again."

"About the lawsuit?"

"Yes." She sighed wearily. "Why do we have the clients sign all those waivers if they are going to try to sue us when they get hurt? It's not like it was our fault. They went off on their own."

"I don't know, Mom. I hope it gets settled soon."

"Yeah, the last thing we need is bad publicity now that things are turning around."

I followed her out of the room. "I know."

I watched her chat with Heather for a few moments and then went to get the Gator. We usually didn't use them for the closer cabins, but the one my mother put her in was on the far side with the best view. With her luggage, it would have been tough to carry them down the path without getting them covered in dust.

Heather helped me with her luggage and climbed beside me on the Gator, saying, "This looks fun to drive."

"It is. I'll let you drive it later."

"Awesome," she said with a smile that gave me pause. I didn't want to like her smile, and I sure didn't want her smile to give me that weird feeling down my spine.

I cleared my throat. "So, your cabin is the farthest one. My mom gave you that one so you had the best view."

"I appreciate that, but the view was for Kari, not me. I'm just filling in."

"Yes, but don't you have to describe things for her, so she feels like she was here?"

"Yes."

I could tell she was staring at my profile, but I kept my eyes forward. "Then you need a place where you can describe it best."

"That is true. You are brilliant, Rob."

I laughed slightly. "Yeah, not sure about that."

"Why not?"

"I don't know. I mean, I know a lot, and yeah, I'm pretty smart, but I know about ranching and making guests happy. I don't know much about other things."

"Other things? I'm sure you aren't giving yourself credit."

"I'm pretty sure I am. I grew up here in Jackson Hole. I've barely ever traveled. I never went to a university, and I have no intentions of doing so. My life is this ranch. My future is this ranch, and that's all I need to know."

I saw her glance around. "Well, it's a huge ranch, so I'm pretty sure you know a lot more than you think you do."

I didn't want to talk about myself, so I changed the subject. "What do you do?"

"I'm an attorney."

I glanced at her. "Now, you are the smart one."

"I am about law, but not about other things—like your ranch."

"Touché. Maybe you can teach me some law this week, and I'll teach you some ranching. What do you say about that?" I pulled up to her cabin and turned off the Gator.

She stuck her hand out. "It's a deal."

I wasn't so sure I wanted to shake her hand again. The whole ride over, I'd been very aware of just how close she was and how when we hit bumps, our shoulders and arms brushed from the jostling. I also didn't want to offend her, so I took her hand in mine. The two of us stared at one another, and neither made an effort to move for a few seconds.

"We should put your stuff away so I can give you that tour."

"Okay," she replied softly but still didn't move.

"Or we could sit here longer holding hands," I replied, and she jerked her hand back, laughing nervously as she practically jumped out of the Gator. I snickered quietly at her reaction and collected the larger of the two suitcases.

She glanced around. "Where is everyone?"

I glanced at the sky, noting the position of the sun. It was around three in the afternoon. "Out on a trail ride. They will be back around four."

I opened her door and let her enter before me. "Wow," she breathed as she stepped in, and I followed. I made the mistake of closing the door behind me as I set her suitcase down. When she turned, I found myself way too close to her, and there wasn't anywhere to escape. "This is incredible."

Oh, I agreed, but I was pretty sure she was talking about the cabin and not me. "Glad you like it."

She nodded, shuffling her feet to the side as she glanced around more. "I do."

I tried to step around her, but she turned back to me at the exact moment, and our bodies collided. My hands instinctively landed on her hips and hers on my chest as our eyes locked.

This was what we called a rattlesnake moment. You could jump away, or you could try to ease back, but either way, there was a damn good chance that you were going to get bit.

As I stared into Heather's beautiful brown eyes, I realized that I had probably already been bitten, and the venom was going to fester in my blood until I either took an antidote or cut off my leg. Now, was she the saw or the medicine? Heather's gaze dropped to my lips, and I couldn't help myself as I tilted my head slightly to the side and went in for the kill.

CHAPTER FIVE

HEATHER

After a brief kiss that I felt in my toes, I leaned back and stared at him. He immediately stepped back, clearing his throat.

"I'm sorry, ma'am. That should not have happened."

"It shouldn't have? You mean that's not the way you normally welcome your guests to their cabins?"

He stood there, wide-eyed, trying to figure out how to answer that, and I laughed. "I'm joking, Rob. Relax. It's okay. If I didn't want to kiss you, I would have stepped away before it happened."

"Yes, but that's not how we do things here."

I cocked my head. "What do you mean?"

"We don't socialize that way with our guests."

"Ah, okay. I get it now. No sleeping with the guests."

"No, ma'am. That is highly frowned upon."

I leaned forward slightly, and he tensed. Did he think I was going to kiss him again? "I won't tell if you don't."

He swallowed, his gaze dropping to my lips again and then back up before he moved back. "Um, thank you." He shifted around me carefully to avoid touching me. "So, you have a small fridge over there and a coffee maker. Your bedroom is up those stairs in the loft, and so is the bathroom. There is a little balcony off the back where you can sit if you are so inclined."

I stared at the stairs and then my luggage. "Please tell me you are going to help me carry my suitcases up those stairs."

He eyed my bags, then the stairs, and finally turned to me and spoke slowly. "Okay."

I held my hands up to him. "I promise not to attack you."

He chuckled and said something under his breath as he turned, but I didn't catch it. Maybe he wanted me to attack him. I could think of worse things to pass the afternoon with.

He allowed me to go first, and I wondered if he was checking out my butt as I climbed the steep steps. If I had been behind him, I would have been checking his out. At the top, there was a large bed along with a chair, a small desk, and two doors. One was open, and I could tell it was the bathroom. I set my suitcase down and popped my head into the bathroom.

"Holy cow, that's a big shower for one person." I suddenly had visions of him in there with me, but when I stepped out, he was already walking back down the stairs. Chicken, I thought to myself before I followed him down.

Downstairs, he seemed ready to bolt. "Do you want to unpack first or get your tour?"

"I'll take the tour, then unpack when I get ready for dinner."

"Okay." He headed toward the door.

"Rob," I called out and stopped him with his hand on the door-knob. I approached him. "Would it make a difference if I said that I had wondered what it would be like to kiss you from the moment I had first met you?"

He compressed his lips and inhaled long and steady. "I appreciate that, Heather. It is nice to know I wasn't the only one thinking that, but it still shouldn't have happened."

"Okay, I understand that, but please, can we just forget about it? I don't want it to make things awkward between us since we are going to be spending a lot of time with one another."

"I would appreciate that," he said with a nod.

"Alright, then let's get going. Show me the ranch."

For the next hour, Rob was a perfect gentleman and kept a proper distance from me while he pointed things out and showed me where everything was. Along the way, I took pictures of stuff to remind myself to write about them later.

Our last stop was the horse barn, and while a lot of horses were out of their stalls, there were still a few inside the barn. "Let me introduce you to your horse," he said as we entered.

He walked down several stalls and paused by a light-brown horse who seemed happy to see him. "This is Hershey."

"Hershey?"

"Yep, like the milk chocolate." He chuckled. "He matches your eyes."

I chuckled as I put my hand out to the horse and let him smell my palm before I pet the soft skin between his nostrils. "You're a pretty boy." He threw back his head and whinnied before putting his face closer to mine.

"He is very docile, but if you work him, he will allow you."

"That sounds perfect. When do I get to ride him?"

"Tomorrow, after you muck his stall, then feed and brush him."

I laughed. "Ah, so that's when work begins."

"Yep. Enjoy your evening because I guarantee by tomorrow night, you are going to be exhausted."

I thought about that for a moment. "I kind of look forward to that."

"Really? Why?"

"Because I'm so used to being mentally tired that it will be nice to be physically tired for once."

"Mentally tired?"

"Yeah, I work twelve- to fourteen-hour days and have had many that are longer."

"Not much different than the ranch, except most of the work is physical."

I glanced around. "Where is your horse?"

He turned and looked down toward the end of the barn. "Miracle is down there."

"Miracle?" I started to walk toward the other side of the barn. "Why Miracle?"

"She almost died at birth, but she pulled through. The vet said it was a miracle, so she earned her name that way."

"How long have you had her?"

A blond horse poked her head over the stall and threw her head up and down as we approached.

"You heard me talking about you, didn't you, girl?" I watched him pet her head and then rest his forehead to hers for a moment. It did funny things to my heart that I didn't want to feel. He turned to me. "Miracle and I have been together for six years."

"She's beautiful." I pet the side of her big head, and she tossed it in the air.

"She is, and she's headstrong too, which is why I ride her. She threw off a lot of riders at first, but now we have an understanding."

I chuckled. "Yeah, and what's that?"

"She doesn't throw me, and I feed her." He grinned. The sight was so deliriously sexy that I wanted to throw my arms around his neck and kiss him again.

The two of us stared at one another again, and I knew he must have been thinking something along those lines because the two of us stepped forward at the same time. Just as we did, voices reached us from outside the barn, and he spun away.

I could see multiple riders dismounting from their horses out in the sunshine. Most of them had happy smiles on their faces. It was easy to tell, even from here, who was a guest and who worked for the ranch. The employees had browner faces from more time in the sun, but they also had wizened looks about them. The amount of gear tacked to their horses was another clue, plus they handled their horses differently than the guests—as if they were part of the animal.

"Come on. I'll introduce you to a few of the guests."

"I'd be more interested in meeting the other ranch hands." He turned to me, his lips compressed for a moment before he nodded. I got the distinct impression he didn't like that I said that.

"How was your ride?" Rob asked a woman who was tying her horse to the fence.

"Wonderful, Rob. It's a shame that you missed out on it today."

"Sorry, Maribel. I had to pick up our newest client. This is Heather. Heather, this is Mirabel. She's here with her husband and those three teenagers over there."

"Family vacation?" I asked, and she nodded.

"Yes, something we have all dreamed of doing for years."

"Are you enjoying it?"

"I am, but my back and thighs aren't so happy." We all laughed.

"Make sure to sit in the hot tub tonight," Rob said to her before he turned to one of the men who was still on his horse.

"Will, this is Heather. She's going to be shadowing me for the next week."

He eyed me from head to toe. "Nice to meet you, ma'am. If you get tired of this bonehead, just let me know. I'd love to have you shadow me."

I saw the invitation in his eyes, and I smiled back brightly, touching Rob's arm. "I think I will be just fine with this cowboy but thank you, my kind sir."

Rob actually stood up a little straighter, and Will chuckled. "Alright then. I see the lady has chosen her stud."

With that, he and his horse walked away, and both Rob and I watched him go as Maribel chuckled behind us and said, "That would be my choice too."

CHAPTER SIX

ROB

I was going to knock his head into a wall the next time I saw him. I peered toward Heather; she was smiling back at Mirabel. At least she wasn't upset by his comment.

Heather wandered around, looking at the horses and talking to some of the guests while I helped Dirk. I lifted my head to see where Heather was every few seconds, and Dirk noticed.

"Mighty fine filly," he said in a low voice that only I could hear.

I frowned. "Why are you saying that about this horse?"

He laughed. "Not the horse, you idiot. I'm talking about your temporary ranch hand."

Immediately my gaze jumped back to her, and I finally got the knot undone. "Oh."

"Don't tell me you didn't notice."

"Oh, I noticed, but that doesn't mean a thing. You know we don't mingle with the guests."

"But I bet you wished that you did," he responded.

I glanced at him and grinned. "Damn straight, I do."

The two of us laughed, and then I returned to Heather's side. "I'll walk you back to your cabin. It will give you time to unpack and get ready for dinner."

"What time is dinner? I'm starved."

"Six on the dot."

She gave a curt nod. "I can do six on the dot, but you don't need to walk me back. I do know where it is."

The two of us started walking away from the group. "I'm just trying to be neighborly."

"Oh, are you my neighbor?"

I grinned at her. "In a way."

"Where do you live?" she asked.

"At the lodge with my mom." He paused. "Does that sound weird?"

"No. Not at all. You help her run this, right? It only makes sense that you live here too."

"I've thought a time or two about building another cabin somewhere on the property for me."

"Well, maybe one day you will meet a woman, and she'll want a place of her own." She stopped walking. "Unless you already have one, and if you do, then I feel horrible for earlier."

I studied her, trying to decide if I should tell her there was someone else. Maybe then she'd keep her distance. "No, I'm not seeing anyone right now."

She grinned and shrugged her shoulders playfully. "Then I am totally not sorry."

I couldn't help but laugh, and the two of us walked back to her cabin. Every once in a while our arms would touch, and I felt it go straight into my chest. I don't think I had ever been so aware of another person before, and I wasn't sure what that meant—not that it had to mean anything.

"Do you like what you have seen so far?" I asked as we approached her cabin. She turned to me, eyeing me up and down. "I meant about the ranch, not me, woman."

She pushed my shoulder. "Sorry, I couldn't help myself. Yes, I do like what I have seen, and I'm going to surprise myself here and say that I'm looking forward to getting on Hershey tomorrow."

"You are?"

She nodded as we reached her cabin and climbed the steps. "Yes. I forgot what it was like being around horses."

"Well, tomorrow, you will get to spend quite a bit of time on one." I looked down at her feet. "Do you have boots?"

"I do. Kari and I are the same sizes, and she gave me the clothes that she had bought for herself for the trip, including good ole cowboy boots."

"Good. I think your feet would be a little too small for mine." We stopped at her door, and I suddenly felt nervous.

"Aw, would you really have let me borrow your boots?"

"Sure."

She put a hand over her heart. "You do know the way to a girl's heart."

I chuckled. "And I thought it was candy and flowers."

She grinned, making her eyes sparkle. "Those don't hurt any, either."

I stepped back, afraid that if I stayed there any longer, I'd be pulling her into my arms.

"Come up to the lodge when you are ready. People tend to congregate in the front parlor before dinner."

"I will do that."

I tipped my hat and turned and walked away, forcing myself not to look back. I was about fifteen feet away when I heard the door open, and I lowered my face, hoping to hide my grin from any prying eyes.

I headed into the barn to find out how things had gone on the ride and found most of the guests were returning to their cabins to clean up for the evening. I spoke to a few of them and then found Dirk and Tom in the office at the back of the barn.

"How did things go?" I asked as I came in and went around the desk.

"Fine. We saw a coyote out on the north pasture watching a few rabbits, but otherwise, it was an uneventful ride," Tom stated.

"How was your ride?" Dirk asked with a smirk.

"I didn't go for a ride," I stated, ignoring the innuendo.

"Oh, did she ride your stallion?"

"Cut it out," I told him, although not harshly. "She's a paying client."

"I thought she wasn't the client, but a friend of the client."

"Either way, she's here for a reason, and it's not to mess around with the likes of us."

"You know, if you want to give her the full experience, you might want to reconsider things a bit."

I shook my head. They were just joking around, but it was hitting a bit close to home. I was already warring with myself over what I felt when I was with her.

"Don't you guys have work to do?" I asked, and Dirk laughed.

"I'm going. I'm going." He disappeared out the door, and Tom took a seat across from me.

"She have any experience on a horse?"

"She does," I told him. "I think she's going to surprise us."

"I hope she does," he replied, and then we switched topics and talked about ranch business.

At five-forty, I was walking into the lodge. Generally, I'd clean up a bit before dinner, but I wasn't filthy since I hadn't been working in the saddle today. I stepped into the front parlor and stopped in my tracks when I saw Heather standing on the other side of the room in a long black skirt, with black cowboy boots peeking out underneath. She was talking to one of the guests and lifted her head, turning in my direction. The moment her eyes landed on mine, she smiled. I felt it deep in my gut, realizing that I was in deep manure here.

I nodded to her and made a beeline to find my mother. She looked weary as she put the phone handset into the cradle on her desk. "Problems?"

"No, same crap I've been dealing with all day." She stood, glancing at me. "How did it go with Heather? Is she going to be able to handle some things, or is this merely going to be an observational week?"

"I think she will do pretty good. She's got riding experience, and she's pretty smart. She seemed to pick up on things fast."

"That's good." She studied me. "If she's going to be alright working at your side this week, why do you look so glum?"

I inhaled sharply and wiped a hand over my mouth before I opened and then closed it again. She lifted a brow. "What's on your mind, Rob?"

I stood. "Um, I don't know."

"Really? You seem unsure of something. Did something happen?"

"Yeah." I frowned. "I kissed her today."

"Who? Heather?"

I nodded and she showed genuine surprise. "Alright, are you upset that you did? Or was she?"

I shook my head. "No, she wasn't, and neither was I." I turned and walked toward the door. "I just wanted you to know that I know we tend to keep our distance from the guests when it comes to a personal nature, but I'm not sure I'm going to be able to do that this time."

"You are a grown man, Rob. I trust you to do what is right for you, and the ranch."

"I appreciate that, Mom."

"Just be careful. Heather goes home in a week, and she doesn't seem like the type of woman to move across the country."

"No, I know that. I just—" I paused. "I feel weird when I'm around her. I don't think I have ever felt like that before."

She came to stand in front of me. "Then see what it is. You never know what could happen. Just don't you decide to hang up your chaps anytime soon."

I grinned at my mom and then kissed her cheek. "Never."

With that, I walked out of the office. I wasn't going to pursue Heather actively, but I wasn't going to say no if things happened.

CHAPTER SEVEN

HEATHER

Dinner was served family style. There were three large tables, and everyone ate at the same time. I was seated between two couples while Rob was at the end. More times than I could count, our eyes locked on one another as I listened to the guests talk about all the fun they'd had so far.

After dinner, everyone retired to the back of the lodge, where there was a large hot tub and a heated pool. A few people went to change to take advantage of the hot water, hoping to alleviate the aches and pains from all the activity.

Rob was absent for a while but finally arrived as the sun began to set. He took a seat beside me on the glider. "Are you having fun?"

"I am, but I am quickly fading. All this fresh air, good food, and a day of travel are catching up to me. I was just thinking about turning in for the night. My boss might appreciate me being awake in the morning."

He grinned at me. "Probably a good idea. I can walk you back to your cabin."

I leaned closer to him, lowering my voice. "Probably not a good idea."

He turned to me, his face only a few inches away. "Why?"

I held up my wineglass. "Because I've had a few of these. I wouldn't want you to take advantage of me."

His body shook with silent laughter. "I promise I'll be on my best behavior."

I gnawed on my bottom lip for a moment. "What if I don't want you to be?"

He looked away, glancing around, then stood. "Come on, let's get you back to your cabin so you can rest up."

That was not the reply I had been hoping for, but he had already told me that they didn't mix business with pleasure here. I stood and set my wineglass down on the bar with a few other dirty ones. Rob put his hand to my lower back as he led me along a path that skirted the back of the lodge.

We were quiet on the way, and I enjoyed the peace. There was little to no silence back home, and my mind was typically running at a hurried pace. It was nice not to have all that noise in my head.

When we arrived at my cabin, he walked me to the door. "I hope you get some rest tonight."

"You could tuck me in," I suggested.

He shook his head with a smile. "As tempting as that is, I think you need to get some rest. At least tonight."

"Tonight, huh?" I stepped closer to him, and he lifted his chin, his eyes darting past me. I turned to see no one was there.

"Yes, tonight, Heather. We can talk about tomorrow when it gets here." He leaned forward and brushed a kiss over my cheek. "Good night. You have my number if you need anything."

He started to back up, and I grabbed his arm. "Wait, I do need something from you."

"What?"

I opened the door. "Come inside for a moment." He eyed me skeptically. "Come on, one minute, and then you are free to go."

"Fine," he said and followed me inside. The moment the door closed, I turned and stepped into him. "Heather."

"I just want one kiss, and then you can go."

He stared at me, a muscle in his jaw ticking for a moment. I could see inside his mind that he was weighing his next move. Finally, he lifted his hat slightly so that it sat further back on his head, and he pulled me to him.

Our lips crashed into one another, and a moment later, our tongues meshed as I wrapped my arms around his shoulders. The kiss lasted longer than I had anticipated, and we were both slightly breathless as we pulled apart.

He stepped back, adjusting his hat. "Good night, Heather. Sweet dreams. I will see you tomorrow."

I was too speechless to say anything in response, and Rob winked at me and then turned and walked out the door. I watched him walk away from the window, and then I grabbed my phone and sent Kari a message.

I think I might be in love.

~

The following day, I was up at three forty-five. I had taken a shower last night and put out my clothes for today so that all I would need to do was get up, dress, brush my hair and teeth, and then head out. Of course, I had to take a few moments to make myself a cup of coffee, but luckily, they kept to-go cups there, and I brought mine with me.

The night was silent, except for a few animals in the distance. Lights lit the path, so I had no trouble seeing where I was going. It was chilly, and I was glad to have a lightweight jacket with me. I knew that by nine, it would be warm enough to shuck it.

I went straight to the barn and found it mostly silent there. A few horses were moving around in their stalls or eating from their feed. There was a light switch on the wall, and I flipped it, illuminating the barn. A few horses poked their heads out to see who had arrived.

Down the way, I found Hershey. He was waiting for me, and after rubbing his nose and talking to him for a moment, I gathered a lead and let him out of his stall so I could brush him down. I attached him to the loop in the hallway and found a brush. Hershey was quiet as I worked, his tail swishing back and forth every once in a while and his ears shifting from one side to the other as he listened to the sounds in the barn.

"You're a good boy," I said to him as I ran the brush over his side.

His eyes perked up, and he shifted his big body toward me a moment before I heard footsteps approaching. I peered over Hershey's back as one of the ranch hands stepped in, looking surprised to find me here.

"Good morning, Heather. You beat me here. That's a first."

I laughed. "I wanted to make a good impression on my boss."

"Oh, you did that already," he said with a grin. "I'm Dirk, in case you didn't know that."

"It's nice to meet you, Dirk."

"Rob is putting you on Hershey, huh?" He approached the horse, rubbing between his eyes for a few moments. "He's a good ride. You should enjoy yourself."

"I hope so. It's been a while since I have ridden, but I am looking forward to it."

Another set of footsteps reached us, and Dirk turned. "That will be the boss. I better get away from you, or he'll have me mucking stalls and fence repair all day."

He winked at me and began to walk away just as Rob appeared in the doorway. "Well, look at you. You beat me out here."

"You said four. I was here at four."

"I said we get up at four."

I shrugged. "What's fifteen minutes?"

"True. How did you sleep?" He patted Hershey for a moment. "Morning, big guy."

"The moment my head hit the pillow, I was out. I don't think I even moved all night."

"Just imagine how tired you are going to be tonight."

"I don't want to," I replied in a slight whine, but I was grinning as I said it.

He came to stand beside me. "Well, I could give you a back rub tonight if your back is bothering you from being in the saddle all day."

I lifted a brow. "What if something else hurts?"

He tipped his hat back, leaning forward. "I might be able to help with that too."

I shifted to close the distance. It wasn't a passionate kiss, just a sweet hello. "I am going to take you up on that."

He winked. "I hope you do."

He walked away and left me staring after him. What had happened to change his mind? Not that I wasn't glad, I was. I didn't have anything against a vacation fling.

CHAPTER EIGHT

ROB

W alking away was a little tricky, but I did it. I was proud of myself for it too. It would have been effortless to lose myself in another kiss. One that led to removing her shirt and pulling off those sexy cowboy boots she wore.

I wanted to make sure this wasn't a mistake, and the best way to find that out was to spend the day with her and get to know her a little better. I wasn't kidding myself with the fact that this wouldn't be anything more than a week of fun.

Heather lived in Baltimore, and she was a big-city attorney. That's what I had been doing last night between dinner and when I went to join the guests on the back patio. I'd been learning what I could about Heather Tate.

Thanks to social media, and her company's website, I had learned enough about Heather to know that this was not her world. That didn't mean I couldn't enjoy her company while she was here.

So when my alarm went off the following day, I was looking forward to getting out of bed and heading out to the barn to start working. We had a lot to get done before the guests began appearing around seven. Breakfast started then and ran through eight. Unlike dinner, breakfast was a more informal setting, and people came in and ordered what they wanted from a select menu that our chef had for that day.

As I stood at the barn door and took in Heather brushing Hershey, I wondered if I were still in bed dreaming. Was this city girl actually out in the barn before I arrived? Holy smokes! She was! She just scored some points.

She also looked cute as hell in her black cowboy boots, jeans, and red plaid shirt. Her hair hung around her shoulders, and her eyes looked bright and rested.

It was fun to tease her a little and surprise her with a kiss. I was pretty sure that as I walked away, she was watching me. Dirk chuckled as I approached him and said in a low voice that she wouldn't be able to hear, "Girl can't take her eyes off you."

"That's the point," I replied and disappeared into the office to check a few things.

A few minutes later, I came out to find Tom, Dirk, and two other hands all hard at work. I glanced around. "Where is Heather?"

Dirk grinned. "She's in the paddock."

I headed to the barn door, slightly worried that she wouldn't be able to handle the horse. Tom slapped me on the shoulder. "Don't worry. She knows what she's doing. Impressed the hell out of me already, and it's not even six."

Heather was in the paddock, going circles in a light trot, her hair bouncing from her shoulders into the brightening sky. She pulled Hershey to a quick stop, then turned him one way before she spun him the other. "Jesus," I said softly, and Tom chuckled. Heather had Hershey walking backward a moment later, then moved him in a big circle. Each time she clucked her tongue, and he moved right along.

"She was made for that horse," Dirk said as he joined us. "Never seen Hershey respond so easily to someone." He glanced at me. "Guess you aren't the only one that likes the lady."

Heather finally noticed that we were watching, and she stopped what she was doing and walked Hershey to us, pausing at the fence. Her eyes were bright, her cheeks flushed. "What a great horse. I forgot how much I loved riding."

"You sure you only did three months of lessons?"

She shrugged. "I'm a quick study."

"You're a natural, Heather," Tom said as he stepped back to return to his work. I climbed up on the bottom rung of the fence as Dirk joined him in the barn.

"Tom is right. You are a natural."

"Well, thank you."

"Now, you need to get off that horse and start helping with the rest of the chores. You will get plenty of time to ride later."

"Do you want me to put him back in the barn?"

"No, just leave him in the paddock. We're gonna head out for a fence check in about twenty minutes. He's fine in there."

I watched as she spoke to the horse, then dismounted with the grace and ease of someone who rode every day. She climbed the fence and threw a leg over, and it seemed only natural to put my hands on her hips and help her down. When her feet hit the ground, she leaned her body against mine.

"Well, hello there, cowboy."

"Hey there, yourself, cowgirl." She snickered, and I kissed the tip of her nose. "Come on, don't get me more distracted than I already am."

"Damn, I was hoping we could skip the work and get to that massage."

"Keep dreaming, ma'am."

"Oh, I will."

～

Our day went from great to fantastic. Heather was a hard worker, and she not only impressed me but all the other guys on the ranch. We quickly learned that she could not only take a joke but dish them out too, and her humor could be even darker than some of ours.

She was incredible on horseback, and I had to wonder how her body was feeling after riding hard and getting on and off Hershey as often as she had. I had a feeling I was going to be giving the woman a full body massage tonight—not that I minded.

We had a picnic lunch out in the south pasture near a stream and then returned to work. When we returned to the barn at four-thirty, she was finally starting to show how taxing the day had been. One of our other hands, Mike, walked his horse toward mine as we came into the main area.

"That girl needs to change jobs. I know she's a lawyer and all, but damn, she can ranch. She worked harder than some of the men I know."

"I agree," I told him. "Although I'm not sure she'll be able to walk tomorrow."

He grinned. "Is that because of the horse or what you two are going to do tonight?"

"Funny," I told him. It wasn't a secret that I had a thing for Heather. We had shared more than our share of looks, and from time to time, we'd even touched one another. Only once had I been unable to deny the urge to kiss her, but no one else had been around.

He chuckled and started trotting away. Heather looked tired as she climbed off Hershey and handed him off to Charlie, one of our junior ranchers that worked in the afternoon to bathe and cool down the horses after rides.

I dismounted and passed my reins over to Charlie before standing by Heather. "I think you might want to either climb in the hot tub or take a long hot shower. Your muscles have got to be hurting."

"What? No, I'm ready to go again." She tried to smile, but I saw the pain behind her eyes and gave her a stern look. "Okay, fine, I'm dead tired."

"Yeah, I thought so. Come on. I'll walk you back to your place."

"If I can walk," she said as she started to shuffle beside me.

"Do you need me to carry you?"

"Ha! That would be a cold day in hell."

"What, you don't like chivalrous men?"

She gave me a dour look. "Throwing me over your shoulder like a sack of grain is not being chivalrous."

I barked out a laugh because if she had said yes, that's precisely what I would have done. "You know me so well."

She ended up walking, albeit slowly, all the way to her cabin, but when she got to the steps, I scooped her up into my arms, and she squealed.

"What are you doing?" She glanced all around, but I ignored her and went up the stairs. We didn't generally lock the doors to the cabins, so I managed to get it open with her in my arms. Inside, I kicked the door closed and headed toward the stairs.

"You know, I like where this is going, but you are right. I need a shower."

"Yeah, well, so do I," I commented as I took another step up.

Her arm tightened around my neck. "Are you suggesting what I think you are suggesting, cowboy?"

I finally looked at her. "I am, cowgirl. You got a problem with that?"

A wicked gleam came to her eyes. "Nope, I'm good with that."

"Good, cuz after watching that cute ass of yours bounce around in the saddle all day, I gotta put my hands on it."

"Just your hands?" she asked with a raised brow.

"Maybe, or maybe not."

CHAPTER NINE

HEATHER

I had never been so physically tired or mentally sated in my life. Each day I was up way before the sun and worked my tail off beside Rob and the others. I learned to mend fences, dig holes, wrangle cattle, and even throw a rope. I wasn't going to win any awards, but I knew the basics of it.

I also figured out which direction was what, which alone was a feat since I could get lost in a paper bag when it came to north, south, east, and west. I had always been boggled when someone said, oh, just head east. Now, I would forever glance to the sky, look for the sun or stars, and know which direction to go from there.

I also learned a lot of other things. Not just about ranching, but about life. Out here, there was stress. There were deadlines and worries to get a job finished before something happened, but you didn't have this overwhelming sense of doom when someone said, it has to be done now. Now could mean in thirty minutes or three hours. It all depended on what needed to be completed beforehand.

In the five days since I'd been on the ranch, I had seen more laughter, friendship, and love than I had in my entire lifetime. I had friends back home, but they were nothing like these men or Patricia. These men had each other's backs and mine. They worked hard, and they never complained. Sometimes we sat in the saddle for nine or ten hours. Other times, we popped on and off the horses two dozen times to handle business. I couldn't imagine any of my co-workers doing such things.

I lay on my side, staring at the lines of Rob's face in the faint light from the window. I never closed the curtains. There was no need to block out the sun since I was awake hours before it rose.

I could fall in love with this man, I thought to myself.

That would be dangerous, though. Rob's life was here. While I loved the ranch—I would never be able to thank Kari enough for pushing me to go in her place—this wasn't my home, and this wasn't my job.

My job was finding loopholes in the law and ways to help my client fight charges and allegations. It was combing through boxes of information and creating strategies. It was hours and hours of searching through statutes and case law to see if I could find a better way to fight the impossible. I hated my job right now.

I rolled to my back and stared at the ceiling of the cabin. Since that night that Rob carried me up the stairs, he had slept at my side. It wasn't a secret that we were together, and many of the guests commented on how cute of a couple we were. Secretly, I thought that too, but I was trying not to look too deeply into this.

I only had one more night here, and tomorrow I would leave on a jet plane. I didn't want to go, but sadly, I knew I had to. I had never hidden from responsibility, and God knew I had a lot of it back home.

I also had a responsibility to Kari. On my breaks, during breakfast, and after a hot shower, I would write my notes for Kari while I lay in bed with Rob beside me. I shared everything that I did, described it as best I could. I had almost filled an entire notebook, and it was going to take her weeks to go through all these notes and organize them.

I slipped out of bed and quietly opened the door to the balcony off the loft. I left it cracked so as not to wake Rob when I shut it. He still had fifteen minutes to sleep before the alarm would go off. I stared out over the ranch, my heart filling with something I didn't understand.

In the distance, I heard horses neighing and cows mooing. A coyote howled somewhere on the property, and crickets sang. I lifted my head and smiled when an owl hooted. You never heard owls hooting in the city.

The door behind me creaked, and Rob's arms came around my waist as he tucked his face against the side of my head. "You're up before your alarm."

"Yeah, I woke up a few minutes ago feeling restless."

"You okay?"

"Yes." I sighed. "I guess the reality is starting to kick in. I'll be leaving tomorrow."

"I know," he whispered. "I wish you weren't."

I squeezed his wrist where my hand lay. "I do too. I love it here."

"Yeah, it does kind of grow on you." He kissed the side of my head. "You could stay."

I laughed softly. "In a perfect world, I could." I turned in his arms. "But this isn't a perfect world, Rob. You are perfect, this place is perfect, but my world isn't quite so ideal."

"Then leave your world and come here."

I studied his face; I knew that he wasn't serious. He couldn't be serious. "I can't do that, Rob."

"Why not?"

"What would I do? I'm an attorney. I deal with corporations and bill three hundred dollars an hour. Despite what I have been doing this week, I'm not a ranch hand."

He pursed his lips and studied me, taking my face between his hands. "You can be anything that you want to be, Heather. Do you think that we don't have attorneys out here? We do. Hell, my mom would probably hire you because she hates the guy she's working with now on this lawsuit." He smiled softly and kissed me on the tip of the nose. "You'd make a damn good ranch hand, but even I know you are better than that. You're destined to do something incredible with your life, and as much as I might want to keep you to myself, I know I can't."

I was frowning at him. "What lawsuit? Is the ranch in trouble? Is someone suing you?"

He sighed. "Yeah, someone is. They got hurt when they were out here, and they are suing us."

"Did they sign the waivers?"

"Yes."

"Your waivers are airtight, Rob. I noticed that when I signed them. Very comprehensive."

He pulled me closer to him. "You know, we could be back in bed making love before we get off to work, but instead, you want to stand here jabber jawing about getting sued?"

I chuckled and wrapped my arms around his neck. "Fine, we can go back to bed, but we aren't done with this conversation."

"Alright, but you have to talk to my mother about it. She's the one dealing with the issue. I deal with the animals; she deals with the people."

"I can do that," I said before I pressed my lips to his and let him lead me back to bed.

~

I was at breakfast when Patricia entered the dining room with a plate of pancakes in her hand and came to sit beside me. "I don't know why I didn't think of asking you earlier, but Rob said he mentioned the lawsuit we are dealing with. Would you mind letting me pick your brain? I'm going to need to figure out what to do, and the attorney we have on retainer is not being very helpful."

"Absolutely, Patricia. I'd be happy to look at what you have and hear what has been done."

"I know you leave tomorrow, but do you mind staying back at the lodge this morning? I think Rob said they are running cattle to another pass today, but you could join them later after we talk if you'd like."

I touched her wrist. "Sounds like a plan. Do you want to tell me about it now?"

She glanced around. "Nope, not around the other guests. It would be better if we talked in my office."

"I'll find Rob after breakfast and let him know."

"Let me know what?" A hand landed on my shoulder as his deep voice filled my ears.

"That I'm going to stay back here and go over things with your mother. I'll meet up with you guys once we finish."

"Alright. How long do you think that will take?" He sat down beside me with a plate filled with eggs and pancakes.

"I don't know, a few hours, I guess."

He took a bite of his food and chewed, then leaned forward. "But don't make any other plans for today."

"Why?"

"Because I have a surprise for you tonight."

"A surprise, huh?" I bumped his shoulder, giggling. "What do you have planned?"

"I'm not telling you. It's a surprise, but I think one you will like."

I did not doubt that I would. Anything to do with Rob, I liked.

CHAPTER TEN

ROB

I stopped by my mother's office before heading to breakfast. "Hey, you might want to take a minute to speak with Heather about that legal issue. She might be able to give you some advice."

"I don't want to trouble a guest with that nonsense."

I chuckled. "I think Heather has shown herself to be more than a guest. Besides, I mentioned it, and she wanted to know more."

"Okay, well, I'll try to find the time to speak with her."

"Mom, she leaves tomorrow. I'd do it now."

She frowned and leaned back in her seat. "Tomorrow? Damn, okay, I will speak to her at breakfast." She studied me for a moment. "You going to be alright after she leaves?"

I sighed as I stared at my scuffed boots. "Yeah. I don't have much choice, do I? She has a life someplace else."

"You two look like you have gotten close."

"We have, and I really like her. If she didn't live in Maryland, we could have had something."

"Why don't you ask her to stay?"

I laughed. "Come on, Mom. She's an attorney who has been pretending to be a ranch hand for research. This is not what she is about."

"Yes, I know, but you should consider asking her anyway. It never hurts to be open and honest."

"I kind of already did, but I don't think she thought I was serious. I'll think about it, but I wanted you to know that I'm going to take her up to the north crest tonight."

"You going to camp out there?"

"Yeah, that's what I was thinking. I might as well go out on a high note and do something she'll probably never do again. At least she won't forget it."

"I doubt she could forget anything about you, Rob. I see the way she looks at you."

"I do too, Mom." I thought for a moment. "I could see myself falling in love with her. Hell, maybe I already am. Who knows. I've never felt anything like this before."

"Well, I'm sorry for that. I know that it will be hard to say goodbye, but you never know what the future holds for you."

"I know."

"You guys will have a great evening. I think that is a wonderful idea."

I asked Jason to gather up the gear we would need for later today. I also spoke with the chef about packing food for a picnic dinner. With that done, I headed out to move the herd. As I worked the cattle, I sat there staring out over the land. I had gotten so used to Heather being here, and yes, I did believe that part of me had fallen in love with her. Would I tell her that? No, probably not. It would just make it harder for both of us.

She ended up joining us around lunchtime, and I watched her fly over the field with her hair streaming behind her. I had never seen such a beautiful sight, and I would miss it terribly.

Late afternoon, well before dinner, I walked our horses to her cabin. I was kind of nervous as I climbed the steps, but I knew that she would enjoy it.

I popped my head into her cabin. "Heather, you here?"

"Yes!" she called from the loft. She peeked her head over the railing. "I'm trying to get some packing done."

"Okay, well, make sure you are dressed in layers and come down here."

"Where are we going?"

"I want to take you to my favorite place," I told her. I liked to go there to think, and I had never shared that spot with anyone before.

"Okay, give me a minute." I stayed downstairs and waited. She came down with a jacket thrown over her arm two minutes later.

When we stepped outside, she stared at the horses. "That's a lot of stuff."

"Yeah, well"—I put my arms around her—"I thought maybe you'd like to spend your last night under the stars with me."

She grinned. "You mean camping?"

"Yes."

She held me close. "I'd love that, Rob. It's a perfect way to end this trip."

"I thought you might enjoy it."

As we headed out, we walked the horses, and she told me about how she'd helped my mother. Perhaps with the information she gave her, my mom would be able to light a fire under the lawyer's ass and get him to do more than tell her to provide them with a settlement.

Heather and I rode for about sixty minutes before we climbed to the area I liked. Once we arrived, Heather sat atop Hershey and stared over the land.

"My God, it's breathtaking."

"It is. I like to come up here when I want to think."

She turned to me. "I'm so glad you brought me here."

I watched her as she turned back to the view, and without her knowing, I took a picture of her. What was breathtaking was her.

We set up our camp and built a small fire before taking out our dinner and cooking steaks right over the campfire. We laughed and talked about all aspects of life, and as the sun finally set, we snuggled with each other and watched silently as the sun disappeared below the horizon on our final day together.

We made love under the stars, and I held her close to me all night long. It was one of the best and worst nights of sleep I'd ever had. We made coffee over the fire in the morning and sat back to watch the sunrise.

"I can't believe I have to leave today."

"I know," I said as I sipped my coffee. "Feels like you just got here."

She laughed. "I don't know about that, but my legs and butt finally got used to being on a horse all day."

"Think you might come back one day?" I asked, staring out at the horizon as if the question didn't mean anything to me.

"Would you like me to?"

I turned to her. "Do you want the honest answer?"

She nodded. "Yes."

"If I had my choice, you'd never leave, Heather. So, the answer to that question would be yes. I do want you to come back. Come back as often as you can, but the next time you do, you stay in my room, not as a guest of the ranch, but as my guest."

Tears filled her eyes as I spoke. "I'd like that, Rob. I really would. I don't know when I'll get to come back, but I would like to."

"Good." I pulled her to me and kissed her passionately for a few moments. "We should get things packed."

"Yeah, we should." We were quieter on our way back, both of us lost in thought, and halfway back to the barn, Heather looked at me. "I need to run one last time."

"Go ahead," I said to her, and she kicked Hershey's flank and encouraged him to run. Her hair streamed behind her, and she flew over the prairie. My heart ached as I watched her go. She was made for that horse—made for this ranch—but I had to let her go.

She circled back after a while, and we rode back to the barn together. We stopped at her cabin and dismounted.

"I need to finish packing."

"Alright, you do that, and I'll take the horses back and clean them up. Let me know when you are done, and I'll have someone come get your bags."

She stood in front of me. "Thank you for the most incredible night, Rob. I will never forget it."

"Neither will I."

She kissed me and hugged me tightly before she turned and went into her cabin. My heart was heavy as I walked the horses to the barn, and instead of handing them off to someone else, I busied myself with caring for them.

I had just finished when I heard her voice at the other end of the barn. She was saying goodbye to Dirk, and I turned to watch her hug him. Every one of the guys had come to love her as much as I had. I wasn't the only one who would miss her.

She approached me, wearing a clean pair of jeans and a blue plaid shirt. "You going to wear those cowboy boots on the plane?"

She grinned. "Damn straight. I might even wear them to the office tomorrow." She glanced at her watch. "Sadly, it's time to go."

CHAPTER ELEVEN

HEATHER

I didn't want to leave. Especially not after the night I had shared with Rob. I had never been interested in camping before, but spending the night tucked safely in his arms had been incredible. My heart had felt so full, and I had been tempted to say something to him, but I had held back.

I was thrilled to hear him say that he wanted me to return. I was already trying to figure out where, in my schedule, I might be able to take another vacation. There was no doubt that I would return here again. It was just a matter of when.

I had said goodbye to everyone, and they had all told me to return soon. Even Rob's mother had expressed such things and admitted that she knew how much her son cared about me. It meant the world to me that she was aware of his feelings and that she seemed to approve.

I made sure to stop and speak with Hershey for a moment before I left the barn. "Goodbye, boy. Thank you so much for letting me ride you." I kissed his nose, and he whinnied and shook his head from side to side as if to say nope, don't go.

As Rob and I drove away from the lodge, several employees stood around the paddock and waved their hats in the air. I waved back from the window and felt my heart begin to crack. Somehow I held back the tears that wanted to break free. I watched the scenery as we drove and was amazed that it had only been a week since I arrived and wondered what I was doing here.

Now, I felt as if I belonged. As if this was supposed to be my home and that city I had left felt foreign. How could a week in one place change all that?

I glanced to my left, my gaze landing on Rob, and I knew. Home is where your heart is, and he had my heart.

He glanced my way and winked before turning back to the roadway.

A sick feeling slithered through my stomach when the airport came into view. I wasn't ready to leave—not this place and not this man. Instead of pulling up to the doors, Rob parked, and we rolled my suitcases toward the terminal with our fingers tightly laced.

I checked in and turned over my bags while Rob waited for me. Like most airports, he couldn't pass through security without a ticket, and we stood off to the side, waiting for a few moments. Fifteen minutes before boarding began, he stood in front of me and rubbed my arms up and down.

"Thank you for all the work that you did."

"Really? After all that we shared, you're going to end with that?" I chuckled.

"Yeah, well, I'm trying to keep my manly dignity here."

I wrapped my arms around him and held him tightly. "Thank you, Rob. For everything, but especially for last night."

"You're welcome, Heather," he whispered against my ear. He pulled back and stared down at me, holding my cheeks in his hands. "Promise me that you'll come back."

"I will. I promise."

Rob kissed me, and while I was never a person for public displays of affection, I didn't care who saw us. We stared at one another as we pulled away. "I lo—"

I put my hands over his lips, begging him softly, "Don't. Please, don't say it, Rob. If you do, I won't be able to leave, and you know I have to. Save it, and when you see me again, if you still feel the same way, you tell me then. You shout it from the rooftops if you want, but not now."

"Alright, I won't." He kissed me one more time, and then he stepped back and let his hands drop. "I'll see you soon, Heather."

I began to step back. "I'll see you soon, Rob."

He tipped his hat, and I turned and walked to security. There were only about twenty people ahead of me in the line, and I looked back at him a couple of times. He was leaning against a pillar, watching me like a hawk. I put my stuff on the conveyer belt and removed my boots.

After going through the line, I collected my things and looked back to see he was still there watching. When it was time, and I heard them calling for passengers to prepare to board, I blinked back the tears and blew him a kiss. He caught it and put his hand over his heart, and I shifted and walked out of view.

When we got outside and started heading to the plane, I let my gaze slide over the mountain range—such majestic beauty. I climbed the steps and followed the other passengers into the plane.

I took my seat by the window, and I glanced out to see a viewing area on the side of the terminal, and Rob was standing there watching. I pulled out my phone and called him.

"Miss me already, darling?"

"Yes. I see you over there."

"You do, huh?"

"I do." I paused. "You know what you were going to say to me in the terminal?"

"Yes."

"Well, I wanted you to know that I feel the same."

I watched him tip his head down and kick something on the ground. "Come back to me soon, Heather, so we can both say those words out loud to one another."

"I will, Rob. I promise I will. I have to go."

"Bye, Heather. Have a safe trip."

"Thank you."

As I hung up the phone and turned it off, I watched him as the tears rolled down my cheeks. I watched him until the plane began to move, and he lifted his hat and waved it. A moment later, the aircraft moved, and I lost sight of him.

I closed my eyes, thankful that the seat beside me was empty, and I could dwell in my sadness for a few minutes in silence.

The moment I stepped outside of the Baltimore airport, I wanted to turn right back around. Gone was the clean, refreshing air and peaceful sounds of nature. Instead, the air was full of fumes, engines roared, and horns honked.

I waited in line for a taxi and then climbed into the back seat, where I wrinkled up my nose at the smell. I had smelled better horse manure.

The ride home was long with the afternoon traffic, but eventually, I arrived. When I got home, the first thing I did was send Rob a message. *I am home, and boy, do I miss you and the ranch.*

I didn't get a reply for a while, but he sent me a picture of Hershey when he did respond. *He misses you almost as much as I do. Glad you made it home safe. Get some rest, and we will talk soon. Got some issues going on right now.*

I thanked him for the picture, and then I poured myself a glass of wine, kicked off my boots, and called Kari.

"Are you home?"

"No, I decided to stay in Wyoming."

She laughed. "Yeah, I doubt that, no matter how good the sex was."

"I don't know. It was tough to leave. It is so beautiful out there, Kari. It was quite depressing to return to Baltimore."

"Oh, come on, Heather. I'm sure it was nice, but you're a city girl. You might be happy there for a little while, but where would you go shopping?"

I almost laughed because the one time we had gone into town, I had spent several hundred dollars in the one shop buying new jeans and another pair of boots. "Shopping is not everything. Besides, they do have big cities around there."

"Oh, I'm sure. Did you get me a lot of good stuff to use?"

"I did. I filled up an entire notebook. I finished all my notes on the way home." The one thing I had left out was my night under the stars with Rob. There was no mention of that hillcrest or dinner over the fire and coffee served in the sleeping bag while the sun broke the horizon. Those memories were just for me. "I'll get them over to you tomorrow."

We set up a time, and then I hung up to get unpacked and ready for work the next day. The entire time I was gone, I hadn't cracked my computer open once. Initially, I had intended to do some work, but work was the furthest thing from my mind once I got there.

Six days later, work was still the furthest thing in my mind. I was trying to keep myself occupied, but none of it seemed to capture my attention as it once had. Not until I received a phone call that would change my life.

CHAPTER TWELVE

ROB

After Heather left, nothing felt the same, and I had difficulty sleeping at night. I pushed myself more during the day and hoped that I was physically exhausted enough at night to fall asleep—it never worked. I would lie there for hours, thinking about every moment of her time here.

We had texted a few times, and we spoke on the phone over the weekend, but our schedules always seemed to cross. The dude ranch was packed with guests, which alone kept us busy. Plus, add in all the usual work for the ranch, and we were working long hours.

I had taken Hershey out for a ride the other day, but he was moody and didn't want to do as he was told. I ended up coming back sooner than expected and let him graze in the pasture.

My mom was overly stressed and had just learned that our attorney had decided to quit. Now she was trying to find another attorney she could trust, but she wasn't having any luck.

I was in her office two days after, and we were talking over options. "Maybe I should just do the settlement."

"You know better than me, Mom, but what did Heather suggest?"

"She told me not to. She gave me suggestions on what to have the attorney research, but he didn't seem willing. Now that he's gone, I have to deal with finding someone who might take it on."

"What did he say about it when you told him?"

"He said that she didn't know what she was talking about."

"But doesn't she deal with those kinds of cases?"

"Not really. I mean, Heather said she handled some personal injury cases in the past, but she mostly dealt with corporate stuff now."

"Why don't you call her and ask her what she thinks. Maybe she might have an idea of what to do now."

"I don't want to bother her," she said with a wave of her hand.

"No, Mom, I think Heather would want you to."

"I'll think about it."

We didn't say anything further, but that night at dinner, when I saw my mother again, she seemed in better spirits.

"I took your suggestion. Heather is going to help us out."

"That's great." I was sure that Heather was happy to help. I knew that she liked my mother, and she'd been worried about what would happen with the lawsuit. I didn't get the chance to ask her about it again that night, and the next few days were busy.

In fact, the next few weeks were busy, and before I knew it, the leaves were changing, and we were preparing for the winter to come. It had been months since I had seen Heather. We video chatted once a week, but otherwise, our chats consisted of text messages.

By November, I began to wonder if I'd ever see her again. It made me sad to think that I wouldn't and that I'd never get the chance to tell her in person how much I loved her.

I knew I did. Even now, after all this time apart, I missed Heather something fierce. Every morning I expected to open my eyes and find her beside me, and each time I was disappointed that she wasn't there.

My mother was in better spirits these days, and when I asked her how things were going, she said that the case was being taken care of. I didn't ask for the details because that was her thing, and I had enough on my plate.

Although the first week in December, she asked me to accompany her to court. For the first time in a long time, I pulled out the one suit

I owned, polished my special occasion boots, and took down my dress hat. If my mother wanted me by her side, then I would be there.

We made our way to the courthouse, and my mother fidgeted in the seat beside me. "Have you spoken to Heather recently?"

"Um, not this last weekend. Heather said she would be busy with some things over the weekend. I'm sure I will talk to her this weekend."

"Ah," she said with a nod. "I'm sure you will."

I thought it was odd for her to bring up Heather, but perhaps the fact that we were going to court brought her to mind.

We made our way into the courthouse and located Judge Norman's courtroom. We found a seat in the back of the room and sat back to watch the attorneys up front discuss another case. I leaned toward her. "Where is your attorney?"

She smiled. "Not here yet." She patted my hand. "But don't worry. They will be."

I wasn't worried, but I'd still like to know where the attorney was. The attorneys and their clients finished up a few minutes later. Someone approached the judge's bench and spoke briefly with him. "We are going to take a ten-minute recess."

Everyone stood as he left the room, and then people began to talk amongst themselves. A few more people came in and some left. Two of the people who entered were our previous guests, and my mother and I glanced at them and then looked away. They were the people that had caused all these issues.

The man had saddled a horse improperly and went out without having one of our men look at it. If someone had checked, they would have immediately noticed it was wrong. Add in that guests weren't supposed to ride alone. A few hours after he left, the horse returned without the rider. We spent six hours searching for him and found him propped up against a tree with a broken leg.

The door opened behind us, and two more people came in. My jaw dropped as I stared at Heather, dressed in a navy suit with a large briefcase at her side. She was talking to the woman beside her, and her gaze skittered over mine and then jumped back.

At the same time, someone called for the courtroom to come to order, and I was on my feet as the judge returned to the bench. Heather smiled at me and then squeezed my mom's arm. "I'll talk to you later, Rob. Come up front with me, Patricia."

I was shocked to see her here, but not only that, she was stepping in front of the galley and sitting down at one of the tables. Why was she here?

The judge banged his gavel and then studied the table where the three women sat. "Ms. Tate, welcome to my courtroom."

She stood. "Your Honor, it is a pleasure to be before you today. My sincerest apologies for my tardiness. My plane got delayed out of Chicago."

"Understood. I also understand that you were just accepted to the Wyoming State Bar."

"I was, Your Honor. I am legally permitted to practice law in your fine state. I have spent the last three years practicing in Baltimore and Washington DC."

He smiled. "Well, I look forward to having you here in my court-room many times."

"I too look forward to it, sir."

Wait, what? Heather could practice law here? Had she done that for my mother? Why hadn't she told me about this?

I sat back and watched her work. It didn't take long for her to contest everything that had been in the initial affidavit and explain to the judge that the suit was unworthy of his attention. It was based on lies and malicious intent on the part of the affiant, who had conducted himself in this manner several times.

My jaw hung open as Heather stated the number of times the couple had filed lawsuits. A whopping twelve times in ten states dealt with being injured while on vacation. The judge frowned, asked the couple a few questions, and then threw the case out after giving a long-winded speech about their audacious behavior not being toler-ated in the great state of Wyoming.

Forty minutes after it began, it was over, and Heather hugged my mother before escorting her down the aisle toward me. My mother waved me into the hallway, and I followed, chomping at the bit to find out what this all meant.

"I don't know how to thank you for everything that you did, Heather." My mother was gushing.

"You are welcome, Patricia. I am glad I could help."

Heather finally turned to me and smiled. "Hi, Rob."

"How are you here? Why are you here?"

My mother laughed and excused herself to use the restroom.

"How am I here? Well, I took a plane, and someone picked me up and brought me here. Why? Because Baltimore just wasn't home anymore."

CHAPTER THIRTEEN

HEATHER

W hen Patricia called me and told me what was happening, all I could think about was helping her. My cases meant nothing to me compared to what she was facing. If the clients won, it could ruin her ranch's reputation, or worse, kill the business.

I knew how incredible the place was, and I wasn't going to watch someone destroy it. The moment I was off the phone with her, I logged onto the computer and started researching the Wyoming Bar Association. It was pure luck that the state bar test was four weeks away, and I would have a week to get my paperwork for reciprocity sent over to them.

I wouldn't have to retake the exam, but I would have to ask to be allowed onto the Wyoming Bar Association. That process took eight to ten weeks after the test was over.

It had taken precisely eleven weeks and four days to get the notice that I was granted reciprocity to practice law in the state.

While I had waited, I searched for jobs, and as luck would have it, I found two firms interested in having me. I took the one that was closer to the ranch.

I also searched for information on the couple who had filed the suit. I unearthed quite a few legal settlements in their names, all from other vacation spots, all from one or both of them getting hurt during their time there. Most of the suits had settled out of court, but two had gone to trial. I was not going to let this one go that far.

There were several times when I almost mentioned what I was doing to Rob, but then something always held me back. What if I was denied? Then I would have gotten his hopes up for nothing. Besides, I figured this would end up being a pleasant surprise if it all went well.

I couldn't have asked for a better expression on his face when I saw him in the courtroom. As much as I wanted to confess how much I loved him, I didn't. I had a job to do, and I needed to prove to the judge and Patrica that I was worthy of being here.

In the hallway, I saw Rob watching me, waiting for me to give him my attention. When I finally did, it took everything in me not to jump into his arms.

"Hi, Rob." His bright-blue eyes bore into mine.

"How are you here? Why are you here?"

Patricia said something about using the bathroom, but I was too lost in his eyes to care.

"How am I here? Well, I took a plane, and someone picked me up and brought me here. Why? Because Baltimore just wasn't home anymore."

"It's not home? What are you talking about?"

I took his arm and pulled him to the side of the hallway out of the way of traffic. "Rob, I took a job here in Jackson Hole."

"You did?"

I nodded. "I did."

"Why?"

I stepped a little closer. "Why do you think?"

"I don't know."

I gnawed my bottom lip. Perhaps I had been wrong to think that he still loved me. "When I left, I told you I would come back. I came back, and unless you don't want me anymore, I'm not going anywhere."

He blinked three times, and then he grabbed my cheeks and pulled me forward. "I want you, Heather. I have wanted you every single minute since I first laid eyes on you." He stared at me for a few seconds. "Are you serious? You are moving here?"

"Yes. I realized that Baltimore is not my home anymore. Jackson Hole is, and more specifically, The Triple G Ranch is home."

"Does my mother know about this?"

I nodded. "She helped me with everything."

"I can't believe she didn't say anything."

I leaned forward. "Rob, are you going to kiss me or keep me waiting?"

Rob pulled my face to his and kissed me with the passion I had been missing for almost six months. It was hard to believe we had been apart that long, but now being back in his arms, I felt like I was finally home after a long unwanted trip.

Someone cleared their throat, and we pulled away from each other, glancing around as we realized where we were. "You two might want to save that for later," Patricia said with a grin.

"Yeah, we probably should."

The three of us walked out of the courthouse, and I held Rob tightly to my side. "Do you have things?"

"They should already be at the ranch," I stated.

Patricia bumped my shoulder. "I wasn't the only one who knew she was coming back. Dirk picked her up at the airport and brought her here."

"Dirk knew?"

I patted his chest. "Yes, and don't get yourself in a tizzy. The kiss you gave me was much better than the one he did."

"He better not have kissed you," he growled playfully.

"Only on the cheek."

On the way back to the ranch, I explained it all to him and how I realized what I now wanted in life. We were in a celebratory mood as we pulled under the gates, and I put the window down and inhaled the crisp mountain air. "Home."

"Yes, you are," Rob said as he lifted my hand and kissed the back of it. Everyone was waiting for us when we pulled in front of the lodge, and I hugged each one of them tightly as I went down the line.

Inside, a big Welcome Home banner hung in the lobby area, and the chef had prepared a feast. Rob and I got zero time alone until things began to wind down.

I stood on the front porch, staring out over the land. It looked a lot different without all the leaves on the trees but just as beautiful.

The front door opened, and Rob came out with a heavier coat in his hands. "I figured you would need this."

"Thank you. It is colder than I thought it would be."

"Just wait."

"You do know that I hate the cold, right?"

"Well, now you have someone to keep you warm. Speaking of someone, I think you need to say hello to a certain fellow. He's been a bear since you left."

We held hands as we walked to the barn, and I inhaled deeply as I stepped inside. "God, I missed that smell."

Suddenly down the way, Hershey stuck his head over the stall and looked at me. "Hey, big boy."

I made my way toward him, and he threw his head back and snorted a few times. "Did you miss me?" He buried his face against my chest and pushed on me. "You did, didn't you? I missed you too."

"You want to take a little ride?"

"Now?"

"Sure."

"Absolutely," I told him, and we quickly saddled the horses. A few minutes later, I mounted Hershey, and the world was right again as Rob and I began to walk into the field.

We rode for about twenty minutes, and my cheeks were numb, but I didn't care. I was in heaven. Rob reached over and pulled my horse to a stop beside his.

"What's wrong?"

"Nothing. I just need to look you in the eye to say this."

"What?"

"I love you, Heather. I loved you the moment I first saw you, and I have loved you every minute that you were gone from me. I don't want to waste another moment without telling you that."

I leaned toward him, and he met me in the middle. "Who would have ever thought that I would find love on a dude ranch? I love you, too, Rob. So very much."

He kissed me tenderly and then sat back and stared at me. "Do you honestly think that you'd be happy with this life?"

"Yes. I do. Will you be happy having me in your life?"

"Darling, I'm the happiest man alive right now."

"Good. Then how about we head back to the lodge, and you show me how you can make me the happiest woman in the world."

He chuckled. "I'd race you, but I don't want the horses to hurt themselves in the dark."

"That's okay. We can race later. We have all the time in the world."

"We sure do, darling."

That night we made love in his bed at the lodge, and the following day at four, we were up and back to work. I wasn't officially starting at the office until next week, so I had a few days to play ranch hand. As we stood in the pasture rounding up the cows to move, I watched the sun climb over the horizon and realized that this had been the best decision in the world.

I glanced at Rob about ten feet away. He winked, and I winked back before I turned Hershey and kicked him. I'd been dying to get him moving since I mounted him this morning, and now that it was light enough for him to see well, it was time to let not only Hershey fly, but my soul too.

THE END

7: FINDING LOVE AT THE FARMERS MARKET

CHAPTER ONE

SANDI

"Sandi, you have no idea how much I appreciate this." Maggie, my best friend, gushed as I collected the keys to her shop from the hook by the door. "You seriously are a lifesaver."

"Maggie, you know I will do anything for you. I'm glad that I could come back to town and help."

"Not that I'm happy that you got divorced, although I always knew Bill wasn't good enough for you. However, I am glad you are divorced." She grinned at me, and I tried to focus on her bright-brown eyes, not the paleness of her cheeks or the dark circles under her eyes. She looked even more tired today than when I arrived a week ago.

I chuckled. "I don't know what you didn't like about Bill. He was a nice guy."

"Ha! He was a jerk. His good looks and smooth demeanor blinded you. You had horse blinders on when it came to him."

"Okay, we can agree to disagree. I'll see you later. Get some rest. You look tired," I told Maggie and then waved goodbye as I let myself out of her house by way of the side door.

When Bill and I decided to get divorced, I hadn't planned on coming back here, but two weeks after my divorce was finalized, Maggie called and said she had uterine cancer, and the prognosis wasn't good. That alone would have brought me back, but Maggie needed a favor. She wanted to know if I could take care of her bakery while she was fighting this horrible disease.

I didn't have a lot of experience baking, and I didn't know all that much about running a business, but I would do anything to help her out. Maggie had told me that the bakery pretty much ran itself, and for the most part, she was right. While she had a great group of employees, they were all younger. She preferred someone with more experience to oversee the financial and business side of things and didn't have the energy to do it during her intense treatments.

The day after I arrived, I jumped in and started learning while enjoying myself and being back in a small town. Maybe while I was back in town, I might find a permanent job and relocate for good.

I climbed into my car and glanced at the list that Maggie had given me. I needed to stop at the dairy for fresh milk and cream, but I needed to do that after I hit the farmer's market for her order of jellies and jams.

I knew that Maggie used some of the jellies in a few of her recipes as fillings. She had also recently added a section in her bakery with unique sauces and seasonings and had two shelves for this incredibly delicious jelly.

The owner of Honeyhill Farms only came to this farmer's market twice a month, and Maggie stocked up when they did because the jars flew off the shelves.

She told me that she had already put her order in but to ask him if he had anything new and, if he did, to grab a few jars to try out with her customers.

I looked forward to seeing how big the farmer's market had gotten. When I was young, I used to love to visit the farmer's market with my mother and older brother. At least once a month, we would walk the rows of booths and fill up the wagon we brought with fresh fruits and vegetables. Plus, Mom always let me pick something special like a new blanket, hair ribbons, or a small room decoration. Shawn always got to pick out something too, but he usually had his attention on the booth at the end where an older man sold comic books.

It was always a fun day, and I hadn't been to the farmer's market since my mother passed when I was twenty. Now eighteen years later, I was excited to visit.

It was in the exact location it had always been, and I parked in the dirt lot near the field and collected the rolling cart that Maggie said I would need before heading toward the booths.

When I arrived at the first one, I paused and looked down the row at the colorful array of tents covering the assorted wares for sale. My heart filled with emotion as I took it all in, and I blinked back a bit of nostalgic moisture as I began to walk.

It was like time had stopped as I glanced around. An older woman I recognized stood near the back of a booth showing a young woman a quilt she had made. My hand flew to my chest. That woman had made the quilt I'd had on my bed for years. Whatever happened to that? I don't think I remember seeing that since I moved away.

I passed booths filled with handmade clothing, scarves, and jewelry and then came upon one with stained glass. I paused and let my eyes scan over things quickly, wishing I had more time to browse. I would have to come back next weekend if I could.

I kept going and finally located the Honeyhill Farms booth. A man was speaking to a customer off to the side with his back to me. I browsed the small jars on display. There were many regular types of jam, like strawberry and peach, but then I blinked and stared at a label that read lilac jam. Who wanted flowers in their jelly? I shifted to the next jar—corn cob.

I laughed. "Corn cob? Seriously?" I continued to read over the labels, sweet lime, spicy lime, banana, Irish stout, bacon, Kentucky bourbon, and then one called Toes. I frowned and picked it up to read the smaller print to find Toes was tangerine, orange, and elderberries. I wrinkled my nose and heard someone chuckle.

"It's better than it sounds." I stood up straight, lifting my eyes to the man behind the table.

His bright-blue eyes studied me questioningly, and I skimmed over his face before I shifted back in surprise. I would know this man anywhere. "Aaron?"

He recognized me a second after I had him. "Sandi Warrenton!" He laughed, and the sound was like a welcoming hug. "Wow!" He came around the counter, and I let my surprised gaze drift over him. *Well, hello!*

"Wow is right! You look fantastic, Aaron," I told him as I took in his handsome face and dark five-o'clock shadow even though it was only eleven in the morning. That alone could have identified him.

He strode purposely toward me, his eyes drifting to my feet and back up before he held out his arms and pulled me toward his body. For a few seconds, that familiar feeling of comfort surrounded me, and I took a moment to enjoy his embrace.

"I can't believe it's you! Do you live around here?" he asked as he pulled back a few seconds later.

"No, I'm helping out a friend," I said and glanced at his table. "But obviously, you do."

"Yeah, I moved back about four years ago. My parents were getting older and having issues, and I needed a break from the rat race in the city."

"I can understand that. How are your parents doing now?"

"My father passed about a year after I returned, and Mom went about a month after him. She said she never wanted to live without him, and a few days before Mom died, she said she was ready."

I grabbed his forearm. "Aaron, I'm so sorry to hear that they are both gone. I have so many wonderful memories of them." My heart ached for his loss.

Aaron and I had grown up on the same street, and he had been best friends with my brother, Shawn. Many times Aaron's parents watched us when our parents were traveling. The last time I saw Aaron was when I was eighteen, and he was twenty-two. My brother had died in a car accident, and Aaron had attended his funeral service.

I was almost embarrassed to admit that I'd had a crush on Aaron when I was twelve until I turned sixteen and my family moved away. When I saw him at my brother's service, I felt those old childhood feelings rush back, but the timing was completely wrong, and I had shied away from him.

As I stood staring at him, I wanted to lean in and stare deeper into his blue eyes. Immediately a familiar childish giddy feeling spread through my limbs as I thought about my crush on him and how I had once, and only once, naively thrown myself at him.

"Thank you. It was rough, but I know they are happy together." He smiled brightly, and I felt my heart sigh. I had always loved Aaron's smile.

"And you decided to stay here and do this then?" I waved a hand toward his booth. Was it destiny that I had come back? That Maggie had sent me to the farmer's market to pick up jams from Aaron?

"Well, this was my wife's business."

I unconsciously shuffled back a step, feeling my excitement immediately wane. "Oh, you're married."

He frowned slightly. "I was. I'm a widower now. Beth passed away."

"Oh, my gosh." I reached out and grabbed hold of his arm. "I'm so sorry, Aaron." I squeezed gently and then let his arm go.

"Thank you. As I said, it has been a rough few years. But what about you? Married? Kids? Work?"

"Divorced, no kids, and I'm between jobs right now."

Aaron put his hand out to touch my arm as he glanced over my shoulder. The warm weight of his palm seeped into my body, and I almost sighed. "Can you hold on one moment? I need to help this customer."

I nodded as he stepped away, realizing that I would probably hold on much longer than a moment if he asked.

CHAPTER TWO

AARON

I didn't want to be at the farmer's market today, but I had two orders that customers needed to pick up. I had been tempted to contact both of them and tell them I would drop them off personally later in the week and ditch the booth.

My old friend, Mr. Guilt, began to harp in my ear. I gave in to his whining and packed my truck with a smaller amount of inventory than I typically did, along with the orders for my customers. That seemed to calm Mr. Guilt into getting off my back—at least for the moment.

I would attend the market, complete my deliveries, and then high-tail it out of there. By the time my standing orders were picked up, I would have sold off most of my regular inventory, and I could hopefully be out of there by around ten.

I had other things that needed my attention today—not that I wanted to do them either.

I chatted with customers and gave out a few samples to new people who stopped by the booth. I had just sold three jars to a regular customer when I turned and noticed a woman frowning as she looked at a Toes jar.

When she lifted her face, I was startled at how familiar she was to me. It only took a few seconds to realize who it was and make my way around the table. I pulled Sandi to my chest and held her. Suddenly, flashes of memories from long ago began to explode in my mind.

I had known Sandi since she was a little girl. Her brother, Shawn, and I were the best of friends all through school and into college.

Shawn and I had even gone to the same college and were roommates. Our senior year in college was when I became good friends with Mr. Guilt.

Shawn had begged me to go with him and his girlfriend Vickie to a concert two hours away, but I told him I had to study for an economics exam. Later that night, I received a frantic call from Vickie stating they were at the hospital after a horrific accident on the highway. Vickie said she would be alright, but Shawn was in bad shape.

I had to borrow a friend's car since Shawn had driven mine and raced to the hospital, arriving a few minutes after he was pronounced dead. I was devastated and blamed myself as I sat in the chair in the busy waiting room. Mr. Guilt took a seat within me and decided to keep me company.

Mr. Guilt told me snidely that I should have gone with them. Shawn hated driving on the highway at night. He never could keep his attention on the road and relied on me to always do the driving— hence the reason he didn't even have a car. Mr. Guilt admonished me. If you had gone, he would be alive. It's your fault. His death would always be your fault.

I was the one to call his parents and deliver the news. It was the least I could do, and as his father sobbed on the phone and his mother cried hysterically in the background, I hung my head as Mr. Guilt patted me on the shoulder, muttering, *get used to it, buddy.*

I left the hospital shortly after that and got trashed. I'd never gotten so drunk, but that became the first of many. When I attended his funeral service, I had a flask in my coat pocket. That was to keep the buzz going that I had started two hours before. I had filled it twice to get through that part of the day.

Even in my alcoholic haze, I had noticed how grown-up Sandi was. The last time I had seen her, she was around sixteen and about to get her braces off. I'd be blind to say that I hadn't noticed her back then, but she was still a young lady and had a lot of growing up to do.

However, when I saw her again at Shawn's funeral, I quickly realized she had completed that task. She had straight teeth and curves in places I had never expected. If my visit had been on different terms, I would have tried to get her alone to find out more about her. However, the grief in her eyes kept me at a distance.

I left as quickly as I arrived, and that was the last time I had seen or spoken to her—until now.

I stepped away to assist a customer, hoping that Sandi wouldn't vanish while I did. Luckily, when I finished the transaction, Sandi was right where I had left her, smiling brightly and waiting patiently. Her blue eyes were bright in the summer light, and her dark-blond hair was pulled back into a ponytail, with little wisps of curly hair hanging around her face.

When she was younger, and it was humid, her hair would get crazy curly and then frizz. She hated it, but I loved it. I was happy to see that she still had that same wild hair.

"So, what brought you back to town?" I glanced at my watch, wondering where my second customer was. Perhaps they would show up soon, and I could get rid of my inventory and invite Sandi out for a cup of coffee to catch up.

"My friend. You know her, Maggie Brooks, the owner of Brooks Bakery."

"Maggie!" I laughed. "I was waiting for her to show up."

"Sorry, you got me instead."

I grinned. "I am not going to complain about that. Don't get me wrong, I love Maggie, but I am thrilled to see you again, Sandi."

"I am too, Aaron. I have thought of you many times over the years."

"I'm glad that I'm not the only one." I winked at her and then had to step away for a few moments to answer a question from another customer. When I turned my attention back to Sandi, I said, "Are you here to get her order?"

She nodded. "I am." She paused, biting her bottom lip for a

moment. "You might not know this; I know that Maggie hasn't told a lot of people, but she's sick."

I frowned. "Sick? What kind of sick?"

I sighed. "The kind where she might not survive."

"Oh, crap, Sandi. What's wrong? Is there anything I can do?"

She shook her head. "No, just good thoughts. She has cancer, and it's pretty advanced. She's always so busy that while she had some symptoms, she didn't take the time to see the doctor immediately."

"Is there any chance she will be able to get rid of it?"

"I don't know. Maggie is trying to be positive, but I see the worry behind her eyes. She goes into the hospital tomorrow to have a hysterectomy and remove what they can. It's uterine cancer, but they said it had already spread much further, and they know it has attached to her bladder. They aren't sure if they will be able to remove that or not, and who knows what else they will find."

"What treatment are they going to give her?"

"I'm not sure of all the specifics, but she told me it would be very aggressive. It's her only chance of surviving longer than a few months."

"Damn, Sandi. I'm so sorry to hear that. Are you sure there isn't anything I can do to help?"

"I appreciate that, Aaron, but I think the only thing I need right now is her order and for you to ensure the shelves stay full. The less stress I can put on Maggie, the better."

"You got it, Sandi."

"She also wanted me to ask if you had anything new."

I shook my head. "No, not this month. I have a few recipes I'm going to try for next month, but I don't have them perfected yet."

"Are they more flower jellies?"

"Hey, I'll have you know that flower jams are damn popular around here, along with corn cob, bacon, and root beer."

"Bacon jam? That's crazy." She laughed, and I lost myself for a few seconds as I let the sound fill my mind.

"You should try it. It might surprise you."

"I'll take your word for it."

I glanced back at the boxes behind the table. "You know, Maggie's order is pretty big this week. How about I deliver it to the bakery when I finish here?"

"You don't have to do that, Aaron." I held up the folded rolling cart. "I brought her handy cart."

"Yeah, well, you'd have to make at least two, if not three, trips for what she ordered."

"Oh." She frowned.

"I'm going to be leaving here soon. I'm almost out of my inventory for today."

"Already? It's not even ten."

"Yeah, it went fast today. As soon as I finish here, I can bring it over to the bakery."

"Are you sure?"

"Yes, I am. Perhaps, when I do, you might have a few minutes to have a cup of coffee with me, and we can catch up a little bit."

A smile filled her face. "I'd love that, Aaron. It is great to see you. Are you sure you don't mind? I need to stop by the dairy farm and pick up her milk and cream order. Then I'll be at the bakery for the rest of the day."

"That should work out well. Let's say about an hour. Does that sound good?"

"Yes, that sounds perfect." She stepped back, still grinning widely. "I'll see you in an hour."

"I look forward to it."

She took a few more steps backward and then turned and walked away. I watched her, and she glanced back and waved. After she was out of view, I realized my cheeks hurt from smiling so much, but that didn't stop me from doing it more.

CHAPTER THREE

SANDI

I giggled as I climbed into my car and pulled out my cell phone to send a message to Maggie. *You didn't tell me that the jelly maker was Aaron Norcini!*

I waited a moment and then saw she was replying. *I thought you might enjoy a surprise.*

Well, that was a surprise. He said you have a huge order, so he will deliver it in about an hour to the bakery.

A moment later, my phone rang. "Wait! Is Aaron going to deliver it to the bakery for you? He never offers to do that for me!" She laughed and then coughed a few times.

"Yep."

"Did he have someone with him? He's usually at the market all day."

"No, he said he was leaving early today. That's why he offered to bring it over and said he hoped we could grab a cup of coffee when he did."

"Look at you! You're not back in town but a week, and you have a date with one of the hottest single men in the area."

"Why did you never tell me he was back in the area?"

"I don't know. I guess I never really thought about it."

"Holy cow, Maggie! Do you not remember the crush I had on him?"

She was quiet for a moment. "Yes, you did have a crush on him. Sorry, I forgot about that, but honestly, Sandi, would it have made any difference? Up until a few weeks ago, you were married."

"Ah, there is that." I chuckled. "Well, I'm not married now, and neither is he."

"Did he tell you about his wife?"

"Only that she passed."

"It was horrible. She was seven months pregnant, and her car skidded off the road during a storm."

I frowned as a vivid memory returned of my mother saying Shawn had died in a car crash. "He lost his wife and child?"

"Yeah, it was awful. Beth was such a sweet person too, and he was devastated. No one saw him for a while after that. A year after she died, he showed up at the farmer's market again and has been there twice a month since."

"Well, I'm glad you told me that. I'd hate to say something that would upset him." I paused. "I can't believe he lost them in a car accident. That's how my brother died."

"I remember. It's ironic, isn't it?"

"Yeah, it is."

"I look forward to hearing how your date goes," Maggie said with a giggle and then coughed again, and I winced.

"It's not a date. It's only coffee, Mags. Two old friends catching up with one another."

"You never know. One coffee could lead to two and then dinner."

"Please! I'm not here to date. I just got divorced. I'm not ready to get involved with anyone. Besides, I have your bakery to keep me busy."

"Yes, there is that." She sighed. "I got a call from the surgery center. I have to be there at six-fifteen."

"Okay, then six-fifteen it will be."

She sighed loudly. "I'm scared of what they will find, Sandi."

"I am sure you are, Maggie, but we will deal with whatever they find. I'm here for you every step of the way." I paused. "Speaking of which, are you doing alright? You sound a little winded today."

"I'm fine. Thank you, Sandi. I'm not sure what I would do without you."

"Well, you don't have to worry about that now," I told her, and we said goodbye a moment later. As I drove to the dairy, I pondered our conversation when she first told me she had cancer.

The doctors had told her that without surgery, she would have about four to eight weeks to live. With the surgery, she could probably extend that to about six months. They had hopes that this intense treatment that she would start a week after her surgery would give her at least another six to twelve months. They didn't think there was any chance she would ever find remission, but they did say stranger things had happened, and sometimes miracles did occur.

I silently prayed for a miracle. I know that Maggie just wanted to make it through the surgery first. The surgeon had told her that it would be tricky, and once they opened her up, they might find things they didn't expect to see.

I just hoped they could clear out more than they anticipated, and it gave her years to live, not weeks.

Forty minutes later, I had pulled up to the bakery with the dairy order and unloaded it through the back door. I checked in with Reba, Dawn, Charlie, and Pam, working at the bakery, to ensure things were going smoothly.

"Did you get the jelly order?" Reba asked as she glanced over the dairy crates. Reba was the assistant manager and an incredible pastry chef. She spent much of her time working on the more elegant items, like wedding cakes.

"It's being delivered," I told her, and she frowned.

"Delivered? It's never been delivered before."

I grinned at her. "Aaron and I go way back. When we saw each other at the farmer's market, he offered to bring it by so we could catch up a little bit."

Her hazel eyes had grown wide. "You know Aaron Norcini?"

"Yes," I replied with a nod. "Why?"

"Because it's Aaron Norcini."

I chuckled. "What's that supposed to mean?"

"I don't know. I mean, he's nice and all. Cute too, but he's a drunk."

"What?" I asked with a laugh. "Are we talking about the same Aaron Norcini?"

"Yes." Reba nodded dramatically. "After his wife died, he became a recluse. People only saw him at the bar or in the liquor store. He started looking bad too, like he was trying to kill himself with alcohol."

I frowned. That sure didn't sound like the Aaron I knew. "Well, he looked pretty good to me."

"Now he does. I guess he's been sober for a while, but I don't know. He freaks me out a bit."

"Freaks you out? Why, because he drank a lot?"

"Hey, my stepfather was an alcoholic, and he was meaner than a rattlesnake. I would never trust a drunk man."

I frowned again, trying to picture Aaron as a mean drunk. I just couldn't make it happen, and I knew firsthand what a mean drunk looked like. "Well, thanks for the heads-up, but I have known Aaron since he was just a kid."

"Okay," she said, shaking her head and carrying one of the crates into the walk-in fridge.

As I thought over the conversation, I felt a bit irritated. It was rude for Reba to have told me what she had. I had never been one for idle gossip, and I didn't intend to start now.

While waiting for Aaron to arrive with the order, I got busy in the office. I reviewed invoices on the desk and the sales figures from the previous night. I sent Maggie a few texts to report on what I found, and she was happy to hear things were going well.

I was preparing the deposit for the bank when Pam popped her head into the office. "You have a visitor."

"Thanks, Pam," I told her and put the money back into the safe before I went out front to find Aaron standing there with his hand truck filled to the top with boxes of jelly.

"Wow! You were right. It would have taken me a few trips with my little one."

"Where would you like me to put them for you?"

"Maggie stores those in her office. Follow me back." He did, and I held the kitchen door open for him to get through, then led the way to the office. Inside, I showed him where to put the boxes and watched as he unloaded them. I thought about what Reba had said the whole time, but I couldn't imagine Aaron having a drinking problem. He seemed so put together, so different than my ex-husband.

Once he finished, he turned to me, and I instantly found myself lost in his blue eyes. "Are you still interested in that cup of coffee?"

"I would love to," I replied. "Where do you suggest?"

"We could have one here, or Amy's Café has a great mild brew just a block down the street."

I thought about what Reba said and realized I didn't want her or anyone else butting their noses into our business. "Alright, then Amy's it is."

"I will put this back in my truck and meet you outside."

"Perfect. I'll be out in a couple of minutes." As he walked away, I thought about Reba's words again. I didn't relish getting involved with a man with a drinking problem, but this was just coffee with an old friend. It's not like it was an actual date. We were just two friends catching up after a long time—that's it.

CHAPTER FOUR

AARON

I was still grinning as I drove away from the market. All kinds of memories had come flooding back to me after Sandi left. I remember when she skinned her knee on a rock at the creek. Shawn and I took turns giving her a piggyback ride on the way home. Shawn only did it for a few minutes, then complained that she was slowing him down, so I took over for the rest of the way.

I remembered another time when she was a bit older, maybe fourteen or fifteen, and doing homework at the table. Shawn had picked up a folder and saw the word Aaron written with a heart around it. "Oh, my God! You are such a loser, Sandi!" Shawn joked with his sister as she turned bright red, grabbed her books, and bolted from the room. Secretly, I was thrilled by that knowledge, but knowing I was several years older than her and she was my best friend's sister, I knew nothing would ever come of it.

I had to rely on those words a whole lot when the night before I was to return to college after Christmas break, Sandi showed up at my window in the middle of the night. I found her standing there shivering with her bed quilt wrapped around her. I hurriedly helped her through the window and realized that she was only wearing a t-shirt and panties under it. I could remember that conversation as if it were yesterday.

"What are you doing here? It's almost midnight, and it's freezing outside."

"I had to come to say goodbye before you left."

I chuckled. "Sandi, you already said goodbye."

She nibbled her bottom lip, then let the quilt fall. "No, I want to say goodbye differently." She took hold of the bottom of her nightshirt and began to lift it, but I jumped forward as I realized what was about to happen and grabbed her hands.

"No! Sandi, you can't be here. You can't do this."

"Aaron, I know you like me. I see the way you look at me."

"Sandi, I'm twenty years old. You're my best friend's little sister. You're not even sixteen yet."

"I will be sixteen next week. Aaron, I love you! I want to show you how much."

I wanted to take her up on her offer. I had imagined kissing her before, even feeling her up a bit, but I had never allowed myself to think any further. She was practically family. I knew there was no way to let her down easily, so I had to be harsh with her. I stared down at her as I pursed my lips. "Sandi, you're too young to even know what love is. I'm not taking advantage of you because you think you care about me."

"Think?" she snapped back in a heated whisper. "I know how I feel about you, Aaron Norcini! I have been crazy about you since I was twelve years old."

"It's just stupid puppy love, Sandi," I snapped back.

"No, it's not," she stated firmly and tried to lift her shirt again. I yanked her hands away.

"I'm not having sex with you, Sandi. I'm not going to be your first."

She lifted her chin. "Who said you would be my first?"

I jerked back slightly. She better not have had sex with anyone else! "Tell me who touched you, and I will break their arms."

She tossed her curly hair back. "I guess since you don't want me, you'll never know."

With that, she rushed toward the window and slipped out before I could *even think of a reply. Before I closed the window, I tripped on her quilt lying on the floor.*

I blinked as I came out of the memory and started my truck. Sandi didn't know that if she had pushed me just a little bit, I probably would have caved in. I did want her, and I sure didn't want anyone else to have her, but the whole best friends with her brother made things tricky. Shawn might not admit it, but he cared a lot about his sister and protected her in any way he could. He would have protected her against me, too—especially the college me.

What would he think of me now? He would probably say I wasn't worth it and tell his sister to get as far away from me as she could. I sighed and put the truck in gear.

Maybe having coffee with her was a bad idea, but maybe not. We were different people now. We hadn't seen each other in twenty years. Twenty years. Wow. It had been almost exactly twenty years since I had seen her.

That childhood crush she had on me would be long gone, and it would be nice to catch up with her a little bit and find out how life had gone for her. She mentioned she was divorced, and I was interested in hearing what had happened with that relationship.

I frowned. I knew that if I asked Sandi about her failed marriage, I was leaving the door open for a conversation about my marriage. That was a loaded topic. As if it weren't for the death of Beth and our daughter, I wouldn't be in the place I am in today.

I glanced at the clock on the dash. I had almost three hours before I had to be at a meeting. It was enough time to enjoy coffee with Sandi and relax for a little while before I had to face reality.

I pushed thoughts of reality out of my mind and brought back a few other memories of Sandi as I drove to my destination.

It seemed almost surreal to walk into the bakery and see her. She looked different, but she still looked the same. Her eyes were still brilliant blue, and her smile was still heart-stopping—maybe even more so now that she was older. Or perhaps I just appreciated it more now.

After unloading the order, I put the hand truck back into my vehicle and waited near the bakery's front door. I didn't have to wait long before Sandi slipped out and came to my side.

For a moment, the two of us stared at one another, and then I held my hand out. "It's this way."

"Oh, yes! Of course." She giggled as we began to walk. "You know, since I saw you this morning, I remember all kinds of things from when we were younger."

"Yeah, I have been too." I chuckled.

"What were you remembering?" she asked excitedly as she glanced my way.

"Um," I hesitated, wondering what she would think if I brought up that last day before she moved and I went back to college. "Just random things."

She pushed my arm. "Just random things, huh? Any of them stick out?"

"A few." I winked at her. "What have you been remembering?"

"Well, I've been thinking about how I used to follow you guys around all the time. It wasn't to spend time with my brother, that's for sure."

I laughed. "Yeah, I remember you had a bit of a crush on me back then."

"A bit of a crush?" She laughed heartily, and I enjoyed the sound. "I was so enamored with you, no other guy could measure up."

"I doubt that," I remarked as I pulled open the door to the café. Sandi stepped in front of me and looked up as she stopped.

"Oh, it was true. I don't think I even seriously looked at any other male until after Shawn died."

I wasn't sure how to respond, and luckily, she didn't seem to want a reply as she stepped into the café. We waited for the hostess to seat us and ordered two coffees as soon as the waitress stopped over.

"I'm sorry about Shawn. I know I told you that at the funeral, but I just wanted you to know that I'm sorry that I didn't drive him that night. I should have. I blamed myself for his death for years."

Her hand snaked over the table and covered mine, squeezing

gently. "Aaron, it wasn't your fault. Shawn died because he wasn't paying attention. That wasn't on you."

"I knew Shawn never paid attention while he drove, especially at night. I should have gone with him."

She squeezed my hand one more time, then pulled hers back. "Do you know why my brother crashed the car that night?"

"Because he wasn't paying attention."

"No, he wasn't, that's for sure, but he wasn't paying attention because his girlfriend was giving him a blow job as he drove."

I stared at her. "What? How do you know that?"

"Because she told me. Vickie came to see me about two months after the funeral and said she had to explain what happened. I guess it weighed heavily on her shoulders, and she needed to let it out."

"Are you serious?"

She nodded. "So, stop blaming yourself, Aaron. That blame falls squarely on Shawn's and Vickie's shoulders. You have no reason to think it was your fault."

I leaned back in my seat, my mouth hanging open as I rubbed a hand over my head. "All these years, I thought it was my fault."

"It wasn't."

I hung my head for a moment as a rush of emotion began to build inside me, and then I put my elbows on the table and covered my face with my hands as two tears leaked out. I heard her chair squeak, and the one beside me did the same before she put her hand on my arm and pulled.

"Aaron, I am so sorry that you have held guilt for that for so long."

I wiped my eyes and took hold of her hand. "Sandi, you have no idea how much I needed to hear that, especially today."

CHAPTER FIVE

SANDI

I hadn't expected Aaron to get emotional. The boy I knew didn't show emotion very much, but Aaron was a man now, and not only that. He was a man who had seen a lot of loss in his life.

"Is today a special day?"

"Um, yeah." He pulled his hand back from mine, and I wasn't sure if I should return to my original seat or remain where I was. At that moment, the waitress returned with our coffee and set it down in front of me. The choice was made.

"What makes it a special day?"

He thought about that for a moment. "I have something I need to confess to you, Sandi. It might change your opinion of me, but I must be honest with you."

"Of course, Aaron." Was he going to tell me that he was seeing someone? I couldn't imagine what else might be important to say to me.

"After Shawn died, I went to a bad place for a while. I had a hard time dealing with life, and everything I did for a while was screwed up. Every relationship I was in went to shit, and work wasn't much better. I changed jobs a few times, but nothing seemed to help. Then I met Beth, and somehow, she managed to help me get my life back on track."

"That's wonderful, Aaron."

"It was wonderful. I finally found a job I liked, and life was going well. Then my parents took a turn, and I moved back. Beth loved it here, and we decided to stay. She had always dreamed of living on a small farm, so I bought the old Miller place out on Settler's Ridge. Do you remember that place?"

"I do!" I said excitedly. "We used to go apple and berry picking there when I was a child."

"Yep, that's the one. Beth loved the orchids and the fields, and we kept the staff and the place running when old man Miller finally decided to move into a retirement home after his wife passed. None of his kids were interested in it." He paused and sipped his coffee momentarily, his eyes skimming off to the side. "Then, about nine months after my mom passed, Beth ran into town to pick something up. I was supposed to do it, but I had fallen asleep on the couch. She left me a note saying she'd be back in a little while, and she left."

I knew what was coming, but that didn't make me any less sad as I wrapped my hands around my cup to ward off the coming chill.

"It was raining, harder than we expected, and she lost control and crashed her car into a ravine only a mile from the farm. When I woke up, I didn't know where she was. I tried to call her cell, but no one answered. I saw her note and figured she wasn't answering because she was navigating the slippery roads." He paused again and stared down into his wide mug. "I was heading to the barn when the sheriff's truck pulled down my driveway. At first, I thought her car might have broken down, and he was giving her a lift home. I knew something was wrong when he stopped his truck a few feet from me. We stared at each other through the windshield, and I saw it on his face. Paul didn't want to get out and tell me. I'd known him all my life, and he didn't want to give me the news."

I reached for his arm, wrapping my hand around his forearm as he continued.

"Finally, he got out and told me that Beth had slid off the roadway, gone down an embankment, and hit a tree. She managed to get out of the car and tried to climb up the hill, but she must have slipped and fallen back down the hill. When she did, she hit her head on a rock, knocking her out. She died before anyone could find her."

I squeezed his arm with one hand and covered my mouth with the other. I quickly swiped at the two tears that had leaked out. "Oh, Aaron, I am so very sorry."

"She was seven months pregnant, too."

"I can only imagine how devastated you were."

"Yeah, remember when I told you that I went downhill after your brother died?"

I nodded.

"Well, I went even further down. I started drinking every day until I couldn't even see straight. I drank for months, barely able to do anything else, until one day, I was driving to the store. I was drunk while I did." He closed his eyes and shook his head. "I was so stupid. Anyway, I was driving, and I got a flat tire about two miles from home. It wasn't until I had gotten out to change it that I realized where I was. I was only about fifty yards from where Beth had died."

"Oh, jeez."

He nodded. "Yeah. I ended up straggling over to the location and slipped down the embankment to where she had died. I sat there for hours, crying, screaming, and sobering up. As I was sobering up, I wondered what Beth would think about all of this. I knew she would have been pissed, and she would have told me to clean myself up. She would have wanted me to get on with my life and not wallow in the grief."

"Smart woman."

"She would have also told me to stop drinking. Years before, we talked about my drinking, and even though I didn't want to name it, I knew I was an alcoholic. I sat there staring at the trees around me, and I knew I needed to get sober."

He stopped for a long moment and sighed before giving me a sad smile. "When I finally climbed my sorry ass up the hill, I found someone had stopped and fixed my flat tire. I had left the spare sitting beside my truck when I noticed where I was. Someone had come by and swapped out the tires. The flat one was now sitting in its place."

"Do you know who did it?"

He shook his head. "Nope, I have no idea, but I was thankful for them. Had I not gotten that flat, I might have gotten into an accident and hurt someone else. I sure wouldn't have stopped at that point in the road or faced the grief and anger I felt."

"Well, I'm glad you got a flat tire, Aaron."

"I am too." We were both quiet for a moment as we sipped our coffee. "When I got back into my truck, I found an address on the seat. I had no idea what the address was to, but I figured I owed the person at least a thank you, so I drove into town and to the address."

"So you did find out who changed your tire."

I shook my head. "No, actually, I didn't. What I found were several people heading into a building. I followed them, not knowing where I was going or why. When I stepped in, someone approached me and welcomed me, and behind him, I saw a sign that talked about the twelve steps to getting and staying sober."

"Oh, wow!" I rubbed my arms. "You just gave me chills, Aaron."

"Yeah." He grinned. "I had them that day too. Part of me wanted to run from the building. The other part made me park my ass in a chair as the meeting started."

"Have you continued to attend them?"

He nodded, slipped his hand into his pocket, then held his hand out to me. "Yes, every single day. This is my eleventh-month chip. One year ago today was when I got a flat tire. It was the day I woke up and saw how bad I was and how a stranger held out their hand with a gift."

"Oh, Aaron, that is wonderful."

"Yeah, I guess so. It hasn't been easy, but they say, one day at a time."

"Yes, they do say that." I gnawed on my bottom lip for a moment. "I have gone to Al-Anon meetings."

He leaned back slightly. "What?"

I thought about how I wanted to express my words and realized that the truth was probably the best way to go about it. "My ex-husband is an alcoholic, Aaron. It is one of the reasons we got divorced."

CHAPTER SIX

AARON

Her words were both a blessing and a curse. They were a blessing because on some level, she understood what an alcoholic's problems were. It was a curse because she had also seen the nastiness of the disease, and it had not turned out well.

I thought for a moment. "I'm sorry about that."

"There is nothing to be sorry about, Aaron."

"Of course, there is. I know how difficult it can be to live with someone with an addiction."

"That is true." She nodded and seemed to think for a moment. "Bill wasn't just an alcoholic, though. His problems ran deeper than that. He was abusive at times, not physically but emotionally. He blamed me for many of his problems and tended to be very controlling."

"Was he always like that?"

"Maybe, but I didn't see it at first. I only saw a handsome man with a great job. At first, he was caring and attentive, but I also know now that is the stage where he was trying to bring me into his web. It wasn't until after our first year of marriage that I started to see things that bothered me. I ignored them, always telling myself that work or something else going on was stressful. It took me years to see the truth, and then I wasn't sure how to get myself out of it."

"How long were you married to him?"

"Eight years. I almost married when I was about twenty-six but found the guy was cheating on me. Luckily, I learned that two months before our wedding, and it was easy to call it off. I met Bill after that. We dated for almost a year before we got married, and as I said, it was good for a while."

"And you never had kids?"

She shook her head, looking sad. "No. He didn't want them. He did when we got married, but later, he said they would interrupt our life. He enjoyed traveling, and it was easy for us to pick up and go away. With kids, he said we couldn't do that. He had other reasons for not wanting them, but that was the main point."

"And did you? Did you want kids?"

She nodded. "I did. I do. I hope to meet someone one day before I am too old and can at least have one. If not, perhaps I can adopt."

I grinned. "Beth talked about adopting too. She said she wanted to have one child that was our own and then adopt at least two more. She was adopted herself."

"I bet I would have liked her very much."

"I know you would. There were times that she reminded me of you."

She laughed loudly. "Yeah, right."

"No, I'm serious. She could be very hardheaded. I remember when we had just married, and she told me something she wanted to do. I don't remember what it was, but she stomped her foot. You used to do that too."

Her eyes widened. "I did not!"

I laughed. "You most certainly did. Whenever Shawn said that you couldn't do something with us, you would demand to be allowed to do it. You stomped that foot quite a few times."

She looked away, glancing around the café, then grinned. "I guess I did."

"Do you still?"

"No, I got over that demanding phase after I got married." Her smile lessened, and I immediately wanted to find another way to bring it back. It was like the sun shining on a gloomy day, and I needed that.

"How long are you in town?" I asked, changing the subject.

"Um, I'm not really sure. My divorce was finalized a few weeks ago, and I came here to help Maggie. I'm not sure what I will do once she gets better."

"Maybe you will stick around for a little while. It would be great to see you more."

The two of us stared at one another for a long moment. "Yeah, it would be great."

Her cell phone rang, and she quickly pulled it out of her purse. "I have to take this. Will you excuse me for a moment?"

"Absolutely, I'm going to use the restroom, and I'll be right back."

She nodded as she said hello, and I moved away from the table to give her some privacy. As I used the restroom, I pondered over our serious conversation. It was strange that I had confided so much in such a short time, but it had felt right. Although she had been much younger, we had been friends, and I would like to see that friendship continue. Maybe she would want to have dinner with me sometime.

I had that thought in mind as I returned to the table but found it empty. I glanced around the room but didn't see her. The waitress paused by the table as I took a seat.

"Sir, your friend had to leave. She said something about a problem."

"Oh, okay."

She quickly dashed away, and I wondered who had been calling her and what the problem could be. I finished my coffee, paid the bill, then walked back toward the bakery.

I paused outside, wondering if I would be intruding if I stopped in to check on her, and decided that if I didn't, I would wonder if she had left for a work reason or if she chose the moment I walked away to make a run for it.

I stepped inside and moved to the counter, where a young woman lifted her head from behind the cabinet and smiled. "Hello, can I help you?"

"Um, yes, I was wondering if Sandi is here."

"I'm afraid that she's not. She came running in, went into the office, and went out the back door, saying she had to take care of something."

"Oh, well, okay. I'll stop by again another day."

"Do you want to leave a message for her?"

I thought about that for a moment, and then I nodded. "Can I leave my phone number for her? She can give me a call when she has a moment."

She happily supplied me with a pen and paper, and I jotted down my number and gave it back to her as another customer entered the store.

I glanced at my watch to see that I had a little time before my meeting, and it wouldn't be worth going home before. Instead, I drove to a local store and picked up a few things I needed for the farm. All the while, I wondered what pulled Sandi away.

All I could do was wait to see if she'd call. I didn't think she had run away from me because of our conversation. Despite the fact that it was a heavy one, it had gone well. I didn't think she thought any less of me for having admitted I was an alcoholic—at least I hoped she didn't.

I dwelled over what she had told me while I shopped, and then I went to the meeting hall early and helped get things set up. Greg, one of the regulars, was there when I arrived.

"You seem to be in a good mood," he commented as I arranged the chairs in a circle. Our group was small. Usually, a dozen or so attended, but we always had extra chairs in case more decided to join us.

"I am in a good mood. I ran into someone I hadn't seen in about twenty years, and we grabbed a cup of coffee."

"Well, that's great. It must have been a woman."

I chuckled. "Why would you say that?"

"Because I can't think of any man I know from twenty years ago that I'd be *that* happy to see."

His comment made me laugh harder. "Actually, it was a woman. Her brother and I were best friends."

He looked concerned for a moment. "Best friends? Wait, is this the sister of the friend who died?"

Greg had been part of this group for three years. The fact that he remembered me telling that story meant more than he knew. "Yes, it is, but I learned something today that has made a positive step in my recovery."

"Did you ask for forgiveness?"

"I did, but come to find out, I didn't have a reason to be forgiven." He looked confused, and I continued. "You will have to wait for that story. I plan on talking about it during the meeting."

"I look forward to it, but I hope that seeing her again doesn't set you back."

I paused and then looked him in the eye. "Honestly, Greg, I feel better today than I have in twenty years. Seeing her again was what I needed, especially today."

"Well, that's good to hear."

It was good to hear, and I hoped I got the chance to let Sandi know that too.

CHAPTER SEVEN

SANDI

"Hello, is this Sandi Warrenton?"

"Yes, this is Sandi."

"Hi, this is Barbara Thorn. I'm a doctor at Mercy Medical Center."

I frowned. "Yes, how can I help you, Dr. Thorn?"

"Maggie was brought in here about an hour ago. She has you listed as her emergency contact."

I froze for a moment. "What? Why? I mean, I know I'm her emergency contact, but why did she go to the hospital?"

"She was having trouble breathing and called an ambulance."

"Is she still there?"

"Yes."

"I'm on my way," I replied, not wanting to discuss Maggie while I was sitting in the café.

"We will see you when you arrive. Ask for me when you get here."

"Okay, thank you."

I grabbed my purse and glanced around to see if Aaron was heading back to the table but didn't see him. I did see the waitress and quickly told her to pass on a message, and then I rushed out the door. Perhaps I should have waited until Aaron returned to the table, but I figured he would forgive me once he knew why. I made it back to the bakery and walked through, stating I had an emergency and was out the back door and in my car before I thought much more about what was happening.

As I started my car, I realized my hands were shaking, and I closed my eyes and tried to calm myself. After a few long breaths, I put my car in gear and headed toward the hospital. It only took me about ten minutes, and I was calmer when I arrived. I was sure that everything was fine as I walked into the hospital, and I was glad that she had thought to call 911 on her own.

I stopped at the desk, asked for Dr. Thorn, and told the young woman who I was. She asked me to have a seat, and I did. It was five long minutes before the doors opened, and a woman wearing dark-blue scrubs and a long white jacket came out and was directed toward me.

"Sandi?"

I held out my hand as I stood. "Yes, I'm Sandi."

She gave me a smile that didn't reach her eyes. Had Maggie's cancer progressed further than we thought? What would this do to her upcoming surgery? Would they have to push it back? She asked me to follow her, and I did without asking the dozen questions floating through my mind.

When she stepped into a small room, I paused at the threshold. The pit of my stomach dropped as she turned to look back at me, and I saw the pity in her eyes. Somehow, I stepped into the room, and she closed the door.

"I'm sorry to tell you this, Sandi, but Maggie passed away about forty minutes ago."

"What?" I stared at her, the words echoing through my mind. "But you just called me about twenty minutes ago."

She nodded. "Yes, and if you hadn't offered to come down here as quickly as you did, I would have given you that information over the phone."

I stepped around her and went to a seat as I felt the room around me begin to spin. "What happened? She was fine this morning. In fact, she was in good spirits and ready for her surgery." Only had she been? She had looked tired, and she seemed winded on the phone.

"She was having trouble breathing, and when she got here, her heart had an arrhythmia. We did a few tests and X-rays of her chest and saw two growths in her chest. It looks like the cancer progressed much further than anyone could have anticipated. One of the masses was on her left lung, pushing against her heart. The other was directly on her heart."

"Oh, my God," I gasped.

"We did everything we could for her, but unfortunately, the cancer was just aggressive. Even if she'd had the surgery tomorrow, she probably wouldn't have survived it, and if she did, she might have lived a week."

I blinked at her, and all those questions I previously had vanished. Maggie was gone. How was that possible?

The doctor explained a few more things to me, but in the end, nothing she said mattered. Maggie was gone.

An hour later, I was sitting in my car, staring out the window. The doctor had led me to the morgue and allowed me to see her before I left. I had stared down at her, remembering her this morning with bright-brown eyes and a pale face. She was even paler now. What if I had stayed with her? Would that have made a difference? I didn't think so.

I started the car and wondered what I should do now. Should I return to the bakery and tell them? Should I go back to her place? What was going to happen to her business and her home? She had no family; her parents had died when she was in college. She had only been married for a couple of years before he left her for someone else. I wasn't aware of any other family I would need to contact, although she had several close friends to whom I would have to reach out.

I couldn't imagine doing that now. I felt numb and lost and unsure of what the future would hold. I started toward the bakery, but when I got there, I sat in the car and stared at the back door. I wasn't ready to go in there and face the questions, the sorrow. I knew how much her employees loved her, and I wasn't prepared to crash their world yet. This news could wait another day.

I backed out of the space and turned toward the house. When I arrived there, I couldn't make myself get out of the car. How could I stay in her home without her there?

I must have sat there for ten minutes before I started the car again and drove away. I drove for twenty minutes before I realized where I was going, and a few minutes later, I turned onto the lane for Honeyhill Farms.

I needed a friendly face, someone who would understand grief and pain. I glanced around as I drove up the drive and took the left lane to the private residence, not the right that led to the barn.

There were no cars near the house, so I turned around and went back down the drive and toward the barn. I parked with seven other cars and climbed out, looking around but not seeing Aaron's truck.

A man stood near the barn, sweeping a pathway, and I approached him. "Excuse me, do you know where Aaron is?"

He lifted his head and smiled. "He's not here right now." He glanced at his watch. "He probably won't be back today."

"Do you know when he will be home?" I asked and then added, "I'm an old friend."

"He usually doesn't get back until around five."

I nodded. I knew that it was almost four. "Do you mind if I wait for him?"

"No, be my guest. The store is open for a little longer if you want to visit there."

"Thanks," I told him and made my way to the small store that sold bundled fruits and veggies grown on the farm. I didn't have an appetite, but I did grab a small bottle of apple cider.

A young woman was behind the counter, and I paid for the bottle and then returned to my car. It was just as I remembered it, and for a second, I almost broke down and started crying. Maggie and I had spent many afternoons here picking apples and peaches for pies. Oh,

Maggie! I closed my eyes, holding back the tears that wanted to burst forward.

After getting back in my car, I drove back to his residence and got out with my cider. There was a swing in the front on the porch, and I made my way to it. I sat there shifting back and forth, sipping the apple cider and thinking about Maggie as I waited.

From time to time, I heard cars come and go to the orchard, but finally, it grew silent, and the sun began to set. I didn't move, though, other than my feet that helped me keep the swing in motion.

A little while later, I heard the sound of an engine coming closer, and I glanced to the driveway to see Aaron parking his truck beside my car. His face was turned toward me, and he looked confused.

"What are you doing here?" he asked as he approached the porch. "Is everything okay? What happened today?"

The minute I opened my mouth, the dam I had been holding back crumbled, and I began to sob. Everything I had been holding back finally burst forward. Aaron rushed to me and sat on the swing as I sobbed out the words, "Maggie's gone, Aaron. Maggie's gone."

CHAPTER EIGHT

AARON

The meeting went very well—actually better than expected. I had been dreading standing up here today because I knew it would bring everything back. Even though this was a huge milestone and one I was proud of, I hadn't wanted to face all the emotions.

Strangely enough, as I stood up to speak, I felt better than I had in a long time. I talked about my journey, where it all started, and how I came to find recovery, and I spoke about my last year, the odd times, the funny times, and the times I wasn't sure I would pull through.

Then I talked about seeing Sandi again after all these years. It was a sign that she showed up today and gave me the information she had provided me. Shawn's death wasn't my fault. I could let go of that blame, and my shoulders instantly felt lighter.

That's what I was thinking about as I drove home. My shoulders hadn't felt this light in years. It was hard to believe that the death of a friend could weigh that heavily on my shoulders, but it did. Compound that with the grief of my wife and daughter, and it had been like a Mack truck sitting on my shoulders.

I would need to speak with Sandi again and tell her how much her words meant to me today. I wasn't sure I had expressed it entirely to her.

When I pulled up my driveway and saw a car sitting there, I was puzzled at first, but then I saw her sitting on the porch swing. My excitement grew that Sandi had come here to see me, and I quickly climbed out of my car and approached her.

However, it didn't take a rocket scientist to realize that she was upset about something, and the moment I sat beside her, she cracked into a thousand pieces as she began to sob about Maggie being gone. Her words shocked me, and I wasn't sure what to do, but I did the only thing I could think of doing. I held her tightly to me as she let the grief out.

Eventually, she began to calm down, and I asked her, "What happened?"

She wiped under her nose with the back of her hand. "I got a call from the hospital, and they said she was there. She was having trouble breathing, and she called an ambulance. The doctor said the cancer had infiltrated her chest cavity and pushed on Maggie's lungs and heart. She had heart failure. They did everything that they could, but it was no use." She swiped at the river of tears rolling down her cheeks. "The doctor said she probably wouldn't have even survived surgery."

"Aw, Sandi, I am so sorry. Maggie was such a great person. Have you told the people at the bakery?"

She shook her head. "No, I wasn't ready to speak to anyone. I went by there but then drove to her house. I couldn't even go inside her house. How can I go into Maggie's house without her there?"

"I know it will be hard, Sandi."

She closed her eyes and shook her head. "I know I need to tell everyone, but I can't do it tonight." She lifted swollen, red eyes to me. "Aaron, can I stay here tonight? I'm not ready to go back there yet."

"Of course, you can, Sandi. I'll put fresh sheets on the guest bed."

Her shoulders dropped in relief. "Thank you. I know I will have a lot to deal with, but I'm not ready to do all of that yet. I thought I would have more time."

"Did you think that the surgery would cure her?" I asked.

She shook her head. "No, Maggie said there was little to no hope of curing it, but we had hoped to at least give her a little more time to enjoy life. This happened too fast."

I tried to smile as I cupped her cheek. "I understand what you mean. When Beth died, I felt like my world had turned upside down, and it took a while to get my feet planted on the ground again."

"I'm sorry for showing up here unannounced. You must have thought I was a horrible person for leaving you at the café."

I shook my head. "No, I figured something came up, and you'd explain later. We might not have seen each other for twenty years, Sandi, but I know you're not the kind of person to just cut and run without reason."

She smiled sadly. "True."

"Let's go inside, and I'll get you some water. Are you hungry?"

She shook her head. "Not really, but I could use some water."

I stood and held my hand out to her. When she got to her feet, I wrapped my arms around her and held her tightly as she tucked her face into my chest. We stood like that for a long time, and I realized how good it felt to hold someone and have someone hold me. I had forgotten what that felt like. I brushed a kiss over her temple and stepped back. "Come on, let's go inside."

Sandi followed me in, and I gave her a quick tour of the first floor of the old farmhouse on the way to the kitchen. She paused in front of a picture of Beth and me and stared at it for a long moment. "She was beautiful."

"She was."

"You two made a beautiful couple."

"Thank you," I replied as she turned to me.

"I'm sorry that I came to you like this, Aaron. I know you are dealing with a lot, and I don't want to add to your stress. If my being here is too much, please let me know. I can pull up my big girl panties and deal with it."

I stepped toward her and cupped her cheek again. "Sandi, I'm fine, and so are you. I'm glad you came to me. I am here for you, whatever you need."

She stepped into my arms again, and I held her tightly for another few seconds. We stared at one another for a long moment when she pulled back. The urge to kiss her grew the longer we remained quiet. She wasn't a young girl anymore, and four years wasn't that much of an age difference. I wasn't married, nor was she, so what was holding me back?

Nothing.

I leaned slowly toward her, and she tilted her chin up to accept the kiss. Our lips brushed once, then twice, before I pulled her a little tighter to me and deepened the kiss. Sandi clung to my shoulders as the kiss continued, and I felt things deep inside me that had been sleeping begin to wake.

After another few seconds, we slowly pulled apart and stared at one another.

"You know I imagined kissing you so many times when I was younger."

I smiled and ran my thumb over her cheek. "Yeah, I have to admit I thought about it once or twice."

She looked surprised. "You did?"

I stepped back from her. "I did, but I knew your brother would kill me if I did."

"True, he might have."

I took her hand. "Let's go get you some water."

I led her into the kitchen and left her by the counter as I went to gather a glass and fill it. "Tell me, was it better than you imagined it would be?"

She looked confused for a moment. "Oh, you mean the kiss." She giggled slightly. "It was much better than I imagined it would be."

I winked at her. "Yeah, for me too." I returned to her and held the glass out. "Are you sure you don't want something to eat?"

She nodded. "Yes, I just need to sit down and process what happened."

We took seats at the kitchen table after I poured myself a glass of water. "What happens to the bakery now?"

She shook her head, both hands wrapped tightly around the glass. "I have no idea, Aaron. Maggie said we'd talk about it later but never told me what she wanted me to do with it. I guess I'll sell it or have to close it." She shook her head. "And her house, car, and everything else inside."

She rubbed her hands over her face, and I reached out and pulled one down to hold. "It is a daunting process, Sandi, but I'll help you."

She smiled sadly. "Aaron, I can't ask you to do more for me than you already are."

"You aren't asking, Sandi. I'm offering. I want to help you. I'm not sure why our paths crossed again, but they did at the perfect time. You helped me today, and now I'm going to help you."

She looked confused. "How did I help you?"

"When you told me today that your brother's death wasn't my fault. You took a weight off my shoulders that I have been struggling with for twenty years. I don't think you know how much that meant to me, especially today, to hear that."

CHAPTER NINE

SANDI

I hadn't felt as safe with anyone as I did with Aaron in a very long time. After Aaron kissed me, I felt peace slip over my soul. I didn't want to look too deeply into the meaning of it. I just wanted to accept it and relish the feel.

Bill hadn't made me feel safe for a very long time. Every time he drank, he got increasingly agitated, and while Bill had never put his hands on me, he had come close. He had thrown things in my direction and smashed other things I cared about. He had demeaned me by saying I was worthless and wished he had never met me. He told me that I ruined his life and that I never supported him in anything he wanted to do.

That was false, and I knew it, but I had sometimes wondered if I could have done more for him. If he were here now, would he have comforted me the way Aaron had? Would he have held me tightly and kissed my brow? Would he have offered to let me stay in his guest room? Or kissed me in such a gentle way that I had felt cherished?

I didn't think so. I couldn't remember the last time Bill had done anything to make me feel good. When I told him I was moving back here, he laughed and made a snide comment about running back to no man's land with my tail between my legs because I couldn't hack the big city. I'd only stayed in the big city because he was there.

Many times in the past, I had longed for a smaller town. For a place where people know you and life was a bit slower. I loved the glitz and glamour of the city, but I hated how fast time flew and how everyone was always in a rush.

With Maggie's death on the horizon, I had come home willingly in hopes that time would slow down. Unfortunately, it sped up, and Maggie was now gone.

Aaron listened to me talk about Maggie for a long while. Eventually, he prepared some leftover stew from his freezer, and while I didn't have much of an appetite, I did eat most of it.

After we ate, he poured us some iced tea. "I'd offer you something stronger, but I don't have anything in the house."

"That's okay. I stopped drinking a long time ago. I removed the liquor from the house when Bill got out of control. Not to say he didn't bring more in, but I decided it was smarter for me to remain sober when he was out of control."

"He never hurt you, did he?"

"No, not physically."

"I'm sorry you had to deal with that, Sandi."

"Yeah, me too."

We sat on the porch swing and listened to the night critters as we slowly glided back and forth. "What are you thinking of doing now?"

"I don't know, Aaron. I have to see what Maggie might have already planned for and make some hard decisions. She doesn't have any other family, and I know she mentioned in passing that she wanted to make me executor of her will, but I don't know if she ever did that."

"Do you know who her attorney is?"

I nodded. "Yes, she has a list of all the important phone numbers on her desk. She was the most organized person that I knew."

"Do you think you will sell the bakery?"

I thought about that for a moment. "I'm not sure I could run it."

"Why not?"

"Because I know how to help her, but I have no clue how to run an actual business. I barely know the ropes of the bakery, and the employees don't know or trust me. How could I possibly manage running it the way Maggie did?"

"You know that you don't have to do everything the way she did. If you keep the bakery, you could change things."

"I don't want to change anything, Aaron. Too much has changed already. I was looking forward to being here and falling into the day-to-day. I wanted Maggie to make the big decisions, so she remained part of it, and I just wanted to help her for a little while."

"I'm sorry things didn't work out that way."

"I am, too," I replied and rested my head on his shoulder. He shifted to put his arm around me, and the two of us snuggled on the swing for a few minutes in silence.

"I'm glad you came to me," he said a little later.

"I couldn't think of anywhere else to go. Luckily, I remembered where you said you lived."

"Well, you are welcome here anytime, Sandi."

I shifted my head to see his face, and he tilted his toward mine. Without thought, I reached up and cupped his cheek. "Thank you, Aaron."

"You don't need to thank me, Sandi. You would do the same for me."

"I would," I replied, letting my eyes drift over his features. He was even more attractive than he was when we were younger. Even the creases around his eyes made him look handsome. "Is it wrong for me to want to kiss you again now? I mean, Maggie died today. Shouldn't I be thinking about her?"

"Everyone deals with grief differently, Sandi. There is no right or wrong answer. You think about what makes you feel better." His voice was soft and husky as he spoke, and I let his words flow over me and fill in the broken pieces of my soul.

"Will you kiss me again, Aaron?"

He nodded and shifted his arms to wrap around me, but instead of kissing me, he pulled me onto his lap. Once there, we stared at each other for a long time. He ran the tips of his fingers over my cheek and jawline. A few moments later, he curled his hand around my neck and brought our mouths back together.

The kiss lasted longer than the first one, and after a few seconds, I felt the desire that had been dormant for so long begin to spark deep inside me. Our kisses deepened, and our hands began to move over each other's bodies, and I realized that I wasn't the only one who longed for this type of companionship.

I pulled back and looked at him. "Do you remember the night before you went back to college when I came to your room?"

He nodded. "Yes, you were wearing a t-shirt, and you told me you wanted to have sex with me."

"And you told me no and sent me home. You said I was too young."

"And you said you had already had sex before."

I grinned. "Well, I lied about that."

"I figured, but if I had learned that you did have sex with someone, I would have hunted him down and kicked his ass."

I chuckled. "Would you have?"

He nodded. "I might have thought that you were too young back then, but that didn't mean I wasn't aware of you. When I saw you at your brother's funeral"—he paused for a moment, then took a deep breath before he continued—"I wanted to spend more time with you, but I knew it was wrong. I felt to blame for his death and thought you would hate me."

"I didn't hate you, Aaron. I could never hate you. I wish you had stayed. I wanted to talk to you more, but we never got a chance, and you were gone before I realized it."

"I'm sorry about that."

"I am too, but—"

"But what?" He lifted my chin with his knuckle.

"But what if there was a reason for all that? What if back then, when I was sixteen, and you were twenty, and then when I was eighteen, and you were twenty-two, we weren't ready for each other? What if we needed to live the lives that we did so we could be here now?"

"You think this is some kind of fate that has brought us together again?"

I shrugged. "I don't know, but maybe."

He stared out over the dark property for a few seconds. "Perhaps it is, Sandi."

I pulled his face toward mine. "I asked you this once, a very long time ago, and I'm going to ask you again. I hope your answer is different this time."

"What is the question?"

I paused, wondering what had gotten into me, but then I threw caution to the wind. Life was too short not to go after what you wanted. "Will you have sex with me now?"

He studied me for a long moment and then slowly shook his head. "No, I won't have sex with you, Sandi." My heart began to fall as he curled his palm around the side of my face. "But I will make love to you. After all this time, it would be more appropriate than just sex."

Aaron kissed me again, and I let myself go. When we leaned back from one another, he smiled. "I want to show you something."

I climbed off his lap, and he took hold of my hand, led me into the house, and up the stairs. At the top of the stairs, he turned right and went down two doors, where he flipped on the light and stepped into a guest room.

I let my gaze travel over the antique furnishings and the bed, and then it jumped back to the bottom of the mattress. I gasped. Folded neatly, lying from one side to the other at the foot of the bed, was my old patchwork quilt.

CHAPTER TEN

AARON

I knew that I would surprise her when she saw the quilt. I never told Beth where the quilt had come from, only that it was special to me, and I wanted to keep it.

Sandi moved to the bed and ran her hand over the quilt. "I can't believe you still have this. This morning when I was at the market, I saw the old lady who made this, and I wondered what happened to it."

"You left it there that night, and I kept it." I shrugged. "I guess I wanted something to remember that night by."

"Why?"

"Because I couldn't have you, but that didn't mean I didn't want you."

"Did you?" she asked as she turned to face me.

I nodded. "I did, but I also knew it was wrong."

She lifted the quilt off the bed and hugged it to her chest for a moment, then spread it out and pulled it around her shoulders.

I chuckled. "You only had a t-shirt and your panties on the last time."

She grinned. "Then maybe you need to help me get undressed."

"I might be persuaded to do that."

"Persuaded, huh?" She gave me a seductive smile. "How might I persuade you?"

I moved to stand before her. "All you have to do is ask."

She lifted her chin, her bright-blue eyes sparkling at me. "Make love to me, Aaron."

So I did.

~

The following day, I woke up to find the bed empty. I quickly threw the covers back and climbed out. I thought it might have been a dream, but I didn't usually sleep in the guest room. I did for a while after Beth died, but I eventually returned to my room.

I pulled on my pants and peered out the window to see her car was still in the driveway. Downstairs, I found her sitting on the porch swing, the quilt wrapped around her as she sipped from a coffee mug.

She turned my way when the screen door squeaked. "Morning."

Her gaze drifted down my body and back up. "Good morning to you. I hope you don't mind; I made myself at home in your kitchen."

"By all means, what is mine, is yours."

I sat beside her and removed the coffee mug from her hands, taking a sip before I handed it back to her. "That's good."

"I have to give the credit to your beans." She chuckled.

I put my arm around her, and she snuggled into my side. "How are you today?"

"Sad, but I'm okay. I dread going back to the house and the bakery to tell everyone, but I can't put it off."

"Do you want me to go with you?"

She turned and looked at me. "The fact that you asked means everything to me, Aaron, but sadly, I need to do this myself."

"Well, I'm here if you need me. I know it won't be easy."

"No, it won't."

"Just take it one step at a time, Sandi."

She chuckled. "I thought it was one day at a time."

I grinned at her. "It is, but sometimes you have to take one step at a time to make it through one day at a time."

"Ah, that is true."

~

Sandi left shortly after that and told me she'd call me later to let me know how she was doing. I invited her back for dinner, but she told me she'd have to see how the day went first.

I worked around the farm that morning and had more of a spring in my step than I previously had. Even a few of the employees noted that I looked happier. I owed it to Sandi.

Not only had she lessened the guilt surrounding her brother's death, but she had given herself to me last night. After Beth died, I wasn't sure I would ever want to be involved with anyone again. I'd had a few local women let it be known that they were available and interested, but none of them were what I needed to move on.

Sandi was, though. I thought about her during the day and wondered what this all meant. Would Sandi sell everything and move away, or would she stay here for a while? I had no clue what she usually did for work or if she even wanted to live in this area. Our conversations revolved around more serious topics. These were the kind of topics that you didn't generally talk about when you were first getting to know someone, but Sandi and I had known each other for a long time. The conversation just flowed, and I had nothing to hide from her. I wanted her to know the demons I dealt with, and I wanted to know the ones that she had surrounding her too.

When my phone rang at three, I grinned as I answered it. "How are you holding up?"

"It's been a hell of a day." She sounded exhausted.

"I am sure it has. How did everyone take it at the bakery?"

"As hard as I knew they would. I gave them the option of closing early today if they wanted to, but they all wanted to keep working. There are quite a few special orders that needed to be fulfilled, and I appreciate their willingness to take care of them."

"That's good. Maggie hired good employees."

"Yes, she did." She sighed heavily.

"You coming out for dinner?"

"I don't know. I'm exhausted and not sure I would be very good company."

"We don't have to talk. I can feed you dinner, and you can take a long bath and then get some sleep."

"That is very tempting," she replied.

"Then take me up on the offer, Sandi."

"I don't want to add any stress to your life, Aaron. I know what you are dealing with and how difficult it must be for you."

"Sandi, I want to be here for you."

"But I don't want it to affect your sobriety."

"It's not."

"Are you sure? It can't be easy thinking about Maggie dying and not thinking about Beth's death."

"I have thought about it, but I honestly haven't once thought about drinking today." I paused. "What if I promise you that I will say something to you if I get to that point?"

"Would you do that?"

"Yes," I answered without hesitation. "Something I have learned in this long process is being open and honest with people around me. I feel I can be that way with you, Sandi."

"I don't want to be the cause of you doing something you shouldn't do."

"Sandi, I want to see you. I want to be here for you. Come have dinner, and then you can get a good night's sleep."

"Are you going to be sleeping with me?"

I grinned. "If you want me to, but if you want me to stay in my guest room, I can give you space."

"No, I want you with me. Let me pack a few things, and I'll be on my way over."

"I'll see you in a little while," I told her before we hung up. As I slipped my phone into my pocket, I grinned from ear to ear. I hadn't looked forward to something so much in years.

CHAPTER ELEVEN

SANDI

Telling everyone at the bakery had been very difficult, and there had been a lot of tears. I was proud of them, as I knew Maggie would also be, that they wanted to keep working. I would not have faulted any of them for taking time off.

Being at her house was also challenging, and there were quite a few tears shed as I walked around her home and looked at all of her belongings. I hadn't been able to sleep here since she died.

Somehow I made it through the funeral, and Aaron had been by my side. He had even helped make the arrangements.

I would fall asleep in his arms at night and wake beside him. It seemed like it had been months that we had been together, and not a little more than a week. I had asked Aaron a dozen times over the last week if I was causing him any stress, and each time he held my face, smiled, and said he was fine.

It had been ten days since Maggie died, and today I had an appointment with her attorney to review her will. I was restless as I waited for the hands of the clock to reach ten. When I finally sat across from Mr. Thatcher, I studied the older man with the thinning gray hair and kind smile and felt my anxiety finally begin to lessen.

This meeting was going to tell me what would happen to everything. The decisions I had been toying with weren't necessarily mine to make.

"Sandi, thank you again for meeting with me today. I am very sorry to hear Maggie passed so quickly. She was a sweet woman."

"She was, thank you."

"I understand that you two knew each other since you were kids."

"We did. We have been best friends since we were in second grade."

"I always enjoy hearing about adults who have been friends since childhood. In this day and age, you don't see that quite so often."

"No, you don't."

"Well, she was lucky to have you."

"I believe I was the lucky one."

He smiled. "You just might be." He turned his attention to the papers on his desk. "Were you aware that Maggie made you the executor of her will?"

"She had mentioned it, but I wasn't sure she had done it."

"Oh, yes, she did. She came to see me about four months ago and had her will drawn up."

"Four months ago?"

He nodded. "Yes, when she learned that she was dying."

I frowned. "But she told me she had just learned that she was sick a few weeks ago."

"Unfortunately, Maggie was aware of it for quite some time. She didn't want people to know, but she had been diagnosed with cancer about six months ago."

"Six months? Why didn't she say anything sooner?" I was shocked to hear this and unsure what to think about it.

"As I said, Maggie didn't want anyone to know. I was the one who encouraged her to tell someone."

I took a moment to process this information, "She knew that she was going to die?"

He nodded slowly. "She did, yes. She told me that they had given her six to eight months. She knew the planned surgery was a last resort, but she felt that she needed to make one last-ditch effort."

"I can't believe she didn't tell me this. She made it seem like the surgery might give her years."

"Perhaps she was hoping a miracle might happen."

"I'm not sure Maggie believed in miracles."

"I don't know about that. I think she might have thought you were her miracle."

"Why would she think that?"

"Because of what she left you in her will."

"What?"

"Sandi, Maggie left you everything. Her home, her car, all her possessions and finances, and her bakery." He let that sink in for a moment. "She told me not long ago when she learned you were coming here to help her that she received her miracle."

"What miracle? She died!" The words burst from my mouth as confusion filled my head.

He gave me a kind smile. "She said that she wanted you home, and she wanted you to keep her dream alive. She knew that you were between jobs and not happy where you were in life. I believed that maybe she was hoping this would be a miracle for you. A new start of sorts."

"A new start? She told you she wanted me to keep the bakery open and stay here?"

"She did, but she knew that you might not want to. She did give me the names of two people who might be interested in purchasing the bakery from you if you choose to sell it."

I leaned back in my chair, not sure what I wanted to do. "Can I think about it?"

"Yes, of course. Maggie also named you the sole beneficiary in her will. She had a seven-hundred-and-fifty-thousand-dollar policy."

"What?"

He chuckled. "She took that out shortly after she opened her bakery. She also had someone appraise her home, and it's worth about five hundred thousand dollars now, and she only owes about half that on the mortgage. If you decided to sell it, you could get top dollar very quickly. The market in town is quite good for sellers right now."

My head spun as he spoke of numbers and other facts I knew nothing about. I was still stuck on the fact that Maggie had known longer than she said that she would die. Why hadn't she told me? Did she think I wouldn't have been able to handle it?

Mr. Thatcher went over some other details and gave me a list of her accounts, along with the necessary documents for me to access them.

I knew that Maggie's business had been prosperous, but I didn't realize just how profitable it had been. Maggie's car was paid off, and she had no outstanding loans or credit cards. Other than taxes and utility bills, there wasn't much more to take care of for her home.

I left the office light-headed and dazed with a stack of papers stuffed in my bag that I would need to review later. Even though Mr. Thatcher had given me some much-needed advice, I was still trying to wrap my head around the fact that Maggie knew she was dying long before she asked me to come here and help her.

I was supposed to go to the bakery, but I needed time to process everything. I could sell it all and walk away with a hefty sum in my bank account, or I could stay and run her bakery. I knew I wouldn't be able to live in her house, but that was the least of my worries.

I returned to Aaron's house and found his truck gone, so I sat on the porch swing and tried to comprehend all the legal documents the lawyer had given me.

Two hours later, Aaron finally arrived home to find me still slightly dazed as I rocked myself back and forth.

"How did things go with the attorney? I tried to call you a little while ago. I was getting worried about you when I didn't hear from you."

"Sorry, I guess my phone is in the house. I've been sitting out here going through all of this since I got back."

He sat beside me. "Did everything go alright?"

"Yes and no."

He chuckled slightly. "You want to elaborate on that?"

"Well, Maggie did make me the executor of her will, but she did it four months ago."

"Really?"

"Yes. Aaron, she knew she had cancer and was dying back then. She learned about it six months ago, but told me that she had just found out."

"Okay."

"She lied to me."

"Sandi, Maggie did what she thought was right for her. She might not have told you the whole thing, but she did tell you that she was very ill."

"But she didn't tell me that she knew she was dying. She even knew that she'd never live through this surgery."

"You can't be mad at Maggie."

"I want to be mad at Maggie!" I snapped. "She should have told me! I could have been here for her sooner. I could have forced her to undergo treatments and helped her try to fight it."

"Maybe that's not what Maggie wanted. Maybe Maggie wanted you here to share in her last days. She didn't want to burden you with everything."

"I don't care! She should have!" I began to cry. "It's not fair!"

"No, life is not always fair, Sandi. I know that well, but you must let the bad stuff go and focus on the good stuff. Maybe Maggie lied to you, but she did what she felt was right for her."

I swiped at my cheeks. "Maybe, but I still hate that she didn't trust me enough to tell me the truth."

"What else did the attorney say?"

"She left everything to me, even her life insurance."

"Everything?"

I nodded.

"And you think Maggie didn't trust you?"

"What?"

"You just said that Maggie didn't trust you to tell you the truth. Maggie left you everything. That means to me that she did trust you, and she trusted you a lot more than anyone else."

"You think so?"

He nodded slowly. "Yes, I do."

"If she knew she was dying, why didn't she sell the bakery before she died? She left behind two names of people interested in buying it."

"Perhaps she was hoping you would keep her dream alive."

"But I don't know how to run a bakery."

"You've been running it since you came back here."

I shook my head, my curly hair fanning wildly around my face. "No, I've been going through the motions of what she has in place, but I have no clue what I am doing. I don't know how to run a business, Aaron. What if I run her dream into the ground?"

He took my hand. "You could learn, Sandi. I could help you, and you could take some business classes to understand better if you think that will help."

Suddenly, I burst off the swing. "I can't do this, Aaron! Maggie had no right to put me in this position! I don't deserve everything she left me, and I sure as hell can't run her business!"

Without another word, I rushed into the house and up the stairs to the guest bedroom, where I slammed the door and then sank against it and cried.

CHAPTER TWELVE

AARON

I watched in shock as Sandi exploded and then disappeared into the house. I wanted to run after her, but I thought she needed a little bit of time to process everything. I reached for the papers she had left behind and began to go through them.

An hour later, I was in the kitchen making dinner when Sandi joined me. A glance at her told me she had been crying, but I didn't say anything.

She poured herself a glass of iced tea and sat at the table. "I'm sorry for freaking out."

"It's okay, Sandi. You don't need to apologize for that."

"I do. I lost my cool. I don't do that very often."

"Yeah, well, I think we all need to lose our cool every now and again." I took the pan off the burner and set it on the back of the stove. Dinner was ready, but I had a feeling that Sandi needed to talk for a few minutes before we ate. I went to join her at the table. "Do you feel better now?"

She sighed wearily. "I don't know. I guess so." She lifted her red-rimmed eyes to me. "Do you think I could do it?"

"Do what? Run the bakery?" She nodded. "Of course, I think you can do it. Maggie thought you could too, or she would have made arrangements with those other buyers to sell it."

She put her elbows on the table. "Yeah, I guess so."

"You don't have to run it. You could sell it. I don't think Maggie would be upset if you did."

"You don't?"

"She left you the option by leaving you the names of people who would be interested. Do you think she would have done that if she didn't want you to know it was alright to sell it?"

"Probably not." We were quiet for a few minutes, and then she finally spoke again. "I'm not even sure I want to stay here."

I didn't want her to know that those words hurt to hear. I had hoped that she would stay and we could continue developing our relationship. "Where would you go if you didn't stay?"

She shrugged. "I don't know."

"Then why don't you stay for a while? Keep running things as they are, and see how you feel in a few weeks. You said you don't want to live in her house, so why not focus on selling that and dealing with her belongings? Then once that is done, you can decide on the business."

She took a deep breath and released it. "I guess that sounds like a good idea."

"You don't need to make every decision right now, Sandi. You just need to take it one day at a time."

She gave me a lopsided smile. "Yeah, one day at a time."

"In the meantime, you can stay here, and I can help you."

"Aaron, I can't keep asking for your help or staying here."

"Why not?"

"Because we didn't even talk about it, and I am suddenly living in your house."

"Then let's talk about it."

"Now?"

"Yeah, why not?"

She laughed slightly. "Okay, let's talk about it."

"I happen to like having you here in my house."

"You do?"

I laughed loudly for a second. "Yes, did you not know that? It's been lonely living in this big house alone. I like having you here."

"But what are we doing? Is this just an affair to you?"

I took her hand. "Sandi, this was never just an affair to me. I think the moment I saw you at the farmer's market, I saw the start of my life again. For the last few years, I have been going through the motions too. I've been trying to take it one day at a time and do what I need to do to stay sober and sane. When you showed up, suddenly, it wasn't hard to do that anymore. I stopped thinking about one day at a time, and I started thinking about the future."

"You did?"

I nodded. "I did. I also thought a lot about the past, and I have come to terms with it. I don't feel guilty for Shawn's death, and I don't feel guilty for Beth's either. You said that life isn't always fair, and I got a raw deal in that one, but I don't want to give up on living because I lost her and my daughter. I'm only forty-two. I have a lot to live for, and I want to start living again—with you. I want us to see where this can go and what we can build together. There was a reason why you showed up at my booth when you did."

She took my hand. "Do you really believe that?"

"I do. I really believe that, Sandi, but the question is, what do you want? You have gone through a lot recently. You got divorced, moved here, lost your best friend—"

"And found you again," she quickly stated. "I found you again."

"You did, but I can't be the only reason you stay here. You have to want to stay here, even if you don't want to keep the bakery. My life is here, and I'm happy here. I don't want to go anywhere else, but I would like it if you stayed."

"Just here in town?"

"No, not just in town, but with me here on the farm. It might seem weird to say this, but I'm already falling in love with you, Sandi. I know we have only been together for a short time, but I know how I feel. You make me happy, and you make me want to give you the world."

"You're falling in love with me?" Her eyes were wide as she stared back at me. "I never in a million years thought I would ever hear those words come from your mouth."

"Yeah, well, you have." I paused. "Do you think you could ever love me?"

Her grin was slow to form but soon filled her face. "I'm not sure I ever really stopped, Aaron. I was in love with you as a teenager, and when I saw you again at the market, I felt those old emotions rush back."

I held her hand tighter. "Then stay, Sandi. Stay here with me. Build a life with me, and we will figure out what to do about Maggie's bakery."

"Are you sure that's what you want?"

I leaned forward until our noses were almost touching. "I can't think of anything I might want more."

Sandi leaned forward the last inch and kissed me, then slipped out of her chair and came to sit on my lap. "Then I'll stay, Aaron, but you have to promise me something."

"What? I'll promise you anything."

"You have to let me work with you at the farmer's market. It's always been a dream of mine to have a booth there."

"Sweetheart, I'd like nothing more than that." I pulled her to me and kissed her deeply again. Dinner was forgotten on the stove, but that was okay. We were going to have a lot more dinners to come.

THE END

FINDING LOVE IN SPECIAL PLACES

I f you enjoyed the stories, please consider leaving a review so others might find and enjoy these stories also. Reviews don't need to be long and in-depth. The best reviews are merely a few words to say you enjoyed the stories, and how they made you feel as you read them.

Finding Love in Special Places

ABOUT THE AUTHOR

Stacy Eaton began her writing career in October of 2010 and, as each year goes by, she releases more and more novels. Stacy took an early retirement from law enforcement after over fifteen years of service, with her last three in investigations and crime scene investigation.

Stacy resides in southeastern Pennsylvania with her husband, who works in law enforcement. She has a daughter in college, and a son who is currently serving in the United States Navy. She also has two grandchildren.

Stacy volunteers with several organizations to help with awareness of PTSD, suicide, addiction and homelessness for veterans. She is also a National Trainer for a company that teaches Active Shooter Response Options for businesses, schools, healthcare and religious organization.

Stacy is also involved in Domestic Violence Awareness and served on the Board of Directors for her local Domestic Violence Center for three years.

Be sure to visit www.stacyeaton.com for updates and more information on her books.

Sign up for all the latest information on Stacy's Newsletter!

STACY BOOKS - PAPERBACK

Rise Again Warrior Series

The *Rise Again Warrior Series* is an intense and emotional journey through the lives of many service members, their families, and their friends. Focusing on the trials that they face after wartime is over, and they have returned home to a nation that sometimes seems to have forgotten what they were fighting for, and what all of these people sacrificed in the name of Honor & Duty. Books Include: Mission: Believe, Mission:Accept, Mission: Repair, Mission: Courage and Mission: Gratitude

Loving a Young Series

The *Loving a Young Series* is a steamy romance series that consists of six books. While these books are all standalone romances, the characters will be seen across the series since this is a small-town romance series about siblings finding forever loves.

Books include: Wesley, Henley, Riley, Kayley & Bradley

The Loving a Winston Series

The *Loving a Winston Series* is a five-book steamy romance series that spins off of the *Loving a Young Series*. Characters from both series will appear from book to book. Each book is a standalone romance with suspense and spicy romance scenes.

Books Include: Cara, Evan, Candy, Coral and Carmen.

The Unexpected Series

The *Unexpected Series* is a steamy romance series where anything can happen and probably will. Each book in the series is a stand-alone happily ever after, or happy for now book. While they are stand-alone, the books are all centered around Safety Zone Security and the employees there. Characters from one book will continue throughout the rest of the series. Books Include: Unexpected Packages, Unexpected Arrivals, Unexpected Trouble, Unexpected Storms, Unexpected Desires, Unexpected Ties.

Paranormal Romance:

My Blood Runs Blue Series

My Blood Runs Blue Series is an adult Paranormal Action/Romance Series with vampires and is intended for mature audiences.

Books Include: My Blood Runs Blue, The Pulse of Blue Blood, Blue Blood for Life, Mixing the Blue Blood, Blue Bloods Final Destiny,

The Return of Blue Blood Series:

This series is 40 years in the future after My Blood Runs Blue. It is a very steamy series intended for mature audiences.

Books Included: Kristin: Blue Blood Returns, Hugh: Blue Blood Compelled, Zander: Blue Blood Reborn, Lena: Blue Blood Desired, Reckoning, Blue Blood Finale

The Twisted Love Series

with Amy Manemann Co-Author

The Twisted Love Series is a continuing Saga of intense police procedures and romantic suspense and contains nine books in total. It delves deep into the world of crime and how it is investigated. Due to that fact, the crimes continue from one book to the next and could leave you hanging till the next one. Not all crimes are solved in the pages of one book. These books also contain strong adult language, violence, and sexual situations. Books Included: Love Lorn, Love Torn, Love Inked, Love Drowned, Love Carved, Love Trapped, Love Crossed, Love Twisted, Love Lies.

Single Titles

Whether I'll Live or Die

You're Not Alone

Garda ~ Welcome to the Realm

Liveon ~ No Evil

Second Shield

Distorted Loyalty

Six Days of Memories

Second Shield II: The Return

Tempt Me Too

Finding the Strength

Finding Love in Special Places:

Stacy's Short Story Series

Sweet Romance about adult topics. Stories include: Finding Love on Christmas Vacation, Finding Love on the Summer Surf, Finding Love with Dear Santa, Finding Love with a Champagne Toast, Finding Love on the High Seas

Heart of the Family Series

The *Heart of the Family* Series is a small-town steamy romance series that is best read in order. Books Include:

Mistletoe & Cocoa Kisses, Roses & Champagne Kisses, Orchids & Hurricane Kisses, Carnations & Hot Toddy Kisses,

Heal Me Series

Love Spicy Medical Romance? Check out the rest of the Heal Me Series for sexy romances that will warm your heart as they deal with life-altering medical and psychological issues. These books do contain language and open door sexual relations. While each book in the Heal Me Series is a stand-alone book, the characters cross between books and are best enjoyed by reading them in order. Books Include: Cured, Revived, Mended and Rescued.

The Celebration Series

The Celebration Series: Celebration Township is made for family, friends, falling in love, and don't forget celebrating the holidays. The first twelve books bring two people onto center stage as they overcome odds and figure out what their futures may hold. There is laughter, love, romance and even suspense when you join these couples as they each find a happily ever after over a holiday. The thirteenth book brings all twelve couples, and even a few special guests, into final focus as the first couple in Tangled in Tinsel prepares for their wedding one year after they met. Books Include: Tangled in Tinsel, Tears to Cheers, Heathens to Hearts, Rainbows Bring Riches, Sweet as Sugar, Making Mom Mad, Sparklers or Spankings, Raffles to Rattles, Flirting with Fireworks, Working Under Wheels, Masquerading at Midnight, Blessing & Beans, Velvet & Vows.

The Sometimes Series:

The Sometimes Series consists of three romances where the passion is a touch spicy and there is a hint of suspense is in the air. Sometimes You Win is a stand-alone story that ends with a Happy-for-Now ending. Sometimes you Lose, Book 2 of the series does end in a cliffhanger and Sometimes You Play the Game will finally give the couple a Happily Ever After. In all three books, you will find adult language and situations. Books Include: Sometimes You Win, Sometimes you Lose, Sometimes You Play The Game.

Pleasure Your Fantasies Series

The Pleasure Your Fantasies series is an ADULT Series with coarse language and intense sexual situations along with suspense. Books Include: Mistletoe Fantasies, Whispered Fantasies, Secret Fantasies, and more coming in 2022.

List Updated 1/18/22

www.ingramcontent.com/pod-product-compliance
Lightning Source LLC
Chambersburg PA
CBHW031026030726
47497CB00004B/1022